LINE
by
LINE

BARBARA HACHA

This is a work of fiction. Names and characters are the product of the
author's imagination, and places and events are used fictitiously.

Published by MediaMix Productions, LLC

www.mediamixpro.com

ISBN: 0983198705
ISBN-13: 9780983198703

To Jim—my husband, best friend,
and *first* first reader, who willingly read
these chapters more times than I can count,
and whose support made all the difference.

And to my mother, Barbara Bezzeg,
who continues to inspire me.

ACKNOWLEDGMENTS

I'd like to thank the following:

My Writer's Group: Sarah Wisely Croley, John Kavouras, and Everett Prewitt, who offered encouragement and—even more important—criticism, making this a far better book than it would otherwise have been.

Mary Lee Corlett, first reader and researcher *par excellence*, who helped ensure I had my historical facts straight and whose many suggestions shaped this story.

My Book Club: My friends and fellow readers for many years—
Gaynell Baker, Marilyn Ferrara, Helen Gozdanovic, Roz Kvet, and Carol Lambo.

Owen Covert, contemporary crafter of hobo nickels, who made sure I got the details right and offered to teach me how to carve.

Tracy Pattison, who lent both her energy and her image.

Cleveland Public Library

In Auburn, NY : Auburn Historical Society, Cayuga Community College Library, Seymour Public Library, and Gail and Gary at Wicher B&B.

Amy Christopher, for introducing me to her grandmother, Needa Simmons, a woman ahead of her time.

Rochelle Swan—Merci!

PROLOGUE—1946

Eddie is coming. The last time I saw him, he was eleven. In my mind he is still my scrawny little brother, but he will turn twenty-six this year. I wonder what kind of man Eddie is now. Does he drink, like our father?

What will he think of me? There's so much he doesn't know.

I walk to my pantry, thinking that I should see what groceries I need to buy to make him a nice dinner, but my eyes are drawn to the second shelf from the bottom. It holds neatly stacked cans of tuna, tomato soup, and beans of all kinds. Hidden behind that food is a box printed with bold, black letters that spell out *Durrand Vineyards*. It's not wine inside that box, no matter what the fancy script claims, and I don't need to open it to remember what it holds.

When Eddie comes, I might let him look inside, let him take out the things in it and see. Each item holds part of my story, and if they are all laid out, they will make a picture. Not like the kind of picture printed on a jigsaw puzzle, with its orderly, neat edges defining a scene as its patterned knobs and notches cleanly snap together, but more like the jagged pieces of a discarded photograph once ripped into pieces and later taped back together. The picture is still there, even if it's distorted by tape and the torn edges don't quite meet.

I've been so hungry I could hardly stand up. Never again. That's the other reason I keep that box in my pantry. When I've used enough food that I can start to read what the box used to hold—Finger Lakes Merlot—I get nervous and go grocery shopping again.

I go to check the guest room for the umpteenth time and add a blanket to the foot of the bed. I remember what it feels like to sleep on cold ground, and I want to be sure Eddie is comfortable. But the pantry pulls me back, and I dig out the box from the second shelf and tug on the twine that has kept my history shut inside for all these years. I reach in and pull out a pair of sturdy shoes that have traveled thousands of miles. The soles, or what's left of them, are so thin that if I wore the shoes again, I'd feel the hard edges of stones beneath my feet. And if it had rained, the mud would ooze into the places where the uppers have pulled away from the soles, where the stitching just plain rotted away and gave up holding things together.

My fingers feel inside the shoes and I panic for a moment, until I find the cellophane that's wrapped around a folded up twenty-dollar bill. The day I bought this house, I cleaned the mud off of the shoes, bought brand-new laces for them, pushed that money inside one of them, just in case, and then laid the shoes in the box. Next to them, I placed a couple of sketchbooks; the smallest is one that traveled nearly as many miles as my shoes.

I pick up the pretty little manicure set that had once belonged to my mother. I wonder if Eddie will remember it. I carried that set with me the whole time. The leather case is shaped like a half moon when it's zipped shut and it has an inset of needlepointed flowers. The oval inset makes me think of a wide-open eye, which is how I learned to see the world, even when I was very young. I unzip the case and look at the tools. Some of them are dinged up and worn, but they're still quite serviceable. A buffalo nickel falls out of the case and rolls across the floor. I pick it up, feel its carved surface, and put it back in the box with everything else. I retie the twine, set the box back on the shelf, and wait for Eddie. It has been fifteen years.

CHAPTER 1—SUMMER, 1931

The train was late. I sat with Eddie on a wooden bench, squinting down the tracks into the late afternoon sun that was turning the rails into blazing strips of metal. I wished I had brought my sketchbook. I would have tried to capture that glow, even though my mother keeps telling me that with times being so hard, nobody can make a living as an artist these days—especially a girl.

"Do you think he likes to go fishing?" Eddie asked.

"Who?" I was distracted, trying to memorize the scene so I could draw it later.

"Raymond! Who else?" Eddie said.

"How would I know?" I shot back. "He lives near the stockyards in Chicago. He's probably never even *been* fishing."

Eddie's face registered disappointment, and I felt a familiar pang of protectiveness. He was eleven—five and a half years younger than me—and I'd looked after him for as long as I could remember. I was the one who made our oatmeal and got us both to school—not my mother, who left early to serve breakfast at the Paradise Diner, and not my father, who at that time of morning usually was snoring off the previous night's bender.

"If he doesn't know how to fish, maybe you can teach him," I said.

Eddie brightened. "Yeah. It's gonna be fun having another boy around."

I hope you're right, I thought. But I had been wiping down counters in the diner when Aunt Ruby read the letter from Lydia, Raymond's mother. *Raymond took the death of his father very hard, and he's become a bit difficult. He just graduated high school and it's time that he finds a job, and of course, there aren't any. I'm worried that he's got too much time on his hands and nothing to do, and he'll get into trouble. I'm hoping that you might be willing to let him visit for awhile, at least for the summer, and maybe put him to work in your diner. Room and board would be all the payment he needs, and I would be very grateful...*

My mother, tight-lipped, had asked, "What do you suppose she means about Raymond being difficult?" I suspected she was worried about having to cope with another male who wouldn't hold up his end. As it was, working at the diner helped her buffer my father's excesses.

"My sister never was very good at handling that boy," Uncle George said. "She pretty much left that up to Mark. Lydia was much better with the girls. Now that his father is dead, Raymond probably thinks he doesn't have to answer to Lydia."

"Or anyone, maybe," my mother said. I heard that from where I was standing, but Aunt Ruby didn't seem to, even though she was sitting right across the booth from my mother.

"Well, we could use the help," Uncle George said. My mother said no more. It is my aunt and uncle's diner.

I felt the train moments before it appeared. The vibrations rumbled through the platform, traveling through the benches and through my bones in passing, as if water had surged from a dam, filling all the inlets and coves in its path as it rushed by. Then the shrill whistle filled my ears and the huge locomotive rumbled into view, spewing steam and black smoke.

The train stopped, and people converged on the platform, exiting from several cars at once. Most of the passengers looked weary. Many of the women wore faded cotton dresses and cloche hats that had lost their smart shape a couple of years ago. Some of the men wore suits that were beginning to get threadbare and shiny. A couple of well-dressed travelers stuck out from the crowd like sore thumbs—people who somehow still managed to prosper while everybody else was trying to make do.

I watched for boys who appeared to be a couple of years older than me. I had no idea what Raymond looked like, but I tried to pick him out anyway. A short, muscular boy with sandy-blond hair sticking out from under a tweed cap strode out of a car. He walked with a springy step, like he was a boxer itching for a fight. Behind him came a taller, stocky boy with dark-brown, slicked-back hair. He was hatless, and he sauntered across the platform, carrying a battered brown suitcase in one hand and shading his eyes with the other.

I guessed that the boxer type was probably Raymond. Besides the attitude, he was carrying two bags; the slick-headed boy had only one. Uncle George stood next to me, watching the crowd, looking at faces. "I believe that's Raymond," he said, motioning in the direction of the boxer type wearing the tweed cap. "He's a spitting image of his father."

I poked Eddie in the ribs. "I should have bet you a nickel I could spot him. I thought it was the boy with the cap!"

Uncle George walked toward the boxer boy and then past him, offering a handshake to the boy with the slicked-back hair. "You're Raymond, aren't you?" Uncle George said.

Eddie grinned and jabbed his elbow into my side. "Yeah, I woulda bet you...so pay up!"

The boy shook my uncle's hand. "Yes," was all he said.

"Well, I'm your Uncle George and these are your cousins, Maddy and Eddie."

"Hullo," Raymond said, barely looking at us.

A little way down the track, the locomotive let off a long, steady hiss of steam. Raymond glanced down the track, following the sound with his eyes, then stared directly at me. His eyes were a dark brown, like his hair, but they weren't friendly. They were just brown, like a shade had been pulled behind them and you couldn't see in. I looked away, feeling uncomfortable, but not before I caught a hint of a smirk as I broke eye contact with him.

Uncle George stepped between us, slapping Raymond on the back. "Welcome to New Harmony, Raymond," he said. "I think you're going to like it here." Raymond shrugged.

Then Uncle George, Raymond, and Eddie started walking shoulder to shoulder toward the diner, leaving me behind. I could have run to catch up, but I was miffed at being forgotten about. I walked slowly, trailing far behind, but no one even noticed.

CHAPTER 2

When I came downstairs for breakfast, I was startled to see my mother sitting at the kitchen table. "Why aren't you at the diner? Are you sick?"

"I'm not serving breakfast today. I have some business to take care of and I want you to go with me."

"What business?" I asked. I looked more carefully at her. She was wearing her dark blue dress with the white pointed collar—the one she had made from a Butterick pattern two summers ago. The dress hugged her slender figure and suited her well. She had also used some scraps of the blue material to fashion a pleated bow that she sewed to the white hat she always wore with the dress. It was a classic but still fashionable look. "We're going into town?"

"Yes." She folded back the newspaper and set it down next to her cup of coffee. "Don't dawdle over breakfast. We need to get going."

My mother and I walked up to Washington Street, past several blocks of tall, narrow houses. Their tiny yards looked ragged, with patches of bare dirt where the grass couldn't bear up under many children playing. We reached the business district, and my mother stopped on the sidewalk at the entrance to the First Union Bank. "Oh my Lord," my mother said, staring past the partly open door into the bank. So many people had crowded into the lobby, it was hard to tell where the lines were. But we pressed our way inside and waited, inching closer to the brass bars of the teller's windows. With so many bodies crammed into that small space, the air became uncomfortably warm and humid. People shuffled restlessly in line. A low murmur added to the tension. Body odors mingled with the smell of overheated wool, making the air unpleasant and hard to breathe. I wondered if I could convince my mother to let me wait outside.

A man in a three-piece suit pushed his way through the crowd, frequently stopping to talk to the customers. Every few minutes, sweat beaded up on his forehead and he dabbed at it with a limp handkerchief. I recognized him from the diner—Mr. Russell, the bank manager. He came in nearly every morning to buy two doughnuts and a cup of coffee for a dime.

He spotted us in line and came over to talk to my mother.

"Iris," he said. "My bank is solid. You don't need to withdraw your money. It's safe here. You have my word."

My mother nodded. "I've always trusted your bank, Mr. Russell, but it just so happens that I need some money today." We stayed in line and she got her money—all of it, which amounted to $106.55. It must have taken her years to save it, squirreling away tips left on the counter—pennies and nickels tucked under the rims of dishes sticky with egg yolk and slippery with bacon grease. It was money I was certain my father knew nothing about, or he would have turned it into hooch and swallowed it.

When we got home, she called me into her bedroom and took out her big blue box of Kotex. She always gave me what I needed each month from this box, which she kept on a shelf in her closet "for reasons of privacy." She put the money into a brown envelope and placed it where my father would never look: in the bottom of her box of sanitary napkins.

"Maddy," she said in a tone so serious that it made my heart lurch, "Your father is never, *ever* to know about this money. Do you understand?" I nodded. "If something happens to me, you take this envelope. It's for Eddie and you to use; it's not a lot, but it could keep you going for a little while. We both know you wouldn't be able to depend on your father." She drew a deep breath. "No one else is to know about our conversation today, okay?" I nodded again. She looked at me intensely, and for the first time, I saw the person inside my mother—she was trying not to be defeated by a life that included a drunk for a husband and hard economic times. I wondered what dreams she had when she was my age. She must still have hope that life could be could be better, I figured, or she wouldn't have saved that money.

"Can I trust you never to speak of this again?"

"I promise," I said, feeling grown up and grateful for her confidence. I watched as she slid the box back onto the shelf. The white cross printed above the T in Kotex promised salvation for Eddie and me.

When we got to the diner, only a few lunch customers remained. "I'm sorry we're so late," my mother said to Aunt Ruby. "I had no idea we'd be gone so long. I was sure we'd be back in time to help with lunch."

Ruby spoke in a low voice. "Several people said there was a run on First Union, so I had a hunch you'd be late. Did you get what you went to town for?"

My mother nodded.

"Thank goodness," Aunt Ruby said. She sighed. "Unfortunately, business is slow today, so we managed without you. It was good to have an extra pair of hands, though." She nodded toward Raymond, who was up to his elbows in soapy dishwater. Eddie brought a stack of dirty plates to him and Raymond made a face that my aunt didn't see. "It's worrisome. I hope this economy turns around pretty soon, or we won't have many customers left."

My mother frowned, but said nothing.

I restocked silverware and napkins and filled the salt and peppers for the supper trade. When my chores were done, I fished my sketchbook out from under the counter. "I'll be back later," I said.

"Take your brother with you," my mother said.

"All right," I sighed. "Come on, Eddie."

"Can Raymond come too?" Eddie asked.

I looked over at Raymond, who still had a pile of dishes and pans to wash and didn't seem to be in any hurry to get them done. At the rate he was going, it would be another hour. "He's not finished with his chores yet. Maybe he can come with us tomorrow, okay?"

We left the diner and turned east, toward the rail yard—one of our favorite places. It has its own music: there's the sounds of locomotives—you can tell how fast they're going by the rhythm of the chugs as they build up or let off steam. There's the metallic squeals and clatter of wheels on the rails, and the sound of couplings grabbing when a train starts out of the yard—the crashes travel like dominoes falling. There's also the smell of coal and hot cinders and sometimes even animals when they come in on cattle cars. Sometimes we'd watch the enormous locomotives take on water at the tower or stand by to see the crew couple and uncouple cars to make up a train. Eddie was fascinated with machinery and the way the welders' torches spewed showers of sparks as men repaired cars in the yard. And I could always find something new to draw.

A commotion at the far end of the yard got our attention. Men and machinery were swarming around the roundhouse. We moved in closer and discovered that a tender brought in for repair had somehow fallen off its track and was wedged on the turntable. The crane operator was backing up, circling around, trying to get his giant hook lined up with the wedged car to lift it back on track. A group of men stood near it, hollering at the driver; each was telling him what to do.

The yard manager spotted us and pointed in the direction we had just come from. "Too dangerous!" he shouted. "Get out of here...now!"

Disappointed, we halfheartedly obeyed and turned around, heading out past the roundhouse. But we circled back to a siding toward the rear of the building, near the woods. Several boxcars and a caboose waited on the rails for maintenance. Eddie and I sat down on a fallen tree. "It's not like we were going to ask to operate the crane," I grumbled. "I just wanted to draw the accident."

"I know. That guy's an old grouch." Eddie picked up some cinders and started tossing them, one by one, at the caboose. Most of the cinders fell short of their target and landed harmlessly in the dirt. One big cinder hit its mark with a solid thump. It broke into smaller pieces and left a smudge on the car's red paint. "Hey, let's go see what's inside!" Eddie said, motioning toward the caboose.

"We're not supposed to go inside any of the cars," I said. "What if we get caught?"

"Nobody's gonna catch us," Eddie said. "Everybody's busy inside the roundhouse. Who's going to see us?"

I was tempted. I had never been in a caboose and I wanted to see what was inside, but of course I was the one who was always expected to know better. I could picture my mother glaring at me, arms crossed, lips tight. "I'm so disappointed in you," she'd say. Then I'd have extra chores and Eddie would get off practically scot-free because he was younger.

"We better not," I said.

"Well, I'm going anyway. You can just *be* a chicken." Eddie took off toward the caboose, grabbed the ladder and scrambled up, disappearing inside.

I ran after him. "Eddie, *come back here!*" Then I was up and inside the car. "Wow," I said, stopping just inside the doorway. I had imagined that the inside of a caboose was pretty much like the inside of a boxcar—just empty space and wooden walls, with maybe a wooden chair or two so the workers could sit down on long trips. Until then, I hadn't given the purpose of the caboose much thought.

"Look at this – it's like a little house," I said. On the right, bolted to the planks of the floor, was a small potbellied stove; a coal box sat next to it, and a few cast iron pots and a skillet were stored in a bin above the coal box. On the left was a partition with an icebox on one side and cans of beans and soup stacked on the other. There were a couple of painted wooden benches to sit on, and at the back end of the car, bunks had been built in to each side. Near the foot of one bunk, a ladder extended up into the cupola. "They actually live here," I said.

Eddie was already at the top of the ladder. "There's another bunk up here," he said. "And you can look out the windows and see the yard."

I followed him up the ladder. If we were going to get caught and punished for trespassing, I wasn't going to miss anything. No sense in doing half the deed if I'd get punished for the whole deed anyway.

When I got to the top, Eddie was kind of crouched on the bunk. I elbowed him over and looked out. One set of narrow windows looked out at the woods, but through the other windows I could see part of the roundhouse and beyond that, the curves of numerous tracks leading into and past the roundhouse. I had never seen the yard before from any height taller than me, and it looked bigger and more orderly than I had thought. I opened my sketchbook to make a rough drawing. Along one of the tracks near the roundhouse, my eye caught something moving. It was a big, burly worker striding toward the caboose.

"Shoot," I hissed. "Somebody's coming!" I scrambled down the ladder with Eddie right on top of me, practically kicking me in the face. We both ran for the door, jumped off the platform, and made a beeline for the trees. We had almost reached the edge of the woods by the time the worker made it to the caboose.

"You kids come back here," the worker shouted. "I want to talk to you. You stay the hell outta the cars!"

Eddie and I kept running, disappearing into the cover of the woods. I didn't know who that worker was, and I wasn't interested in finding out. I also hoped that he wouldn't find out who we were.

When we were convinced the worker wasn't following us, Eddie and I slowed to a walk, catching our breath, and headed for the river that flowed behind the rail yard. We sat down on some boulders at the river's edge to figure out what to do next.

"I'm not going back through the rail yard," I said.

"Me neither," said Eddie. "But how are we going to get home?"

"Be quiet and let me think," I said. Then, I couldn't resist. "You got us into this mess, you know."

"Yeah, I know."

I glanced over at Eddie. He scooped up some flat stones from the river's edge and turned away from me as he tossed them into the water. I knew he was embarrassed, and I felt a little rush of satisfaction—I had been right, after all. But it wasn't much comfort. I watched as Eddie skipped several stones. One large stone plopped heavily into the water, splashing back at Eddie.

"We'll have to follow the river," I said. On hot, steamy days we often swam in the river just a few blocks north of the diner, by Fourth Street. But we had never followed the river as far as the rail yard, and I didn't know how far it was or whether there were any paths along the riverbank. "We'll just have to keep walking until we reach the Fourth Street bridge," I said.

"How far is that?" Eddie asked.

"I have no idea. But it's the river or the rail yard."

We started off in the direction of town, following the gravelly bank for quite a distance as it paralleled the gentle turns of the river. The walking was fairly easy until we came to a sharp bend. Then the gravel disappeared. A tangle of thick undergrowth extended right to the water's edge, where bushes had collapsed, their roots undermined by the flow of water around the bend. They dangled, half dead, over the water, low enough to catch river litter in their branches. It was impassible.

"Now what do we do?" Eddie asked.

I looked around for a minute. "We're going to have to backtrack a little and find a path through the woods—away from the riverbank."

"Is that going to work? What if we get lost?" The fear I heard in Eddie's voice mirrored my own.

"It's going to have to work," I said. "We'll just keep listening for the river. As long as we can hear the water, we won't get lost." I led the way toward the woods, striding with a confidence I didn't feel.

We hiked for a while, following narrow animal paths that wound through the woods, never losing the sound of the water, and we both started to relax. As the woods thinned, we were able to make our way closer to the river. Just ahead, I could see another thicket, but this one looked odd. As we got closer, I saw that branches had been piled up deliberately to form a wall. Someone had built a shelter—several shelters—at the edge of a clearing. In the center of the clearing, a circle of rocks surrounded a fire pit. Alongside the pit, several logs provided a place to sit.

"Wow, do you think somebody is living here?" Eddie said.

"Ssshhh! I don't know." We seemed to have stumbled on someone's... what—camp, lair, hideout? Although I felt uneasy, more powerful was the thrill of discovery and an intense curiosity about whose place this was. I made plans to return without my brother.

"We better keep going," I said. A well-traveled path led from the camp to the riverbank. We followed it down to the water's edge, turned a bend next to some shallow rapids, and then saw that the Fourth Street bridge was in view farther up the river. We both yelled, "There it is!" We ran along the riverbank, which was again mostly gravel, and scrambled up the bank to the bridge. From there, it was only a few blocks to the diner.

"You've been gone for hours," my mother said. "Where have you been? It's suppertime!"

I furtively glanced at the customers sitting on the stools at the counter. Several were railroad workers. I looked back at my mother. She looked tired. Her blonde hair was escaping from the pins she used to keep it pulled back and off her neck. Her complexion was pale; no color showed in her cheeks. This, I knew, was actually a very good sign, because when she was angry, her cheeks became flushed. She was annoyed that we were late for dinner, but she didn't know about the caboose—at least not yet. It occurred to me that the phrase "forgive us our trespasses" must have been written for the curious. Lots of people must go where they weren't supposed to, or it wouldn't be included in that prayer.

"We've been down by the river," I said. I crossed my fingers and hoped she wouldn't ask more. "Sorry we're late. We lost track of time."

My mother sighed—a long, exasperated sigh. "Maddy, I depend on you to see that you and your brother are where you're supposed to be."

I glared at Eddie when my mother wasn't looking. "I know. I'm sorry," I said.

CHAPTER 3

I woke up to a familiar racket. My father was stumbling on the steps that led up to my parents' bedroom, which is down the hall from mine. My mother whispered angrily, my father started to shout, and my mother shushed him. I waited to see which way it would go. There were only two paths, like where a switch divides the railroad tracks. One way would end with my father stomping back down the steps, and I knew we'd all have to tiptoe around him snoring on the davenport the next morning. The other way would end with someone crying, and then it would get very quiet. My mother would come downstairs by herself the next day, and my father would get up in time for lunch. I wasn't good at predicting which way it would end. I suppose it depended on who was pulling the switch.

Eddie always slept through the whole miserable scene. He slept hard, even through thunderstorms. My mother always said a freight train couldn't wake him if it went right past his head. I sat at the edge of my bed and looked out at the stars, wondering why it was always like this, wishing on every one of them for something to change. Finally, I curled up on my bed and inhaled long, deep breaths, trying to focus only on my breathing and lull myself back to sleep.

It felt like I had just dropped off for a moment when my mother was at my bedroom door. "Time to get up, Maddy. I'm leaving for the diner."

"What?" I fought my way back through muddy consciousness.

"It's time to get up," my mother insisted. She spoke firmly but softly. That meant my father was sleeping upstairs.

"Can't I sleep in?"

"I already let you sleep in a little. You need to get up now. Get yourself some breakfast and then come to the diner. We need you to help for a couple of hours this morning, and then you can have the rest of the day to yourself." She stood in the doorway, waiting.

I sighed and sat up. There was no chance for a few more minutes of sleep. "What about Eddie?" I swung my legs off the bed and felt the coolness of the floor pull the warmth from my toes.

"He left about an hour ago to go fishing with Raymond."

"Oh." So he didn't have any chores this morning. I was irritable and tired, and I thought about pointing out that it wasn't fair, but I knew I'd just hear about how I was older and more was expected from me…blah, blah, blah.

"Don't wake your father," my mother said as she turned to go.

"I wouldn't dream of it," I muttered.

"What did you say?" She stepped back into my doorway.

"I said don't worry—I'll be quiet."

My mother nodded, then walked away. I heard the third step from the top creak as she made her way downstairs. I took my time getting dressed, fixed myself some oatmeal with lots of brown sugar, and then left the house. I paused for a second on the back step and then pulled the door shut—hard. It made a satisfying bang that rattled the kitchen window. I knew there was only a slight chance that it woke my father, but I hoped I at least disturbed his sleep. Fair is fair, I thought.

Already the day was heating up and getting sticky. I ambled along for several blocks before I noticed that off to the west, a line of thick gray clouds had overwhelmed the blue sky and was pushing quickly over the town. I heard the low rumble of thunder, and the inside of the clouds glowed for a second and then flickered. I picked up my pace. The diner was only about a block away now. I headed for the side door, cutting across the grass, and reached out to push on the screen door, but the sound of raised voices stopped me.

"Why do you put up with that? You deserve better!" Aunt Ruby said.

"He promised me he would quit," my mother answered.

I quickly drew my hand back away from the door and stood to the side so that I wouldn't be seen. I felt a little guilty, but I wanted to hear what was going on. My mother and aunt hardly ever argued, so this had to be important.

"*When*, Iris," Aunt Ruby asked. "After he loses his job?"

"Jack is still good at what he does," my mother said. "I don't think they'll fire him." She didn't sound too sure, though. My father was a tool-and-die maker and a drunk, and he was very good at both occupations. I started to worry about what would happen if they did fire my father.

"How long do you think that's going to last?" Aunt Ruby demanded. "How long do you think they're going to put up with a man who spends most of his shift drinking at a speakeasy and they have to go find him and drag him out when they need a fixture or a mold made? You're just lucky they haven't found another tool-and-die man to replace him."

"They know why he drinks," my mother insisted. "I think they're making allowances because of Stephen."

This really got my attention. My mother hardly ever talked about Stephen, who was born two years after me. But I knew she kept a photo of Stephen and me in her dresser drawer. I'm about three years old in that picture. Our faces are a study in contrast—mine is solemn, framed by straight, dark-brown hair, and my blue eyes look seriously at the camera. Stephen, with brown eyes and blond, curly hair, like my mother's, is laughing. I'm holding Stephen on my lap, but I don't remember him at all.

"He's not the only man who ever lost a child," Aunt Ruby said. Her voice was quieter now. "And Stephen was your child, too. Jack should be paying attention to you and the kids, to the members of his family who are still here, not drinking himself into oblivion."

"I know, Ruby," my mother said. I heard her blow her nose, so I was pretty sure she was crying. "But I understand how he feels. It's been thirteen years and still not a day goes by that I don't think of Stephen."

Another rumble of thunder blocked out the conversation, and then I heard Aunt Ruby say, "But you haven't turned your back on your family, and *you're* not drinking!" She blew her nose, so now both of them were crying.

There was a long pause. Several large drops of rain splattered on my arm and cheek and I started to go inside. Then my mother spoke again, stopping me in my tracks. "You know, Jack blames himself for Stephen's death."

"That doesn't make any sense. It was a flu epidemic, for pity's sake," Aunt Ruby said. "How could that be Jack's fault?"

"Well, Jack got sick first. He says it's his fault—that he's the one who brought the flu into our house."

My aunt made a sound that was a cross between a snort and a laugh. "And so," she said, "he drinks."

I wondered if it was true that my father drank because of Stephen. If Stephen had lived, maybe my father wouldn't drink so much, and maybe my parents wouldn't fight. Would Stephen and I have been close, like Eddie and I are now, or would Stephen and Eddie, being boys, be the ones to do things together? There was no way to tell. For Eddie and me, Stephen never existed; he was like the rings that form when a pebble is tossed into a pond. It disturbs the water for a short while, and then disappears. Anyone who comes to the pond later never sees the rings.

"Don't you have enough sense to get out of the rain, kid?"

I jumped, startled by the rough male voice, and the man pushed past me into the diner. I waited for a few seconds, collecting myself, becoming aware of the rain that was coming down harder now. A flash of lightning streaked above the diner and I scooted inside.

I was surprised to see only one customer. He sat facing me at a booth at the far end of the diner, and I could see him dipping a square of toast into the runny yolks of fried eggs with one hand while forking up pieces of ham with the other. I recognized him from the rail yard. He was the grouchy yard manager who had sent Eddie and me out of the roundhouse. I avoided eye contact with him, afraid that he might recognize me and put two and two together. But he was watching the man who had just come in ahead of me, who was now standing at the counter talking to my mother. A fringe of salt and pepper hair framed his bald head. He seemed familiar, but his back was to me, so I couldn't see his face. I stepped around to the short side of the counter, where we kept the silverware and napkins, and I made myself look busy. The rain pounded on the metal roof of the diner, and the man spoke loudly over the racket. His gruff voice filled the diner.

"This is the second time, Mrs. Skobel. The rent payment is due on the first of the month, not the fifth. And the rent is $24, not $20."

"I'm very sorry, Mr. Bentley. My husband must have made an error." A flush of red crept up my mother's neck, and two bright spots grew on her cheeks. She gestured toward the red stools at the counter. "Would you like to sit and have a cup of coffee?"

"No, I would like the rest of the money that is owed to me."

"I'll speak to my husband this afternoon..." my mother's voice trailed off. She looked like she wanted the earth to swallow her up. The yard manager was openly staring at her, and Aunt Ruby stood a few steps away, listening.

"I'll do my best to see that you have your money tomorrow morning... but I might need an extra day..."

Mr. Bentley started to speak, but Ruby stepped up to the cash register. She hit the lever to open the drawer. The No Sale flag popped up in the Amount window and Ruby withdrew four dollars and gave them to my mother. "Why don't we save Mr. Bentley some time and settle this today?"

My mother's hand shook a little as she accepted the money. "Thank you," she said. Her cheeks burned even brighter. She handed the money to Mr. Bentley. "Sorry for your inconvenience."

He just grunted and stuffed the money into his shirt pocket. He stepped out the front door, and I watched as the rain bounced off his hat. At the back booth, the yard manager pushed his plate away and slid across the seat. Ruby rang up his meal—22 cents—and gave him change. "You have a good day, now," she said, extra cheerily.

The screen door banged shut behind him, and then the diner was empty, at least of customers. But it was filled with my mother's shame and the unspoken words between my aunt and my mother. They both stepped into the tiny kitchen and I picked up the yard manager's dishes and wiped down the back booth. He had left my mother a quarter. I carried it over to the white coffee cup she used to hold her tips and dropped it in, not sure whether she'd be grateful or embarrassed.

Snatches of hushed conversation drifted over to me while I stood wiping water spots off the silverware.

"...seems like things are getting worse..."

"I'll pay you back..."

"...What do you mean he's never done this before?" Ruby's voice was louder, full of exasperation. "Your landlord just told you this was the second time! I'll bet it won't be the last, either."

"What do you expect me to do? Throw him out? He's my husband, Ruby. He's a good man when he's not drinking..."

"And when was the last time you saw that 'good man'?" Ruby demanded.

She had a point, in my opinion. I tried to remember a time when my father wasn't drinking, but I couldn't.

"I can't throw him out," my mother said. "Everybody in town would know. And how would I pay the rent?"

"You're my sister," Ruby said. "You and your kids could always come live with George and me until you get on your feet."

"I can't, Ruby."

"Why not?"

"Because..." There was a long silence. I waited. "Because I've got to give Jack one more chance."

I threw the dish towel on the counter and walked out the door. One more chance, one more chance. My feet stamped out the rhythm—One... More...Chance—as I strode down Fourth Street, crossed Oak and then Cherry. My shoes sent out splashes of water from puddles that collected where the concrete had cracked and tilted. The rain had stopped, but storm hadn't cleared the air at all, just made it more humid. The musty smell of drowned earthworms drifted up to my nose. It wasn't that I wanted to go and live with Aunt Ruby. But all my mother ever did was give my father chances. And nothing ever changed. Why didn't she see that?

I looked up and realized I had reached the Fourth Street bridge. A few people sat fishing here and there along the riverbank, but not Eddie and Raymond. They were probably at the other end of the bridge where the fishing was usually better. That suited me just fine because I instantly made a decision. I followed the dirt path down the embankment at the side of the bridge and crunched through a wide bed of shale, reaching the river's edge. Satisfied that nobody would notice me, I turned downstream, looking for the trail we had discovered just a couple of days ago.

High above the trees, a couple of hawks circled gracefully, scouting for dinner. I wondered how it felt to be so free—what was it like to glide on the air, supported by the wind? Was it easy to steer? And what did the river look like from that height?

Further down the river, I saw another fisherman. His dog was running around him and jumping. The sound of the water intensified, and I noticed an area of shallow rapids. Just past the rapids, the patch of woods thickened, and I saw the path. I hesitated only for a moment, and then I turned onto the path and followed it into the woods. I stopped at the edge of the camp. This time, the camp seemed to be inhabited. Under one of the shelters was a rolled up blanket. A man's shirt and a pair of brown socks hung from a length of rope stretched between two trees. A small fire smoldered in the fire pit; next to the fire, a beat up frying pan and a tall, battered tin can sat on a flat rock. No one was around, but the camp had a presence, as if a play was in progress but I had come at intermission. I stood at the end of the path, staring at the scene in front of me and wondering who these things belonged to.

"What are you doing," said a voice right behind me. It was more of a demand than a question. Startled, I jumped and whirled around. Standing in the path was a man holding a pole and a stringer of fish. His hat shaded his face and I couldn't see whether he was angry, but there was no smile in his voice. A brown and white dog stood at his side, the fur on his legs wet and muddy. They both looked at me, waiting.

"I was just walking...I wasn't...I didn't mean to..." I tried to get my composure. My heart was beating so loud I was sure he could hear it, too.

"This ain't no place for kids," he said.

CHAPTER 4

Nervously, I shifted my weight from side to side. Should I run? He was blocking the path back to the river, so I'd have to run deeper into the woods. That seemed like a bad idea. Besides, I could never outrun the dog. I swallowed hard. "I didn't know it was yours; I didn't know it was a... fishing camp," I said, eyeing his stringer, which had quite a few good-sized catfish on it. I realized that he was probably the man I had seen further down the river.

"So what *are* you doing here?" he asked again.

I shrugged. "I don't know, exactly. My brother and I were cutting through the woods a few days ago and we found this place. I just wanted to see it again."

He stared at me for a minute.

"I didn't mean any harm," I said. He scowled, which I could now plainly see under the shadow of his hat. "Yeah, I suppose not," he said. "Sometimes trouble comes even when you're not looking for it, though—kinda like stepping on a yellowjacket's nest."

"What?"

He grinned. "What's your name, kid?"

"Maddy," I said.

"Maddy...that short for something?"

"For Madeline, which I don't care for much," I said.

"Well, Maddy, you might as well sit for a bit by the fire and satisfy that curiosity of yours. You hungry?"

"Maybe a little," I said. It felt like something had passed over us and gone—like the way a cold wind keeps the heat of the sun from touching you, and then the wind stops and you feel warmth on your skin again.

"You like catfish?"

"Yes, sir. I like to catch 'em and I like to eat 'em."

"Well, I caught plenty today, so there's enough for the three of us," he said.

"Three? Is someone else here?" I asked, looking down the path to the river.

"Nope." He cocked his head toward his dog. "Just you and me and Jigger. Hearing his name, the dog pricked up his ears. Jigger was staying close by, obviously interested in the fish. He was a handsome dog, a little on the thin side, like his master, but he looked healthy and his eyes were a bright, warm brown. "So do you want some lunch?" the man asked me.

"Yes, thank you," I said. I sat down on one of the logs and waited. I was excited to be allowed to stay for bit. I couldn't have known it then, but that day was the start of a practical education that would keep me alive over the next couple of years.

CHAPTER 5

"Name's Henry," he said. He sat down on the opposite log and added a small amount of wood to the fire, blowing on the embers until they glowed and sent up fingers of flame. He piled more wood on the fire and began cleaning the catfish. I watched as he made quick, sure cuts with his knife, stacking one fillet on top of another until all the fish had been cleaned. Jigger sat close by, following Henry's every move, not taking his eyes off the fish for a minute. As Jigger watched, drool dripped rhythmically from his mouth—a sight I found both funny and disgusting.

When the fire had settled into a steady burn, Henry placed a makeshift grate over it and got a few items from a bundle he had in the shelter. He scooped out a dollop of lard from a can and dropped it into a frying pan, which he placed on the grate. The lard sizzled and melted. Henry quickly dredged the fillets in cornmeal and set them to frying in the lard. He set out several pie tins and put the plump, golden fish in them as each piece got done. The air grew thick with the aromas of frying fish mingling with campfire smoke.

I watched all this quietly, and Henry didn't speak, either. When the fish was finished, Henry took a long stick and poked around in an area of the fire that wasn't directly under the grate. He pushed out a couple of charred-looking lumps, which I hadn't noticed earlier, and he nudged them to the edge of the fire and swept them into a pie tin. He carefully pulled blackened tin foil off the lumps, and I saw that they were potatoes.

"I didn't know you could cook potatoes like that!" I said.

Henry smiled. "I usually do three or four at a time if I have them; they keep for a couple of days and I can either eat them cold or reheat them in a fire."

"How long do you stay when you come here?" I asked.

"Depends." He pushed several pieces of fish and a potato onto a pie tin, added a fork, and handed it to me. "Maybe a few days, maybe a week or two." He cut up some fish in another tin, mashed some potato in with it, and set it down for Jigger. Finally, Henry fixed a plate for himself. I waited until he began to eat, and then I joined him.

"This is the best catfish!" I said between mouthfuls.

"Happy to share," he said.

"So is this your camp?" I asked. "Where do you live?" I was still trying to remember if I had seen him at the diner.

"I live nowhere and everywhere. This ain't my camp, either." Henry looked at me. "You don't know what this is, do you?"

I stopped chewing and looked back at him. "I guess I don't," I said. I had thought it was some kind of camp for fishermen. Now I wondered if Henry was on the lam and we were sitting in some kind of gangster hideout.

"This is a jungle, kid. It's a place where hobos stay when they're passing through."

"Hobos? You mean, like bums?"

For a moment, Henry looked very angry. Then he spoke quietly. "First thing you need to know is that there's a difference between hobos and bums," he said. "Bums can't or won't work. Lots of them are messed up on drink. But hobos work for food or a bed; they don't take handouts."

"You're a hobo?" I asked.

"Yep."

"Then where do you work?"

"Anywhere I can," he said. "I started hopping freights, hoping I could find another job after the steel mill in Pittsburgh shut down. Ain't no jobs out there, though." He ate a few more bites and then said, "So I survive on spot labor...anything from washing windows to pearl diving."

"Pearl diving?" I asked. We were hundreds of miles away from the ocean, but if there were pearls to be found in a nearby lake or river, I wanted to know about it.

Henry laughed. "Washing dishes."

"Oh." I was disappointed, but his words sparked a memory. One day Uncle George was ill, and a man had come to the diner asking to work for food. Aunt Ruby had been happy to hire a substitute dishwasher for the day. Later she said she wished she had a regular job for him because he worked hard, even mopping the floor and wiping down the tile during the slow part of the day when there weren't any dishes to wash. She gave him a meal and paid him besides. I had only gotten a few quick looks at the man, though, because Eddie and I were forbidden to visit with him. "No distractions," Aunt Ruby had said firmly. Now I was fairly sure that the dishwasher was Henry.

He gathered up the pie tins and cooking utensils. "All right, then," he said. "One rule of the jungle is that you clean up after yourself. If you don't, other 'bos will tell you to go build your own fire." He had a can of water heating up at the edge of the fire, and I helped him wash the dishes with it. He carried them over to one of the shelters and tucked them behind a small mound of rocks heaped at the back. I could see a couple of other cooking pots and several tins of food—beans and salmon. At least he had something for supper.

"Can I come visit you again?" I asked. I wasn't sure how I was going to do it, but I'd find a way to bring him some food. I thought about how he had shared the food he had, and I hoped he and Jigger still had enough to eat.

He studied me for a moment. "This really ain't no place for kids. Especially girls," he said.

"I want to bring you some food, to replace what I ate today. Will you still be here tomorrow? I could come in the afternoon."

"You don't give up easy, do you?" he laughed. "I guess that's a good thing these days. All right, I'll still be here tomorrow. If you have food to share, I'd be grateful for it."

I turned down the path to the river.

"If by chance you have an onion, that would be just the thing for tomorrow's stew," Henry called after me.

When I got back to the diner, Eddie was sitting at the counter, grinning from ear to ear. "Guess what, Maddy! We're going fishing tomorrow morning. Just the men, dad said." He spun round and round on the stool, and I was sure he was going to fly off.

"What? Dad said that?"

"Yeah! We're going fishing. Dad, me, and Raymond."

"Don't get your hopes up," I said, instantly regretting it, Eddie stopped spinning and his face drained of joy.

"We are too going," he said. He crossed his arms and glared at me. "You're just jealous."

"No, I'm not." He was right, though—at least a little. I could only think of one really good memory of my father. I was probably nine or ten at the time, and my father spent an entire afternoon with me, trying to teach me how to ride a bicycle. I remember how I tried hard to please him, and I came close to getting my balance. My father gave me a quick hug and said we'd try again the next day. So I got my bike out and sat on the front steps, waiting for him to come home from work, but he didn't come home until it was already dark—and he was drunk. "I just don't want you to be disappointed if Dad doesn't come through."

"We're going to go fishing together," Eddie insisted. "You wait and see!"

The next morning I woke up to a quiet house. I looked over at my clock. 9:30. I crept quietly downstairs for breakfast and found a note propped up next to an empty cereal bowl. *Maddy, I let you sleep in today. The boys have gone fishing—why don't you just enjoy the day yourself? If you come to the diner in time to help with supper, that will be fine. Love, Mom.*

I studied her neat handwriting. *The boys have gone fishing.* Did that mean they were with my father, or did they go by themselves because my father was still sleeping off last night's binge? I hurried through my breakfast and tiptoed upstairs to peek in my parents' bedroom. It was empty, and the bed was made.

"Wow, everybody's gone," I whispered. I was free for the day and I knew exactly what I wanted to do.

CHAPTER 6

At the Fourth Street bridge, I stopped to make sure my father and Eddie were nowhere in sight, and then I quickly made my way down the river. I found the path easily, but when I got within sight of the jungle, I stopped. There were three figures sitting on the logs around the campfire. I knew one was Henry because I could see Jigger sprawled by his side. But I didn't know who the others were, and I wasn't sure if I should approach. Still, I had promised Henry that I would bring him food…

Jigger decided for me. He bolted upright from his sleeping position and came running at me, barking. All three men jumped up and moved toward me. One man grabbed a thick stick. Panic surged through me and I wanted to run, but my legs seemed frozen. Henry was the first man behind Jigger, and when he recognized me, he whistled for his dog. "Here, boy!" Jigger turned and ran back to Henry. "Good boy…it's Maddy…it's okay," he said. Then he called to me. "Come on, kid. Meet my friends."

My heart was still thumping wildly, and my legs felt like rubber, but I stepped closer to the campfire. "Jigger scared me, Henry. I didn't know if it was safe to come closer."

"You got to call out his name as you come up the path," Henry said. "He'll greet you nicely if you call to him first."

"I'll remember that," I said.

Henry turned to his friends. The man standing closest to him was older, lean, and clean-shaven. The dark dress pants and a light-colored button-down shirt gave him an air of authority. The other man was much younger; he wore a crumpled brown fedora and he had reddish-brown hair and a beard. He was also thin, and his clothes hung on him, giving him the appearance of having borrowed his older brother's clothes. Henry introduced him first.

"Reedy, this here's Maddy."

Reedy grinned and tipped his hat to me. "It's a pleasure," he said.

Henry looked at the older man. "And this is Professor," he said.

Professor bowed. "Pleased to meet you, Miss," he said very properly.

"Thank you, it's nice to meet you, too," I said to both of them. It was Reedy who had grabbed the stick, ready to use it as a club. I watched as he sat back down on the log and laid the stick against it, still within easy reach.

"Don't you give this any mind," he said, patting the club. "I keep it just in case."

"One never knows," Professor agreed, nodding.

I handed Henry the bag of food I had brought. One side of the brown sack was quite wrinkled. I must have squeezed it hard when Jigger came after me. "I hope this stuff is still okay," I said.

Henry smiled, a warm smile that felt like friendship. He dug into the bag, pulling out one item at a time. The peanut butter sandwiches had gotten a little squished, but they were still recognizable. Next was a red and white can. "Oxtail soup! We can make stew," he said. At the bottom of the bag was an onion. He held it up and grinned. "You remembered! Stay if you can, Maddy. We're going to have us a good mulligan!"

Henry taught me how to make mulligan stew that day. I watched as he got it started in a tall, battered tin can. He balanced the can on rocks that had been carefully positioned in the campfire. He cut up the onions, Reedy brought him a small piece of sausage, and Henry let that start to cook in the bottom of the tin. In just a few moments, the smell of onions cooking in pork fat filled the air. It smelled delicious already. Jigger sat next to Henry, his nose quivering like a rabbit's as he took in the smells. Henry dumped in the soup and added water. "The soup is a bonus," he explained. "You can make mulligan without it, but it gives extra flavor." Professor added several potatoes, and Reedy had gotten a soup bone and a couple of tomatoes. I could see that it was both expected and a matter of pride for each man to contribute.

Henry passed around the peanut butter sandwiches, and with Henry's approval, I fed one to Jigger, who was now becoming my buddy.

"Why did you name him Jigger?" I asked Henry.

He laughed. "I'll show you," he said. Henry walked a short way away from the campfire, then turned and took a little bite of his sandwich. Jigger watched, his ears pricking to attention. Then, in a very honeyed voice, Henry began talking to Jigger. "Oh, what's the matter...poooor puppy dog. Come here, puppy..." Henry crooned. Jigger got up and began limping over to Henry.

"Oh my gosh!" I said. "He's hurt!"

Jigger made his way to Henry, and then held up his paw for Henry to inspect; Henry gave him a chunk of sandwich. All three men broke into noisy laughter.

"What's so funny?" I demanded.

"He's faking!" Henry said, still laughing. "When I first found him, he really did have an injured front leg. I took care of him, and he learned fast that if he could get someone's sympathy, he'd get some food. He's been doing that act ever since." Henry returned to the campfire with Jigger bouncing along beside him. "So I named him Jigger. That's what we call someone who does a jig—a 'song and dance'—pretending to be hurt to get a handout."

We sat around the campfire while the stew cooked, and I listened as Henry's friends talked. Turned out that Professor really was a professor, of sorts. He was a high school teacher—had been for twenty-two years in some small town in Illinois until times got so bad they couldn't afford to keep the school open. I couldn't believe they would actually close a school. I turned that thought over in my mind for a few minutes, thinking what it would be like. Sure, it would be fine not having homework and exams, but I would miss my friends and some of my favorite teachers. It would also mean that I'd either have to spend more time working at the diner, or I'd be at home, trying to stay out of the way of my father. Neither option was very appealing.

"Maybe you could teach in my school," I offered.

Professor shook his head. "I keep checking. They hired a new man last January, but they're not hiring now."

I nodded. Mr. Otis was the new teacher. He took over my eleventh grade class halfway through the school year, replacing Miss Graham. The trouble had started over the summer when Miss Graham, who had taught at the school ever since I entered first grade, became engaged. She came to school in the fall wearing a modest engagement ring, and we were deliciously shocked.

"But she's *old!*" Martha Robbins had whispered to me from across the aisle.

"I know!" I whispered back. "She's probably thirty!"

"Do you think she's too old to have babies?" Martha asked.

I shrugged. "Maybe not. But if she wants a baby, she'd better get busy!"

Martha giggled and her cheeks turned several shades of pink. "Shhh! Stop it!" she said.

Then, over Christmas break, Miss Graham and her fiancé got married, which promptly resulted in her being fired. Times were so tight and jobs were so scarce, the school administration said, that a married woman had no right to a job. Turns out that our school, and about half the schools in the country, had a policy that actually said so. Miss Graham wasn't even allowed to finish the school year. I was still mad about that, but Mr. Otis had won me over. Not only was he a good teacher, he was an artist. He helped me with my drawings, and he'd even given me a sketchbook that he said was just going to waste.

"What about schools in some of the other towns, like Dennison?" I asked Professor.

He shook his head. "I've been looking for another teaching job for two years. A lot of schools have closed. There's no money to keep them open."

"Professor keeps riding the high iron looking for a classroom," Henry said. "We don't see him often, but at least he brings us the news when he comes in."

Professor laughed at my puzzled look. "The fast trains that run long distances ride over the higher sets of tracks. Those tracks are built to take bigger loads and greater speeds." For a few minutes he was a teacher again. "The rails for the branch lines are lower. Those trains don't travel as fast or as far and their loads are lighter."

"More people ride the high iron, too," said Henry. "They travel from one end of the country to the other, looking for a job, like Professor here."

"Do you do that, too?" I asked Henry.

"Nope. Used to, for a little while. But then I found out I could make a bit of a living riding the branch lines and finding odd jobs. Most 'bos are sticking to branch lines now. It's too crowded on the main lines."

"Really?" I had seen plenty of people riding the passenger trains, but it was hard to imagine crowds of people riding freight trains.

"Oh, yes," Professor said. "You should see what happens when a train starts to leave a yard. Hundreds of people emerge from woods or fields, wherever they've been concealed. They all run along the tracks, hopping into boxcars and onto reefers and gondolas; they grab ladders and pull themselves up on top of boxcars. They ride anywhere they can."

My mind was reeling with questions. "Isn't that dangerous? Why don't they get on the trains before they start moving?"

"You bet it's dangerous," Henry said. He stirred the stew and the smell of onions wafted into the air.

"The railroads don't want people riding for free," Professor said. "They don't care that half the nation is out of work and has no money to buy tickets." Professor seemed to be building up his own head of steam. "So they've hired police—bulls, as they are called by everyone else—to keep people off the trains. Some of the bulls are nasty men, very mean. They won't let anyone catch out—hop on—if they can help it, and those who do often have to face a swinging club. More than one hobo has had to take his chances jumping off a moving train, or face being clubbed to death." Professor paused, taking a deep breath.

I was horrified. Killing someone for hopping a freight? I thought about the day Eddie and I nearly got caught exploring the caboose. Was that man a railroad bull, and would he have hurt us if he had caught us? My heart started racing. I took a deep breath.

Professor looked at me for a moment and then spoke quietly. "They're not all like that, though. Some will keep you off the cars until the train moves out of the yard. Then they'll turn their back and pretend not to see the swarm of people catching out. But they can't let anyone get on the trains in the yard or they could lose their job. If you want to catch out, you have to do it while the train is leaving the yard, before it gets going too fast. You learn to count the chugs. If they're slow, you can grab a ladder. If they're quick, the train is going too fast."

I stared into the campfire, picturing the scene Professor had described. I knew times were bad, but I didn't know that so many people were out of work that they were risking their lives riding freight trains across the country in the hopes of finding a job—and that others were willing to hurt or even kill the people riding the trains. I wondered why President Hoover hadn't done something about all of this. Surely he knew what was happening. Surely he had the power to stop it.

Gradually, I became aware of music. I recognized the tune – *Wildwood Flower.* My mother had sung it to me when I was a little girl. But it wasn't my mother's voice I was hearing; it was an instrument. Still, I could hear the words playing in my head.

> *I'll sing and I'll dance, my laugh shall be gay*
> *I'll cease this wild weeping, drive sorrow away.*

Startled, I looked up. Reedy was blowing softly into a harmonica. When he saw that he had my attention, he winked at me and began playing louder. I laughed and sang with him:

> *Though my heart now is breaking, he never shall know*
> *That his name made me tremble and my pale cheeks to glow.*

He played another verse and then we ended together:

> *I'll live yet to see him regret the dark hour*
> *When he won, then neglected the frail wildwood flower.*

Reedy smiled kindly at me. "You sing very nicely, Miss Maddy." He studied me for a moment. I noticed his eyes were the color of the slate in the riverbed – a bluish gray. "Don't let Professor's stories upset you too much," he said. "Mr. Hoover keeps saying prosperity is just around the corner. Who knows, maybe we're about to turn that corner."

"That's been Mr. Hoover's song, all right – Prosperity Is Just Around the Corner," Professor said. "He's singing it, but nobody is dancing to it."

Eddie was practically dancing, though, when I came in the back door to the house late in the afternoon. "Look, Maddy!" He dragged me over to the fridge and pointed to a plateful of filleted fish sitting on the top rack.

"You caught all those?"

"Yep. Me and Raymond—and *Dad*!" he said. "And that's not all of the fish, either. We sent a bunch with Raymond to give to Aunt Ruby."

"Wow, today was your lucky day," I said, referring more to his spending time with our father than to the day's catch. "Where is Dad, anyway?"

"Upstairs. He said he had to shower off the fish scales. Mom said you didn't have to go help with supper at the diner. She's coming home and we're all having fish tonight!"

"That's amazing," I said.

"What, that we're having fish?"

"No, silly. It's amazing that we're having supper together. When was the last time *that* happened?"

"I know," Eddie said. "But Dad said things were going to change from now on."

"Hmmm." I didn't believe it. But I wasn't going to rain on Eddie's parade today.

"And guess what else? Dad said we could go again tomorrow. He's going to come to the diner to get us after his shift ends, so we should get our chores done early."

"Us?"

"Yeah, don't you want to go?"

"Sure. I always like fishing." I let a little seed of optimism grow inside me. Maybe things really would be different. People changed sometimes, didn't they? Maybe my father could change.

CHAPTER 7

"Did you enjoy your fish last night?" Ruby asked as the three of us—my mother, Eddie, and I—came to the diner.

"It was *excellent*," my mother said. She looked happier than I'd seen her in a long time. She'd put on a little makeup that morning, too. With a touch of lipstick and a bit of rouge, she looked pretty.

"I'm glad," Ruby said, smiling.

"We're going fishing again today," Eddie announced, "as soon as Dad gets off work."

"Well, well," Ruby said, raising her eyebrows. "That should be fun."

Eddie and I set about doing our chores while my mother helped with the food prep and Ruby started her big pot of chili. Lunchtime came, and business was steady, but it wasn't a crowd by any means. We had the diner cleaned up by early afternoon, and there wasn't much left to do. I pulled out my sketchbook and Eddie grabbed an old *Saturday Evening Post* and started flipping through it. He kept glancing at the clock, which my mother also noticed. "You won't make it move any faster by staring at it," she teased.

"I know," he moaned. "I just want it to be 3:30 already!"

By 3:45, my mother was also checking the clock every few minutes.

At 4:00, gloom had settled into the diner. No one was talking. No one wanted to say it—that my father wasn't coming. Finally, at 5:00, as business picked up a little, my mother sent us home. "Maybe your father got to work some overtime," she said, but we all knew there hadn't been any overtime in several years. "Maddy, why don't you start some supper in case your father gets home in a little while."

Eddie and I walked home in silence. I didn't know what to say to him, he looked so miserable. I had a knot in my stomach, too, and I could have kicked myself for being so stupid, believing that things might change.

"What would you like for supper?" I asked, looking in the icebox for something to make. There was some leftover fish, but I decided not to mention that.

"I'm not very hungry," Eddie said.

"Me, neither." I sighed. "You just want some cereal?"

"Yeah, okay."

I cooked a pot of oatmeal, throwing in some raisins at the last minute because I knew Eddie liked them. Just as we finished eating, the back door opened and there was my father, standing in the doorway to the kitchen. "Where's supper?" he demanded.

"Well, I didn't exactly make anything...we weren't too hungry...Eddie and I had cereal." I scrambled to find words to answer him.

"What the hell kind of supper is that!" he bellowed, glowering at me. "That's a goddam breakfast."

"Well, we weren't very hungry," I said again.

"Well I'm hungry and I want some supper!" He was still yelling, but he stepped closer and the reek of alcohol and cigarettes rolled off of him, filling the kitchen.

I stood up quickly. "Okay, I'll make you something. I don't know what we have...I'll look."

For some reason, this angered him even more. "I don't know what we have...I'll look," he said, mocking me, his voice hateful and sarcastic. "Tell you what," he shouted. "I'll look!" He lurched over to the cupboards, flung open the metal doors, and started throwing boxes and cans of food over his shoulder, into the kitchen.

"Here's soup, crackers, macaroni, cereal, tuna fish..." He tossed each item as he named it. Food flew everywhere. I stood rooted to the kitchen floor, not believing what I was seeing and not knowing what to do. Then a can of soup hit my left foot and a box of crackers thudded against my right shoulder. I ran to the living room, pushing Eddie ahead of me through the doorway. We watched as my father systematically emptied the cupboards, strewing food everywhere. When he finished, he stood staring at the mess on the kitchen floor. "There—that's what we have! Make something! Oh here, I forgot. You need something to cook with." He yanked out a drawer, turned it upside down, and dumped it out. I watched, mute, as spoons, forks, knives, spatulas, and a can opener became part of the mess.

Eddie and I froze, too frightened to move. My father stood looking at us, his arms crossed across his chest, his anger apparently spent. "The hell with you!" he said, and he turned and staggered out the door.

"The hell with *you!*" Eddie yelled back. I heard the catch in Eddie's voice and I knew he was trying not to cry.

"It's okay now, at least he's gone," I said. "Help me clean this mess up before Mom comes home."

"Clean it up yourself," Eddie said. "You're the one Dad got mad at!" He stormed through the kitchen and started up the stairs to his room.

I could feel hot tears pushing their way out. "It wasn't my fault!" I shouted. "You come back here and help me." The door to Eddie's room slammed and I stood in the kitchen by myself, surrounded by chaos and choking on rage—rage at my father for being a drunk, rage at my mother for marrying a drunk, and rage at Eddie for blaming me and deserting me.

Slowly, I started cleaning up the mess, picking up the boxes and cans first. Most of the cans had suffered small dents, and I stacked them the best I could in the cupboards. Some of the boxes had their corners bashed and some boxes had broken open. I got adhesive tape from the bathroom medicine cabinet and taped up the broken boxes before I put them back on the shelves. Finally, just the utensils were left, strewn among bits of cereal and macaroni that had spilled out when food went flying. I got the broom and swept everything into a pile and into a dustpan. Then I picked out the spoons and knives and spatulas, blew them off and put them, deliberately, back into the drawer without washing them. All the while, I kept hearing my father's voice as he said, "The hell with you."

CHAPTER 8

I was first up the next morning and went downstairs for breakfast. Eddie came in a few minutes later, but I refused to look at him or talk to him. He sat down with his bowl of cereal, choosing the chair opposite me, and after a few minutes of silence, he said, "I shoulda helped clean up. It wasn't your fault. But I was so mad at Dad, and then he said 'the hell with you' and..." Eddie's voice trailed off and he stirred his cereal around in the bowl, pushing down on the flakes, drowning every flake in milk. "Why doesn't he like us?" Eddie asked.

I wasn't going to answer him. Even though I had gone to bed last night soon after I cleaned up my father's mess, I was tired today, and still angry. But since Eddie had offered an apology of sorts, I briefly gave in. "I think he only likes booze. I don't think he even likes Mom." I applied a blob of grape jelly to a piece of toast, carefully spreading it, transforming the bread into a slab of sticky purpleness right to its edges. I tried to imagine what my father would be like if he didn't drink, but to imagine him not drunk seemed like I was thinking about someone else's father.

My mother walked in, wrapped in her faded yellow bathrobe. She looked small and worn out, as if she was shrinking in response to the load my father put on her. It occurred to me that probably another few years of living with my father and she'd disappear entirely.

She opened the cupboard to reach for the oatmeal and her hand paused in midair. "What in the world!" she said. In the morning light, it was almost comical. I had neatly lined up bashed boxes mended with white strips of adhesive tape on the upper shelves, and the scuffed, dented cans were balanced precariously against and on top of each other on the lower shelves.

The emotions of the previous night surged fresh again, but collided with what I now saw as a ridiculous array of battered food. I covered my face with my hands while my emotions fought it out; what would it be— tears or laughter? For a few seconds, tears came; then laughter started to bubble up.

"What happened?" my mother demanded.

"Dad." Eddie said.

"What do you mean?"

"Dad was looking for supper," Eddie said.

This was too much. Eddie's simple explanation struck me as hilariously funny and I snorted with laughter. Looking out between my fingers, I could see both Eddie and my mother watching me in astonishment.

"So you didn't have supper ready, and your father got mad," my mother said. "I'm surprised at you, Maddy. You should know better."

At that, my emotional battle was over. Laughter and tears gave way to an overwhelming feeling of betrayal. "Why are you defending him?" I shouted. "You always defend him!"

"You shouldn't make him mad, Maddy. It only makes things worse."

"How could things be any worse!" I stormed up the stairs to my room, but not without a parting shot. "Why did you marry him, anyway? You should have known better!"

CHAPTER 9

"Where are the other hobos?" I asked, as I gave Henry a can of beans and two onions I had taken from home.

"They come and go just like I do," Henry said. "Can't predict, unless they leave a message."

"A message? How could someone leave a message?"

"On the water tower, usually," he answered.

"Ohhh." I said. Sometimes Eddie and I watched the railroad crew preparing a locomotive for the next run. They'd drive the engine under the coal chute to fill the tender and then stop at the water tower to fill the boiler. There was always a lot of writing scrawled on the tower, and sometimes scratchy, simple drawings, too. I never gave it more than a quick look; it didn't make much sense so I figured that probably some of the boys from town had done the scribbling.

"Do the hobos do the drawings, too?" I asked.

"Yep. Those are all messages we leave for others."

"What do they mean?"

"Well, it depends," Henry said. He scratched a large X into the dirt, drew a circle on both the right and left sides of the X, and then added a semicircle above the X. "This means 'safe camp.' It's on the water tower, with an arrow pointing in the general direction of this place."

"So that's how people find this camp!" I said. I wondered if the crew in the rail yard knew about the hobos. "What else do the signs mean?"

He drew rapidly in the dirt. "This one is a warning that there's bad water, this means there's good water, and these are directions." He drew circles with lines and arrows passing through and coming out of the circles. "See—this means 'good road to follow'; this one means 'turn right here'; this one means 'turn left here'; and this shows you which way to go at a crossroads. Sometimes you'll see signs drawn on fences by someone's house." He drew a horizontal line with two lines angled under each end that made me think of two legs of a table. "This means you can get sit-down food here, and this one," he drew a line drawing of a cat, "means 'kind-hearted lady.'"

"Wow! It's like a secret language!" I said. Henry laughed, and the skin around his eyes crinkled. "I guess you're right," he said. He stood up and scuffed up the dirt to erase the signs. "But most people either don't notice or don't care about the signs."

"Well, I care!" I said. Tomorrow I'd go take another look at the water tower.

CHAPTER 10

I think Eddie gave up on our father the night he threw food around the kitchen. Eddie started spending more of his free time with Raymond, which was okay at first. I figured Eddie could use a friend, and I also felt sorry for Raymond. I thought it would be tough to lose your father, if you had a decent father, and then get farmed out to relatives because there weren't any other jobs. As time went on, it seemed to me that the friendlier Raymond was to Eddie, the more disagreeable he became to me. Raymond was even downright mean at times, but it was always when no one was looking. I'd be busing tables and Raymond would walk by and bump me, shoving me into a table. "Oops," he'd say. "I didn't see you." Once when I brought over some dishes for him to wash, he sprayed my hand with scalding hot water as I set the dishes down. "Sorry, I didn't see you," he said with sarcasm in his voice. I yelled and dropped the dishes. A plate shattered and Aunt Ruby came over.

"Maddy, please be more careful!" Ruby said. Raymond smirked, but Aunt Ruby didn't notice. She never gave me a chance to explain, and I had to clean up the broken crockery besides. The next time I brought in dishes, I set them down hard on the soggy counter next to the sink. They slid heavily into the sink, splattering Raymond with bits of garbage and dirty dishwater. I got some on myself, too, but it was worth it. "There," I said to Raymond, "I bet you see me now."

He glared at me as he grabbed a towel to wipe off his face and arms. "You'll be sorry, you little bitch," he muttered just loud enough for me to hear.

After that, I kept my distance from Raymond. I tried to do more things with Eddie, but I found that Eddie preferred to spend his free time with Raymond. Somehow, things had shifted and I was the odd one out.

I complained to my mother. "I tried to be nice to Raymond, and now I'm the one getting left out."

"I know, Maddy," she said. "But you're seventeen now, and your interests will soon become very different from the boys' anyway. Most girls your age are already thinking about getting married."

"Well, not me." *I'm going to become an artist,* I added silently. "And I don't see what age has to do with it, anyway. Raymond is older than me! Why are Raymond and Eddie so buddy-buddy? Eddie's only twelve."

I saw a flicker of something cross my mother's face. It was quick, and then it was gone. "Raymond never had a brother," she said after a moment. "I think Eddie is kind of a little brother to him."

"Fine!" I said, "I guess I don't need a little brother, then. Raymond can have mine!"

"Maddy, try to be a bit more understanding. Raymond needs friends right now, and Eddie seems to be about the only person Raymond wants to be friends with. Give it time."

I dropped it. My feelings were hurt, but there was more to it than that. The so-called accidents in the diner were bad enough, but sometimes when I was working, I'd look up and Raymond would be staring at me with that cold look in his eyes; one corner of his mouth turned down in what seemed like a sneer. I could feel his scorn; it made me uneasy, like the way I felt sometimes when I had to walk home alone in the dark. I didn't know why Raymond was like that and I didn't know what to do about it. I knew it was pointless to tell Aunt Ruby, and now it seemed hopeless to say anything to my mother.

I decided to talk to Eddie about it one night. It was a hot summer evening, and the two of us sat on the front porch at dusk, drinking lemonade, waiting for the stuffiness in the house to be replaced by a cooling evening breeze. Up and down the street, yellow light appeared in windows—a dim yellow at first, like it was stifled by the heat—and then it got brighter as the dusk turned to night. The heat encouraged the crickets and cicadas, and their sound was loud and energetic.

"You and Raymond are getting to be pretty good friends," I said, not sure how to start.

"Yeah, he's okay," Eddie said.

"Raymond likes you, but he doesn't like me," I said. "I don't know why."

"It's simple. He doesn't like girls," Eddie said.

"Raymond doesn't like girls?" I pondered that information for a few moments. "You mean...he's a...a *homosexual*?" I whispered the last word.

"No! Don't be stupid!" Eddie said. "He just doesn't *like* girls. He thinks they're bossy. And brainless."

I was stunned. I wasn't expecting an answer like that. Maybe something like *because you talk too much* or *because you don't like to play catch*, neither of which was exactly true, but not an answer as cut and dried and unreasonable as *because you're a girl*.

"But..." I couldn't think of what to say. I took a deep drink of my lemonade and chewed up a piece of ice. "How do you know?" I finally asked.

Eddie shrugged. "He told me, stupid."

I scowled, noticing that my brother had called me 'stupid' twice in the last five minutes.

"He told me he didn't get along with his sisters." Eddie said. "Raymond said they were always telling him what to do and he got tired of it. He said he didn't think his dad liked girls much, either. He and his dad did a lot of things together, but his dad didn't pay much attention to Raymond's sisters. Plus, his mom and dad fought a lot."

"Well, that seems to be what married people do," I said.

"Yeah, well...Raymond said his dad would get fed up and hit his mother. That would stop the fight."

"He'd *hit* her?" Everybody knew that men weren't supposed to hit women, just like boys weren't supposed to pick a fight with someone smaller or younger. *Pick on someone your own size* went through my head. I'd heard it often enough at school, when boys got into a scuffle. "Didn't Raymond ever try to stop him?"

"I guess a couple of times," Eddie said. "But then he started figuring his mother deserved it."

"Then Raymond's the one who's stupid!"

Eddie shrugged. "Maybe his mother did deserve it. How do you know she didn't? Maybe she was bossy! Raymond said he had a girlfriend back in Chicago who was bossy. He said he hit her to show her who was in charge, and that settled it."

A surge of hot anger traveled through my body and into my face, burning my cheeks. I leaned over so that my face was inches away from

Eddie's. "Men shouldn't hit women, period!" I hissed. "And if you don't know that, you're more stupid than Raymond—if that's even possible!" I got up and went inside. Now there was no getting away from the heat.

The only good thing about that summer was the jungle. I think Henry and his friends just tolerated me at first, but they were always happy to get the food I scrounged from the diner. I had discovered a while ago that appearing busy made me invisible to my mother. If I was occupied, even if I was filling salt and peppers that were already full, it was much less likely that I would be assigned some other, possibly unpleasant, chore. Being invisible also meant that I could squirrel away food without attracting any notice. I'd grab a roll that a customer hadn't eaten or wrap up several pieces of sausage and stash them under the counter. I'd wait until the coast was clear, then I'd gather the food I had scrounged and head for the jungle.

Sometimes the newer hobos were suspicious of me, but Henry and his friends made it clear that I was a friend they would protect. They began to trust me, and I learned more about what I thought of as their "secret world." I often stopped at the water tower to look at the symbols. "What does this mean?" I'd ask, drawing a new sign I'd seen in the dirt. One sign looked like an X with a two-headed arrow drawn horizontally through it. Underneath was written J.D. 7/12/31.

"That means someone with the initials J.D. left the railroad to travel the highway on July 12," Professor explained.

"Why would they leave a sign like that?" I asked.

"Probably J.D. gave up waiting for someone and left a message, just in case."

"Huh, so people leave messages for each other, too." I said.

"Sure," Professor said. "It's cheaper than sending a letter, and the post office doesn't deliver to the jungles, anyway." He grinned, and I laughed. Professor hardly ever joked.

Henry and Reedy were the mainstays of the jungle, and Professor, too, although he spent much more time traveling. Other hobos that camped there were only passing through, on their way to what they hoped was something better.

One hobo, named Marcus, was my age. Seventeen. He was traveling north from somewhere in Kentucky and planned to go out west to follow the fruit harvest. As we sat around the fire, he told us that his father had lost his job and the family was having a tough time making ends meet. Marcus had five younger brothers and sisters and his father couldn't afford to feed everybody; he said it was time for Marcus to make his own way. "I didn't want to go," he said, "but I had no choice." He looked away, but I saw tears welling up in his eyes.

"What about your mother?" I asked. "What did she say?"

Marcus just shook his head. "She don't ever say much. Especially to my father."

I thought my about mother in her faded yellow bathrobe. "Yeah," I said. "I know."

CHAPTER 11

By the end of summer, the Depression was choking the life out of New Harmony. Aunt Ruby and Uncle George held onto the diner by a thread, mainly because of the big pot of chili Aunt Ruby kept simmering at the back of the stove. On the weekends, it was mostly a small group of railroad workers who came in. Sometimes, on Saturday night, young couples would come for an inexpensive supper at the diner and then go to the movies. You could buy a bowl of chili for a nickel. A ham sandwich and a bowl of soup cost fifteen cents. If you added in the price of a movie, a couple could enjoy an entire evening's entertainment for a little more than a buck. And what could be more romantic than starting the evening in Paradise? Everybody joked about that, and Aunt Ruby would laugh every time, like it was the first time she had heard it.

Four of us sat around one Saturday morning with very little to do. My mother tidied up, stacking dishes on the shelves beneath the counter, and I sat on a stool, wiping water spots off the silverware Raymond had just washed. Ruby had cooked breakfast for about eight customers and it would be a while before anyone came for lunch. If they came.

"You and Raymond could use some time off," my mother said. "Why don't you go home for awhile? Maddy and I can take care of lunch." She sighed. "Seems like it's going to be slow again today."

Ruby gratefully accepted my mother's offer. Raymond hardly said anything, mumbling something like "Okay, see you later," and he didn't say "Thanks" either, which didn't escape my mother's notice.

"That boy could be a bit less surly and a little more polite," she said, watching him stride back to the house. She set out two cups and saucers and poured us each a cup of coffee. Working in the diner, I had acquired a taste for the pungent flavor of coffee, and now that I was in my last year of high school, people had finally stopped telling me I was too young to drink it.

"He acts like that because he doesn't like us," I said.

"Why do you say that?" My mother turned to look at me. "I suppose he's still adjusting to being here, but I wouldn't think..."

"I mean he doesn't like *us*," I said, "as in *girls*."

"Is this about you feeling left out?" she asked, frowning.

"It's about Raymond telling Eddie that girls are bossy and brainless," I said.

She laughed—a short, acid laugh. "He said that?"

I nodded, still miffed that she had questioned my motives.

"Raymond has a lot to learn," she said. "He'll change his mind as he grows up. When times get better, he'll find a regular job and he'll be looking for a wife."

"Well," I said, adding milk and sugar to my coffee, "I don't want anybody I know to marry him."

"Why not?" She picked up her coffee and sipped it slowly.

I felt a little panicked because I knew this conversation had gone too far to stop. I was about to betray what was probably a confidence, but then, Eddie hadn't actually told me not to tell. "Because he thinks it's okay for men to hit women."

"What? Maddy, that's a terrible thing to say!" She set her cup down heavily and coffee sloshed into the saucer and onto the white countertop.

"It's true! Ask Eddie! Why would I make something like that up?"

"What did he tell you?" she demanded.

"Raymond told Eddie that his parents used to fight a lot, and his father hit his mother...because she deserved it!" I swallowed hard. "And that's not all. Raymond had a girlfriend in Chicago and he hit her, too."

My mother was now visibly upset, and I worried about what I had just done and what the consequences might be. I watched as she soaked up the spilled coffee with a napkin, the brown liquid wicking into the white paper. "I don't want you to talk about this to anyone else," she said. "I will handle it now, understand?"

"Okay," my stomach was in a knot. The coffee tasted flat as I drank it in a gulp.

Eddie came in later that morning. "Raymond says he got some time off. We're going fishing, okay?"

"Not today," my mother answered.

"What? Why not?" Eddie said.

"I have some things for you to do."

"Can't it wait until later?"

"No."

"But Raymond's off today!"

"Sorry, there's work to be done."

I kept busy wiping down the tile. I was afraid of what would happen next. I didn't know what my mother was going to do, but I was sure her refusal to allow Eddie to go fishing with Raymond was because of our earlier discussion. Nothing more was said, but my mother kept us both going all day. The entire diner sparkled and not one thing was out of place when Aunt Ruby came in to take over before dinnertime.

"The diner looks wonderful, and I feel so much better!" she said to my mother. "Sometimes you need some time to put your feet up and just sit. Iris, why don't you go home now and do the very same thing? I'm sure I can manage by myself for a while, and Raymond will come in later to help me close up."

"I'll stay for a little longer; maybe there'll be a dinner rush," my mother said. "Maddy, you go on home and make sure your father has something to eat when he comes in."

"All right." I turned to leave, wondering what made my mother think my father would stagger home before midnight. Eddie started to come with me, but my mother stopped him.

"Eddie, you stay with me and bus tables if we need you to."

As I had figured, there was no sign of my father when I got home. I put a can of tomato soup out on the counter and set the can opener next to it. If my father happened to show up, I could open the soup quickly and say that I had supper started. I wasn't going to give him a chance to empty the cupboards again in a fit of anger.

I went to my room and got out my drawing materials. Lately, I'd been trying to draw people, but it was hard to find a model. My mother always said no, she was too tired, and she didn't want me to draw a tired old woman.

Aunt Ruby didn't sit still long enough, and I didn't take my sketchbook to the jungle because some of the hoboes were suspicious and uncomfortable. I drew a couple of sketches of Eddie, and even did a drawing of some railroad workers once when they sat down in front of the roundhouse to eat lunch. But I rarely found a willing subject when I had time to draw.

It had finally occurred to me to do some self-portraits, and I started working on one that evening. I dragged a chair over in front of my dresser and positioned a lamp so that it cast a strong shadow on my face. I propped my sketchbook up so that I could see my image in the mirror as I drew.

The front door slammed and I heard voices—first my mother's, then Eddie's. I was poised to run downstairs if I heard my father's voice, but there was no sign of him—no big surprise, and if anything, I felt relief. I was used to life like this, but every now and then I wished for a real father. One that didn't have drunken rages. I didn't have a clear idea of what that would be like, but I knew it would be different, and better. Maybe a real father would look at my sketches and smile, even hug me, and encourage me to keep trying. Maybe a real father would let me try to draw him.

I had abandoned one sketch and was deep in concentration, focused on a second drawing when Eddie burst in to my room.

"Traitor!" he yelled. "You're a stupid traitor!"

I was speechless for a moment, trying to bring myself back into the present and make sense of Eddie's angry intrusion.

"What are you talking about?"

"Why did you have to go and tell Mom that Raymond's dad hit his mother?"

"It just kind of came out. I didn't tell her on purpose. Besides, you didn't tell me not to tell." Eddie's face was red and puffy. A little bubble of spit clung to the corner of his mouth.

"Why are you so mad, anyway? It's the truth, isn't it?"

"Because now I'm not allowed to spend time with Raymond unless we're at the diner when mom is around. It's all your fault! We can't go fishing or stuff like that. You've ruined everything!"

"I'm sorry," I said, but the truth was I was only a little bit sorry. There weren't many kids that lived near us for Eddie, or me, to be friends with.

I had been lucky to meet Henry and the others in the jungle. Raymond was the only friend Eddie had right now, but Raymond was mean, and I didn't want Eddie to become like him.

"Maybe Mom will change her mind," I said.

"Yeah, sure!" Eddie turned and stomped out of my room. "Traitor!" he said again under his breath.

I tried to talk to Eddie over breakfast the next morning, but he was barely speaking to me.

"Look, maybe you shouldn't be friends with Raymond, anyway," I said. "It gives me the creeps that he thinks his mother deserved to get hit. Doesn't that bother you?"

"Just drop it. I heard it all last night from Mom when we walked home—the big lecture—okay? Are you happy?"

"But..."

"*Drop it*, Maddy!"

CHAPTER 12

Life had become pretty lonely. Eddie was still mad at me, Raymond was almost openly hostile to me, and my mother spent most of her time at the diner, even if she wasn't really needed. My father was nearly always drunk and things were getting uglier at home.

My friends in the jungle kept me from feeling abandoned. Because business at the diner was slow, I had time many afternoons to go down to the camp and talk with Henry and the others for a while. It was almost September and the weather was getting cooler. I could usually smell the campfire as I approached. That smell lifted my spirits; it was as comforting and welcoming as the smell of freshly baked bread. Sometimes I'd get there early enough to help make the mulligan, and then as the stew simmered, I'd lean against a log and watch as the late afternoon sun streamed through the trees, streaking the woods with rich, warm light.

After one such happy afternoon, I returned to the diner to find my mother and my aunt sitting at the counter, talking seriously and looking very distressed.

"It's bad news, Maddy," my mother said as soon as I slid onto a stool. A stream of possibilities raced through my mind. Had something happened to Eddie? Was the diner going under? Had my father left town? I hung onto that last thought for a moment. I would have considered that good news, although I knew it would upset my mother.

"What happened?"

"The school isn't going to open next week," Aunt Ruby said.

"What do you mean? Are we starting later this year?"

"No," my mother said. "They've closed the school. Period."

"Closed it! But why?"

"There's no money," Aunt Ruby said. "People don't have money to pay their taxes, businesses have shut down. There's no money to run the school. The teachers have been let go and the school is locked up."

I felt a lump growing in my stomach. I remembered Professor talking about his school closing, but I didn't think it would happen here. I had even hoped that he could get a job teaching at my school. Now Mr. Otis and the other teachers no longer had their jobs, and as far as I could tell, all of us students no longer had much future.

"What are we supposed to do?" I asked.

"I don't know, Maddy," my mother said. "We have to hope that things will get better soon. In the meantime, I guess you'll have to do the best you can to study on your own." She sighed. "You and Eddie can study at home or bring your books here to the diner."

"What books?" I asked. "How are we going to get any books?"

"The library is going to store the school's books," Aunt Ruby said. "You can check out the ones you need."

"How am I supposed to know what to study?" I was shouting now, but I couldn't seem to stop myself. "How am I going to *graduate*? I was supposed to graduate this year, remember?"

"Maddy, everyone has to make do," my mother said. "I'm sure they'll reopen the school as soon as times get better. For now, you'll just have to do the best you can to keep up on your schoolwork."

Sure, without a teacher. That'll be great, I thought. And then another thought hit that made me feel like I had just gotten the wind knocked out of me. *No more art classes with Mr. Otis.* I could feel hopelessness swallowing me up—whole.

CHAPTER 13

"I'm going up east to Pennsylvania tomorrow," Henry said. He was cutting up potatoes and adding them to the steaming mulligan. "Might be awhile before I come back this way again."

"Really? How long will you be gone?" I asked.

"Hard to say. Heard there might be some work in Pittsburgh. If that's true, I'll stay for as long as there's work."

I nodded, feeling a surge of apprehension. There was always the possibility that he wouldn't return to New Harmony. He might find a real job or—I tried not to think about it—something could happen to him on the trains. Henry had become a good friend, and soon, with the school closed and Henry gone, I wouldn't have anybody to talk to. I swallowed hard. "Are Reedy and Professor going, too?"

"Don't think so. Haven't seem them in a couple of days. I might see Reedy in Akron, though. He heard there might be some temporary jobs at the rubber plant."

"Oh. What time are you going?"

"I'll probably catch out on the 11:15."

"Do you need some food?"

"It's not necessary." Henry gestured toward his bedroll, where Jigger was sleeping peacefully. "I've got some bread and a coupla cans of beans. I'm always grateful to have some more, though," he said with a grin.

"I'll try to get here before you leave," I said.

That evening, Aunt Ruby came out behind the counter just as I stuffed a pork chop someone had left untouched on his plate into a sack. "What have you got there, Maddy?" she asked. I had never asked her if I could take the leftovers. The way I saw it, if you weren't sure that you'd get the answer you wanted, it was best not to ask the question. I took the leftovers because I couldn't see throwing away perfectly good food when Henry and his friends—and Jigger—needed it.

"Just some leftover food," I said.

"Let me see what's in there," she said. She reached out and took the bag, unrolled the top, and looked in. I had wrapped up some string beans, which had been the vegetable of the day today, some leftover boiled potatoes, and a half dozen rolls that were getting stale. I had just added a half-eaten ham sandwich that I knew Jigger would like.

She looked puzzled. "Are you planning to eat this?"

I scrambled for a believable explanation without telling her about the jungle. "Um...no. It's just that...well, there was this man who came to the back door and he was hungry, and I thought that since this food was going to waste...I said maybe he could come back later..."

Aunt Ruby sighed. "So many people are hungry. It gripes my soul that Hoover isn't doing anything about it. He thinks volunteers should take care of feeding the hungry, but it's not his stomach that's empty and it's not his kids looking at him for something to eat! People shouldn't have to beg for something to eat."

I was confused. Was she saying it was okay to take the leftovers to feed people, or was Hoover supposed to do it?

"I want to show you something," she said. She led me to the cash register and pulled out a stack of guest checks from the bottom drawer. "Do you know what this is?"

I shook my head no, although I had an idea about them.

"They're IOUs. Credit I've extended to people who have been good customers for years. They all needed a meal and didn't have money to pay for it. I had to stop, Maddy. I'd have gone broke if I kept giving credit." She looked out the diner window. I followed her gaze, but she didn't seem to be looking at anything in particular. Across the street was the Kessler's house. They were an older couple, and I knew they had been renting out rooms since the Depression started, trying to make ends meet. They had lost most of their life savings when the Washington Street bank folded. I noticed their front steps were sagging, and the roof was streaked with soot from the trains. Everything looked tired.

A couple of railroad workers were walking home, past the diner. They waved, and Aunt Ruby and I waved back, but they didn't stop in. "Do you know how hard it is to say no to your friends?" she asked.

I stood there quietly, not knowing what to say, watching Ruby watch the workers as they made their way home; I still wasn't sure if I was allowed to take the leftovers. She turned away from the windows.

"You go ahead and give that man the food this evening," she said. "But I don't want you to keep doing this. If people find out they can get a handout here, I'll have hundreds of people coming to my back door. I can't do it. I hope you understand. I can't feed everybody!"

It was getting dark, and the last few customers had just paid their bills as my mother came back to the diner to help us close up, although Ruby had sent her home in the late afternoon to get some rest. "You've been working too much, and you look tired," Ruby had said, avoiding saying the truth—that my father's behavior was the source of my mother's exhaustion. "Maddy and Raymond are here, and we can handle the dinner trade without you tonight, Iris. Go home. Get some rest."

She had gone, willingly, and she might have slept for awhile, but then I think she found it hard to be alone with her thoughts. Eddie had gone off to do some night fishing; the smallmouth bass were starting to bite now. So my mother came back, saying that she needed to stay busy. Ruby just clucked at her, but she didn't try to send her home again.

Shortly after, there was a commotion at the side door of the diner. Several people spoke urgently to my mother and Ruby. Turned out that Ernie Foster, owner of the speakeasy on Third Street, had neglected to make his monthly payment to the police. The payoff money bought Ernie advance notice of impending raids, but since Ernie's payment was late, they raided his cellar and arrested everyone, including my father, who was quite drunk, and who punched out one of the officers, possibly breaking his jaw. My mother had to go down to the police station, and she begged Ruby to go with her. "I can't face this alone," she said.

"All right," Ruby said. "Maddy and Raymond, just finish cleaning up and lock the door when you're done." Without waiting for an answer, they left. But on their way out, I heard Ruby suggest to my mother that some time in jail might benefit my father.

I was furious at my father for getting himself into trouble. Ruby was right, in my opinion, and I hoped my mother would just let my father sit in jail. I really didn't care how long he was there. I hurriedly wiped the counters and filled the salt and peppers. Raymond was finishing up the dishes. I only had the booths to finish and I could leave. It was already dark and I just wanted to get out of there and get home.

As I reached the booth in the back corner, Raymond said, "I'm done. Time to go home." He clicked off the lights in the diner.

"Well I'm not done. Turn the lights back on!"

"You should have worked faster." The scorn in his voice cut through the dark.

"Turn the lights back on and leave. I'll shut them off when I'm done."

"You're just like the rest of them," he said. His voice was closer now and as my eyes adjusted to the dark, I could start to make out where he was. "Bossy! Always ordering people around."

He was walking toward me and I felt afraid now, but I wasn't about to show it. "Yeah, and brainless too, I suppose." I said, speaking with as much sarcasm as I could muster. "I heard all about it."

"You heard all about it and then you told, didn't you?" He stepped closer to me. I could smell the dishwashing soap on him, mixed with his sweat. It was a sickening combination. I tried sidestepping him, but he blocked me. "You fixed it so Eddie couldn't be friends with me. You wanted things your way, so you told about my father!"

"Yeah, I told about your father. And about you, too! I didn't want you teaching Eddie that it's okay for boys to hit girls. It's not right, and you know it!"

"Some girls deserve to get hit," he said. "Like you." Pain and light burst at the left side of my face, like a firecracker had exploded too close. Raymond had hit me, but I didn't see it coming in the dark, so I had no chance to try to defend myself. My cheek and jaw throbbed, and for a moment I was too stunned to speak. Then fear released adrenaline and I reacted.

"I'll tell about this, too—so you better leave me alone! Get out of my way!" I started to sprint past him, but he reached out in the darkness and pushed me. I couldn't get my balance and I fell against a table. Another shove and I fell face down into a booth. Then he was on top of me, pushing his knee into my back, pinning me against the seat. "Nice girls don't tell!" he hissed into my ear.

I could hardly breathe. I tried to yell, but I couldn't get enough air. His weight was crushing me.

"Eddie told me everything you said. You called me a queer!"

"I didn't! Eddie just said you didn't like girls... and I thought..." My voice came out muffled, the sound absorbed by the seat covering.

"Just shut up! He tore at my blouse and started groping my breasts. "I'll show you I'm no homo!" He was pushing my skirt up to my waist. Terror enveloped me and I struggled to break free, but he pinned me with his body, and then I felt him ripping my underpants and fumbling with his trousers. He shoved his knees between my legs, pushing them apart, and then I felt searing pain travel up my body. "I'll show you!" he kept saying as he pushed himself into me. "I'll show you, I'll show you." For a few moments it felt like I had left my body and was watching this unspeakable act from somewhere else. Then the horror and pain descended on me again, and I felt sure he was going to kill me when he was through. I lowered my head to gasp for air, and I caught the glint of something underneath the booth. I could barely reach it, but I got it into my hand and realized it was a fork. I grasped it hard, twisted my arm around, and shoved it with all my strength into what I hoped was Raymond.

"Shit!" he screamed, falling off me and onto the floor.

I scrambled out of the booth and kicked hard at his groin. He screamed again, rolling onto his side, and I ran toward the door. "You goddam bitch. I'll kill you next time I see you!"

CHAPTER 14

I don't remember getting home. It was like a fog descended and then time and place became shapeless and shadowy. I remember stumbling around in the dark house and filling the bathtub with water as hot as I could stand and removing my clothes, which were torn and blood stained. I forced myself into the steaming hot water, immersing myself completely, feeling the sting on my skin and a throbbing burn between my legs. I covered myself in soapy lather and I scrubbed hard, except for my face and crotch, which were quite tender, and I tried to purge every trace of that horrible attack. Then I stood up and drained the tub, willing the night's violence to disappear with the spent water. I filled the tub once more with hot water and I submerged my body for a second time, soaking long enough that my fingertips started to pucker. When I got out, I dried myself and stepped over the discarded clothes. I stood, wrapped in a towel, and stared at the clothes. Then I scooped them up and stuffed them into the bathroom trash. I would never wear those clothes again.

An idea had taken shape. From my parent's bedroom, I took a pair of my father's trousers, one of his shirts, and a gray tweed cap that I had never seen him wear. I carried these back to my room and began dressing. My father wasn't a large man, and when I put on his clothes, they fit me as if they were hand-me-downs from an older sibling. I combed my still damp shoulder-length hair, twisted it up, and pinned it on top of my head. I pulled the tweed cap over my hair, drawing the bill down over my face a little. I looked in the mirror and studied the person looking back at me. Medium build, dark hair, blue eyes, angular face—except for the puffy cheek and swollen bottom lip. I saw what could be an older version of Eddie. *This will do*, I thought. I touched my cheek and lip. *And this will heal.*

I pulled some underwear from my dresser drawer and a change of my own clothes, laying these items on top of the tan wool blanket on my bed. I tossed my comb, toothbrush, and a bar of soap onto the pile. I bent down to pull the sturdiest pair of shoes I owned from my closet, and as I stood up, I felt a warm trickle between my legs. I was still bleeding. My stomach tightened, but I willed myself to stay focused on what I was preparing for and not think about what had happened.

I went to my mother's closet and took some Kotex—one for now and several for later—from her blue box. The box looked new and bright. Hoping that she transferred the brown envelope each time she bought a new box, I dug down and found the money she had shown me before. I took two tens and a couple of dollar bills. My mother had said, *If something happened to me...it's for you and Eddie to use.* She hadn't said *If something happens to you*, but how could she have known that the "something" would happen to me, not to her?

As I left the room, a zippered case on my mother's dresser caught my attention. It was made of brown leather and had an oval-shaped inset, like a wide-open eye, with a needlepointed rose sewn into it. Inside were manicure tools: scissors, tweezers, a nail file, and several other items for cleaning fingernails and tending cuticles. My mother often used this set. "If you're going to serve food, your hands had better be clean," she'd say. She was fastidious enough for both of us. I can't say for sure why I took that manicure set, but I did, stuffing it into my trouser pocket. Looking back on it, I suspect it had a little to do with hygiene and much more to do with wanting to carry something meaningful of my mother's. It was a way to have her with me.

Back in my room, I wrapped the wool blanket like a cocoon around the items I had selected. I wrote a short note to my mother and left it where I knew she would find it eventually—tucked into her box of Kotex.

Sept. 1, 1931

Dear Mother,
I'm sorry but I can't stay here any longer. You can ask Raymond why. He's a despicable ~~human~~ being. He deserves to have something horrible happen to him, but he should at least be sent back to Chicago, away from you and Aunt Ruby and especially Eddie. I took some money to keep me going for a little while. I hope you understand. I promise I'll pay it back when I can.

Don't worry about me. I'll write if I can.

Love,
Maddy

P.S. I took your manicure set. I promise I'll take good care of it.

I tucked my bundle under my arm, and as I left the house, I grabbed one of my father's jackets from the line of pegs by the back door. The cool night air felt soothing to my face, but the rest of me started to shiver. I put on the jacket and headed toward the river. My way was lit here and there by street lights, but as I came closer to the river, darkness pressed around me. A few spots of light glowed near the Fourth Street bridge. Night fishermen. Eddie would be fishing at the far end of the bridge— his favorite spot. I could have stopped to find him, to talk to him, but I needed to keep moving, as if my forward motion would create a wake that could close behind me and then disappear, covering my trail. I had to leave New Harmony. I promised myself that I would never step foot inside that diner again.

CHAPTER 15

I caught a faint smell of campfire as I turned up the path to the jungle. I had never been there at night and things looked different. I had to pick my way carefully, concentrating so that I wouldn't wander off the trail. My toe caught a fallen branch and the snap echoed through the woods, reaching the sensitive ears of Jigger, who came snarling and barking at me in the darkness.

"Hey, Jigger. Whoa. It's me!" I had traveled this path often enough that I knew Jigger would stop if you called his name. But tonight Jigger was making such a fuss that he wasn't hearing anything. "Jigger! Jigger— whoa!" Finally, my voice penetrated Jigger's racket and, as if a switch had been flipped, he began bouncing around me, greeting me, sniffing and looking for food.

Henry hurried down the path after Jigger. "Who's there?" he called out.

"It's me. Maddy."

"Maddy! What the hell are you doing here? I said I'd be okay without you bringing food. You shouldn't come here at night!"

"I didn't bring any food. I had some, but I left it. I need a place to sleep," I said. "Just for tonight...I'm leaving tomorrow."

"What are you talking about?" He sounded annoyed, and I suddenly felt very alone. "Come on," he said, turning back toward the jungle. "No sense standing there in the dark. Let's go talk by the fire."

He motioned me over to the log closest to the shelters, on the far side of the fire. Nobody else was there tonight. Just Henry. He had a small fire going; a pot of coffee sat off to the side. It was still steaming. I sat down and set my bundle behind me.

"I was about to let this fire die out," he said. "It's getting late. But I guess I can keep it going for a while yet." He stirred the embers, added several small logs, then blew on it until yellow flames flared up, throwing light onto a larger circle around the fire, casting light on all of us. That was when Henry looked over at me. The expression on his face transformed from annoyance to disbelief to something else that I couldn't quite read.

"What the hell is going on?" he asked, taking in the men's clothes I was wearing and my swollen face. He spoke gently now, and I no longer felt alone. I felt the warmth of his friendship. "Who beat you up?" He was angry, but not at me.

His concern made me feel so vulnerable that I couldn't speak. I just shook my head in response. I huddled closer to the fire, trying to get warmer so that my shivering would stop.

"Do you want some coffee?" he asked. I nodded, and he poured some into a tin can and brought it to me. I took it carefully, not letting his hand touch mine. "Thank you." My voice sounded strange to my ears. I sipped the coffee cautiously, avoiding touching the can to the side of my lip that was swollen.

"Maddy, are you okay?"

"I guess so... Yes...No...I don't know."

"What happened?"

I searched around in my mind for the right words, but all I could see were images: flashes of the diner, darkness, red seat cushions, Raymond, blood. How could I tell these things to Henry? And I was still so cold; my shivering hadn't stopped, and it was so distracting. Maybe if I got warm I could tell Henry what happened. "I can't say," I finally spoke. "If I could just get warm, I'd feel better." My lip hurt when I talked.

"It ain't that cold, Maddy," Henry said, looking very seriously at me, but he reached for another log and added it to the fire. "Thank you," I whispered. I noticed that if I rocked as I sat, the shivering wasn't as bad.

"We've got to do something for your face," Henry said. "I should get some cold water from the river. We can dip a cloth into it and put it on your cheek. Bring down the swelling."

"No cold water," I said. "I'm already cold."

"Look, I'll keep a fire going so you can warm up, and you can wrap up in my blanket if you need to, but it'll be a lot better if we can get the swelling down on your face."

"All right."

"Good. I'll be right back. Jigger, stay here."

Henry left and Jigger stayed. He sat by me and I petted him. Somehow, pushing my fingers through his soft, warm fur soothed me. After a few minutes, he rested his chin on my thigh and calmly looked at me while I stroked his neck and back. "You're a good pal, aren't you boy?" I said to him. At that moment, that dog was what I needed. Sitting by the fire with him was like sitting next to a friend—just being together, sharing space and time, no pressure to talk, and your friend liking you no matter what you look like. When I thought about it more, I realized that Henry was a friend like that, too.

He came back from the river, handed me a can of cold water and a cloth, and I started applying cold compresses to my face. After awhile, my face felt better as the swelling went down. True to his word, Henry kept the fire going and he didn't pressure me to tell him what had happened. I needed to talk, but not about that.

We talked about the job he used to have at the mill and some of the places he'd traveled to by train. He told me about his family, too. Both his parents were dead, and he had a younger brother, Pete, who lived out in Oklahoma now. "Several years ago, before the mill closed, Pete said he'd had enough of Pittsburgh and dirty cities," Henry said. "He took his savings and his wife and went out west to try to make it as a farmer. I think they did okay for awhile. But I heard there was a drought there this summer, so I imagine they're just scraping by, like everybody else." He poked at the fire, pushing some unburnt wood toward the flames. "Pete and I were never close," he said, "even when we worked together at the mill. Now we just barely stay in touch."

All this was new to me. Henry had never talked about his family before. It wasn't that he was secretive; the subject just never came up, maybe because I had never asked. Tonight he seemed quite willing to talk, so I asked more questions. "What about you? Do you have a wife?"

Henry looked down at the fire. "Nope. I almost had one, though." He looked at me and grinned a little, but it wasn't really a grin; the corners of his mouth turned up but his eyes clouded with sadness.

"What happened?"

"It's kind of a long story. You sure you want to hear it?"

I nodded.

"Well, I started working at the mill in 1914, right after I graduated high school. I worked there for about three years and saved some money. I was planning to marry Anna—she was my high school sweetheart—as soon as I had put enough money aside. But when the World War broke out and the United States got involved, I enlisted. They sent me to France. I spent three years over there."

Henry was silent for a few minutes, and I wondered if he decided not to say any more. Then he cleared his throat and went on.

"When I came back, I started working at the mill again and I was all set to ask Anna to marry me, but then the mill closed and I couldn't find any other work," he said. "No woman in her right mind's going to marry a man who can't support her."

"What happened? Did she marry somebody else?"

"No. At least not that I know of. That was two years ago, though."

"So maybe it still could work out when times get better," I said.

Henry just shook his head. "Maddy, I'm thirty-five years old now. Even if she hasn't found somebody else, I still don't have a thing to offer her. I find it hard to believe I ever will."

"But why?" I wasn't willing to accept unfulfilled dreams for this man who had become my friend.

"Sometimes a man gets caught up in things he can't control. When I enlisted, I left a job that paid $1.35 an hour and traded it for the army, which paid a buck a day. When I got my discharge papers, I couldn't get my same job back at the mill, but at least I got one. Lots of vets didn't. We all lost ground during that time we were overseas. Then times got hard and the mill closed. I spent my savings trying to keep a roof over my head while I looked for work. But there ain't no work. And if there's ever work again, which sometimes I wonder about, I'll be too old to make much headway." He paused and then said, "It's just how it is, I guess."

"But it's not fair!"

"No, it ain't." He stirred the fire. Sparkles flew into the air from the embers, then burnt themselves out and fell back, spent, into the fire. "It's getting late. Do you think you could get some sleep?"

"I don't know," I said. I realized I had finally stopped shaking. Physically I was exhausted, but my mind seemed to still be churning over and over, not letting the day's events rest. "Maybe in just a little while."

"Do you want to tell me what happened?" he asked.

I looked over at Henry and swallowed hard, trying to push down the feeling of panic that started to rise in my throat. But Henry's face showed concern and kindness, and I felt that I could trust him, like he had trusted me tonight, when he told me personal things about himself.

"My uncle's nephew...he came from Chicago...he never liked me..." I took a deep breath. "I tried not to be around him, but I had to work alone with him tonight because my mother and aunt had to go get my father..." A flash of anger at my father; it was partly his fault, too. "Raymond shut off the lights. We argued. Then..." It was so hard to talk. "...then he hit me and he pushed me down and he ripped my clothes and he...he...attacked me." As I finished the last few words, the panic that had risen in my throat took physical form and I dashed over to the bushes and vomited, throwing up the night's violence. The hot baths had cleansed the outside of my body, and now I was purging the rest of it from the inside.

Henry followed me to the edge of the bushes. I heard him asking me if I was all right. "Please, just give me a minute," I said. I got my toothbrush, brushed my teeth, and splashed the cold river water on my face. *It's over*, I reminded myself. I tried to believe it. Gradually, I felt that I was gathering control and I walked slowly back to sit by the fire. Henry was waiting, pacing, and then he sat down next to me. After a moment, he spoke.

"Maddy, I'm real sorry. It's terrible what happened to you. I don't know what else to say." He put his hand on my shoulder and for the briefest instant, I recoiled, but then I stopped myself, deciding at that moment that I would not allow that...attack...to put physical distance between me and people I cared about. "Are you really okay?"

I nodded, and placed my hand on top of Henry's.

"What are you planning to do?" he asked.

"I'm leaving. I can't stay here anymore."

"You sure? What about your folks?"

"Look, Henry. My father's a drunk, and I don't think he even remembers he has kids most of the time. He'd rather drink than do anything else. My mother is barely surviving. If it wasn't for my aunt and uncle, we'd probably be out on the street by now. I don't know what they'll do about Raymond, but even if he gets what he deserves, I'm not stepping foot back inside that diner. Ever." It didn't matter anymore if Henry knew my family ran the diner. I looked over at him, but he didn't seem surprised. "I'm seventeen years old and I've got nowhere to go. They've closed the school, too. So it's either home with my hungover father or the diner...Nope. I'm not going back."

"So what are you going to do?" he asked.

"I'm going to hop a freight and get out of here—see what life is like somewhere else."

"Life ain't so good most other places, either," he said.

"Well it sure ain't pretty here, is it?" I said.

We sat in silence for a few minutes, and then Henry spoke. "How about if we get some sleep. We can talk more in the morning."

"Okay," I said.

Henry let the embers burn out, and as the fire died, I took my bedroll into a shelter to try to sleep. My body ached and my lip still throbbed a little, but I rolled up in my blanket and closed my eyes, focusing my attention on the night sounds—the crickets and the frogs. Jigger was nearby, and Henry went to one of the other shelters, but after a few minutes, Jigger trotted over and curled up right next to me. I reached out to stroke his soft fur. I must have fallen into a deep sleep then, because when I awoke in the first light of morning, I was disoriented, as if I was trying to swim to the surface of murky water. Quickly, though, conscious-ness returned, nearly overwhelming me as I remembered where I was, and why. I touched my lip. It was still tender, but not as bad. I got up and walked a good distance into the bushes, away from the camp, to relieve myself. I had stopped bleeding, so I removed the pad, still pinkish with last night's blood, and I buried it.

When I returned, Henry was up, too, blowing life into a morning fire. We warmed ourselves by it as we drank coffee and ate bread and peanut butter for breakfast. The day promised to be beautiful—a September day rich with blue skies and the smells of late summer mixing with first signs of fall.

"You feeling better today?" he asked.

"Yes, I am." I hesitated. "Thanks for your help last night."

He nodded. "You're a nice girl. I'm sorry you had all that...trouble."

Me, too, I thought. We sat by the fire for a while longer, drinking coffee and not saying much, but it was a comfortable silence, the kind of silence that comes with friendship, and I felt lucky to have a friend like Henry.

"You still planning to leave today?" he asked.

"Absolutely."

"You sure you don't want to talk to your ma first?"

"I told you last night—I'm sure!" I snapped. "What's my mother going to do? She can't even stand up to my father when he's drunk and can barely stand up himself. And I already said, I'm never stepping foot in that diner again!"

"All right, all right." Henry put his hands up, trying to stop my outburst. "Then we got some work to do," he said. "I'm gonna show you some things you ought to know about riding the rails. Might help keep you out of danger." He scooped dirt onto the fire to smother it and motioned for me to follow him. "Just leave your stuff here for now. We'll come back for it later.

"Where are we going?"

"To the rail yard."

"What if someone sees us?" If a railroad worker spotted us and recognized me, it could cause big problems. I had no idea what was happening at home right now; I didn't know if my father was still in jail, I didn't know if my mother had even found my note, but I knew I wasn't ready for any confrontation—not with my mother, my aunt, my father, or especially, with Raymond.

"Don't worry," Henry said. "You'll be fine."

I decided to trust him. We tromped through the woods, with Jigger darting on and off the path in front of us and circling around behind us. Henry led me to a siding at the far end of the rail yard, well away from the activity. Workers were busy making up trains closer to the roundhouse, but the siding was deserted.

"Okay," Henry said. "If you're going to ride the rails, it's good that you're dressed in men's clothes. Keep to yourself and nobody'll pay any attention to you. But you've got to do a few things to stay safe." He dug through his pockets and handed me a couple of lengths of twine. "Those wide pant legs are risky," he said. "Tie this string around your ankles so your cuffs don't catch on anything."

He watched as I did as he said, and then he led me over to a boxcar. "Best thing is to find an open boxcar," he said. "If you can spot one in the yard right before the train moves out, climb in if nobody's looking and count your blessings. But if the railroad bulls are watching, you'll have to catch out on a train that's moving. Then you got to run alongside the car and grab onto the handle and heave yourself inside. If you can't keep up with the car when you're running, don't try to get on. The train'll be going too fast and you'll probably get killed."

"What if I can't find an open boxcar?"

"Yeah, I'm getting to that. Sometimes there ain't no open boxcars, and sometimes they're full. Stay off the reefers and the flatcars—they're too dangerous. Too many people been killed riding those. It's not so good, but you can ride on top of boxcars if you have to. If you can't wait for another train, here's how you do it."

He walked me over to the ladder at the front of a car. "Always get on at the front of the car, because if you miss, you'll slam against the side of the car and with any luck you'll bounce off. But if you grab on at the back and miss—well, you'll probably fall onto the couplings between the cars and end up greasing the rails."

I flinched at Henry's straightforward description of death on the rails. I had seen some gruesome pictures in the newspapers. Some of the tabloids were publishing those pictures, hoping to discourage people, especially young people, from hopping freights. But they rode anyway. When you ran out of hope in one town, they said, there wasn't much else to do but try another. I knew riding freight trains was dangerous, and I hoped I would always find an open boxcar when I needed to. Still, I wanted to know what it was like to climb up the side of a car, so I reached up to grab a rung and swung my foot up. "Wait!" Henry said. I stopped, poised for action with my right hand and foot already on the rungs.

Henry moved in close. "Look," he said. "If the train is moving, the forward motion can make you slide sideways down the rungs." He pushed against my arm and foot to demonstrate, and my hand and foot slid, just like he said. "Now you don't have any place to put your left foot," he said. "How are you going to hang on and get up to the top of the car?" I saw his point.

"So what you do is grab on first with your back foot and hand." He gently pushed me off the rungs and had me do it again. "Your back foot is always on the side closest to the cars if you're running alongside the train. In this case, it's your left side. Now grab on." I did as he said, and again, he pushed against my arm and foot, sliding them down the rungs. "Now look," he said, pointing at the rung. "You got room to swing yourself in and plant your right foot."

"Hey! That's a pretty nifty trick!" I said.

"Yeah, make sure you don't forget it. Now go ahead and climb up."

I worked my way to the top of the boxcar, feeling excitement rising in me with each step up the ladder. I crested the top of the car and peered out over the top.

"If you have to ride up there, you make sure you loop your belt through one of those runners. That way, you won't get bounced off," Henry warned from the ground.

I climbed down and he stopped me just as I was ready to jump off. "Now if you have to get off a moving train, it's hard to tell how fast the train is going. You can get hurt bad if you jump off when it's going too fast."

"So what do you do?" I asked.

"You stand on the lowest rung and hold on to the rung just above your feet. Then lean your rear end out and touch the ground lightly with one foot. If your foot shoots back up and kicks you in the butt, the train is going too fast. You got to wait until it slows down some. When you can touch the ground without kicking yourself, it's safe to jump off."

I practiced what Henry showed me, pretending the car was moving, and then I jumped off, away from the boxcar.

"That's good, Maddy," he said. "You just might stay alive." His voice was serious, but he was grinning, too.

CHAPTER 16

Back at the jungle, Henry and I gathered our things. Jigger waited expectantly while we packed up; he seemed to understand it was time to go. I suppose over time he had learned to watch Henry and read his signals. I wondered if Jigger had any favorite places along the circuit that Henry traveled, or if he was just happy to stay someplace for a while and then move on. For Jigger it would mean new terrain and new smells. I wondered if he liked life on the road.

Would I like life on the road? I was about to find out. The three of us—Henry, Jigger, and I—made our way through the woods by the jungle until we reached a place not far from the rail yard where the railroad tracks made a bend through the woods. We were close to the yard, but out of sight of it. It was the perfect place to hop a train unseen, and before the train built up much speed. I smiled at Henry. "Now I get why the jungle is where it is!"

"Yep," he said. "Close to the tracks and close to the river, too. Keep that in mind when you're traveling, and you'll probably be able to find a jungle wherever you go."

"I'll remember." We set our bedrolls, *bindles* Henry called them, on the ground. I tied string around my pant legs, like Henry had shown me.

"That's good," he said, nodding approval. "Another thing is, if you brought any money, put most of it in your shoes. Just keep a little bit in your pocket. That way, you won't lose much if you take a spill off a train—or if someone shakes you down."

He watched as I dug into my pockets and put a ten-dollar bill in each shoe. "You keep your wits about you," he said.

"I will," I promised.

We waited. Excitement rose up in me as sure and as swift as the flood waters rose up in the river every spring. I wasn't scared, either. Even when Henry reminded me he would only go with me as far as Akron. "Do you have a plan?" he asked. "Do you know where you're going?"

I shook my head. "Nope. Not really. I want to go north to see Lake Erie because I've never seen it, and then I'll decide. I might go east, or I might go west. I guess I'll just make up my mind when I get to the lake."

Henry just nodded and we were quiet. A long whistle broke the stillness; its sound seemed to bounce off the tree trunks and surround my head. For a moment, that sound was all that existed in the world. Then I looked at Henry and he grinned back at me. "I believe that's your train, ma'am. Please have your ticket ready and watch your step."

We heard the measured chugs of the steam engine as it slowly made its way along the rails. The great black iron giant rumbled into view and Henry motioned for me to step back a few feet into the woods. "Out of the engineer's sight," he shouted over the noise. The locomotive and then the tender passed not ten feet from us. Black smoke spewed from the engine, pinging my face with bits of cinders. My body vibrated with the shuddering of the engine; my heart seemed to be keeping time to the pulsing of the pistons. And then we saw a lovely, long string of cars stretching out behind the tender. I knew it would take a long while for the train to build up speed with so many cars attached. Henry and I stepped out again, watching the approaching cars. He pointed to a boxcar about eight cars away. Its door was partially open. He watched it as it got closer, and then he shook his head no. "Wait," he yelled over the clatter. I was disappointed, and I hoped that we didn't just miss our only opportunity. But I trusted Henry and waited. The racket of the engine lessened as it traveled farther down the track. More cars passed, but the boxcar doors were tightly shut. Then Henry pointed to another car just coming into sight. Its door was wide open and the boxcar looked empty. He watched the car for a minute or two and then said, "This is it—you ready?"

My heart leapt into my throat as I nodded yes. We started walking alongside the train, gauging its motion, which was still very slow, and as the boxcar came even with us, Henry picked up Jigger and boosted him into the boxcar. "Throw your bindle in first and then grab the handle!" he yelled as he tossed his bindle in after Jigger. I did as he said and heaved myself into the boxcar. Henry pulled himself in right behind me.

There I sat, in the middle of a boxcar, wearing the biggest possible grin my face could make. The gentle side-to-side rocking of the boxcar mixed with the forward motion and the sounds of metal wheels against metal rails—and through that huge open door, I saw the world opening before my eyes. I was both part of it and passing through it, and I experienced a feeling of freedom unlike anything I had ever felt before. I knew I had just left my childhood behind, for good.

I hugged my knees to my chest and soaked it all in for a while. The train picked up speed and the wheels struck a hypnotic rhythm on the rails. Henry settled back, using his bindle as a backrest, and Jigger had curled up next to Henry and was peacefully sleeping.

"Why didn't you want to get on that first boxcar?" I asked.

"It looked like it had a flat wheel," Henry said.

"How could a metal wheel be flat? They don't have any air!" I pictured the pneumatic tires of a Ford car; plenty of drivers had to change flat tires on the roadway that ran near to the tracks by the rail yard. There was a lot of debris from the cargo the trains carried, some of it sharp enough to do damage to tires.

Henry laughed. "Sometimes when the conductor has to make an emergency stop, some cars kind of skid along the track. A wheel can heat up and the skidding can wear a flat spot on it."

"Is that dangerous?"

"Well, it ain't good for the track, but mostly it's just damned uncomfortable.

When the train gathers speed, the wheel causes the boxcar to bounce around and vibrate like crazy. Ain't no sleeping when you're riding like that. And sometimes you get bounced around so much you have to hang on to the sides of the car the whole trip. It ain't a pleasant ride. You suffer through one of those and you learn to look before you choose your car the next time."

"I'm going to remember that," I said.

"That's good," Henry said. "Else you'll learn the hard way."

We didn't talk much after that. I couldn't pull myself away from the open door of the boxcar. I felt like the world was revealing itself to me and I didn't want to miss a thing. Not only could I see the countryside, I could smell it. We passed by farmers' fields, and the sweet smell of hay filled my nose. We crossed over rivers and I could smell the water. It seemed like hardly any time had passed when Henry said we were almost in Akron. I could smell that, too. The country smells gave way to the sharp, pungent odors of smoke and rubber.

The train started slowing down as we approached the city, and we passed through some residential areas. The houses closest to the tracks were modest houses with small yards. I knew that these were the houses of the men who worked in the factories and labored for a living, if they still had jobs. The well-to-do always took the best places for themselves—usually the places far from the tracks—the places with the best views and the best locations, like near the river or close to town, where they could build their big houses for everyone to admire. They didn't want the racket of trains disturbing their dinner or their sleep. I knew this was true in my town and I expected it was true most places.

"This train should keep heading north," Henry said. "You can probably safely stay in this car, but stay out of sight until you pull out of the yard. But if you feel the train back up, get off and wait and see. Could mean they're going to put some cars on a siding, and one of those cars could be this one. Just keep your wits about you and be sure you're heading north, if that's where you want to go."

I nodded. "Lake Erie," I said.

"You sure you're going to be okay?" he asked again.

"I'll be fine." I hesitated. "Thanks, Henry, for all your help."

"You're a good kid," he said. "Hate for anything bad to happen to you." He dug around in his pocket, scribbled on a scrap of paper, and handed it to me. "I hope to be in Pittsburgh for a while; that's where I'll be if I can find work. Maybe you could send me a postcard every now and then so I know you're all right. If I ain't there, I'll be on the circuit again, so I'd be sure to stop at New Harmony from time to time. You might reach me there, too."

I took the paper. *Henry O'Connor, General Delivery, Pittsburgh, Pennsylvania,* it read. "I'll write when I can," I promised.

The train had slowed to a crawl; it was approaching the rail yard, and Henry was getting set to go. He picked up Jigger and tucked him under his arm. With his free arm, he threw his bindle out the boxcar door and then grabbed onto the handhold and jumped off. He hit the ground softly and set Jigger down. It was all one smooth combination, like a dance he had done a thousand times. "You take care now," he said. I stood in the doorway and watched as he retrieved his bindle. "I will," I said. Then I called after him, "You take care, too."

I watched as Henry and Jigger got smaller and smaller and I felt more and more alone. I wanted to jump off the train and run after them, shouting, "Wait! Can I go with you?" But I'd made my decision back in New Harmony to make my own way, and I was determined to stick to it.

The train creaked slowly along for some distance. I sat against the side of the boxcar, opposite the door but toward the front of the car. I could still see out, but I wouldn't easily be seen by any of the railroad crew.

Finally, all motion stopped. I waited. After a while, I began to wonder if I should get off the train and investigate. But then I heard the brittle clang of metal against metal traveling toward me from the front of the train. The couplings were engaging. The sound got louder. One by one the cars were lurching, like dominoes, and I sat waiting to see which direction the dominoes would fall. Finally I heard a loud clank and I felt my car shudder. The motion pitched me toward the back of the car. I smiled. Now I knew we were moving forward, and I settled in for the ride north—to Cleveland and Lake Erie.

CHAPTER 17

The vastness of the lake surprised me. Maybe it was because I had learned in school that Lake Erie was the smallest of the Great Lakes. Maybe, because the lake looks small on a map, I had somehow expected to see across it. I don't know. But I wasn't prepared for that huge expanse of calm, blue water, which is what I saw that day I got off the train in Cleveland. I was immediately enthralled with the color and the sound of the water. Eventually, I became aware of the marine smell of the lake—a combination of fish and green seaweed and cool air heavy with moisture. But I didn't discover the smell until later, when I stood on the shore and pushed back against a northerly breeze. Otherwise, the smells of the steel mills overpowered the freshness of the lake.

I had hopped off the train in a rail yard near the mouth of the Cuyahoga River and found myself in the heart of an industrial area of machine shops, steel mills, and iron works clustered along the flat banks of the river. A coating of grime gave the area a dark, dusty look. More than a few factories were boarded up. There was activity along the river, but it was low key. It seemed like the workers had gone, taking some of the life of the river with them. Probably the boarded up factories had taken some of the life out of the workers, too, the same as in New Harmony.

It was easy enough to find a secluded spot that was near the lake and not far from the railroad tracks. The first night I was afraid—it was the first time I had ever slept outside by myself. I found a piece of driftwood I could use as a club, if needed, and then I spread my bedroll out on the sand and stretched out to look at the sky. It was a clear, warm fall night, and the stars seemed close and distinct. The sound of the waves splashing gently on the shore soothed me, and I tuned into the peaceful rhythm of moving water. I slept fitfully, still clutching my makeshift club, hearing every noise. Finally, night gave way to the early morning sun reflecting brightly on the water and the ruckus of gulls squabbling over fish.

Hunger drove me from the shore into the city. I followed the sweet smell of baking bread and found a bakery where I could buy day-old bread. Across the street from it was a family-owned lunch counter where I could eat cheaply. Cleveland was so much bigger than New Harmony, and to my small-town eyes, every street revealed something new and interesting. I spent one day making the long walk to Terminal Tower, where I discovered I could watch the passenger trains come in and depart. I made my way to the observation deck on the forty-second floor, and when I crossed the tile floor and leaned out the windows to see the view, my knees got rubbery and I had to grab the rail to steady myself.

A voice spoke close to my right ear. "Are you all right, miss?"

I turned toward the voice. An older man, portly and bald, smiled at me. I tried to smile back as I wiped my sweaty hands on my pants. "Yes, thank you. It's just that where I come from, the tallest building is only three floors. I've never seen anything like this."

"It's quite a sight," he agreed.

Below me was a dizzying view of the city, stretching out for as far as I could see. The streetcars looked like toys, and people on the sidewalk seemed to be about a half an inch tall. Then it occurred to me that if they looked up, I'd look the same way to them, if they even saw me at all. When all's said and done, I realized I didn't take up much space in this world, and I felt small and unimportant.

I studied how the river twisted around the city, passing under a huge, elegant, arched bridge and one smaller one that swung open to let boats pass through. I wished I had some drawing paper and colored pencils. From high above Cleveland, I looked out at the lake, huge and blue, sparkling in the afternoon sun. I thought I might have spotted Canada. The excitement I had experienced on the train returned, and I felt the power of possibilities; it was up to me to choose my next destination.

Eventually, I tore myself away from the view. Down at street level, I passed a newsstand that had a rack of postcards. There were many views of Cleveland, each one showing blue skies and a few puffy clouds, as if the weather in this city was always perfect. I selected a card with the Terminal Tower printed on its linen surface, bought a stamp from the clerk, and borrowed a pen, too. At the edge of the counter, I quickly wrote:

Dear Mom,
I hope you found my note and understand now why I had to leave.
I'm in Cleveland, and today I stood on the 42nd floor of this
skyscraper and saw Lake Erie. It's so big, you can't imagine it!
I don't know where I'm going next, but I'll write when I can.
I hope you're not mad at me, and I hope Raymond is on his way
back to Chicago.

Love,
Maddy

I passed a corner mailbox as I started the long walk back to where I was camping; I pulled open its metal jaw and dropped the postcard into its steel belly, sending the card on its way to a town that I never wanted to live in again.

The morning of the fifth day, I awoke to a cold wind coming off the lake. The water had turned dark and gray; it churned fiercely in every direction, spewing white froth as the waves crashed into each other. Out by the lighthouse, the wind drove the water into the breakwall, throwing spray high into the air. I was amazed that a huge body of water could have such moods and change so rapidly. It was as if the lake had its own personality. Yesterday it was calm and welcoming, and today it was hostile and wild.

I was cold, but I was also fascinated. I drew my blanket tightly around me and hunkered down to watch until I became very hungry and so chilled that I was forced to start moving. Reluctantly, I turned away from the lake and made my way to the bakery to buy some bread. As I moved away from the shore, the wind lessened a bit, blocked by the buildings and thwarted by the trees, and I started to warm up a little.

Today the wind drove the scent away from me and all I could smell was the sharp odor of the city. But when I pulled open the door of the shop, I walked right into that comforting yeasty smell. "Good morning, what can I get for you today?" the shopkeeper asked me. Her manner was as warm as her bakery.

"Do you have any day-old bread?" I tried to smile at her, but my cheeks resisted, still numb from the cold wind.

"I've got a couple of loaves of cracked wheat, dearie. But I have cinnamon buns fresh out of the oven." She smiled at me and waited.

I hesitated. I was being very conservative with my money. I didn't know how long I would have to make it last. But I was so hungry, and the smell —and the thought—of a warm cinnamon bun was overpowering.

"Okay—I'll take one cinnamon bun and a loaf of day-old bread."

She wrapped up my purchase, and as I gave her the money, she touched my hand. "That wind must still be whipping around out there. Your hands are cold as ice!" she said.

I nodded. "I was down on the beach this morning watching the waves. The lake was wild."

"It's that north wind riling up the lake," she said. "The wind will cut right through you and chill you to the bone." She sighed. "Summer's about over, I guess. Once the weather turns, the lake will be like that until it freezes over for the winter."

I paused to consider this. I hadn't even thought about winter coming on, and the prospect was daunting. I'd have to get settled somewhere before the weather got really cold.

"You from around here?" she asked, studying me for a moment.

I shook my head no. "Just visiting," I said.

"I thought so," she said. "Wait there a minute." She disappeared into the back room and returned with a steaming mug of coffee. "I just made some fresh," she said, handing me the mug. "Warm up a bit before you go." She waved off my attempt to pay for the coffee. "Where are you headed?" she asked.

"Out West." It was a decision I made on the spot. I sipped the coffee slowly and nibbled on the cinnamon bun, savoring each mouthful and considering which part of "out West" would be my new destination. Maybe I'd try to make it to California to pick fruit; it sounded like a fine place to spend the winter.

"Seems like lots of people are going out West," the shopkeeper said. "Too many, I think. It's hard to find a job there, too, I hear. But maybe you'll have some luck. Dressing like that might help you," she added, eyeing my men's clothes. "Chances are they hire the men first."

I reached up, realizing that I had forgotten to tuck and pin my hair up this morning. I'd have to pay better attention to that.

"I hope so," I said, "I hope I can find a job, I mean." I didn't think hiring men first was at all fair. "Anyway, I've got to try." I started out the door. "Thanks for the coffee. It was just what I needed."

"Be careful out there," she said. "And remember to keep your hair under your cap!" she called out after me.

I found a spot near the rail yard where I could sit and wait, unnoticed, for the next freight heading west. About an hour later I heard the slow chugs coming my direction. I tried to keep in mind everything Henry had taught me, and as the cars moved past me, I chose an open boxcar and started trotting alongside, getting ready to grab on. As I reached out for the handle, I was startled by the motion of other people running near me. I hadn't known that anyone was nearby. I lost my concentration for a moment and nearly tripped, but I held on, caught my balance, and heaved myself into the car with the aid of a push from behind by a pair of unidentified hands. I half tumbled into the car and was even more surprised to find three men already occupying it. Two more scrambled in after me.

"Thought you were going to lose it there for a minute, kid," one of the men said.

"Me, too," I said in a low voice. "Thanks for your help." I was shaking and I sat apart from the men and took some deep breaths. The train picked up speed and I tried to calm down. I felt foolish expecting to be the only person on the boxcar and nervous about being there with five men. As long as they thought I was a boy, I'd be okay, I told myself.

We passed through town after town in Ohio. The train announced its presence with blasts from the steam whistle. Two long, one short, one long. Before each crossing it slowed down, and then it picked up speed again between towns. Nobody in the boxcar talked much. One man pulled out a deck of cards and three of the men started to play. The other two men slept.

I sat where I could keep an eye on the men and yet watch the world go by through the open doors. Sometimes I could even catch the names of the towns. I remember seeing a sign by a crossroads that said *Welcome to Vermilion*. Vermilion. I first saw that word on one of the tubes of paint Mr. Otis kept in a cigar box; it means *bright red*. Mr. Otis even used it as a spelling word—one "l," not two. What was it about that town that caused it to be named after a color? I imagined a make-believe town of brick red streets and all the houses painted bright red. Maybe red glass in the streetlamps so the town was bathed in red even at night.

The train slowed down almost to a crawl as we came into Vermilion. It just looked like an ordinary town with the usual row houses near the tracks; I was disappointed that not a single one of them was red. But as I studied the nearby houses, a large group of people emerged from a wooded area near the tracks and ran to the cars. Two more men pulled themselves into my boxcar. They were followed by a family—a mother, two children, and the father. Still other people climbed on top of the car. I was beginning to see for myself the scenes Professor had described back in the jungle.

I watched the family for a little while, although I tried not to stare. The youngest of the two children was a boy, probably about four years old. His mother called him Lewis. He was very dirty. Of course, none of us was spotless—you have to expect some smudging when you're riding in a freight car. Lewis had the sweetest smile and bright blue eyes. Most of the grownups in the car were quiet and serious. But Lewis had a spark. He plainly was enjoying the trip—too young to understand that most people didn't want to live their lives in freight cars and hobo jungles. He wasn't boisterous, just happy. Little by little, he lightened the mood in the car.

I spent the night in a camp somewhere in Indiana. It was too big and sprawling to be a hobo jungle. Shanties, shacks, and lean-tos of all kinds stretched along a section of track just beyond a rail yard. The shelters were made of cardboard, scrap metal, anything that could be salvaged. This wasn't a camp just for transients; many people, even whole families, actually lived here.

I wandered through the camp, looking for a place to set down my bedroll. I passed near a small group of people sitting by a fire, stirring a soup. "Hey, buddy! Come and sit," one of the men called out, pointing to their campsite. "Have some soup."

I moved toward them, grateful for the invitation and glad that I still had bread to share.

"Where you headed?" asked a tall young man who introduced himself as Mike. He made room for me and I dropped my bindle into the spot and then sat down and leaned back against my blanket. Mike handed me a tin of steaming soup.

"California, I guess," I answered.

Mike's traveling companion, whose name was Sam, laughed. "Isn't everybody?" he said.

"Not me," said a dark-haired man sitting across from me. "We're staying here long as we can. I hope my luck will change and I'll find some work soon." He pointed to the thin, worried-looking woman sitting next to him. "I've got to find something before the baby comes."

I took a quick glance at the woman's belly. By the looks of it, they only had a month or two to get luck on their side. The only thing I could do was to make sure she got a good-sized piece of bread.

The next morning I moved in close to the rail yard. I could hear them making up a train and I was planning to be on the first one out. This yard was guarded, though. A big, brawny man with a club walked the length of the tracks. *Bulls*, Henry had called the railroad police. I knew to stay just outside the yard and out of sight, and when I heard the familiar clank of couplings grabbing, I got ready. The locomotive slowly rolled past, the guard turned his back, and a mass of people swarmed out of the woods and onto the train. They climbed into and on top of boxcars, on reefers, flatcars, and anywhere there was space. I tried to get into an open boxcar, but it was already full of people. The train was beginning to pick up speed as I ran alongside, and my only choice was to climb on top of the car. I was afraid, and I remembered Henry telling me how dangerous it could be. "If you can't wait for another train, here's how you do it," he had said when he showed me how to grab on. I started to reach out for the grab bar and then some little part of my brain reminded me that there wasn't any good reason that I couldn't wait for another train. I dropped back away from the cars, slowed my steps down to a walk, and noticed that my knees had a strong inclination to buckle. I laughed out loud, relieved that I had given up the chase. It took a good fifteen minutes to stop shaking, long enough for me to decide that I'd rather get on a train when it's standing still.

Several hours passed before I heard the sounds of cars being moved. I cut through the woods and worked my way—unseen, I hoped—deeper into the rail yard. I waited at the edge of the woods, watching as a line of cars was moved off the siding and added to the train. A bull was patrolling, club in hand, while the crew was busy checking couplings. I spotted several open boxcars; one wasn't very far from where I stood. I crouched in the woods and watched for awhile as the bull strode up and down. When he turned to make another pass down the line and his back was to me, I stepped quietly out of the woods and walked slowly to the first open boxcar. I wasn't probably more than fifty feet behind him, but I knew if I ran, he'd hear me. I was betting that if I held my breath and walked quietly, he wouldn't sense me behind him.

I grabbed the handle and pulled myself into the car, trying not to let my feet scrape across the wooden floor. I scrambled to the far corner, hardly daring to breathe, sitting down away from the doorway so that the bull couldn't see me if he passed by the car again. From farther up the track, a voice started yelling. At first, I couldn't understand the man's words, and then the voice came closer. "Check those damn boxcars!"

My heart started pounding. There must have been another bull patrolling who had spotted me. A second voice answered the first. "Sonofabitch! Which car?" And then from the back of the train I heard him pounding his club against the cars as he came toward my car. "Goddam it, no one's riding on *my* train!"

I stood up and clutched my bindle in front of me, ready to deflect a swinging club. But then the train jerked to a start and I lost my balance and fell to the back of the car. Both men were still yelling, and I leaped to my feet, hoping it was a short train that could build up speed in a hurry, before either bull got to me. Inch by inch, the locomotive pulled metal wheels across metal rails. Seconds ticked by in slow motion while I watched the doorway, and then a head burst through the opening in the boxcar. A thick fist closed over the grab handle and a beefy man swung himself into the car, waving his club and swearing.

"You goddam tramp! You're gonna be sorry you ever hauled your sorry ass onto this train!"

He took a step toward me, but fear made my legs so heavy that I couldn't pick up my feet from the floor of the boxcar. Then there was more commotion as people who were waiting at the edge of the yard ran to hop the train. Another face appeared in the doorway and the bull turned to the unlucky man. "Get away from the goddam train!" he yelled, and hit him in the head with his club. Blood spurted from the man's forehead as he fell away from the boxcar. Outrage unlocked my feet and I took the only chance I knew I'd get to defend myself. I jumped at the distracted bull, throwing every bit of my weight on him. I was no match for him, but I knocked him off balance and he went flying out of the car. I hit the edge of the doorway with my shoulder and bounced back to the floor of the car. I heard people yelling, and in the distance, the other bull shouted at people to get off railroad property. Suddenly my boxcar started filling up with men, a few women, and even a couple of children as the train picked up speed.

I squirmed my way closer to the door so I could see out. Down the track, the bull I had pushed lay sprawled face down in the cinders. "Good one," someone said, slapping me on the back. "He deserved it." "Sure did," another voice agreed.

I nodded and rubbed my arm. He did deserve it, but I couldn't gloat that the bull was eating dirt. I knew it would have been my head split open with the bull's club if it hadn't been for that one man trying to climb on. I felt bad that he was suffering and there was no way I could help him. It was my fault he got clubbed.

Finally, the train cleared the yard and I caught my breath, waiting for my muscles to stop shaking. I looked at the people sharing the boxcar and thought about what had just happened. The bulls would start over again with the next train—except maybe for one bull who would be picking cinders out of his nose—and people would be scrambling for a car or for a ladder to get on top of a car. There would be another batch of riders on the next freight out, and the next one after that, and the next one after that. The reality of it washed over me like one of those fierce waves I had seen hitting the breakwall in Cleveland. Most of these people were hoping, like me, to pass the winter in a warmer climate, probably picking fruit. There was no way that all these people heading out west were going to find work, including me.

I decided I wasn't going to starve in California. I rode for a while longer, and when the train slowed for another town, I grabbed my bindle and hopped off the boxcar. I crossed over the tracks and walked a couple miles, hoping to find a place where I could get a decent but cheap meal while I made new plans.

Shorty's Lunch Counter drew my attention. It was in a tiny storefront at the corner of Main St. and State St., next to Blakey's Hardware, but I can't remember exactly which town it was. Every small town has a Main Street, and usually a State Street, too, and most of the time they're lined with two- or three-story brick buildings with attached canvas awnings that keep the sun off your head or drop water down your neck, depending on the weather.

Shorty's had a faded green awning that matched the faded green leather on the stools that lined the counter. Most of the stools had been patched here and there with black electrical tape, giving them a shabby but oddly uniform appearance.

Only two other men were sitting at the counter, but it was afternoon, and pretty late for lunch for most people. I needed to use the washroom; I hesitated for a moment, but dressed the way I was, I had no choice but to use the men's. I pushed on the door and was thankful that no one was standing at the urinal. There was only one stall, and I ducked into it, trying to hurry before anyone came in. As I finished, I glanced down and noticed a small red stain in my underwear. Relief flooded through me. I had hoped I had gotten Raymond off of me in time, but now I was sure. I dug around in my bindle for the Kotex I had brought from home, pinned one into my underwear, and rearranged my clothes. As I finished washing my hands at the sink, the door opened and one of the men who had been sitting at the counter walked in. I gave a quick tug at the roll of white linen toweling and dried my hands, leaving the men's room without making eye contact.

It had been a long time since my breakfast of bread and coffee, and I was ravenous. I ordered Shorty's special—a ham sandwich with hash brown potatoes and a slice of apple pie and coffee. I let myself eat only half of the sandwich and wrapped up the rest for later. The pie was heavenly, and in the spirit of celebration, I ate the entire piece and washed it down with probably a half gallon of coffee.

As I ate, I caught pieces of conversation between the men sitting at the counter. From time to time, the owner—whose name really was Shorty—joined in. The three men covered topics ranging from the weather—unseasonably warm, they agreed—to the town's affairs, including a juicy one: the mayor is sleeping with his secretary, one man claimed. While Shorty was occupied with talking about town politics, I slipped a knife, fork, and spoon into my trouser pocket. I didn't have anything to eat with in the camps, and unless someone had a spare utensil, I had to use my fingers. I didn't think Shorty would miss one place setting. I looked over to be sure no one was watching, and then I reached for the salt shaker and added that to my pocket. Might as well have some seasoning, too.

I sipped my coffee, wishing I had stirred some more sugar into it before I stuck the spoon into my pocket. Shorty was saying how darned mad he was about how Hoover was running the country, and the two customers were agreeing; they were out of work and discouraged about their prospects for jobs.

"I heard Tomco Machine might be hiring temporarily, but I stopped in and the owner just shook his head. Said he was going to have to cut back some more if things didn't turn around soon," one of the men said.

"You think things couldn't get worse and then they do," said the other man. "I don't know what would happen to us if Miriam hadn't found that job up on Wintergreen Hill. It's only domestic work and it don't pay much, but at least it's something. Sure gripes my ass to have her supporting us, though."

The first man nodded sympathetically. "I know what you mean. Guess she was lucky to get that one, though."

Shorty agreed. "I think those domestic jobs are about all anyone can find right now," he said, "and there's not a lot of them, either."

I had heard enough to know that there wasn't any point in sticking around that town to look for work. I paid for my food and left Shorty's, walking carefully out the door so that the silverware I filched didn't clink. I bought some bread at a bakery and walked back to the railroad tracks to wait for an eastbound train. California had been a bad idea. I decided to go back east and follow Lake Erie for a bit and see where it would take me.

For several weeks I rode the rails along Lake Erie's shoreline—through Toledo, back again through Cleveland, then on to Madison, Ashtabula, and Conneaut, to name a few of the towns I remember. I stayed a day or two in each place, always looking for work and having no success. Not even spot labor. I ate as cheaply as I could and slept outside, sometimes in hobo jungles and sometimes just making camp in a good spot.

In Conneaut, the weather turned ugly. It was the first week of October and a frigid wind came screaming off the lake, pushing its way onshore and penetrating every bit of clothing I wore. That day I had camped close to the harbor in a jungle that was occupied by only one other traveler—a hobo who went by the name of Blackjack. We kept a fire going to try to stay warm, but we couldn't escape the wind. It would frequently whip smoke and ashes into our faces.

I got nervous when I sat, alone, across a campfire from a man. I liked it better when there were several people in the jungles. We'd all share some food, and then I could move away from the fire to a spot near the edge of the clearing and keep to myself. I didn't want anyone to figure out that I was a girl. But I soon discovered that I passed quite well for a boy, and the other hobos were helpful and sometimes a little protective, I guess because of my age.

Blackjack was friendly enough, but under the surface he seemed sad. He sat kind of slumped, like he was carrying a weight, and he didn't smile very much, although he seemed glad to have someone to talk to. He was on his way to California to find a job in the fields, he said, helping with the harvest.

"I hope you have good luck," I said. "I started to go out West, but the trains were so crowded. I didn't figure I had much chance to get hired once I got out there."

"Probably right. I've heard they're not too friendly to young people out there," Blackjack said. He glanced at me and then looked away. "Guess they figure that the boys ought to be staying with their families and helping out. Some of the towns don't want the boys hanging around at all. If they're caught on the trains, they're jailed for a night and sent packing the next day—if they're lucky. If their luck isn't so good, they end up on a work farm for 30 days, providing unpaid labor."

"Well, some young people have damn good reasons for not staying with their families," I snapped, flashing back to the Paradise Diner. "And back in a jungle in Ohio, I met a boy who couldn't go home, even though he wanted to. His family sent him away."

"Don't get pissed off," Blackjack said. "I'm just telling you what I know. I'm sure you got your reasons for being on the road."

We both sat silently for a few minutes. Blackjack poked at the fire. "Anyway, I'm hoping that maybe someone will hire a veteran if there's a job to be had."

"You were in the service?"

"Yep, in the Army for two years—1917 to 1919. I was overseas for most of the time." He grinned. "Got real good at playing cards with my Army buddies, too, while we were waiting for action."

I laughed. "Hmm. I bet you played a lot of blackjack."

"Turned out to be my game." He pulled a deck of cards out of his jacket pocket and grinned. "Want to play a few rounds?"

"Not for money!" I said. "I've got to conserve what I've got." I had about five dollars left: three dollars in my shoe and two dollars and change in my pants pocket. I didn't know how long I'd have to make my money last. Besides, I didn't want to admit that I didn't know how to play blackjack. I knew very little about any betting card games. My father had played poker sometimes, which made my mother very unhappy because my father usually bet heavy and lost. It was one more thing they fought about.

"Yeah, well it's too windy, anyway," Blackjack said, tucking the deck back into his pocket.

By mid afternoon, it became obvious that the wind wasn't going to settle down. My hands and feet were getting numb and I was chilled to the bone, no matter how close I got to the fire. I decided I had had enough. I started packing up my stuff and rolling it into a bindle. "There's got to be another train or two coming through here this afternoon," I said to Blackjack. "I need to get away from this lake. I'm going to freeze to death if I stay here tonight."

Blackjack nodded. "I'm thinking the same thing myself," he said. "Time to head west." He stood and stretched his long legs. "I'll put this fire out. You go on. If you want, go back through the rail yard and stay close to the eastern edge. You'll see that one of the sets of tracks starts veering southeast. If you catch out from that track, it'll take you into Pennsylvania—away from the lake."

"Thanks. That's where I'm going, then." I reached out and shook his hand. "You take care—and good luck."

"Yep. You too," he said.

I started toward the track, walking slowly—my feet and legs were stiff from the cold.

"Hey, one more thing," Blackjack said. "A piece of friendly advice."

I turned back toward him. "What's that?"

"Don't be admitting to people that you have any money." He stepped forward. "They might try to take it from you." He lifted his hand, and I saw metal flash. "Empty your pockets, kid."

"What...you're not...serious..." I stared at his hand, trying to understand why he was gripping a knife.

"I said empty your goddam pockets." His voice suddenly sounded menacing and I reached into my pockets with trembling hands, pulling out a couple of crumpled dollar bills and a small amount of change. "Put it on the railroad tie by your foot," he said. I bent down to do what he said, hoping my shaking legs would let me stand back up.

"Now pull your pockets inside out."

I did. There was nothing more in them.

"That all the money you got?" he asked, his eyes narrowed.

"Yes," I squeaked out through dry lips, trying not to think about the money in my shoe.

"All right. Turn around."

I faced down the track in the direction I had started to go only a few minutes before. I wondered if he was going to stab me in the back so he didn't have to look at my face as I died.

"Now you got one minute to run like hell and get out of my sight. If you slow down at all, I'll send this knife right into your kidney. Now git."

I grabbed my bindle and took off running, fueled by adrenaline. I tripped on a tie and nearly fell, but I headed for the cinders at the edge of the track and dug in, running full out for as long as I could. Finally, my burning lungs couldn't get enough air and I stopped, gasping and coughing.

CHAPTER 18

When I looked back, I was surprised to see how far I had run. There was no sign of Blackjack. He was long gone, with my money in his pockets. "Damn you!" I screamed down the empty track. "Damn you to hell!"

I sat down hard on top of my bedroll and let the tears come. *Stupid, stupid, stupid*, I told myself. *How could you be so stupid, blabbing to a stranger about money like that! It's a damn good thing Henry told you to put some money in your shoes, or you'd have lost it all. Keep your wits about you, Henry told you. But you didn't. And look what happened! You could have been killed.*

I blew my nose and took some deep breaths. When I calmed down I realized that in one way, I was lucky. I wasn't hurt or dead. Just poorer. "Well, I certainly hope you learned something!" I said out loud, sternly. I shouldered my bindle and started walking.

That incident hammered home Henry's lessons, and I made up two new rules besides:

Rule Number One: Either travel in a group or travel by myself.

Rule Number Two: Don't go blabbing to strangers, period.

I followed the tracks for a while until I came to the edge of the rail yard. There were people milling around and I hung back, watching, until I was satisfied they were just travelers like me.

The yard was patrolled, but the bull didn't carry a club and he half-heartedly ordered people away from the tracks. "This is the property of the Penn-syl-van-ia Railroad," he said in a singsong voice. "The Penn-syl-van-ia Railroad don't want nobody riding for free. Please step away from the tracks." I was part of a small group of people, and he made us move back into the woods, off railroad property. "Just doing my job," he said. Then he turned on his heel and walked away. "Don't let me see you get on," he said quietly over his shoulder.

A tall, gaunt man standing next to me kind of chuckled. "I guess all the bulls ain't bad," he said.

A man wearing a torn denim work shirt spoke up. "Most of the bulls would just as soon club you as look at you. Glad there's a few with a little humanity in 'em."

Several men murmured agreement, and then we stood in silence, waiting for the familiar chugs announcing our ride out. When we heard the train, we fanned out to choose a car. The train creaked along so slowly that this time I wasn't afraid to grab on. I chose a boxcar, threw in my bindle, pulled myself in, and the tall, gaunt man pulled himself into the car right after me.

Nobody else got in our boxcar and I was mad that I already had to break my brand new Rule Number One. We nodded to each other, and then I sat opposite the door so that I could enjoy the view and keep an eye on my unwanted traveling companion, who chose the back corner. He promptly stretched out and went to sleep. We rode for quite a while, passing through one town after another—some of them hardly more than a crossroads.

The side-to-side rocking of the boxcar was hypnotic, but I was beginning to find myself in a predicament. I had to pee. I sat there for awhile, trying to decide what to do. I didn't want to get off the train in the middle of nowhere, and we were moving along at a pretty fast clip besides, but there was no way I could think of to relieve myself when there was a man in my boxcar, even if he was asleep. I tried to think about other things—I thought about school, about Henry and Jigger, about Lake Erie—but it was very hard to concentrate on something other than the growing pressure on my bladder. Then the tall, gaunt man woke up, stretched, and walked over to the open door of the boxcar.

"Man, I gotta take a leak," he said.

I heard the sound of his zipper, and then he urinated out the door, aiming his stream down the track, in the direction we had just come from. I willed myself to hide my embarrassment. *As far as he knows, we're both men*, I reminded myself. But his relief made my physical discomfort even worse. Finally, as I was close to bursting, we approached a town and the train slowed. We crossed a river, and the sound of swift water added to my misery. When the train reached the other side and I could see the town stretching out in front of the train, I grabbed my bindle and bailed out without so much as a word.

I hit the ground pretty hard and tumbled forward, but scrambled to my feet quickly and ran into the nearest clump of bushes, unfastening my trousers as I ran. When I came back out, feeling much more comfortable,

I walked toward town, trying to get my bearings. A distinct petroleum smell was in the air, and then I saw the sign that named what my nose already knew. *Welcome to Oil City.*

The railroad bridge spanned the Allegheny River, and a large rail yard extended along its northern banks. It didn't take me long to discover the location of the hobo jungle, which was near the intersection of Oil Creek and the Allegheny River. Dusk was creeping in when I walked into the campsite. Five hobos sat around the fire; one was tending to a large pot of mulligan. Most everyone was eating. They all turned to look at me when they heard my footsteps. I nodded to them and laid my bindle down at the edge of the clearing. Unlike the Hoovervilles, hobo jungles sometimes had hierarchies, I had learned from Henry, depending on who was a "regular" in the camp. I waited.

A man with a reddish beard called out. "Hey kid—you hungry? Come get something to eat."

"Okay," I said, walking toward the fire. I had eaten a paltry lunch with the knife-wielding Blackjack back in Conneaut, but it had long worn off, and my stomach had been gurgling and growling all afternoon. "I don't have anything to give, though."

"There's plenty for tonight," a man wearing a tattered flannel shirt answered. "If you're staying, you can bring some food back tomorrow."

"Thanks," I said. "I'm really hungry!"

The man with the reddish beard ladled a good portion of soup into a well-used tin can and handed it to me. I fished out my spoon from my bindle and ate a mouthful of the soup. It was full of chunks of potato and carrots and meat. I couldn't quite identify the meat. It had a familiar flavor, but it wasn't exactly like anything I had eaten.

"This is good," I said, pointing at the soup with my spoon. "What is it?"

"Turtle soup," said the man in the flannel shirt. He pointed at a square-jawed man with brown hair. "Walt caught him this afternoon."

"I never ate turtle before," I said. Its flavor was a little different, but real hunger takes away anybody's inclination to be a picky eater. "I like it, though."

"Yeah, tastes just like chicken, don't it?" Walt said.

Everyone laughed. "Sure, chicken drowned in a river," said the red-bearded man. "It's not too bad," he acknowledged. "Could use some salt, though."

I jumped up. "Maybe I do have something to give," I said, and I dug the salt shaker out of my bindle, unscrewed the top so I could remove the paper I had put over the opening, screwed the top back on, and handed the shaker to the red-bearded man, who passed it around.

The red-bearded man shook his head and laughed. "Ain't never seen a hobo carry a damn salt shaker before." He stuck out his hand to me. "People just call me Red," he said.

I shook his hand. "People call me Matt," I answered, giving him the male version of my name that I had started using on the road. Red then pointed to each man sitting around the campfire, naming them: Walt, Frank, Gus, and ending with the man in the flannel shirt, whose name was Owen.

We sat around the campfire for a long while after dinner. No one seemed in a hurry to turn in for the night. Gus and Frank talked about the merits of going out west for the winter. Frank said he was going to give it a try. "At least I can be warm," he said.

"Yeah, and what're you going to eat—warm dust?" Gus asked. "The drought is getting worse out west and there ain't no jobs."

"If I can't find anything closer, I might just go all the way out to California and see about picking fruit or something," Frank said.

"You're more likely to end up standing in a food line with a thousand other people." Gus shook his head. "Nope. I'm sticking to the branch lines. Less competition. I can usually find a couple of odd jobs to tide me over."

I half listened to the exchange. I had already decided to stay east and stick to the branch lines, like Gus—and like Henry. I wondered if Henry had found a job in Pittsburgh. I missed his friendship. It surprised me that it felt like the time we rode together had happened a long time ago. But in actual time, it had just been a little more than a month.

I brought my attention back to the fire. Near my right foot was an empty paper sack left over from some food one of the hobos had brought to the camp. I reached down to pick it up and throw it in the fire, but stopped, thinking maybe we'd need it for the next morning's fire. I smoothed it out with my hands, Feeling the rough texture beneath my fingers sparked another desire; near the fire pit, I found a small piece of wood that hadn't been fully burnt—a piece of charcoal—and I began to draw with it.

Gus and Frank were still debating, which involved quite a lot of gesturing. Red, however, was sitting quietly, listening to the discussion, so he became my model. I started sketching him in the firelight—first the shape of his face, then his eyes and nose, which were strongly shadowed by the fire, then his eyebrows and hair, the outline of his beard, the set of his shoulders, the bend of his right arm against his thigh, the angle of his wrist and his weathered hand, his outstretched left leg, the tip of his worn boot. Eventually, I became aware of the sound of the crackling and hissing of the fire. Then I realized it was the only sound. I looked up, and all five men were watching me.

I felt my face flush. "Uh...I was just...in school I used to...I was just fooling around," I finally stammered. When I faced five pairs of staring eyes, I realized that any one of these men could take offense at being drawn without their permission.

Red burst out laughing. "You look like a deer caught in a hunter's crosshairs, kid!" he said. "Let's see what you're doing."

Silently, I handed Red my drawing. He studied it for a few minutes and then he said, "Man, I need a haircut!" The other men laughed, and Red passed my drawing around. Owen was the last to look at it, and he studied it for a while. "Not bad, Matt," he said, finally, handing it back to me.

"What are you going to do with it?" Red asked.

I shrugged. "Nothing special. I was just passing the time."

"You planning to finish it?" Red asked me.

"Well, sure, if you don't mind...," I said. I was ready to toss it into the fire if it was going to cause trouble.

"Nah, I don't mind," he said. He lowered his voice. "But I was thinking if I could have it when it's finished, I'll send it off to my sister in St. Louis. Haven't seen her in quite a while. She might like it."

"It's yours," I said, and I picked up the charcoal and went back to work. I made it a point to finish it before I turned in for the night. I looked at it with a critical eye before I gave it to Red. My drawing skills were rusty, for sure; I could have done better with the lower body. But Red's face was pretty good—it seemed recognizable enough—and I hoped his sister would like it.

The next morning, I planned to walk into town to look for work and to buy some food to bring back for stew. I was running out of money. All I had left were the few dollars in my shoe and fifteen cents I discovered in my shirt pocket. It wouldn't buy much more than a week's worth of meals. I really needed to find a job. I felt a bit of panic rise from the pit of my stomach, creating a lump in my throat. I swallowed hard to push it back down.

I looked up. Owen was watching me. "You look worried, kid," he said.

I shrugged. "I've got to find a job. Soon."

He studied me for a minute. "After watching you last night, I think I can show you how to stretch your money farther than you think," he said.

"What do you mean?" I asked. I was very suspicious. If he even mentioned playing cards, I was going to run like crazy.

"Got a nickel?" he asked.

I frowned. "Why?"

"For Crissakes, kid," he said. "I'm not going to take your money!" He dug into his pocket, pulled out a coin, and flipped it to me. "Here, look!"

I caught it in the palm of my hand and looked at it. It was a buffalo nickel; nothing out of the ordinary. "I don't get it," I said. "It's a nickel."

"Turn the damn thing over," Owen said.

I did. On the front of the coin was a man wearing a derby hat. The detail was striking. The derby had a band with a pattern etched into it, and the man had a neatly trimmed beard and mustache. He wore a shirt with a pointed collar. "What in the world!" I said. "Isn't that supposed to be an Indian's head? Is this some kind of new coin?"

"Nope," Owen beamed. "It's a buffalo nickel all right. I carved it. I changed the Indian head to a man with a derby."

"Wow! How did you do that?"

"You just need a few simple tools, a little drawing ability, and a lot of time and patience," he said. "The drawing you did last night was pretty good, so I figure you can learn how to do this if you want. I can help you with the tools."

"But I don't get why you do that," I said. "Won't shopkeepers refuse to take the nickels if you've changed them?"

"Nope, just the opposite," he said. "The carved nickels are a little piece of artwork, a conversation piece. People like 'em. You can usually trade 'em for something worth more than a nickel."

"Really?"

"Yep. Once I even got a room for the night *and* a meal for one of those nickels."

"No kidding! And you'd teach me how to do it?"

"Why not? An old 'bo I met in Chicago taught me. Kept me from starving more than once. It'd be a way to return the favor," he said.

I hadn't forgotten that I was honor bound to bring some food to the camp that day. "Could you show me as soon as I get back from town? I have to go get some meat for stew today."

Owen nodded. "If you want, we can go together. I've got to get some food, too."

It was maybe a 15-minute walk to town, and we stopped at the closest grocery store. We went inside and when we reached the meat counter, Owen grinned at me and said in a low voice, "Well, let's see what happens."

"Sir," he said to the shopkeeper, "I'd like to buy some beef, and I'm wondering if you would consider taking this special coin in trade."

The shopkeeper eyed us both, taking in our worn clothing. I studied him, too, especially the blood-stained apron that he wore over his clothes. It looked like he had been painting with two colors: brown and red. But it was old blood and fresh blood staining his apron. "What special coin?" the shopkeeper asked, his face clearly conveying his doubts that either of us had anything of value.

Owen handed him the nickel. "This one," he said.

The shopkeeper turned it over in his hand and studied it. "Well look at that," he said. Now his face showed quite a bit of interest. "Where did you get this?" he asked.

"I didn't get it," Owen said. "I carved it."

"Is that right?" the shopkeeper said. "Well, maybe I would be interested in a trade. How much meat do you want for it?"

"You give me what you think it's worth," Owen answered.

We watched as the shopkeeper weighed out about a quarter's worth of meat. I looked over at Owen. A little smile played at the corner of his lips. I worked real hard to keep my astonishment from showing.

"Is that satisfactory?" the shopkeeper asked.

"Yes, sir," Owen said. "Like I said—whatever you think it's worth."

"There you go, then," the shopkeeper said, handing the package to Owen. "If you got any more, I might be interested in another one," he said. "One of my customers likes unusual coins, too."

"Thank you," Owen said. "I'll remember that."

I walked over to the vegetable bins and selected about a nickel's worth of vegetables—a couple of turnips, some snap beans, and an onion—and handed the shopkeeper a dime. He rang up my purchase and handed me back a nickel in change. Now I had two nickels I could work on.

Outside the store, I couldn't contain my excitement. "He gave you five times what that nickel was worth!" I said to Owen.

Owen looked pleased. "Can't always depend on that," he said. "But if someone's interested, they'll always give you more than the face value."

"I can't wait to learn how to make those!" I said. If I could trade carved nickels for food, I thought, I could actually buy some time to find a job.

We returned to the jungle and gave the meat and vegetables to Walt, who had said he'd cook that day. Walt smiled broadly when he saw the contents of our packages. "A good trip into town," he said.

"Yep, a good trip," said Owen. Then he turned to me. "Now you and I have some work to do." He got me set up with simple equipment, if you could even call it that. We used things that most people would've probably just stepped over or kicked aside and thought nothing of it, even during the Depression.

Owen had several pieces of scrap wood; one of the pieces had a couple of nails sticking out of it. He used one of the scraps for leverage and worked the nails out of the other one. Then he showed me how to file down the sides of a nail by scraping the point against a rock. It took a while, but when I was done, he said, "Okay, now that's your flat chisel."

Then he took a small piece of scrap metal and, using a rock as a hammer, he gouged out and pounded a circular depression into one of the wood scraps. "This'll hold your nickel so you can work on it," he said. "Now give me one of your nickels and I'll show you what to do." I handed one to him and he slipped it into the depression and then fished a screw and a washer out of his pocket. I watched as he set the washer to cover the top edge of the nickel and then using his pocketknife, he tightened the screw to hold the washer. The nickel was trapped pretty securely. "You can always put another screw in at the bottom if the coin wants to slip," he said. "But sometimes the screw'll just get in your way."

Next, Owen set up his own jig and set a nickel into it. "Best thing is for you to watch what I'm doing and then work on yours," he said. "I'll show you how I made the nickel I traded today." He took a nail and carefully scribed the shape of a derby over the head of the Indian. I followed suit, except that my hat looked like it was some kind of bowl sitting on the Indian's head—not quite a derby. Owen looked at it. "Not too bad for the first one. You'll get better with practice," he said. Then he took his own nail chisel, wrapped a rag around it for grip, and started carefully removing the parts of the Indian's hair and feathers that were outside the derby marks. "This is where you have to have patience," Owen said. "If you try to cut away too much metal at once, you'll get deep gouges you'll never get rid of."

I wrapped a bit of rag around my nail chisel and started working on the feathers. The metal was tougher than I thought. "This is going to take a while," I said. We worked away for quite some time and I started to get a feel for making the small, smooth cuts that made a nice finish. Owen nodded approval. "You're getting it," he said.

When that part was done, the coin looked like an Indian wearing a derby of sorts. It was an odd-looking combination, and it made me laugh. Owen chuckled, too. "You end up with some weird looking characters before you're done," he said.

Next, we chiseled away the Indian's braid and smoothed out the neck area. Owen showed me how he took a little of the bony part of the nose away to soften the man's features. Once all the removing was done, Owen said, "Now we can add to the coin."

He pulled out a small assortment of broken drill bits, the tip of a screwdriver, odd bits of metal—anything that would make a pattern. I watched as he used these tools to put a pattern in the hat band and form an ear where the Indian's braid had been scraped away. "This is the hard part," he said. "You have to have a bit of an artist's eye to get the ear right, and if you make a bad cut, you're stuck with it." He cleaned away more metal from the ear, giving it dimension.

I set to work on mine and got a decent-looking ear the first time, which pleased both of us. "That's what I thought," Owen said. "When I saw your drawing, I figured you could make a nice nickel."

But there was still more to do. Owen started to work on adding facial hair to his man; I watched for a few minutes, and then remembered the manicure set I had taken from home. I got one of the pieces, which was made of hard steel, and used it to give my man a curly beard. "Now you're thinking," Owen said.

The set had several usable tools, including a nail file that I used to smooth out some chisel marks. I thought about my mother; I hoped she and Eddie were okay, and I wondered if my father had spent much time in jail. More than anything, I hoped Raymond had got what was coming to him.

Owen and I worked on those nickels all day, stopping only to eat, but at the end of the day we had two good-looking nickels. Owen's was more finely carved than mine, but I wasn't ashamed of my first effort, and I was pretty sure I could trade it for food. I remembered one conversation I had with my mother over my drawings. *You're not going to be able to make a living with your artwork,* she had said. Maybe not, I thought, but if I can eat, it's a start.

The next morning, I awoke with the first light. The smell of fall was heavy in the chilly air and I was wrapped up tightly in my blanket. I forced myself to throw it off so I could walk down to the river to bathe. For the last two days I had to settle for just washing up because the men at the camp were nearby. But now, no one was near the river. Owen, Walt, and Red were still sleeping, and Frank had caught a westbound freight the day before. Gus was gone, too; he said he was headed to Titusville to try to find some odd jobs. Even so, I walked down the river quite a ways so that I wouldn't be seen. The water was cold enough to take my breath away when I plunged in, but it felt so good to strip off all my clothes and scrub down.

By the time I got back to camp, Red had a small fire burning under a makeshift coffee pot. Walt was ambling toward the river, and Owen was trying to shave, peering at himself in a cloudy mirror he had tied to a low-hanging branch of a maple tree. There wasn't much to eat, just some chunks of stale bread, but the coffee warmed me. I drank it from a small can I wrapped with a rag to keep from burning my fingers.

Red poured some coffee into his cup. It was made from a tin can, and he had wrapped some sturdy wire around the top and bottom rims, attaching the wire to a piece of wood that served as a handle. "Coffee's kind of weak," he said. "That's the last of it."

"I'll try to get some today," I said. I was secretly excited about going back into town to see what my hobo nickel would buy.

"Good," he said. "I'll work on getting something for dinner."

"Me, too," said Owen, who had finished shaving and was now drawing close to the fire. "Matt, we should try different sections of town with our nickels. How about I go east of the stem and you go west?"

"That's okay with me," I said. I knew he meant the main street. I finished my coffee quickly and stood up to go. I was trying to adjust to eating one meal a day, but it was hard to be hungry most of the time. I hoped I could find a bakery on the west side of town. If I could get some bread, I knew I would feel much better.

I walked for several blocks looking for a bakery. I had trouble at first because the odors from the refineries permeated the air. I imagined that to the owners and workers who still had jobs in the refineries, the air smelled like money, but to me, it just plain stank. Finally, I located a bakery, but by seeing rather than by smelling. *Antonio's Bakery*, the sign above the door read. The letters were painted a deep green, and the dot over the i in Antonio's had been turned into a rectangle of three vertical stripes—green, white, and red—the flag of Italy. In the window stood a small display of pastries and bread that had been arranged around a cardboard model of the tower of Pisa.

I pushed on the door and a bell jangled. An old, heavyset man with a full head of white hair shuffled out to greet me. "Yes, sir," he said. He stood, looking at me, waiting.

"I'd like some day-old bread, if you have it," I said.

"Sold out," he said.

"Oh," I said. I couldn't tell if he was grumpy or just a man of few words. "Well, thank you just the same," I said. I wished I could afford fresh bread, hungry as I was, but I took a step back toward the door.

He raised his voice to stop me. "But my idiot son-in-law put two loaves too close to the side of the oven, so they burnt where they touched the oven. Can't sell them looking like that. You want them?" he asked.

"Yes," I said, hoping they weren't terribly burnt. "I could pay you day-old prices."

"Nope," he said. "I just said I can't sell them. You can take them or you can leave them."

"Well, then, I'd be happy to take them," I said. *Grumpy*, I said to myself, trying not to smile. He seemed to be a man of many words, after all.

The old man shuffled into the back, muttering as he went. "You'd think he'd learn by now. Working here fifteen years and he still puts the damn bread too close to the sides of the oven. Don't know what Lucy saw in him..." He returned with two loaves. Each one had a dark brown streak on its side, near the top, at the place where the loaf mushrooms out before the pan confines it, but they certainly weren't burnt by my definition.

He wrapped them up and gave them to me. "You come back another time and try some of my *good* bread," he said.

"I certainly will if I can," I said. "Thank you."

I waited until I had walked about half a block from the bakery, and then I tore a small chunk of bread from one of the loaves and popped it into my mouth. The bread was moist and luscious and full bodied. If that old man considered this *bad* bread, I thought, his *good* bread would probably overwhelm me. I pulled several more chunks of bread from the loaf and ate as I walked. My stomach was grateful to have something to work on. My hunger was like a fire smoldering deep in my belly and the bread was putting it out.

Several blocks away I found a Kroger's. Hardly anyone was in the store. I wondered if business was bad because times were bad, or was it too early in the morning for many people to be out. Inside the store, a man stood on a stepladder, taping papers to the plate glass window announcing the week's specials. Frankfurters 10¢/lb., Lemons 15¢/doz., Proctor & Gamble Soap 10 bars/32¢, Peanut Butter 15¢/2 lb. jar.

Peanut butter. I wanted so badly to scoop a spoonful of peanut butter into my mouth and feel it stick to my teeth, my tongue, the roof of my mouth.

I worked up my courage to approach the man. I hoped he was the owner. "Excuse me, sir." He looked down at me from his perch and I immediately lost my nerve when he spoke. "Can I help you?" he asked.

"Uh...where would I find the coffee?"

"Aisle 2," he answered. "The grinder's there, too. You can grind the beans however you like."

I hesitated. "I don't have a lot of money," I began. "Would you consider taking a special coin in trade?" I used Owen's words, hoping they'd work for me, too.

"What coin?" he asked, frowning. He stepped down from the ladder. I dug in my pocket and showed him the nickel. "It's really a little piece of artwork," I said, and I was embarrassed as soon as those words left my lips. I didn't feel like an artist. "I carved it."

"Hmm," he said as he looked closely at the bearded man with a derby. "That's remarkable! This was a buffalo nickel?"

I nodded.

"How did you do it?" he asked

"I have special tools," I said, thinking how he would laugh if he saw my filed-down nail chisel. "It takes a couple of days to carve one."

"You want to trade this for coffee?" he asked.

He seemed quite interested, so I went for broke. "Coffee and a jar of peanut butter, if you're willing." I said.

He looked at me for a long moment. "All right, then. I can do that."

I left Kroger's feeling absurdly happy. Further up the street, I spotted a small city park with a few benches situated under the trees. That's a great spot for a *real* breakfast, I thought.

I settled onto a bench and opened the jar; then I tore a chunk of bread from the loaf I'd been working on and used it to scoop out some peanut butter. I popped the whole gooey chunk into my mouth. The peanut butter clung to my teeth and tongue and blended with the taste of wheat; I was in heaven, or darn close to it—a cup of coffee would have been perfection. I ate a little bit more, savoring every mouthful, and then I put everything away. I wanted to have enough to share back in the jungle and still have something to eat tomorrow.

The next order of business was to look for a job. I crossed back over to the main business district, but it didn't look promising. Several stores were deserted; only their names painted above the doors revealed what had occupied the space: Gail's Clothing, Oil City Furniture. Their empty interiors looked black against the morning sun, and as I walked past the stores, here and there I saw a few dead flies lying belly up on the window sills. A couple of store windows were covered with yellowing newspaper, as if to block the sight of failure from the eyes of townspeople passing by. *Closed,* a handwritten sign claimed on one door. But the door was also padlocked, and the storefront was vacant.

I stopped in every business that hadn't yet locked its doors in defeat, but I ended up being the one defeated. Each time, I asked about a job, and each time I was turned down. Not hiring, they said. Then I'd ask after odd jobs, again without success. After a while, I gave up. I didn't feel like facing any more rejection that day, and I returned to the jungle. Owen had started a stew, and the smell of simmering onions and beef filled the air. Owen grinned when he saw me. "I had good luck with my nickel," he said. "How about you?"

"Not bad," I said, showing him the peanut butter and coffee.

"Very good!" Owen said, handing me the can that served as a coffee pot. "I could use a cup of coffee about now. How about you make some?"

"Okay," I said. I stood up to go down to the river to fill the can with water. "And if you're hungry now, here's some bread to go with the peanut butter." I held up the second loaf—the one I hadn't torn into for lunch.

Owen whistled. "Coffee, peanut butter, *and* bread!" You got good mileage out of that nickel."

"Nah, the bread wasn't part of the deal," I said, turning the loaf to show Owen the brown streak. "I just got lucky and found a baker who was very unhappy with his son-in-law."

Owen's laughter warmed me and buoyed my spirits. After I got the coffee going, I got out my tools and sat down to carve another nickel. This time, I decided to try a man with a watch cap. I scribed the lines in and went to work, stopping only for supper, which was a satisfying mulligan brimming with beef and vegetables.

"Best we've had yet," Red said.

We all ate our fill, mopping up our tins with pieces of bread to get every bit. I helped Red with the cleanup and then worked a little while longer on my nickel until the light got too dim to see. I turned in early that night, wrapping up tightly in my blanket to try to ward off the increasingly chilly night air. Tonight I could see my breath. It was mid October; time was getting short to find someplace to pass the winter. I tried not to worry. I reminded myself that I could always catch a freight west if I couldn't find anything here. If the weather got miserable before I got settled, it would only take me a few days to get out of it and into a warmer climate. The weather didn't concern me nearly as much as the possibility of starving.

The cold air seeped into my blanket overnight, finding its way through the fibers and settling in my bones, waking me very early in the morning. I tried to get back to sleep, but I was too cold. There was only a hint of first light, but I arose, wrapped up Indian style in my blanket, and worked on starting a fire. Last night's fire wasn't completely dead, and I was able to blow some life back into several embers. I fed little bits of twigs to the wisps of fire and soon the twigs caught, shooting up little tendrils of yellow flame. Even the tiny bit of heat given off by the twigs eased the coldness of my fingers. I added more twigs and as they caught, I added bigger pieces of wood, and soon there was enough heat that I could do without my blanket. I set a couple of cans of water to heat over the fire—one can for coffee and the other to provide some warm water so I could wash up a little.

Red and Owen were both stirring, and Red sat down across the fire from me. "Damn, it's cold!" he said.

"I know," I said. "I was so cold I couldn't sleep."

"At least we got coffee today," he said.

I glanced at the coffee pot. The water was starting to steam. In a few more minutes, it would start to bubble. "Shouldn't take too much longer," I said.

Red added some sticks to the fire. "I'm heading out this morning," he said. "I think we've about reached the end of Indian summer."

A short distance from the fire, Owen coughed, as if to punctuate the end of good weather.

"Where are you going?" I asked Red.

"Time to travel my southern route," he said. "I'll go through southern Ohio, along the Ohio River for a while, and then into Kentucky." Red looked over at me. The light from the fire added more color to his red beard. "Maybe that would be a good route for you, too. Get you out of here before winter."

"Maybe," I said. But I had no intentions of going back to Ohio. Not while Raymond was there. Maybe not ever. "But I'm going into town again today. There's a few more places I want to try. I keep hoping I'll get lucky and find some kind of work."

"I don't know," Owen said, warming his hands over the fire. "I don't think you could even buy a job around here!" He sighed. "I guess I'm going to be on my way soon, too. I'll stay one more night while I decide where to go next."

We sat in silence then, sipping coffee and passing around bread and peanut butter. A formation of geese passed directly overhead, honking noisily as they flew. We all looked up and watched as the ends of the long V disappeared over the tree tops. Red watched them for a few minutes and then said, "Did you ever notice that one side of the V is always longer than the other side?" We nodded. "Do you know why?" he asked. Owen and I thought about it. In school, I had learned something about birds flying in a V shape so they could balance the wind turbulence, but I didn't know why one side of the V was always longer than the other. Apparently, Owen didn't either.

"Well, I don't know," I admitted. "Why is one side of the V longer than the other?"

Owen nodded, waiting for the answer.

"Because," Red answered slowly and seriously, "there's more geese on one side of the V than the other!" He threw his head back and burst into raucous laughter.

"Hee, hee, hee," Owen snorted. "You got us on that one!" I laughed, too, and then we all settled into a happy companionship where no words were needed.

As the morning light got stronger, I got out my tools and started working on my nickel. My goal was to have it finished before I went into town.

Red finished breakfast and started packing up his few belongings, rolling them tightly into his bindle. He came back over by the fire and then stuck out his hand to me. "I'm off," he said. "I'm catching out this morning. Maybe we'll meet up again sometime, Matt."

"I hope so," I said, shaking his hand. "You take care."

"Will do," he said, turning to shake hands with Owen.

"Be careful out there," Owen said.

"Yep. You, too."

Owen looked over my shoulder at my nickel. "Hey, that one looks even better than your first one!" he said.

"I'm almost done," I said, sitting back to look at my work. This man sported a curly beard and mustache, and a little bit of hair peeked out from under his knit cap. I had carved the ear pretty well on this one, too. I leaned forward again to carve a bit more away from the man's profile to define it a little better.

"That watch cap looks good," Owen said. "You don't see too many of those."

"Well, I thought it might be easier than the derby," I admitted, "but then you have to carve away more metal. So it takes longer. I guess I'll have to work on derbies and other hats with brims."

"You'll get it," he said. "The ear is the hardest thing, and you got that already."

I unscrewed the nickel from its holder and looked at it closely. "Does everybody work on the Indian?" I asked Owen. "What about the buffalo? Can you do anything with that?"

"Sure," he said. "Some people carve the buffalo. I think it's harder, though, so I just stick to the Indian head. But I've seen people change the buffalo to an animal—rabbits and donkeys and turtles especially—and sometimes they change it to look like a man with a walking stick and a pack on his back."

"How in the world do you make this buffalo into a man?" I asked, staring at the buffalo grazing.

"Turn it sideways," Owen said, showing me. "Now the buffalo can be carved into a man walking upright, and the ground turns into a walking stick." He pointed to show me. "See, the buffalo's hump gets changed into a pack."

"Whew—that's a lot of carving," I said.

"Yep. That's why I stick to the Indian," he laughed. "They're real pretty, though, if they're done right."

"I think I'll be sticking to the Indian, too," I said. "Owen, thank you for showing me how to do this. You've already helped me stretch my food money."

"I'm glad you took to it," he said. "Like I said before, an old 'bo showed me how, and I'm returning the favor by showing you. Maybe you'll show somebody else some day."

"I'd sure be willing if the right person came along." I stood and stretched. "I think I'd better go into town now. Are you going?"

"No. I think I've about given up on this town," Owen said. "It's warming up a bit, so I think I'm going to sit by the river and fish. Then I'll figure out what's next."

"Okay," I said. "Should I try to get something for supper?"

"Well, if you get something, make sure it goes with fish," Owen grinned.

I would try one more day to find work in this town, I decided, and then I'd have to move on. I took the long way into town, past the refineries along the river. I stopped everywhere I could to ask about a job. Nobody was hiring. Not even for spot labor, although I wasn't sure I could carry off doing any heavy labor like a man would, even if I had the chance.

"I wish I had a nickel for every person who's asked me for a job," the manager at Woolworth's said, shaking his head.

"I know," I said. "I wish I had a nickel for every place I've asked for a job." I hesitated for a moment and then added, knowing it was futile, "I'd do any odd job if you had one," I said.

"The problem is," he said, "I can't pay anybody for odd jobs."

I tried to hide my disappointment; I stared at his shirt pocket, which had a name tag pinned to it. *Mr. Dawson*, it read.

"Unless you wouldn't mind being paid with a meal," he said.

I raised my eyes from his name tag to his face. His brown eyes looked at me seriously. "No sir, I wouldn't mind that at all," I said.

"All right," he said. "I've been trying to get the front of the store and the window trim painted before the weather caves in. If you're interested in doing that, I'll make sure you get a good lunch."

"Yes, sir," I said. "I'd be more than happy to do that."

Mr. Dawson pulled a can of paint and a couple of brushes out from under the counter, and then he retrieved a stepladder from a storage area. "Here you go, then," he said. When you're done, come over to the lunch counter and I'll make sure you have plenty to eat."

"All right, thank you." I went outside and got to work. The smell of paint mingled with the fresh fall air. The morning was warming up and the sky had become a sparkling blue, interrupted haphazardly with luminous white clouds that made the blue all the more stunning. The word *cerulean* came into my thoughts, almost as if someone had spoken it; for a moment I wondered how I had learned that synonym for blue, and then I realized that, like vermilion, it was both a paint color and a spelling word from Mr. Otis's class. It seemed so long ago that I was in school. I hoped Mr. Otis had found another job teaching somewhere. I hoped I'd get to paint pictures again, too, not just storefronts, although it felt very good to hold a paintbrush. Even a big one.

As I painted, a small group of people passed by the store. A few watched me work as they stepped around my ladder. Some lingered to look at the window display, and I heard snatches of conversation. Two women stopped briefly. They were both in their forties, and they both looked tired and a little gritty. One of the women peered into the store window, and the other pulled out a mirror and quickly applied a dab of red lipstick. "That's better," she said, looking at her reflection.

"How's your daughter?" the other woman asked the one with the lipstick.

"She's fine, I guess. I haven't gotten a letter from her lately, though."

"Is she still keeping house for that doctor up in Auburn?"

"I imagine so. I haven't heard different. But she was a little worried in her last letter. She thought she might be pregnant."

"Oooh! Your first grandchild!"

"Yes, that part is exciting. But then she'd have to give up her job, and her husband lost *his* job about a month ago. I don't know if he's found any work since." She cupped her hand against the pane of glass to get a better look inside the store. "I wish I'd get a letter from her!"

I glanced down and saw that she had left a smudge on the window from her hand, and for a moment, her wish to receive a letter was caught in a spot of moisture left on the glass from her breath. But as she stepped back, the wish vaporized.

By the time I was done, it was nearly lunchtime. I found Mr. Dawson and gave the leftover paint back to him. "Go get yourself a good lunch," he said, nodding toward the lunch counter. "Alice will get you whatever you want."

Several people were already eating sandwiches and sipping steaming cups of coffee. I stood by the lunch counter and was greeted by a tall young woman, probably not much older than me. She had strawberry blond hair, and a sprinkling of freckles decorated her nose. "Mr. Dawson said you could have as much to eat as you want," she said. "What'll it be?"

"Um, how about a couple of ham and cheese sandwiches?" I said.

"Okay. With some potato salad and a pickle? We've got cherry pie, too, for dessert."

"Sure! That would be good," I said. "Uh, if you don't mind, I'd like to take my lunch with me...to eat in the park."

She shrugged, "Okay by me." She wrapped up my lunch and placed it carefully into a paper sack. "You want to take something to drink, too? How about a Coke?" She pushed the neck of a green bottle into the opener and after the initial *pfffft*, she retrieved the cap and pushed it lightly back onto the opening so the fizzy brown liquid wouldn't spill as I walked.

"Thanks!" I said.

"Sure thing," she said. As she slid the bottle of Coca-Cola and the package heavy with food toward me over the counter, she winked at me. For a moment I was taken aback, but then I realized she was winking at the young man I appeared to be. I smiled, tipped my cap to her slightly so that I didn't free my hair, and then I winked back.

I polished off every bit of one sandwich and pickle, washing it down with the syrupy soda, but I saved the potato salad and pie and the second sandwich, even though I was still a little hungry. When I got back to the jungle, I picked up a clean tin can and went looking for Owen. He was still sitting down by the river fishing. "How's it going?" I asked.

He pulled up a length of rope he was using for a stringer and showed me two catfish. "I had three, but I cooked one for lunch. Fishing is a little slow this afternoon, but if I get a couple more, we'll have plenty for supper," he said. "How did you make out today?" He looked at my brown bag. "Did you trade your nickel for what's in that bag?"

"Nope. I didn't have to," I said. "I painted the front of Woolworth's in exchange for lunch, and this is a sandwich and a big helping of potato salad I saved for us for dinner. We've got cherry pie, too."

"You found work?" Owen asked, raising his eyebrows.

I sighed. "Not exactly, just an odd job."

"Well, at least you got that."

"Yeah, but I think that was the only odd job in this whole town. I guess it's time for me to think about moving on, too."

"Where you gonna go?"

I shrugged. "I don't know yet." I tied a piece of twine around the can, put the food in it, and lowered it into a jog in the riverbank where the water was quiet. When the can was about three-quarters submerged, I tied it off to a branch, satisfied the food would be cool and protected until suppertime.

Owen and I sat in silence, watching the river flow by. He jerked quickly up on his pole, which he had made from a stout length of sapling, and pulled up a small crappie. "Shoot," he said. "Too small to keep." Carefully, he disengaged the hook from the fish's mouth and tossed it gently back into the river.

While Owen fished, I went back to the camp and settled in to work on another nickel. I worried about being nearly out of money, and I wanted to have a couple of nickels at the ready if I could. The man on this nickel, I decided with my scribe tool in hand, would have a decent derby. I worked for several hours, chiseling away bits of metal and scrutinizing my work in the afternoon sun as it appeared and disappeared behind clouds. The woods around the jungle had become a blaze of color. The maples turned into transparent crimson and gold as the sun backlit them and changed them into jewel tones. The afternoon light cast a warm orange-gold color on my work. Every now and then a leaf drifted down to the ground near me, having lost its ability to hold on.

As late afternoon began its transformation to early evening, the quality of light changed; I stretched and looked up through the canopy of trees, and noticed that huge thunderclouds had formed. The color of the leaves had become soft and muted against the dark gray of the thunderheads. The wind was picking up, and off in the distance, I could hear the low growl of thunder.

Owen came back from the river carrying the can of food and the two catfish he had caught earlier in the day. "Fishing was lousy this afternoon," he said, shaking his head. "I guess these will have to do."

"We'll have enough to eat," I said.

"Yeah, I guess so," Owen said. "I think there's one heck of a storm coming in, though, by the looks of those clouds. I think we'd better find some cover."

"How are we going to do that?" I asked, thinking again of what little money I had left. No way could I afford to pay for a room anywhere, and I was pretty sure Owen couldn't, either.

"Let's pack up our things and head east over to the bridge," Owen said. "We can get out of the weather underneath the bridge supports."

"Good idea," I said, feeling foolish that I hadn't thought of that. I still had a lot of survival tricks to learn.

We hurried along the riverbank, stashed our bindles under the bridge, and then went scrounging for firewood. The thunder was rapidly moving closer and it grew louder and more ominous. Owen dragged some fallen branches over to the bridge. "Grab a couple more if you can," he shouted over a loud roll of thunder. "We'll break it up later." A clap of thunder boomed overhead and shook the ground around us. Big drops of rain pelted us as we scrambled for cover under the bridge, and soon there was such a downpour that as the water ran over the sides of the bridge, it formed a curtain on either side so dense that I couldn't see anything but water.

"Whew! That storm came in fast," Owen yelled over the racket of pounding water and crackling lightning. "We're lucky we got here in time."

I could only nod in agreement. Words would have been blown away by the wind and lost in the storm. The thunder echoed and bounced around under the bridge, hurting my ears. I covered my ears with my hands, trying to block out the loudest booms.

Owen started breaking up branches, piling the bigger pieces off to one side and heaping small twigs in a spot where I could see he intended to build a fire. We had managed to stay dry, even with the rain cascading off the bridge, but the air was very damp, making it hard to get a fire going. I worked on coaxing a small fire out of the pile of kindling and tended to it while Owen, still staying under the protection of the bridge, took the fish closer to the river to clean them.

I finally got a fire stable enough to cook the catfish, but the wind was gusting wildly, swooping under the bridge and scattering sparks and cinders in every direction. Our fish was coated with ashes. We ate quickly. We had no choice but to douse the fire and wait out the storm.

The rain let up a bit, but spectacular lightning drew jagged lines across the evening sky, the way a crack in a pane of glass travels through a window as it breaks. Sometimes the entire sky lit up and the trees near the bridge were frozen in an eerie brightness for an instant and then disappeared into darkness. The sounds of thunder became more distant and I hoped the storm had passed.

"Maybe that's the worst of it," I said to Owen.

He shook his head. "It don't feel right," he said. "The air is still muggy. I bet it ain't done yet."

We sat in silence and in darkness for a short while. It seemed like the wind had calmed down enough that maybe we could make it to the rail yard and look for a nice, safe boxcar. I was just about to suggest it to Owen when off in the distance we heard one long roll of thunder closely followed by another.

"Yep, there it is," he said.

"Shoot," I said.

Owen just laughed. "You'll get used to it," he said.

The trouble was, I didn't want to get used to it. I felt very defenseless sitting under a bridge in the middle of a storm. It felt like I was in danger, like the time I tried to catch out on a moving train. At least that time, I had a way to stay safe—by waiting for another train. This time, I had no choice.

"I'd rather be sitting in a nice big, dry boxcar," I said.

"Well, sure," Owen said. "But there's no time to get to the rail yard. We'll just have to wait it out."

I shrugged, trying to look unconcerned as one storm after another rolled through, driving water and wet leaves under the bridge and fear into my gut. The air got colder as each storm barreled through, and the wind hardly let up before it picked up again with each squall. To escape the blowing rain, we had to squeeze high up under the bridge into the space where the ground forms an angle with the steel girders. It was a small space, but more protected, and although we avoided getting soaked, we were cold and damp. There was no way to build a fire and the wind blew right through our blankets.

With every blinding burst of lightning, I imagined the bridge being struck, or a nearby tree, and the lightning traveling along the wet ground until it found us and left nothing but scorched corpses. I shut my eyes tightly, but that only screened the flashes and turned them pink. Finally, I concentrated on hearing the thunder that followed each flash. If I can hear the thunder, I told myself, lightning hasn't struck me.

I passed the night that way, trying not to drown in my fear. I couldn't sleep, and at first when I looked over at Owen, he was awake, too, and hunkered down into his blanket. Later, I saw that Owen had dozed off. I couldn't imagine how he could sleep, but I concentrated on the thunder for both of us. When morning finally came and brought clear skies with it, I was exhausted, and my muscles were tight and stiff.

We slowly scooted out from under the bridge and stretched our cramped muscles, feeling the moist, chill air that seemed to have had every trace of pollution from the oil refineries washed from it. The air smelled fresh and new, and it seemed like last night's storm brought the morning into sharp focus. Everything I looked at was bright and clear.

"Whew! That was a helluva night," Owen said, massaging his neck.

"Yeah, and a real long one, too," I said. All of my muscles ached. "I've got to try to get a fire going so I can warm up. I'm so cold my muscles don't want to work!"

Owen laughed. "Matt, you got to toughen up. You sound like a girl!"

I looked at him quickly, but he seemed to be joking.

CHAPTER 19

I think I appreciated that morning's fire the most of any since I had been on the road. The heat took my aches away and I started to feel better. Owen made us some coffee, and as I sipped the hot liquid and enjoyed the warmth of the fire, I let go of last night's fear.

"I'm definitely leaving today," Owen said. "No sense in sticking around waiting for more lousy weather."

"Where are you going?" I asked.

Owen shrugged. "South, I guess. Too many people are going west. Maybe Red had the right idea. I might even try to find some work in the stables in Kentucky. I like being around horses, and sleeping in a barn don't sound too bad right now."

"Yeah, nice and dry and warm with lots of hay for a bed," I said. It sounded pretty good to me, too, except I didn't know anything about horses. I wasn't about to follow Owen, either, like some little kid. I wanted to find my own way.

Owen started packing up, and I put out the fire. "Are you going into town first and get something to eat?" I asked.

"Nah, I'm just gonna go," he said.

I watched as he cinched his bindle with a piece of twine. His hands were a little weatherbeaten, but strong, and the fingers of his left hand had several little gouges, half healed now, which I knew were from missed strokes of the nail chisel he used to carve his nickel several days ago. Suddenly I had a hunch about why he wasn't going into town for food. That nickel he had traded the day before must have been his last nickel, period.

"Owen," I said, "I hope we'll meet up again, but in case we don't, I want you to take this." I reached into my pocket and pulled out the money I had left. It came to one dollar and thirty cents, all in change. I counted out sixty-five cents and tried to give it to Owen.

"I can't take that," he said.

"Yes you can!" I said. "You showed me how to make those nickels, and if you hadn't, I'd be out of money by now. The least I can do is share what I've got left with you!"

Owen hesitated, and I was afraid he was still going to refuse me. "You've got to let me give you something," I said. "Besides, this way we've each got a little money for food and a nickel to carve, too."

He looked at me for a minute, not saying anything. I held out the money to him. He didn't budge. Finally, he spoke. "I told you I learned how to carve nickels from an old 'bo. He didn't charge me nothing...How can I take your money?"

"You didn't charge me anything, either," I said. "This isn't a payment for you showing me how to carve. That's worth a lot more than sixty-five cents! I just want you to have this—because you're my friend, okay?"

At last, Owen grinned, and I relaxed. "Okay, then," he said. He took the money and put it in the pocket of his faded brown pants. "Thanks, Matt." He picked up his bindle and slung it over his shoulder, and then set it back down again. "I just thought of something," he said. "You should take one of these." He dug around and pulled out a little snuffbox. He opened it and picked out a length of fishing line and a hook. "Here," he said, "if you have one of these, you have one less chance of going hungry—at least if you don't stray too far from water."

"You sure you can spare this?" I asked.

"Yep, I have extra," he said. He picked up his bindle again. "Do you know where you're going next?"

I shrugged. "I heard a lady in town talking about Auburn. Do you know where that is?"

"I'm pretty sure it's up by one of them Finger Lakes in New York," Owen said. "That where you're going?"

"I might," I said. Who knows—it could be that there's a doctor up there in need of a housekeeper, I thought, remembering the conversation I had overheard. "I'm going into town first, though, to see if I can get something at Antonio's bakery. Change your mind?"

Owen shook his head. "I think I'll just go ahead and catch out," he said. "Might as well get an early start." He patted his pocket and the change jingled softly. "I'll find something to eat as I head south. You take care," he said as he turned and walked toward the rail yard.

"You take care, too!" I called after him. I watched him walk away and felt a hole opening up where his friendship had been.

I pushed on the door of Antonio's, making the bell jingle. I inhaled deeply, savoring the sugary, yeasty smell of fresh-baked breads and pastries. A male voice called out, "I'll be right there!" The voice wasn't the old man's, although it had a trace of an accent, and I waited to see who the voice belonged to.

After a minute, a man came to the counter. He was probably in his early thirties. His dark hair was receding, but he still had a handsome, boyish face, and he was compact and well-built. He wore a dark blue apron that was dotted with flour. A smudge of flour streaked the right side of his face, too, giving him a slightly harried appearance. His dark features reminded me of some of the Italian men who were regulars at the diner when the factories were still flourishing, and I wondered if he was Antonio. Or was it the old man who owned the bakery?

"Sorry to make you wait," he said. "The bread had to come out of the oven."

"It's okay," I said. "You wouldn't want the bread to burn."

"No, I'd never hear the end of it," he said. I smiled, figuring that this was probably the son-in-law the old man had been disgusted with.

"What can I get you?" he asked.

"Do you have any day-old bread?"

"No, I'm sorry. Yesterday's bread is all gone. I have fresh bread, of course, just warm from the oven. And there's *sfogliatelle* if you want something a little sweet."

"What's that?" I asked.

"*SFO–lia-TEL-eh,*" he said slowly and carefully. He pointed in the direction of the cardboard tower of Pisa. On either side of the tower, small doily-lined plates were covered with fat, seashell-shaped pastries sprinkled generously with powdered sugar. "It's puff pastry filled with sweet ricotta cheese and a little citrus," he said. "My father-in-law insists on making them once a week." He smiled. The corners of his mouth crinkled a little, forming a couple of deep dimples that framed white, even teeth. "You'd think he doesn't know there's a Depression right now."

"But some people buy them, don't they?" I asked. I glanced back toward the tower of Pisa. The pastries looked wonderful, but I certainly couldn't afford any.

"They used to," he sighed, "but not so much nowadays; money is too tight. Bread is our biggest seller."

"Why does he keep making them, then, if people aren't buying?"

He smiled and shrugged a little. "They don't go to waste. He eats the *sfogliatelle* for breakfast. He says it reminds him of Italy. It's not so bad if it makes an old man happy. And if he's happy, my Lucy is happy. And if Lucy is happy..." he winked at me, "then I am happy!"

I laughed. "I see," I said, but I was thinking about the old man's complaint that he didn't understand what his daughter saw in his "idiot son-in-law." *I understand what she sees*, I answered the old man in my thoughts.

"So you've never eaten *sfogliatelle*," the man said. "You must try one." He plucked one off the paper doily, set it on a napkin, and held it out to me. He took another for himself.

"Oh!...no, thank you...I can't..." I said, trying to politely refuse something I didn't dare spend money for.

"Please," he said. "On the house. It will make my father-in-law happy to see that some are missing from the plate."

"Well, thank you," I said, feeling that to refuse would be an insult to this man. I bit into the pastry and my mouth filled with the flavors of butter, cheese, and a hint of lemon and cinnamon. "This is so good!" I said. "I can see why your father-in-law likes them so much."

The man smiled again. "I'm glad you are enjoying it, too."

I had planned on buying only day-old bread, but I couldn't leave empty-handed after accepting the pastry. I chose a sturdy, round loaf of bread. *Pane casareccio*, he called it. "It means 'country bread,'" he said, as he wrapped it for me. It cost ten cents and I planned to make it last for as long as I could.

"Please stop in again," the man said as I walked toward the door. "The *sfogliatelle* is fresh every Tuesday."

"I'll keep that in mind. Thanks for the pastry," I said.

"Ciao!" he called after me as I shut the door.

I stopped one more time at the grocery store for a small jar of peanut butter, and then headed back to get my bindle. It was still early, and I wanted to get to the rail yard and catch a freight north as soon as I could. Now that I had decided to go, I was impatient to move on.

I worked my way to the north side of the rail yard, staying out of sight of the bulls. This was a big yard; it was sure to be guarded. Last night's storm had left its mark here, too. Bits of tree litter were scattered along the track bed and a fat limb had broken off a tall maple, creating a hole where sunshine now streamed through. It looked like a fine place to eat a little breakfast and wait for a train. I sat down on the severed branch and let the sun warm my skin as I pulled small chunks of bread away from the loaf and spread them with peanut butter. With coffee, it would have been perfect. I only ate a little, though, and then made myself put it away. This food had to last.

After an hour or so, I heard the chugs. I had chosen a good spot; the chugs were slow, and I knew it would be easy to hop onto a car. I stayed out of sight as the great black machine labored past me, working to build up a head of steam. Partway down the track, a couple of open boxcars swayed and creaked into sight, and after checking to be sure the train was clear of bulls and brakemen, I trotted alongside and pulled myself into one of the cars. It was empty, to my surprise, and I hoped it would stay that way. I was exhausted from last night's storm, and I planned on curling up in a corner and sleeping for a good while. But within a minute, two men pulled themselves up and into my car. We nodded to each other and I sat up straight. Now I'd have to stay awake.

The train picked up speed and one of the men sprawled out on the floor of the boxcar, using his bindle as a pillow. Within a few minutes, he was asleep, his head bobbing slightly in time to the movement of the boxcar.

"Where you headed?" the other man asked me.

"Auburn, New York," I said.

"Got family there?"

"Not exactly. Just moving on."

He nodded. "Going to Warren first, then?"

"If that's where this train is going, then I guess I am."

"Well, let's see," he said. "You'll probably want to go to Salamanca from Warren, and then go a little east to Olean. You can catch a northbound Pennsy out of Olean and head toward Rochester. Find a New York Central line up there and work your way east." He grinned. "Is that what you had in mind?"

"Something like that," I said. Inwardly, I was panicking. When I first got on the train, I had no idea how I was going to get to Auburn. I was just glad to be in the shelter of the boxcar and moving to a new destination, and I was happy enough that I was heading north to the state of New York. But now that this man had described an actual route, getting to Auburn sounded next to impossible.

"Where are you going?" I asked him.

"Maryland," he said.

"Where in Maryland?"

He shrugged. "Don't know. It doesn't much matter. I'll try Baltimore first. If I can't do any good there, I'll probably aim for the Chesapeake Bay. At least I can fish there. Better than going hungry."

I started to calm down. This man's outlook was reassuring in a way. *So what if you can't find Auburn,* I told myself. *What does it matter? You'll end up somewhere.*

"You sure seem to know your way around," I said. "Have you been riding the rails for long?"

"Over a year now," he said. He shook his head. "Can't believe I've been looking for work for a damn year!"

"Have you found any?"

"Just odd jobs here and there," he said. "What about you?"

"Just odd jobs, too," I said. It was half true. I had at least gotten one odd job.

He looked at me for a long moment. "I meant riding. You been away from home for awhile?"

"Not as long as you," I said.

"Didn't think so," he said. He was silent then, and I sat there wondering how he had known I hadn't been on the road long. I didn't ask, though I wanted to.

We rode for a time without talking, and I watched though the door as we passed farms and fields dotted with bales of hay ready to be picked up and stored for the winter. Sometimes the track ran alongside a river and through patches of woods, and then we'd pass through one small town after another— some only as big as a crossroads, some that had a feed store for the farmers and a small freight depot, and some that had a patchwork of streets lined with modest houses crammed together and separated by their tiny yards. Usually, a little way into these towns, but not too close to the tracks, a church steeple or two poked into the sky, breaking up the orderly pattern of rooftops.

I concentrated hard on these scenes as a way to fight off the desire to fall asleep. The rhythmic rocking of the boxcar and the repetitive *ka-chung ka-chung* of the wheels on the rails nearly put me into a stupor. My body craved sleep but I couldn't allow it. Not until I was traveling alone. To distract myself, I took in every possible detail outside the boxcar door: the way the towns were lit by the afternoon sun, the way the shadows fell, creating long lines between the trees, the reflection of a bridge over the river it spanned—as if there were two bridges connecting the river banks, one above and one under the water—and even the jagged edges of a broken windowpane in a freight station as we rumbled slowly past it.

"Next town is Warren."

I jumped as the voice broke my concentration. The last time I had looked, both men were asleep.

"This train'll have to take on water. You better get out and find yourself a train heading east. This one'll be going to Chautauqua."

I nodded. "Thanks." I felt the train slowing down, and soon we came into a freight yard. Metal squealed against metal as the train stopped, and I threw out my bindle and jumped down behind it.

It took some time, but I found the east-west tracks and sat down to wait for an eastbound train. I ate a little more while I waited, trying to quiet my hunger. I really wanted a hot meal—even soup or stew would be wonderful, but that wasn't possible now, so I tried thinking about other things. Several westbounds came through, heading for the yard to drop off freight or take on coal, I figured, and then they would continue west. For a minute I was tempted to change my plans and hop one of them. But then I remembered the crowds of people trying to get out west, and it seemed just plain stupid to do that again.

Finally, I heard an eastbound train approaching. This time, I waited until many cars had passed me, hoping that if other people were catching out they'd choose one of the cars toward the front of the train. I spotted a boxcar toward the end of the train and pulled myself into it. It smelled of grain, and the car was covered with a fine dust, but the car was empty. As I sat against the back wall, the train picked up speed and I knew I had gotten on just in time. Best of all, I'd have the car to myself, at least for a while, because now the train was going too fast for anyone else to jump on. I curled up into a corner, arranged my bindle as a headrest, and gave in to the rhythm of the wheels. After nearly two days without sleep, my body was aching for it. I slept the heavy, deep sleep that comes with exhaustion.

CHAPTER 20

I'm sitting on the steps that lead upstairs from the front hall. Tables laden with food are set up against the wall opposite the stairway. From my perch I can see the platters and casseroles, the stacked dinner plates, the silverware and white napkins. Smells of ham, cabbage, chicken, and warm pastries drift up the stairs and assault my nose. I want some food, but I can't get to it—the room below is too packed with people. They are milling around, talking in low tones at first, but as the room becomes more crowded, voices rise. I'm sad; something bad has happened. I think someone has died, but I'm not sure who it is. These loud voices upset me and I try to tell people to stop, to show some respect, but no one notices me. I hear someone laugh and the sound of it cuts through the wall of noisy chatter. I am outraged that someone is laughing and I stand up to shout, to demand silence, but nothing comes out of my mouth. Someone passes me on the stairs and bumps me, not seeing me, and I start to tumble down the steps, but I reach out and grab at the wall, jerking myself, hard, to a stop. And then I'm sitting in darkness, disoriented, hearing the high-pitched whistle of the train and getting jolted as the boxcar bounces over a bad section of track.

I don't know for sure how long I had been asleep, but through the open boxcar door I saw that the moon was high in the night sky, lighting the fields and casting shadows over scrub bushes and clumps of brush. The car was still rocking violently and I didn't dare stand up to look out the door until we reached a better section of track. I tried to shake off the creepiness of my dream, but it felt like it surrounded me in layers and I had to peel it off, one layer at a time. It took a great effort to get free of it. I knew it was a dream, but it felt so real that I kept wondering if somehow it had really happened.

My stomach was in knots and growling loudly besides. It had been a long while since I had eaten. I pulled out the last of my bread and fished around for the peanut butter. I spread it thickly on the bread and thrust a chunk into my mouth. My mouth was dry—I needed some water, but that would have to wait for the next town. I sat in the dark and kept working on the bread and peanut butter. The ride seemed to be smoothing out and I needed to stretch my legs. I started to stand up, but as I pulled myself to my feet, the boxcar lurched badly, throwing me against the back corner and sending my things flying. My jar of peanut butter flew across the car and rolled crazily around the floor. I couldn't grab it, and I watched it roll to the doorway and drop out of sight.

I felt hot tears pushing their way to the surface, but I bit my lip and sucked in big breaths of air. I refused to cry—refused to feel sorry for myself. I'm no worse off than most people, I thought. I'll find a job in the next town, I told myself, and then I'll have plenty to eat.

I heard the clatter of other cars hitting that bad rail and I suddenly realized that if the track was bad enough, the train could derail. I had seen the result of one derailment when I was about nine years old; it was a sight I'd never forget. Cars had been strewn every which way, two and three deep in some places, laying on their sides along the railroad tracks, their cargo spilled all over the tracks and in the ditches. The railroad had to bring in all kinds of equipment and it took days to clean up the mess. If anyone had been riding in those cars, they wouldn't have survived.

There were pictures on the front page of the newspaper, but everybody in town went to see for themselves, including Uncle George and me. We got right up to the mess and George stood with one foot propped on some twisted rail, talking to a railroad worker.

"The engineer is lucky to be alive," the worker said to Uncle George, "but one of the brakeman wasn't so lucky." He wouldn't say anything more, but I looked in the newspaper. The man's neck had been broken, the paper said. He had been riding in the caboose and it had flown across the tracks, the last car in a terrible game of crack the whip.

I had no idea what to do if the train started to derail. If I stayed in the car, I'd get thrown around and probably be killed, and if I tried to jump out, I'd most likely be crushed. I held my breath and listened as the train bounced over the bad section of track. My muscles were so tense they hurt.

Finally, the last cars passed over the bad section of track and I felt the regular rhythm of the cars settle in. I had had enough, and I gathered my things and curled up again in the back corner, wrapping up in my blanket and going back to sleep.

It was the quiet that woke me. I sat up in an effort to get my bearings. It was daylight and the air smelled like damp earth. Outside, cloud shadows crept across a field, first blocking the sunshine and then letting it through. Something didn't feel right, and it took a few minutes for me to realize that I heard no train noise. The boxcar wasn't moving.

I got up, stumbled over to the door and poked my head out. I could see up and down the empty tracks. I hopped out and then saw that my boxcar was one of five cars that had been left on a siding. I couldn't believe that I had slept through the whole process—the slowing down, the switching, and the uncoupling. I had no idea where I was and how close or far the nearest town was, or even which way to walk to find a town. The only structure nearby was a small shed by the siding. Tracks led to it from a dirt road, and I guessed that this siding was used by farmers. I knew from hanging around the rail yard in New Harmony that the railroad would drop off empty boxcars on sidings for farmers to fill with hay or grain, and they'd be picked up later and shipped to another town where their contents would be sold. Farmers sometimes had their own sidings, and many small businesses did, too, like Miller & Sons, the barrel manufacturers who had a small factory a couple of miles west of town.

Now what, I wondered. I had plenty of choices, but I didn't like any of them. I could move away from the tracks and investigate the dirt road, hoping that some hospitable farm would be within walking distance. But then what? Or I could walk westward along the tracks and hope I'd come into a town. But that would be backtracking, which made little sense. I could sit right where I was and wait for another train, but chances are it would be going too fast for me to get on. Or I could walk eastward along the tracks and hope I'd come into a town, but there was no telling how far I'd have to walk.

Well, I guess moving is better than sitting still, I thought. I gathered up my bedroll and started walking eastward. At least I'd be heading in the right direction.

The area was desolate and I walked a long while on a narrow path beside the tracks, seeing only woods and no signs of humans except for the tracks that humans had once laid.

Twice I heard a train coming toward me from the east and I had to move a safe distance away from the tracks. Turned out I was right about the speed. The train sped past me, going far too fast for anybody to hop on. The second train was a passenger train. It was going slower, but still too fast to catch a ride, even if a person wanted to go west, but it went slow enough that I saw people in the dining cars eating their meals.

"I guess not everybody is suffering from the bad times," I said out loud to no one. That quick flash of diners passing by made me all the more aware of my hunger. Last night's "dinner" of bread and peanut butter was long gone, and I had been walking for the better part of the day with nothing to eat. I had a few pieces of change in my pocket, but even that would do me no good unless I found a town with a store and a sympathetic proprietor.

Finally, as I rounded a bend, I saw a water tower further down the track—not the type of tower that supplies a town, but the kind that provides the water for the locomotives. My spirits lifted and I picked up my pace a little. I knew that once I got to the tower, I could wait until a train stopped to take on water and catch out then.

I didn't feel so alone as I rested for a bit and studied the marks left on the water tower by the hobos who had passed this way before me. Some of the signs had been scratched into the metal years ago, a rusted history left by men who had probably chosen their way of life, unlike recent travelers forced into living life on the road and in the jungles.

A fresh mark on the tower grabbed my attention. It pointed eastward. *Go past the crossroads*, it meant; following it was a large X contained within a circle—*good chance for food*.

"I wish you had said how far it was to the crossroads," I muttered. I tried to decide which was better: staying and waiting for a train to stop for water so I could catch out, or walking, no telling how much farther, to find some food—if I was lucky.

I became more and more aware of my hunger pangs as I stood there trying to decide. "All right, then," I said, "I'm not getting any closer to food just standing here."

CHAPTER 21

I had to walk the tracks, which I don't like to do—it's awkward. The ties aren't spaced right for the human stride. To stay on the ties, you either have to shorten up your steps and walk hobbled, like a girl wearing a tight skirt, or you have to stretch out and lumber along like a gangly boy. The best thing is to walk in the dirt alongside the track bed, but sometimes it's too muddy, like it was that day, and I had no choice but to walk between the rails. I was too tired to keep adjusting my step to stay on the ties. Step on a tie, crunch in the gravel; step crunch, step crunch, crunch step. The unevenness made it sound and feel like I walked with a limp. I kept on, though, walking in the direction indicated by the mark on the water tower, hoping it wouldn't be much farther.

I could see some hay fields and the edge of a small town ahead in the distance. I walked for a while longer and came to a point where a road crossed the track. Off to my left, a short distance from the track, was another road that crossed the first road. Beyond that, a row of modest houses stretched out, neatly lined up and running parallel to the rails, like small squares in a quilt block. Some of the back yards of the houses along these tracks had been fenced years ago, but they had been neglected. The fence boards were the dull gray of weatherbeaten wood, the whitewash long since removed by summer storms. The odor of wet mud rose up from the water stagnating in the ditches along the railroad grade and mixed with the pungent smell of the damp cinders I disturbed as I walked.

Just ahead on the left, partially obscured by wild blackberry canes, I saw the other sign—a mark left by an earlier traveler—an X drawn on a fencepost. I hurried toward the mark, glad the blackberry canes hadn't grown tall and thick enough to conceal it. The bank dropped down sharply from the edge of the railroad bed. I had to side-step down and jump over the ditch, but I couldn't jump quite far enough and my foot caught the muddy edge. I entered the yard by the fencepost, trying to stamp off the mud before it oozed into my shoe.

Near the house, a child's red wagon sat by a sand pile that bore the scars of a recent dig. A solitary child's shovel had been thrust into the sand; only its handle showed—a wide oval at the top, like an open mouth.

By the time I reached the back door of the house, my stomach hurt so much I could hardly stand up. I couldn't say for sure whether it was hunger or dread that caused it. I was desperately hungry. I wanted food, but I didn't want a handout. I remembered many conversations in the jungle when Henry would insist that he was a hobo, not a bum, and that there was a big difference between the two. *Hobos pay their way,* he had said. *I don't panhandle and I work for a meal. Bums don't want to work; they're happy to mooch meals and beg for spare change on street corners.* I had decided back then that if it ever came to that, I would work for my food. Now it had come to that.

I took off my hat and unpinned my hair. I hoped that the occupant of the house would be sympathetic to a girl asking for food. I knocked. After a moment, the door opened. The woman who answered was in her early thirties and obviously pregnant; a hint of darkness under her eyes made her look tired. Even so, she didn't seem unfriendly.

It was one of the hardest things I've ever done, and I'll always remember it—the first time I ever knocked on a stranger's door to ask for food. I forced myself to speak. "Ma'am, I'm wondering if you might have any chores that need doing...in exchange for something to eat?" I said.

The woman stared at me for a moment. "How long since you've eaten?"

"Nearly two days, I think." I stood there shifting my weight from one foot to the other. My legs were getting rubbery.

She hesitated. "I have some chili left from yesterday. You could have that."

"I'd be very grateful," I said. I would have been happy to get anything—even some bread or beans—but chili sounded like fine dining. It also sounded like Ruby's Paradise Diner, and for a moment, the memory of all the smells of the diner overwhelmed me.

"You better come in and sit," the woman said, motioning me toward the kitchen table. She pulled the chili from the Frigidaire and started heating it on the stove. She poured a cup of coffee from her percolator, added milk and sugar, and set it in front of me. "You can start with this," she said.

I curled my hands around the cup, feeling its warmth, and I brought the cup to my lips, sipping slowly at first, wanting to savor the comfort and sweetness of fresh, percolated coffee. But I was so thirsty that I drained the cup in several long gulps.

"My name's Doris," the woman said, her eyes widening slightly when she saw my empty cup. She took it from me and refilled it. As she handed it back to me, a little girl suddenly peered around the doorway; she was probably four years old, maybe five.

"That's my daughter, Lizzie," Doris said. Lizzie smiled coyly, studying me and my clothes, her curiosity winning out over her shyness.

"Why are you dressed like a boy?" Lizzie asked.

"Lizzie! Don't be rude," Doris said."

"It's all right. I don't mind her asking," I said. "Because it's easier, and safer, to travel when I look like a boy," I told Lizzie, knowing as I spoke that this wouldn't satisfy her.

"Why?"

"Lizzie, that's enough! Go and play," Doris said as she slid a steaming bowl of chili in front of me. Next to it, she added a plate of thick-sliced bread.

The aroma of the food filled my nose and I picked up my spoon and forced myself to eat slowly, although I really wanted to shove huge, heaping mounds of chili into my mouth. I'll never forget that meal. I can still remember biting down on those chunks of beef and how that flavor just exploded in my mouth. I tasted onions and spices and felt the texture of the beans on my tongue. The bread was fresh and yeasty and crusty.

"You haven't told me your name," Doris said.

"It's Maddy," I said. I pointed at the bowl. "This is wonderful," I said. "Thank you!"

Doris offered me more chili, which I accepted, and then she cut a piece of apple pie and refilled my coffee again. Finally, I could eat no more. It was the most heavenly feeling to be full. The sharp pains in my stomach had disappeared, and it no longer hurt to move. Besides that, I was clear headed again; it felt like my brain had come out of a fog.

"I can't thank you enough," I said. "I've never been so hungry as I was when I knocked on your door. And now please tell me what chores I can do for you so I can repay you for this meal."

She sat down across the table from me and sipped a cup of coffee she had just poured for herself. She was wearing a man's shirt, her husband's, probably, and the fabric strained across her belly, the buttonholes stretching a little, pulling against the buttons. "I don't have any chores for you," Doris said. "I had extra food and you were welcome to it. Times are hard."

Feelings of panic surfaced. I had just experienced the humiliation of begging for food, and now I was going to suffer being a bum unless I could find a way to repay her. I explained—insisted—that I didn't want a handout. She shook her head. "Just tell me a little about where you've been," she said. "I've never been anywhere outside of the state of New York."

"New York?" I said. "That's where we are right now?"

"Well, yes," Doris said. Her brow furrowed a little. "You didn't know?"

"No, ma'am. I got off the train near the water tower. I had no way of knowing where I was."

"Well, you're just outside of Steamburg," she said.

I laughed a little. "Well, that's good that I know the name of the town, but I still don't know where I am. I'm sorry to say I've never heard of Steamburg."

Doris smiled. "Steamburg is about midway between Jamestown and Olean, and a little south of Salamanca. Have you heard of any of those towns?"

"Well, yes, as a matter of fact," I said. "Someone I was traveling with the other day told me about Salamanca and Olean." I was excited to discover that I still seemed to be traveling in the right direction to get to Auburn, at least according to that hobo who was headed for Maryland. "How far to Olean?"

"Probably twenty miles or so," Doris said. "Is that where you're going? To Olean?"

"It's my next stop, I guess. But I want to get to Auburn. How far is that?"

"I'm not exactly sure," Doris said. "More than a hundred miles. Maybe a hundred and fifty. I've never been there," she said. "I've heard it's nice, though. There's a big amusement park there, and they even have a dance hall. Maybe someday I'll go."

"I hope you do," I said.

"I'd like to," she said. "I'd like to go a lot of places. I probably won't, though," she said, patting her belly. "But I can dream. So tell me about where you've been...what you've seen."

Lizzie poked her head around the corner again. She was carrying a rag doll that looked like it had traveled many miles. It brought to mind the Raggedy Ann stories I read when I was younger, which gave me an idea. "Okay, I'll tell you about Cleveland and Lake Erie if you want, but I'd also like a piece of paper and a pencil," I said. Doris looked a little puzzled, but she sent Lizzie for it. Lizzie came back with a pad of paper, a couple of pencils, and an orange crayon.

"Lizzie, stand next to your mother and I'll draw you a picture," I said. Lizzie grinned and went to stand by her mother's chair, clasping her doll to her chest, her eyes following my hand as I picked up a pencil.

"Well, first of all, Lake Erie is enormous," I said. "I think it must look a lot like the ocean. But it seems kind of...moody. One day it's calm and the next day it's riled, full of dark, frothy waves." I drew as I talked, sketching in Lizzie's heart-shaped face, dark eyes, and hair that had just enough curl to make it charmingly unruly. "You can stand on the shore and see nothing but beach stretching out on either side of you," I said. I drew in an outline of the rag doll and then sketched in Lizzie's arm hugging the doll to her chest, choke-hold style. "And in front of you, there's nothing but water for as far as your eyes can see. Behind you is the city of Cleveland. I went up in the tower of the train terminal right in the heart of the city. There's a platform on the forty-second floor where you can watch passenger trains coming in and out and the streetcars on the main street below. You can see where the steel mills were along the river, because of the smoke and soot. But the lake! Even from up in the tower, the lake spread out for what seemed like forever."

Lizzie was too short to see what I was drawing, but she watched intently. When I picked up the orange crayon, she started jiggling impatiently, trying to see what the color was for. I added color to the doll's hair and dress and then turned the paper so Doris and Lizzie could see the portrait.

Lizzie grinned and ducked under the table. Doris smiled. "You really caught my daughter," she said. "You have a talent. Where did you learn to draw?"

"A teacher at school helped me," I told her, "before the school shut down."

"You should keep doing it," she said. "It's a gift."

I shrugged. "Well, maybe some gifts are just meant to be used on special occasions." I thought of my mother's good silverware, a wedding gift from my grandmother, packed away in a cupboard. It had been years since my mother had used it. There weren't many family celebrations that I could remember, and very few times that we even sat down as a family to have a real Sunday dinner. I handed Doris the pad of paper, Lizzie's face smiling up from it. "I'm glad you like the drawing. It's a thank you for giving me a meal." I stood up, ready to go.

"Wait," Doris said. She went to her cupboards, pulled out some items, dropped them into a sack and held it out to me. "Here, take this."

"I can't repay you for this food," I said.

"Yes, you can. Maybe you could come back again—after my baby is born—and do a drawing of him...or her. I'd really like to have a drawing of each of my children."

"I never know from one day to the next where I'll be," I said.

"I know that, but even if it takes awhile before you can come back, that's okay. And if you never come back, I'll understand, but if it's possible..." Her voice trailed off, but she looked at me directly.

"All right, I'll come back sometime, if I can. If you'll give me a scrap of paper, I'll draw myself a little map so I won't forget how to find your house."

She carefully removed the sketch of Lizzie and then handed me the pad. "Your gift for drawing is meant to be used. You keep this pad of paper," she said, "and these pencils, too. Maybe they'll come in handy."

"You never know," I said, smiling. "Thank you again." I made my way through her back yard, returning to the railroad tracks, but I stopped at the fence post. In the sketchbook, I drew a map of her house relative to the water tower and the crossroads. Then I turned my attention to the fence post and added another mark above the X—a line drawing of a cat. Kind lady, it meant.

CHAPTER 22

Drawing suspends time and place for me. When I'm putting pencil to paper, that's all that exists for the moment. Everything else fades into hazy, gray patterns, and I leave reality for a little while. I see whatever I'm drawing in sharp focus, like I'm looking through a lens, and I hear the scratching of lead on paper. Line by line, the marks on the page become a scene, a person, even a memory. When I'm finished with a drawing and set my pencil down, I feel like some kind of creature suddenly awakened in the bright light of day, blinking, trying to get my bearings.

After I left Doris's house, I drew every chance I got. Inside the next boxcar I rode in, I sketched the view from where I sat—a view that included my legs crossed at the ankles, my feet wearing muddy shoes framed by the open boxcar door, and beyond the door, a blur of vegetation.

As I changed trains and made my way east, I made quick sketches—a small town that wasn't much more than a whistle-stop, a view I had of a distant railroad bridge spanning a wide river, and even other hobos who pulled themselves into my boxcar. I drew them cautiously at first, but to my surprise, no one seemed to mind—except once.

Just past the marker for Silver Springs, a hobo dressed in baggy denim overalls swung into my boxcar. He sat opposite me at the far end of the boxcar and pulled his brown tweed cap down low over his forehead. He didn't make eye contact; he crossed his arms, slouched against the wall, and stared down at his shoes. The sole of his right shoe was just about worn through, I noticed. After a few minutes, he seemed to be going to sleep, so I turned to a fresh page in my pad and started sketching him.

I drew quickly, outlining his body the way it leaned against the boxcar wall. His left leg was bent and his left arm was slightly askew, resting on the edge of his bedroll, which he had tucked behind his back for padding against the wall. I was concentrating on getting the angle of his head, which was turned toward me but had dropped forward on his chest, when he looked up and saw me studying him, pencil in hand.

"What the hell do you think you're doing?" he snarled, eyes narrowed, glaring at me.

"I'm just doing a little sketching," I said. "I didn't think you'd mind."

"Well you thought wrong. I *do* mind!"

"I'm sorry." I was embarrassed and a little scared. He was hopping mad, and I couldn't imagine why he'd be so angry. I wondered if he was running from the law. "I guess I should have asked."

"Damn right you should have asked!" he said, scrambling to his feet. "And I would have told you to keep your eyes to yourself!" He came toward me and I jumped up quickly. "Let me see what you've got."

I felt I had no choice but to hand over my sketchpad, so I held it out to him, trying to keep him at a distance. My hand was shaking and my heart was racing. I hoped he wasn't going to hit me. In my mind, I was frantically trying to decide if it would make matters better or worse to reveal that I was a girl. "I didn't draw your face yet, if it makes any difference," I said as he grabbed the pad from my outstretched hand."

"Damn good thing you didn't," he growled. He looked at the drawing and then settled down a little. "Or I would have thrown this book out of the train, and you after it."

Something about the tone of his voice struck me as more blustery than threatening, and I guessed that he probably wasn't going to hit me or throw anything, including me, off the train. We stood opposite each other as we swayed in time to the motion of the car, and I got a better look at him. His round face was about level with mine, so we were about the same height. He didn't weigh much more than me, either. I figured maybe I could hold my own if I had to, if I had judged wrong and he really did take a swing at me.

We stared each other down; neither of us wanted to be the first to look away. His dark eyes were framed by dark eyebrows knit tightly together in a scowl. Then I saw it—a slender lock of dark hair dropping down from behind his ear and looping back up again under his cap. I stepped back and took a deep breath—and a big chance. "I think you and I have more in common than just being in the same boxcar," I said.

"What are you talking about," he said, still glaring at me.

I reached up and took off my own cap, exposing my pinned up hair.

"I don't believe it!" my adversary said, staring at my head. "You're a girl!"

The train jerked around a curve in the tracks, throwing us both off balance. But we both stayed standing, quickly putting an arm against the boxcar wall to steady ourselves, each making a mirror image of the other.

"My name's Maddy," I said, as we stood face to face. I watched as the scowl etched into her forehead softened a little.

"Mine's Rita," she answered.

The train jerked again and we both sat down, relieved to call off the showdown.

"How did you know?" she asked.

"A piece of your hair came untucked," I said.

"Darn." She patted her head below the cap and found the wayward strand. "It must have come loose when I started to doze off."

"You've got to pin it up better. Either wet it and twist it tight before you pin it, or braid it if it's long enough."

She nodded and was quiet for a few minutes. "That's not a bad drawing," she said, finally.

"Thanks. Why did you get so mad?" I asked.

"Hopping freights scares me," she said. "Especially because I'm by myself. I found out that if I'm disagreeable enough, people will leave me alone and there's less of a chance someone'll find out I'm a girl. When I looked up and saw you staring at me and *drawing* me, I got really scared."

"If it makes you feel any better, the way you got so mad scared the heck out of *me*," I said.

Rita grinned. "No kidding? Did you think I was going to throw you off the train?"

"I thought you might punch me," I said. "But when you threatened to throw me off, I didn't think you'd make good on it."

"Oh," she said, clearly disappointed.

"Sorry," I said, and then I smiled at the ridiculousness of it all. There I sat, being sympathetic to a fellow hobo for not being threatening enough—to me!

"By the way, I wasn't staring," I said.

"Sure you were," Rita said.

"Well, kind of, I guess," I admitted. "But not how you think. I was looking at shapes and shadows."

She looked doubtful, but then shrugged.

"So where are you from?" she asked.

"Southern Ohio. What about you?"

"Detroit," she said. "How come you're riding the rails?"

"Let's just say it's because of family problems and leave it at that." I wasn't about to tell some stranger my life history. "What about you?" I asked, not expecting a real answer.

"I guess I could say 'family problems' too," Rita said, giving me a quick look, "but I think maybe my family problems are a different kind." She drew her legs up and hugged them to her chest. "My father and my brother worked for Ford Motor. Well, my brother still does, but my pop lost his job about a month ago. Henry Ford is an s.o.b., don't let anyone tell you different. Some people think he's the greatest man since Jesus Christ, but the people who think that don't live in Detroit, and they sure as heck don't work for Ford Motor."

I opened my mouth to speak, but Rita only paused long enough to take a breath. Her voice rose above the clatter of the train and she clenched and unclenched her hands as she spoke.

"Henry Ford is supposed to be some big hero for inventing the production line so he can make cars cheap enough so more people can buy them. But he sucks the life out of the workers and then spits out what's left. He keeps speeding up the production line until the men are falling down from exhaustion at the end of their shift. And do you know what happens if the men get behind?"

I had a feeling I did know, but Rita didn't wait for an answer. "They get fired and Ford hires younger men to take their place! Keep up or you're gone. That's what happened to my pop. He hustled for Ford for fourteen years until one more speedup on the assembly line broke him." She took a deep breath. "I don't remember ever seeing my pop when he wasn't dog tired. And for all that work, my pop never made much money. We had food on the table and a roof over our heads, but nothing extra. Now my brother will be the next one in the family to get eaten up by Ford."

I didn't know what to say. How could having a job be lucky and unlucky at the same time?

"The day my pop got fired, he came home mad as a hornet. 'A union is what's needed,' my pop said. 'A union would put an end to Ford's under-handed ways,' he said." Rita's voice got softer. "Yeah, he was really mad. But later, I saw him cry. Did you ever see your pop cry?"

Not when he was sober, I thought. I ignored her question. "Did your pop find another job?" I asked.

Rita looked at me like I was an idiot. "How could he? There's no jobs in Detroit—unless you work for Ford!"

"Do you think the workers will get a union?"

"If they do, it'll be over Henry Ford's cold, dead body," Rita said. "Any of the workers who even whisper the word 'union' get fired. Matter of fact, any worker who's friends with someone who talks about unions could get fired. Ford's got what he calls a Service Department, but it's really a bunch of company spies. There's spies on the assembly line and even in the bath-room! My pop told us once about those goons actually grabbing a worker and throwing him out of the building. They said he was talking about unions while he was washing up."

A long whistle and several short blasts punctuated Rita's story. The train was approaching a crossroad.

"I hope your brother will be okay," I said.

"Me, too," Rita said. "I hate knowing what it's like for him to work that line every day, but if he loses his job, my family will be out on the street."

"Seems like you're already out on the street," I said.

"Yeah, well I'm trying to help out," she said.

"By leaving?"

"Well, sure—I had to leave! I'm not going to find any work in Detroit."

"Don't get your back up. I didn't mean it that way," I said. "I was just thinking about a hobo I met a while back. He was sixteen, and his father had sent him away so that there'd be one less mouth to feed."

"Oh, that's sad," Rita said. "That poor boy...but it's not like that for me. I have a cousin up north in New York, in Pulaski. She said there's a hotel next door to this lighthouse on the Salmon River, and it's pretty busy. I'm hoping I can find a job there. My cousin said I could stay with her for a little while. If I can find a job, I can pay for room and board and still send some money home."

I nodded. "Where's Pulaski?"

"Well, I take this freight to Syracuse, and then I have to find a north-bound train. It should take me right into Pulaski. Then I just have to find the Salmon River and follow it till I find the Lighthouse Hotel." Rita said. "What about you? Where are you going?"

"Auburn," I said.

"Why?" she asked.

"Same as you. I'm hoping to find a job."

"Do you have people there?"

"No."

"Then why Auburn?"

I shrugged. "Because if you're on a trip, you have to have a destination."

CHAPTER 23

Some friendships grow slowly over time and take a lot of nurturing. But sometimes a friendship will simply burst into bloom, like flowers in the desert after a rare shower; the seeds were there all along, just waiting for an opportunity. That's how it was with Rita and me.

We rode in silence for awhile, but now it was comfortable. The earlier tension between us was spent and I was glad to have a female traveling companion, at least for a short time. Through the boxcar door, I watched as long afternoon shadows stretched across fields and woods and the color of the light changed from yellow to orange-gold.

"You hungry?" Rita asked.

"A little," I said, trying to make myself believe it. The meal I had eaten at Doris's house yesterday had stayed with me a long time, but I hadn't eaten since then. Ever since the late afternoon light started fading, my stomach had been pleading for supper. But I only had the food Doris had given me, and no money to speak of, except for an unfinished nickel I was carving. My plan was to wait until the end of the day to eat. That way, I might be able to sleep through the night without being awakened by hunger pangs.

"Well I'm starving!" she said. "And I have to pee, besides. What do you say the next time this train slows down, we jump out and camp somewhere for the night?"

"All right," I said. "But I can't do much about supper." I rooted around in my things and held up a can of beans that Doris had given me.

"That's a start," Rita said. "Let's hope for a town soon. I've got a little bit of money, so I can buy something to add to dinner."

Before long, the train slowed to a crawl; we threw our bindles out and jumped. Rita ducked into a patch of woods and I waited near the tracks. The train shuddered to a stop. When Rita returned, we picked up our bedrolls just as three young men—boys, really—ran past us, toward the boxcar we just vacated. We watched as the first boy swung himself in and then extended a hand to the second and third boy. All three disappeared into the boxcar. A moment later, the couplings on the cars snapped to work and the train slowly crept along again.

Rita turned to me. "Well, thank goodness we didn't have to share that car with them!"

"Yeah," I said, thinking about one of my earlier experiences. "Probably wouldn't be long at all before one of them would be peeing out the door."

Rita whooped and laughed out loud. "So that's happened to you, too!" she said. "I couldn't believe it the first time some man did that!"

"Me, neither! What did you do?" I asked.

"Well, we were both standing by the boxcar door watching the scenery, and this man was talking to me, telling me about getting caught by the railroad bulls and going to jail," Rita said. "Next thing I knew, he was watering the bushes as we were passing by." Rita started laughing again and she got me to laughing, too. "So what did you *do?*" I asked again.

"At first, I kept eye contact with him, because I didn't want to look anywhere else," she said. "But then he kept watering and watering and *watering* those bushes, and you can only keep eye contact so long when someone's peeing. Where are you supposed to look, anyway? And I thought I might burst from trying to keep a straight face."

Picturing Rita wide-eyed and attempting to be nonchalant while she stood next to some guy answering nature's call made me laugh so hard I had trouble catching my breath. But Rita kept on, "Finally, I glanced up at the sky and then pointed to a hayfield a little ways away and said, 'Do you think it might rain? That hay looks awfully parched!'"

"You didn't!" I shrieked between peals of laughter.

"Well, it's hard to think about anything else when you're hearing water running!" she said, grinning.

"What did that man say?"

"He didn't say a word," Rita chuckled. "He just gave me a funny look, zipped up, and went inside the boxcar to stretch out. I stayed by the door, in case I needed to get off quick," she said. "So now if I find myself sharing a boxcar with another traveler, I always pretend to sleep. It's a lot simpler."

We started walking along the tracks toward town, our shoes kicking up little puffs of dust in the dirt alongside the tracks. "Looks like it's a little parched here," I said, grinning.

Rita laughed. "Nothing I can do about that! Anyway," she said, "it's not like I've never seen a man pee. I have a brother, after all. But when it happened on the train, I wasn't expecting it!"

"I have a brother, too," I said, and I was surprised at how I barely finished the sentence before my throat tightened so much I could hardly speak.

Rita glanced over at me. "Is he younger or older?"

I cleared my throat. "He's younger. He's twelve."

"What's his name?"

"Eddie." My eyes were swimming a little, and I blinked several times to clear them. "What about your brother?"

"His name is Daniel. He's older—he's twenty," Rita said. "Do you miss Eddie?" she asked.

"Nah," I lied.

"Yeah, me too," Rita said.

The town closest to the crossroads where the train had stopped was called Canandaigua, and it was near a lake with the same name. Rita and I walked into town and found a bakery on South Main that sold small loaves of rye bread. Rita bought a couple and we hurried to set up camp close to the lake before it got dark. We had nothing to cook and no cans to serve as pots or pans even if we had had any food that needed cooking, but we built a fire for warmth against the chilly fall evening.

I opened the can of beans and Rita split the loaf of bread lengthwise. I poured the beans onto two halves of bread, put the loaf back together, cut the loaf in half, and then we sat back to eat bean sandwiches. I ate slowly, concentrating on each bite, trying to stretch out my suppertime. Rita finished first.

"Here, hand me that empty can," she said. "I'll go get some water from the lake. We can boil some water and have a little coffee." She disappeared before I could ask any questions. When she returned, she dug around in her bedroll and held up a little package. "Chicory root," she said, adding some to the water and putting the can near the hot coals. "I found some by the roadside a couple of days ago and roasted it in the coals of a campfire. It's pretty good."

She let the chicory steep and as the sun went down, we drew close to the fire and passed the hot, coffeelike drink between us, each taking warming sips as we talked a little about our travels.

The next morning was sunny and clear. Rita woke up first, built a small fire, and started some of her chicory coffee. "I'm going back to that bakery," she said, pulling on her shoes. "I've got to get something to eat. I feel like something's gnawed a hole right through my stomach!"

I knew exactly what she meant. Last night's bean sandwich had quieted the hunger pangs enough that I had been able to sleep through the night, but this morning, my stomach was loudly demanding food. A cup of hot chicory coffee might trick it into quieting down, but only for a short while.

"I've got one can of soup left, but that's all I have to offer," I said.

"Well fine. Then we've got something for supper," Rita said. "I'm going to get us some breakfast!"

The day was shaping up to be warm and breezy. While I waited for Rita to come back, I decided to take advantage of the weather and bathe in the cool waters of the lake. I scrubbed my body and washed my hair and felt energized as the sun warmed my skin and dried my hair. Naked and clean, I ran the short distance back to our camp, grabbed my bindle and took it to the lake, where I washed everything I could, starting with my blanket and my underwear. I was standing in chest-deep water soaping up my socks when Rita returned.

"Hey," she called, trying to wave, although both of her arms were occupied. She held a large tin can and a small paper sack in one arm and something blue in the other. "Come on out and have some breakfast!"

I climbed out of the water, still naked, and Rita threw me the blue thing, which turned out to be a man's shirt.

"What in the world!" I said, as I put the shirt on. "Where did this come from?"

"See, you were doing exactly what I was thinking. It's such a great day today that I wanted to wash everything, except that would leave me with nothing to wear. But on my way back from the bakery, I noticed that someone had forgotten to bring their clothes in from the line yesterday," Rita said, grinning. She held up another shirt, a green plaid, "so when I saw these, I thought we could borrow them for awhile."

"You *stole* some man's shirts?" I said.

"I didn't say 'stole,'" Rita said indignantly. "I said 'borrow.' We can return them when we're finished with them."

"I can't believe you took some man's clothes!" I said. "He's no small man, either. Look at this!" His shirt hung nearly to my knees and was wide enough around that I could have belted it like a dress. The cuffs of the sleeves nearly touched my fingertips. "You better hope he doesn't come looking for his shirts."

Rita rolled her eyes. "You worry too much," she said. "Besides, he probably doesn't even know they're gone."

"Maybe not, but I bet his wife does," I said, as I tossed some sticks on the fire to keep it going.

Rita ignored me. "Look, I found this can behind the bakery," she said. "I think it had preserves in it. Anyway, I'll go wash it out and we can use it for cooking."

Rita made more coffee. We set the can of steaming coffee and the loaf of bread on a flat rock and sat side by side, sharing breakfast in the truest sense as we took turns eating and drinking. Rita had chosen cinnamon-raisin bread, which filled my senses with the scent, flavor, and texture of pungent cinnamon and plump raisins. We could easily have eaten the entire loaf, hungry as we were, but we forced ourselves to save some for later.

Then Rita got busy washing everything she owned, and I washed the set of clothes I had planned to wear while my other set was drying. When we were finished, socks, underwear, shirts, pants, and blankets hung everywhere from low tree branches. The camp was festooned with cloth of various shapes and colors, and everything fluttered in the day's warm breezes. Our campsite looked almost festive, and Rita and I, dressed in oversized men's shirts, looked like oddball hosts of a costume party.

While our clothes were drying, I got out my jig and tools and set up the buffalo nickel I had started on back in Oil City. Rita came over. "What are you doing?" she asked, peering over my shoulder.

"I'm turning a nickel into a meal," I said.

"Looks to me like you're wasting it," she said. "Nobody's going to take that nickel if they can't tell it's a nickel!"

"That's what I thought," I said, "until I watched a hobo trade one of these for a nice chunk of beef."

"What? Are you pulling my leg?"

"Nope," I said. "And I traded the last one I made for a jar of peanut butter and some coffee."

"You're kidding!" Rita said. "What exactly are you doing to that coin?" She leaned in to get a better look.

"I'm giving the Indian a different face," I answered, "Which I can't do with you blocking my view."

"Sorry," she said, backing away a little. "Well if you hurry, maybe we could have some beef stew tonight, right?"

"I'll never have this done in time to buy food for supper," I said. "It takes a long time. I've got several days into it already. If I'm lucky and everything goes well, I might finish it tomorrow."

"Darn," Rita said. "You got me thinking about beef stew."

"I guess you'd better think about something else," I said, smiling. "Better yet, why don't you go fishing and see if you can catch us something for supper?"

"Very funny. What am I supposed to catch fish with – my bare hands?" Rita said.

"I've got a hook and line," I said. "All you have to do is tie it to a nice green stick."

"If you've got a hook and line, I can catch fish," Rita said. "I used to go fishing with my brother a lot in Detroit. Before he started working at Ford, though. Once he started working there, all he wanted to do on his off time was sleep!"

"Yeah," I said. "I used to fish with my brother, too, until my cousin came to town."

Rita looked at me with raised eyebrows, waiting for me to say more, but I just stood up and got her my hook and line. "Happy fishing," I said.

Rita reached out to take the line. Her dark eyes were drilling into me, like if she looked deep enough, she might see inside me. *Burnt umber*, I thought. Rita's eyes reminded me of that rich brown color Mr. Otis had squeezed out of a paint tube onto a palette. I ignored Rita's inquiring eyes and sat back down to work on my nickel.

Rita looked like she might say something, but then changed her mind and pointed south along the lake to a rocky area on the shoreline. "I bet there's some smallmouth bass hiding out in those rocks," she said. "Keep that fire going. I'll be back with some fish!"

I focused my attention on my coin, using the sharpened nail chisel to carve moustache hair above the man's lip. The derby on this nickel looked much better than the first one I had carved; the way the derby sat on his head, I imagined this man to be a banker, so I made his moustache very neat. "Well, I hope your bank didn't go belly up," I said. "Maybe you were one of the lucky ones." I wondered if the people who had lost all their savings when the banks failed would ever get their money back. I still couldn't figure out what happened to all of it.

As I scraped away on the coin, I thought about my mother. I was glad she had gotten her money in time. I felt a tiny twinge of guilt about taking some of it, although right now I wished that I had taken a little more while I was at it. I tried to picture my mother's reaction when she found my note. Surely she would have needed Kotex by now. In my mind, I could see her reading my note, but I couldn't decide how her mouth looked. If she was angry, the corners of her mouth would turn down a little and form a hard edge. If she was upset, her lower lip would appear and disappear as she bit it and released it.

My thoughts were interrupted by the sound of footsteps, and I turned to see Rita walking toward me, following the water's edge. The late afternoon sun flashed off two glistening, coppery fish that she carried, one in each hand, and she wore a grin that pretty much connected one ear to the other.

"Just look at these!" she exclaimed, barely pausing to breathe. "I bet they weigh three pounds apiece! I knew I could catch some smallmouth. Did you keep the fire going? Let's cook these beauties and eat them!" Suddenly, Rita's grin disappeared, replaced by a look of distress. "But how are we going to cook these? We don't have any pans!"

Now I grinned. "I know how. At home, I watched fishermen do it when they got hungry but the fishing was too good to leave." I stood up. "Come on," I said, walking toward some young maple trees. "First we need to get a couple of long green sticks from these trees." We snapped off two slender but sturdy branches and took them back to the fire. I pushed a pile of glowing coals off to the side of the fire, making a thick, hot bed. "Add some more firewood to the main fire," I said to Rita. "We're going to have to keep adding coals to this." I gutted the fish and then took the two sticks and impaled the head of each fish on a stick, threading the stick through the gill area into the mouth. I jammed the free end of the stick into the ground at a low angle, suspending each fish over the hot coals.

"Wow," Rita said. "I'm impressed!"

"Thanks," I said. I was feeling a little pleased with myself, too. "But I have to admit that I don't know how long it'll take to cook these. I've seen fishermen do this, but I've never actually done it myself."

Rita shrugged. "I guess it will take as long as it takes," she said. "We ought to be able to tell when the fish are done, don't you think?"

"I guess so," I said. Already I could imagine the taste of freshly grilled fish.

Rita pushed hot coals from the main fire over to our cooking embers to keep the heat steady, and I kept working on my nickel. The smell of fish cooking drifted up to my nostrils and made my stomach growl. When the fish were done, the skin and spine peeled easily away from the flesh, and we feasted on tender, flaky chunks of bass.

"This sure beats soup!" Rita said between mouthfuls.

Before the sun set, we pulled our laundered clothes from the trees. The air was getting cool but our clothes smelled like sunshine and the afternoon breeze. I folded my pants and shirts, accounted for my underwear and socks, stacked everything neatly, and then I wrapped up, Indian style, in my blanket. "I'm not wearing any of my clean clothes until tomorrow," I said. I noticed that I smelled a little like fish, and so did the man's shirt I was wearing. "I want one more bath in the lake first."

"Good idea," Rita said. "Let's hope it doesn't get real cold tonight." She pulled her blanket around herself and settled in close to the fire. Although the evening was getting cooler, it was still warm enough to inspire the frogs and crickets, which were plentiful around the lake, and as night fell, we had to talk a little louder to hear each other over the racket.

"Tomorrow I've got to be on my way to Pulaski," Rita said. "I imagine my cousin will be looking for me soon."

I sighed. "Yeah, I've got to keep moving, too." *But I don't have anyone looking for me like you do*, I thought. I felt a little sad about that, but I was more sad to be saying goodbye to Rita. I'd only met her two days ago, but I felt like I'd known her a lot longer. "I'm glad I met you," I blurted out, feeling shy. Then I grinned. "Even if you did threaten to throw me off the train."

Rita chuckled. "Yeah, but you weren't worried. So I guess I'd better work on my 'tough act,' huh?" She poked at the fire and then spoke quietly. "I never expected to make any friends while I was hopping freights. Maybe I could send you a letter once I get to my cousin's. I'll let you know what the Lighthouse Hotel is like. If Auburn doesn't work out, maybe you could come to Pulaski."

"Okay," I said. "I'll check at the post office every now and then. And I'll write back and let you know what Auburn is like. If you don't like Pulaski, you could come back this way to Auburn."

"That's good," Rita said. "It's always good to have another plan."

CHAPTER 24

Little tendrils of mist floated gently over the surface of the lake. Here and there the long rays of the early morning sun grabbed the slender wisps and lit them—pale cadmium-yellow shapes drifted over the blue-gray water. The air was crisp and fresh, but Rita and I threw off our blankets and ran headlong into the lake. Compared to the air, the lake felt warm, and we stayed up to our necks in water for comfort. But we didn't stay long, and Rita and I scrambled to the shore, making a beeline for the fire.

As we warmed ourselves and got dressed in our own sets of men's clothes, we drank chicory coffee and finished yesterday's cinnamon bread; then we braided or twisted our wet hair and pinned it up, giggling a bit and talking about things in general, like music and the movies. Turns out we both liked Gary Cooper, Greta Garbo, and Our Gang. Rita said she even had a picture of Our Gang on a movie card she had gotten at the Oliver Theatre in Detroit. "Pete's got a hold of the seat of Stymie's pants and Wheezer is standing by laughing," Rita said.

"I always wanted a dog like Pete," I said. "But we weren't allowed to have a dog—not even a small one."

"Well, maybe you can get a dog when you get settled."

"Maybe," I said, although we both knew it wasn't likely.

We packed up and then put out the fire. "We should each take one of these cans, in case we need to cook something," I said.

"Just give me the small one," Rita said. "You might need the larger one to make soup or stew or something. I'm planning to make it to Pulaski before I have to cook."

I pointed to the men's shirts that Rita had taken. "I hope you remember where these came from. We should return them before we catch out."

Rita rolled her eyes. "You sure you don't need an extra shirt?"

"Not that bad," I said.

"All right, we'll take them back," she sighed.

We walked toward the tracks and Rita pointed to a small frame house. Behind the house was a cinder-block garage that had a clothesline strung between it and a metal post a short distance away. The clothesline was empty. "That's the place," Rita said. "Looks like they brought in the other clothes."

"Either that," I said. "Or the poor guy doesn't have anything left to wear."

"Well I noticed I wasn't the only one to put the man's shirts to good use!" Rita said.

We tied the shirts on the line, pulling up the sleeves and knotting them over the top of the line. We walked away, leaving two empty shirts hanging there, looking like they were holding on for dear life.

Just outside of Auburn, the freight train we were riding pulled onto a siding to let a passenger train go by. "I better get off here," I said. "No telling if this train will slow down again once we get into Auburn." I stood up and Rita stood up with me.

"If you want, I can give you my cousin's address," she said. "That way, if Auburn doesn't work out, you can get in touch with me. Maybe there'll be something in Pulaski."

"Okay." I dug out my sketchpad and a pencil. "Write it in here so I'll be sure to keep it." The last car of the passenger train passed, taking the clatter of its wheels on down the track. As I tucked the sketchpad back into my bindle, the freight engaged and lurched. We both grabbed onto the walls of the boxcar. "This is how we started, isn't it?"

Rita laughed, but then she stepped forward and quickly hugged me. "Be careful out there," she said.

"You, too!" I said, as I jumped down to the cinders below. The train whistled as it began pulling away. I waved at Rita, who was standing in the doorway of the boxcar. "Write!" I shouted over the whistle. I watched for a minute as she got smaller, and then I turned away, still feeling the warmth where Rita had hugged me.

I followed the tracks to Auburn's freight depot. Just beyond it, the tracks crossed a wide road, Clark Street, and I turned onto it, walking briskly toward town, elated that I had successfully made it to Auburn and excited at the possibilities that lay ahead of me. My new life!

In my mind, I had pictured Auburn to be like New Harmony, but Auburn was so much bigger than I had imagined. Clark Street intersected with State Street, which intersected with Genesee Street, which was the main street, but it looked nothing like Main Street in my former home town. For one thing, I couldn't see the end of it. Three- and four-story buildings, big stone churches, and brick storefronts stretched along both side of the road. Blocks of side streets crisscrossed Genesee, and they were lined with impressive buildings, too. Cars chugged past me, their black bodies glinting in the afternoon sun as they made their way through the city.

In New Harmony, it wouldn't have been hard to find the wealthy section of town and make inquiries about families in need of household help. But as I walked block after block in Auburn, doubt began to creep in, the way a toothache begins sometimes. At first, there's just a few twinges and you try to pretend it's nothing, but deep down, you know it's going to blossom into something that can't be ignored. I began to realize that finding the well-to-do doctor I had heard about who *might* be needing a housekeeper would be like finding a needle in a haystack, especially since I didn't even know the doctor's name.

My stomach growled loudly, reminding me that many hours had passed since I'd eaten. Across the street, near the end of the block, I saw a sign that said Imperial Coffee Shop. *Maybe if I get a little something to eat, I can figure out a plan.* I crossed the street and entered the coffee shop, breathing in deeply to enjoy the smell of fresh coffee mingling with food. I sat at the counter, sliding onto the stool closest to the register. The rest of the stools were empty, and only a few men sat at the tables. They were reading the newspaper, barely aware of what they were eating, it seemed to me. I couldn't imagine ever again sitting down for a meal and not paying full attention to the flavors of the food as I ate. You never know if a meal is going to be your last one for a while and all you'll have is the memory of it.

A tired-looking, middle-aged waitress came over. "What can I get you?" she asked.

I had hardly any money left, but the daily special was cheap enough—chili and cornbread for a dime. "The chili special, please. And coffee."

She nodded, poured a cup of coffee, and set it in front of me, along with a rolled up napkin holding silverware. She disappeared into the kitchen and came back a few minutes later with a steaming bowl of chili and a large hunk of cornbread.

"Here you go. Anything else?" she smiled a little, but it looked like it took some effort.

"This will be fine, thanks." I dug into the chili, and the waitress moved down the counter and started filling salt and pepper shakers. I watched her as I ate, remembering all the times I did the exact same thing at the Paradise Diner.

"Maybe you can tell me something..." I said, feeling a bit of kinship with her. "I'm new in town, and..."

The restaurant door opened and a woman walked directly over to the waitress. She was a slight woman, but she wore high-heeled shoes, a stylish dress, and a dark blue narrow-brimmed hat with a high crown, which gave her added height. Under her smart hat, her hair, streaked with gray, was pinned neatly at the back of her head. She was probably in her forties. She carried a small stack of papers and an air of authority.

"Millie, dear," she said to the waitress as she brushed past me, "the Ladies' Auxiliary is sponsoring a dance to benefit the orphanage. I'm taking flyers around town. I've already talked to your boss about it. I'd like to post a flyer in the front window."

"If Mr. Delinks said it was okay, go ahead," the waitress said, shrugging.

"Yes, of course. Would you get me some tape, dear?"

I thought I saw the waitress roll her eyes as she turned to get a roll of tape from next to the register. She handed it to the woman, who then walked the short distance to the window to hang the flyer, her heels clicking sharply on the linoleum floor.

The waitress turned her attention back to me. "So what were you saying?"

"Uh, well...Like I said, I'm new in town and I'm wondering... I need to find a job and...maybe you could give me a couple of suggestions about where to look?"

She refilled my coffee, set the coffeepot down, and shook her head. "I don't think you're going to find a job in this town. Lots of people are out of work."

The woman came back to return the roll of tape, but stopped right by my stool. "Young man, let me offer you a bit of advice about looking for a job," she said.

"All right," I said. She seemed like she knew some of the business owners. I hoped she could point me in the right direction.

"My advice is that you should keep moving. Frankly, Auburn doesn't have enough jobs for its long-time residents. *Transients* aren't welcome. You won't find work here."

"I see," I said, feeling my cheeks burn. "Well, thanks for your advice," I turned back to my meal and I took a bite of cornbread, but it tasted like ashes in my mouth. "Thanks for nothing," I muttered as the woman turned on her heel and strode out of the restaurant. That was the second piece of "advice" I had gotten since I left home. The first time I nearly got stabbed and now this time, that woman practically slapped me.

"Don't mind her," the waitress said. "Mrs. Hunter is a pain in the neck and everybody knows it. But her husband is a hotshot in city government and her nephew is on the police force, so nobody wants to get her dander up. She's right about the jobs, though. Like I told you, I don't think you're going to find any work in this town."

I sighed. "I don't suppose you could use a dishwasher here, either."

Millie shook her head. "Sorry," she said. "I really am."

I paid for my meal and went back out on the streets of Auburn. Further east, I discovered that Genesee Street bridged a river—Owasco River, the sign said—and I turned off the city streets to follow the river and find a place to camp for the night. It was a chilly evening and the clouds were clearing out. As the stars peppered the black sky with dots of white light, I felt small and cold. I rolled up tightly in my blanket, afraid to call attention to myself by building a fire, and I slept fitfully, waking at every night noise.

Morning finally came. I made a small fire to get warm and heat some water. I washed up hurriedly in the chilly morning air and dressed in my men's clothes, but left my hair down. If I wanted to find a job as household help for *anyone*, they'd have to know I'm a girl. I followed the river for awhile and discovered it emptied into Owasco Lake. There was an amusement park on the northern tip of the lake, like Doris had said, and I sat down to rest near a pavilion. The building next to the pavilion housed a carousel, and beyond that, a huge roller coaster sat, imposing but idle, at the end of an inlet. Signs everywhere declared the park was *Closed for the Season*. It looked like everyone had gone home from a party. There I sat, with the weight of discouragement on my shoulders and feeling foolish, to boot, for choosing to go to Auburn on what amounted to a whim.

I pulled out my sketchpad and tried to draw a few quick sketches while I was thinking about what to do next, but my fingers quickly got cold. The wind had picked up, blowing unhindered across the lake and easily penetrating the weave of my trousers, and I decided to start walking. Hoping to find a windbreak, I walked up Lake Road into a residential area lined with trees. The wind followed me, pulling red and orange leaves from the maples and swirling them at my feet. But the oaks held stubbornly to their brown leaves, answering the wind with a brittle hiss.

The streets off Lake Road were lined with tall, narrow houses sitting shoulder to shoulder on small yards. Most of the houses had front porches, and when I turned a corner and looked down Swift Street, all the porches on the block lined up, creating a tunnel of pillars and wood. I followed the sidewalk alongside the tunnel, trying to memorize how it looked so I could draw it later.

Partway down the street, someone had taped a cardboard sign to an inside corner of their front window. *PIES OF ALL KINDS,* blocky letters declared. Underneath, in smaller letters, *Cakes Made to Order*. In the opposite corner of the window, printed on white paper, was *Raisin Cakes for Sale*.

I stopped on the sidewalk and studied the house, fingering the buffalo nickel that was in my pocket. The coin wasn't quite finished. I planned to define the man's face and smooth out the background a little, but maybe I could still trade it for food. If not, at least I could step out of the wind for a few minutes and warm up.

I walked up the porch steps. Another hand-lettered sign was attached to the front door. *Please Walk In.* I pushed lightly on the door. It felt a little odd to just walk into someone's house, even if the sign encouraged it. A bell bumped and jingled against the door as I shut it behind me and stepped into a sparsely furnished front parlor. Two armchairs had been pushed against the side wall, and an old leather-topped oak table sat between them. A ceramic lamp gave off a thin yellow light, overpowered by the late morning sunlight that streamed through narrow leaded-glass windows. Against the back wall of the parlor, several card tables were lined up. They were covered with a long checkered tablecloth, but their spindly metal legs poked out beneath the fabric, which stopped about a foot above the scuffed hardwood floor. The tables held an array of pies and several cakes, and the sweet smell of sugary fruit baking wafted through the parlor, the aroma unmistakably coming through the doorway separating the parlor from the kitchen.

"I'll be out in a moment," a female voice called from the kitchen. "Please have a seat. The cake is not quite ready."

I didn't know how to respond, so I just kept quiet and studied the assortment of pies. The crusts were lightly browned, with perfectly fluted edges. I read the handwritten labels and discovered that the pies were grouped by category. Fruit pies were on the left—apple, apple-raisin, lemon meringue, peach. In the middle was a small, colorful grouping of meat and vegetable pies: Sausage and Pepper, Ham and Cheddar, Spinach and Onion. (*Quiche*) was hand printed on each label. But the pies on the far right interested me the most. They were striking, latticed-topped pies with a dark filling. *Francine's Lemon-Raisin Pie*, the tag read. I looked more closely at the tag and saw that it was actually a folded recipe card. The first few ingredients showed: 2 cups raisins, 1 cup sugar, 2 Tbsp. cornstarch, 2 tsp. ground lemon rind... the rest of the recipe disappeared under the fold. Why would a bakery give out the recipe for its specialty pie, I wondered. Aunt Ruby never would have given out her recipe for chili, even if the President of the United States asked for it. Especially President Hoover.

"One more minute, please," the voice called out from the kitchen. I heard some muttering and then footsteps. "So sorry to keep you waiting.

The cake isn't...Oh! I beg your pardon. I thought you were someone else."
In a glance, she took in my men's clothing and my bindle. "You must
be visiting someone in the neighborhood?" She smiled warmly; it was an
infectious smile, and I couldn't help but smile back. She was a beautiful
woman, probably in her early thirties, with blue-gray eyes and fair skin.
Her light brown hair curled softly around her face.

"Yes," I said. "I was, um, out walking and saw your sign..."

"Ah, I hope you came for my pies," she said. "Perhaps one of my lemon-
raisin pies?"

She must be Francine, I thought, glancing again at the recipe card.

"My cakes are delicious, but to decorate them is, well, more difficult."
Her speech had a trace of an accent, but I couldn't identify it. She laughed,
a pleasant, musical laugh that made me grin. "When I heard the bell,
I thought you were here to pick up the carousel." She lowered her voice to
a mock whisper. "It's not ready—I'm still trying to get it right."

I had never met someone so outgoing, and I wasn't sure what to
make of her. But her manner was friendly and engaging, and I liked her
immediately. "Oh, you mean the carousel by the lake? I just came from
there."

"Yes. Here—let me show you. See what you think!" She disappeared
into the kitchen and quickly returned, carrying a sheet cake. It was smoothly
covered in creamy white icing and both the upper and lower edges of the
rectangle were piped with green ribbons of frosting. On the top of the
cake was a rendering, in frosting, of the carousel I had sat near in the park.
Except it didn't look much like the carousel. It was a stiff, rather clumsy
attempt. I bit my lip, searching for something to say.

She burst out laughing. "It's terrible, isn't it? I can see it in your face."

"Well, I...it's...not *too* bad," I stammered, then inhaled deeply, trying to
be nice. I pulled out my sketchpad and pointed at the quick drawing I had
made earlier. "But you need to use perspective to get the roofline right,
and the horses are out of proportion to the carousel, and..." I couldn't help
myself. I giggled a little, and as it bubbled up, Francine started laughing
again—that same, musical laugh as before, only louder. Soon we were both
laughing uncontrollably and Francine was wiping tears from her cheeks.

"Oh, dear," she said as we settled down. "You certainly seem to know what's wrong with it. Can you help me fix this?"

"I don't know," I said. "I've never tried to draw with frosting before." But it seemed like it was a good opportunity for me to earn some food if I could fix the drawing. "I can try."

"Drawing with frosting isn't hard," Francine said. "It's *drawing* that's hard! I can make roses and ivy with frosting—it's my specialty for cakes, mostly because that's what I draw best—but my customer didn't want roses and ivy. She wanted the carousel on her granddaughter's birthday cake because Beatrice loves those horses! I stupidly said I could do it." She motioned for me to follow her. "Please. Come into the kitchen."

She set the cake down on the countertop. "What do you think? Can you fix it, or do you need to start over?"

I surveyed the cake. "I think," I said slowly, "it might be easier to start over. Is that possible?"

"Certainly," she said. She picked up a narrow spatula and swiped it across the cake, deftly removing all traces of the carousel. Then she dipped the spatula into a bowl of icing and swirled a fresh, thin coating onto the cake. "There's your canvas," she said.

"Can I practice on something?" I asked.

"Certainly!" she said again. She took a triangle of parchment, rolled it into a cone, slid a metal tip into the narrow end, and spooned white frosting into it. "Try this. You can draw on a sheet of waxed paper."

The tube of frosting felt squishy in my hand, but I soon found the amount of pressure I needed to apply to control the stream of icing.

"Very good!" Francine said. "See, drawing with frosting isn't hard." She pointed to an assortment of colorful tubes of frosting she had prepared earlier. "There's the colored icing I used in my pathetic attempt. Use whatever you like. Some of the tips will give you different shapes, too."

I hesitated. "Do you have a picture of the carousel? My drawing is pretty sketchy."

"There's a postcard on my desk. I'll get it for you." She walked into a shelf-lined room that adjoined the kitchen. It looked like it had once been a bedroom and now served as an office and a pantry. She handed me the postcard. *Enna Jetticks Park*, it said in white letters.

I was a bit timid with the frosting at first, but as I got used to the feel of the tubes, I became better and better at controlling the ribbons of color. I drew the umbrella-shaped roof, the lattice supports, the brightly colored poles, and started in on the festive-looking prancing horses. Francine bounced around me, looking over my shoulder and nodding approvingly. "That's it! It looks wonderful!" she said.

I even added some shrubs and other greenery to the park before I stepped back to survey my work. I was pleased. It wasn't perfect, but it was a major improvement over what Francine had done.

"Oh, thank you!" Francine said. She picked up a tube of blue frosting. "Now I'll just write 'Happy Birthday, Beatrice' on it and it will be ready. I am so happy you walked through that door! I didn't want to face Evelyn Hunter with that terrible-looking carousel. She's hard to please anyway, and that cake would have been the kiss of death. I never would have gotten another order from her, and she would have told her friends as well."

Evelyn Hunter? Was it possible, I wondered, that this cake was for the same Mrs. Hunter who was so unpleasant to me yesterday in the restaurant?

The bell on the door jingled and a woman's voice sang out, "Hel-lo! Fran-cine, are you there?"

Mrs. Hunter, Francine mouthed to me. "I'm coming," she called as she started to put the cake into a box. I wanted to hide, but there was nowhere to go.

"I hope you don't mind, dear, but I'm in a bit of a hurry," said a commanding voice from the doorway. I turned to look at Mrs. Hunter, the very same Mrs. Hunter, who was now standing at the entrance to the kitchen.

"Oh, I didn't realize you had an... assistant, Francine," Mrs. Hunter said, surprised, looking at me and the tube of frosting I still held in my hand. Mentally, I prepared for more unpleasantness, but there wasn't even a flicker of recognition in her eyes. It might have been because I looked different as a girl, but I suspected the real reason was because to be so unpleasant to a stranger, you can't really see the person in the person.

"Yes, today I have a helper," Francine answered, "but I see you're in a hurry—so we will save the chit-chat for another time." She handed the cake to Mrs. Hunter. "I hope Beatrice will like it. Please wish her happy birthday for me, won't you?"

Mrs. Hunter looked like she wanted to say something else, but changed her mind. She looked down at the cake. "It's very nice," she said, with a touch of disbelief in her voice. "Beatrice will love it. It's good that you can manage something other than roses. I'll come by in a day or two to arrange for a cake for the church supper. The church façade might be nice on a cake, don't you think?" She paid for the cake and swept out the door, shutting it firmly. The bell jingled noisily, celebrating her departure.

Francine laughed out loud. "I love to string her along. She can't stand not knowing everything that's going on in the neighborhood, or in the whole town for that matter. She'll be back tomorrow to ask about you."

Francine motioned for me to sit at a little wooden table in the corner of the kitchen. "Let's have a cup of tea," she said, "and you can tell me who you are.

Francine set a steaming cup of fragrant tea in front of me and then poured one for herself. Next, she cut a generous piece of raisin pie and slid it next to my tea. "Please try a piece," she said.

By this time I was famished, and I immediately set to work on the pie. When I pushed my fork into the crust, I lifted out a heaping mound of plump raisins surrounded by flaky pastry. The crust was as tender as it looked and the sweetness of the raisin filling was perfectly balanced by the tang of lemon. "This is the best pie I've ever had!" I said, trying not to talk with my mouth full, but not wanting to stop eating, either. "You must sell out of these every time you make them."

Francine laughed. "I do sell a lot of them, but I don't always sell out. I wish I did, but times are hard. Some of the people in the neighborhood are still doing all right, but a lot of people have lost their jobs." She sipped her tea and then said, "I still don't know your name."

I swallowed another bite of pie. "It's Maddy."

"Maddy as in Matilda – or Maddy as in Madeline?"

"Madeline."

"Ah, like the pastry. When I was a little girl, my French grandmother taught me how to make Madeleines. But the French spell it with l-e-i-n."

"I don't know what those are. Do you make them for your bakery?"

"No," Francine said, giving it some thought. "I don't think they would sell well right now. It's better to make the raisin pies. So—Maddy. You said you were visiting? Who are you visiting?"

I studied my china teacup. A spray of violets decorated the outside of it, and a smaller cluster had been painted near the rim on the inside of the cup so that violets would be revealed to a right-handed tea drinker as the cup emptied. I set the cup down, noticing how its fluted pedestal base fit neatly onto the saucer. "I'm visiting Auburn in general," I said. "But no one in particular. I came to see if I could find a job." I was too embarrassed to tell her how I had come hoping to find a doctor who possibly needed a housekeeper.

"I think you are going to have a difficult time," she said. "People who have lived here for many years can't find work. It's gotten so bad that hundreds of people apply for any job, even if it's just a rumor."

The bell jangled and Francine rose. "Please excuse me for a minute," she said, and she disappeared through the doorway. I caught only snatches of conversation. When Francine returned, she was smiling. "This is a good day," she said. "I just sold the last of the raisin pies and an apple-raisin pie, too."

"That's good," I smiled back.

A timer dinged and Francine pulled two pies from the oven. "These are a special order—sour cream and raisin pies. When this customer comes to pick them up, I can close for the day." She sat down across from me again and poured more tea for both of us. "So, Maddy—do you have somewhere to stay?"

I hesitated. "Not yet. I'll find a place, though," I said, thinking about the lake near the park. I figured I could probably find some sheltered patch of woods not far from the water to set up camp. It would have to do until I either found a job or moved on.

"You saved me from great embarrassment today. I wish I could offer you a real job, but..." Francine shrugged and chuckled and waved her hand at the kitchen, "this isn't much of a bakery. But I have a little room off the pantry," she said, motioning with her head. "There's a bed in it and not much else, but you'd be welcome to stay for a few days. I know Mrs. Hunter will be back to order another cake that I won't be able to decorate, and if you could help me a little in the bakery and decorate Mrs. Hunter's cake, I can at least offer you a place to sleep and something to eat."

"Oh, thank you," I said. "That would be wonderful!"

"Good. Then why don't you get your things," Francine said, "and you can bring them back into the room."

I retrieved my bindle, which I had left in a corner of the parlor, and followed Francine into the pantry and through another doorway into a small room. The room was tiny, but it held a bed and a straight-backed chair, and it looked magnificent to me.

"Will this be all right?" she asked.

"This will be perfect!" I said. I couldn't believe my good fortune. Tonight I would sleep in a real bed—the first time in almost two months.

"There's a bathroom off the hallway behind the kitchen," Francine said. "Why don't you get settled, and then after I close, we'll have some supper." Francine left the room and I smiled at the thought of "getting settled." I unwrapped my bedroll, set my sketchbook, the manicure set, and my carving tools on the chair, and then I hung my single set of "girl clothes" on a hook next to the bed. *There, I'm settled,* I thought.

I heard the bell on the front door jangle a couple of times, and when I went through the kitchen to find the bathroom, I heard Francine talking to a customer out front. I brushed out my hair and washed up, still hardly believing my luck.

When I returned to the kitchen, Francine still wasn't back, but I surveyed the countertops, which held various mixing bowls, utensils, pie pans, and baking sheets from the day's work. *Well, if there's one thing I learned in the Paradise Diner,* I said to myself, *it's how to clean up.* I rolled up my sleeves, filled the sink with hot, soapy water, and went to work.

Francine came in a few minutes later to box the sour cream and raisin pies. "Maddy," she said, surprised. "I thought you might want to rest for a little while."

"Well, I'm not sure I should admit this," I said, "but it actually feels good to have my hands in hot water."

Francine laughed. "We'll see if you still think so by the end of the week."

For supper that evening, Francine warmed a meat and vegetable pie she hadn't sold. "The French name for this is *quiche*," she said as she served me a large piece chock full of sausage and green peppers. "People around here call it an egg pie, but I think they should know its real name."

"Nobody makes this back where I come from," I said. "I've never heard of quiche before, but it's very good!"

"Where are you from?" Francine asked.

"Southern Ohio. People there want meat and potatoes."

She laughed. "So do people around here, for the most part. But some have become fond of my quiche. And some people still think French food is quite stylish. Of course, Phillipe and I eat quiche quite often."

"Phillipe? Is he your husband?"

"No," she smiled. "Phillipe is my brother. Actually, I have two brothers. Armand and his wife, Louise, live not too far from here—between Cayuga and Seneca lakes. Phillipe works with Armand, so he stays there during the week and then comes home over the weekend." Francine pointed to the raisin pie we had sampled earlier. "Would you like a piece for dessert?"

"Maybe a small piece," I said. The sweet taste of raisins highlighted how much better today had turned out than yesterday. There was no way to guess what tomorrow would bring, but today I had plenty of food and tonight I'd have a real bed to sleep in—more than I ever would have hoped for. Maybe coming to Auburn wasn't such a bad idea after all.

CHAPTER 25

I awoke early the next day, at dawn. Over the past two months on the road, my body rhythms had become strongly tied to nature's clock. I had gotten used to the first light waking me as it spread across the fields and into the woods, rousing the birds, whose songs signaled what I had come to think of as the shift change. The nocturnal animals would be heading to their shelters for sleep, and the creatures of the day, which included me, greeted the morning, stretching sluggish muscles and thinking about food.

But this morning felt different, and it took a moment before I remembered where I was. My body was warm, enveloped in covers that trapped warmth and held it lightly around me. I felt the weight of my limbs and torso pushing down against the bed, and it seemed as if the bed gently pushed back. The pillow embraced my head and I felt like I was suspended in a warm, calm sea. I lay there like that for probably an hour, floating, listening to the muted birdsongs that came through my window and enjoying the luxury of a real bed. Eventually, I heard noise coming from the kitchen, and I forced myself to throw off the covers and get up.

Francine had coffee percolating and was starting to make piecrust. "Good morning," she said brightly. She was, I soon learned, one of those people who jumped out of bed fully awake, bursting with energy, ready to enjoy the day. "Did you sleep well?"

"Better than I've slept in months," I said.

Together we rolled out crusts and made lattice tops. When it was time to make pie fillings, Francine went into the pantry and came back with two large bricks of raisins.

"I've never seen raisins packaged like that," I said. "Do they come like that because you buy so much for your pies?"

"They come like this because that's how we preserve them."

Francine laughed at my confusion. "The raisins come from my family's vineyard," she explained. "Since Prohibition, we sell some of our grapes to home winemakers—at least that's not illegal. We sell as much of the grapes as we can as juice and for jams and jellies, and then we dry the rest of our harvest. We can sell the raisins through the winter—or put them in raisin pies. I think my *grandpere* turned in his grave, though, the first time we had to sell good wine grapes for jelly."

"Your grandfather was a winemaker?"

"Yes, my family came here from France and settled first in California," Francine said. "Then my grandparents came east. Everyone else was going west, but the Durrands have always gone 'against the grain,' so to speak. My grandfather believed he could grow wine grapes successfully in New York, and he set out to prove it. Planting a vineyard is an act of faith, though. It takes four years before you know if you're successful. Three years for the vines to mature and the fourth year to harvest and make wine. After that, you know how the wine will taste. Durrand wines were some of the finest wines in the United States, not just in New York State." She measured out sugar and added ground lemon peel to the raisin filling. "We still have the family vineyard. Armand and Louise live on the property with their two boys, and Phillipe spends most of the week there, too, working. We hope that we can someday return to making those wines, but for now..." she shrugged and motioned toward the pies in process.

By nine thirty the last pies, the quiches, were coming out of the oven and the raisin and fruit pies had cooled. Francine glanced at the clock and handed me a small stack of folded recipe cards. "I like to open for business by ten o'clock so people can buy their pies for lunch or supper. Here, put one of these cards with each raisin pie," she said, "and we'll wrap them up and put them out on the tables."

"I noticed these yesterday," I said, looking at the heading. *Francine's Lemon-Raisin Pie.* "And I wondered why you would give out the recipe for your specialty pie."

"So now you understand," Francine said. "It's the best way to sell more raisins." She laughed. "And if the customers buy the raisins, I don't have to make so many pies. I hate making those lattice tops!"

We arranged the pies on the tables in the parlor and then Francine made a fresh pot of coffee. We sat down at the wooden table in the kitchen, and each of us sipped a steaming cup of coffee and nibbled on a piece of pastry. The bell on the door jingled and Francine started to get up.

"Hel-lo, Fran-cine," a familiar voice sang out.

Francine sat back down and covered her face with her right hand, shaking her head. She chuckled softly. "What did I tell you," she whispered. "Mrs. Hunter," she called out as she stood up and walked to the parlor, "what a pleasant surprise."

"Well, dear, I had some errands to run, and I just had to stop by and tell you how much Beatrice loved her cake. She was just thrilled with those horses!"

"I'm so glad," Francine said. "And it was so nice of you to stop in specially to tell me."

"You're welcome, dear. Ah...tell me...the girl who was here yesterday. Did she help with the cake? Who was ..."

"Oh, yes. She's an able assistant," Francine cut Mrs. Hunter off midsentence. "Now, if I remember correctly, yesterday you mentioned that you might want to order another cake?"

"Yes, I suppose I should make arrangements as long as I'm here..." Mrs. Hunter said. From where I sat in the kitchen, I could hear irritation creeping into her voice. I knew Francine was stringing Mrs. Hunter along, as she had put it yesterday, and I was glad that the two of them remained in the parlor so Mrs. Hunter wouldn't see me grinning. It served her right for Francine to have the upper hand.

"You mentioned something about the church building," Francine said. "Is that how you would like the sheet cake decorated?"

"Yes, *if* you can do it. And write 'Thank you, Volunteers' on it, please. I'll need it for Saturday morning."

"Fine. It will be ready then," Francine promised.

"You're sure you can manage the church façade? It's not too difficult to do?"

"Mrs. Hunter," Francine said, "Drawing with frosting is not hard."

I was happy to hear the bell signaling Mrs. Hunter's departure, because I thought I might burst from trying to hold in laughter. When Francine came back into the kitchen, she didn't hold anything back. Her musical laughter filled the room. "I suppose I'll go to hell for being so mean," she said, looking rather pleased with herself. Then suddenly, she looked stricken. "You *can* draw the church building with frosting, can't you, Maddy?"

For one moment, I was tempted to continue the game of stringing someone along and tell Francine I could only draw animals, people, and carousels, but then I thought better of it. Once she got over the shock, she probably would have laughed, but I wasn't going to risk offending her. Decorating that cake meant I could at least stay here until Saturday. "Sure," I said. "I'll have to go take a look at the church, but it should be easy to draw."

"Easy for *you*," Francine said, relieved.

Francine's pies sold well before lunch, but business slowed to almost nothing by mid afternoon, except for a few customers who came in to buy blocks of raisins. Half a dozen pies and several quiches sat unsold on one of the card tables. "Some days are like that," Francine sighed. "I'm just glad my bakery doesn't provide my only income."

"Where do your customers come from?" I asked, as an idea formed in my mind.

"Mostly from the neighborhood," she said. "People who know me know about my raisin pies. Why do you ask?"

"What about the rich people?" I asked. New Harmony had its well-to-do section of town—the families who owned the factories and the stores. I figured Auburn had a section like that, too. "Do they know you?"

Francine shook her head. "Probably not. Many of the wealthier people live over on South Street. They don't come this way often."

"What if I took your pies to them? I could go door to door and try to sell them."

Francine's mood brightened. "You would do that? Oh, but Phillipe has the truck! I have no way to drive you there. It's a little far to walk, especially carrying pies!"

"I'm very used to walking," I said. "Just point me in the right direction."

She looked at me solemnly for a minute. "If you're serious, I thought of just the thing to carry the pies," Francine said.

"I'm serious," I said.

I followed Francine out to the garage and watched as she moved some boxes and old tools out of the way. From a dark corner, she pulled out a child's wagon. "This was Phillipe's when he was a boy," she said, wresting a rear wheel free from the tines of a garden rake. She rolled it out into the daylight. The wagon was covered with dust and its wooden sides bore the scuff marks from Phillipe's childhood, but I could still read the faded and scratched paint that spelled out *Liberty Coaster*. "It was a favorite toy of Phillipe's," Francine said. "I wanted to give it away to some neighborhood children, but he wouldn't let me. I couldn't imagine that we'd ever have a use for it, but it seems I was short-sighted." She laughed and wrinkled her nose. "Of course, Phillipe doesn't have to know that we've put his wagon back into service. Maybe I'll just forget to mention it."

We cleaned up the wagon and oiled its axles and wheels. I pulled it toward the house, turning it this way and that to test how it would steer. "It behaves well," I said to Francine. "Let's give it a job to do."

We boxed the pies and quiches and arranged them carefully in the wagon, padding them with newspaper so that they wouldn't shift. Then I was off toward South Street, determined to come back with an empty wagon.

It was already late afternoon, and I worried that by now people would have their dinners planned and maybe even in the oven. I walked quickly, pulling the wagon behind me, covering a good distance from Francine's neighborhood, but I started knocking on doors before I got to South Street. Tomorrow I could walk there and work my way up and down the street, I thought, but for today, I'll try to sell the pies on my way out.

I knocked on one door after another and was turned down time and again. "No money for extras," people said. "Times are too hard." "No job, no money." I was discouraged and frustrated, but I kept going. I didn't want to face Francine's disappointment if I returned with a wagon still full of pies.

Finally, the street sign announced that I had reached South Street. The houses were large and stately, set back father from the road. They sat on bigger lots, which gave them a more dignified appearance than the houses hunkered together in Francine's neighborhood. I felt a twinge of hope and strode up the walk to a large brick home with green shutters. When I walked back down that walk, both my wagon and my spirits were a little lighter—I had sold two pies! By the time I finished ringing doorbells at the next few houses, I felt like I had struck gold. Francine's pies were selling well, and several people invited me to stop again when I returned to the neighborhood. South Street was a long street. By the time I had covered several blocks on one side of the street and got halfway down the other side, my wagon was empty and I was overjoyed.

I had walked a long way, though, and as I walked back to Francine's, I thought about the real bed I had slept in last night and imagined how cozy it would be tonight. I could almost feel the warmth of the covers and the mattress soothing my tired legs.

Francine must have been listening for the clatter of the wagon because she burst out of the back door to greet me as I pulled the wagon toward the garage. "Did you sell anything?" she asked, and then stopped to stare at the wagon. "You sold *everything*?" she exclaimed. "Maddy, I can't believe it!"

"Yep. Turns out not everybody is suffering from the Depression. Lots of people on South Street were glad to have your fresh-baked pies. And some of the customers even knew what quiche is."

"Well, I'm surprised at that. But that's good. Maybe I will get some new customers. Put the wagon back in the garage and let's celebrate. Oh, I hope you don't mind having a quiche for dinner?" Francine said.

"What?" I teased. "You kept back something I could have sold?"

"Yes. My mistake," Francine said. "Now I'm afraid we'll be forced to eat it."

In the kitchen, as Francine warmed our dinner, I took the money I had collected from selling the pies and set it on the counter. I straightened out several crumpled dollar bills and stacked up the change. "Here you go," I said.

Francine gathered it up, but handed a small amount of change back to me. "You should have this," she said. "It's a little compensation for all the walking."

I shook my head. "But I'm staying at your house and I can't pay you, except by helping out."

"Yes, but you have helped me very much and you should have a little bit of money in your pocket," she said. "I insist. Think of it as a small sales commission."

I hesitated. "Well, all right. Thank you!" I took the money reluctantly, but Francine was right. I needed to have a little money. After Saturday, I would be on the road again, once Mrs. Hunter's cake was finished.

As we got ready to eat dinner, Francine disappeared down the cellar stairs. She returned a few minutes later, carrying a dark green bottle. "This will be just the thing for our celebration," she said. "A little bit of Durrand wine with our quiche will be perfect."

"But, I thought...well, with Prohibition and all..."

"Maddy, dear. Don't look so shocked. Do you really think people are going to stop drinking because of some stupid law? We aren't allowed to sell wine anymore, but it is no one's business what we drink. The French have a long history of enjoying fine wine with dinner, and I have no intention of giving that up, no matter what the so-called temperance people think."

"I know people still drink," I said. *My father might still be in jail because of it,* I thought, although his being in jail was actually because he punched a cop when he was drunk. I wondered what Francine would say if I told her that. "But I thought you said you weren't making wine anymore."

Francine smiled. "Look at the label, Maddy. This wine is twelve years old." She pulled a corkscrew out of the silverware drawer and twisted it smoothly into the bottle, pulling sharply up on the cork, releasing it with a pop.

We sat down to dinner and she poured some of the ruby red liquid into two wine glasses that sparkled even in the ordinary light of the kitchen.

Francine picked up her glass carefully, holding it by the stem, and swirled the liquid gently as she held it up to the light. "Excellent color," she said. "Only the tiniest bit of sediment."

I held my glass up to the light, too, but I didn't attempt to swirl it. "It's beautiful," I said, admiring the rich red color. "It's like a jewel."

"Thank you!" she said. "This wine is one of my favorites." Francine touched her glass to mine. A clear bell-like chime rang out from our glasses and quickly disappeared. "*A la Sante*," she said. "To your health." She passed the glass under her nose and inhaled softly before she tipped the glass to her lips and sipped.

I did the same, not wanting Francine to know that I had never tasted wine before—that my mother, in fact, had never let me get within ten feet of a drink, except when it was sloshing around my father's brain. The liquid in my glass smelled nothing like the alcohol my father drank. The soft, fruity scent of ripened grapes filled my nose and I took a little sip. The taste surprised me. It was nothing like grape juice, yet I tasted grapes and even a hint of cherries. I took a second sip. The wine wasn't sweet, but it wasn't sour, either. It was smooth and rich, with a bit of tartness.

I looked up. Francine was watching me. "This is very good," I said. "Do you put cherries in your wine, too? I taste some in here."

Francine raised an eyebrow. "That is the grape that you are tasting, but it has what we call a cherry undertone. It is the mark of a good *merlot*." She motioned toward our plates. "And it's very good with the smoked bacon in this quiche."

Suddenly, I was very aware of how hungry I was and I dug into the quiche, which, as Francine suggested, tasted especially good with the wine. I also realized how tired I was, although I was surprised to notice that my legs didn't ache anymore and I felt relaxed and warm.

By the time we finished dinner, I was getting sleepy. I kept thinking about the bed that waited for me beyond the pantry. Somehow, Francine seemed to know that. "Today was a long day for you," she said. "You walked a good distance. I will clean up tonight. You go on to your room and I'll see you in the morning."

I didn't argue. "If you're sure...thank you. Goodnight, Francine." I stood up and slowly walked through the pantry. *Your room*, she had said. I knew that after Saturday, when Mrs. Hunter picked up the cake, I would have to leave, but the words still bounced around in my head—*your room*.

For the next several days, Francine and I followed the same pattern. We got up early and made pies together. Then, in the afternoon we packed anything that hadn't sold into the Liberty Coaster and I went out in search of customers. Again, I knocked on doors of big houses on South Street and the streets that intersected it, and I managed to sell nearly everything.

I was happy to feel like I was earning my keep, and as I walked back to Francine's on a Thursday afternoon, I hummed a tune to the rhythm of the wagon wheels bumping over the sidewalk. I turned my attention to the song that my brain had selected and realized that it was *Wildwood Flower*. I thought of my mother, who had taught me that song, and I remembered sitting in the jungle with Henry and singing as Reedy played his harmonica. I felt a small ache growing in center of my body. Maybe I would send some postcards soon, I thought, if I could find a way to stay in Auburn long enough to get an answer back.

Francine was delighted with the nearly empty wagon and again gave me a small sales commission. "Sales of the raisin blocks have picked up this week, too," she said. "People I don't know are stopping here to buy raisins. They must be from the neighborhoods where you've taken my pies."

"That's good news," I said.

"It certainly is. Selling many blocks of raisins will help us get through the winter." She paused, her eyes twinkling. "And it means I won't have to bake so many of those raisin pies! Phillipe will be pleased, too. You'll get to meet him tomorrow night. He's coming home from the vineyard and he'll stay for the weekend."

"I'm looking forward to meeting him," I said. *But what if he doesn't like it that you let me stay here this week?* I worried. *What if he wants me to leave right away?* I could camp by the lake for a couple of days if I had to,

I figured. But even the days were getting chilly, and the nights would be uncomfortably cold. At least I had a little bit of money again, and I could buy a few groceries.

"Here's my idea for tomorrow," Francine said, interrupting my internal planning session. I snapped back to the present. "You can help me prepare the pies tomorrow morning, but we won't make as many as usual. Hopefully, we'll sell them all, or at least most of them, from the house. In the afternoon, I'll bake Mrs. Hunter's cake while you go to the church to do a drawing. Then you can decorate the cake either Friday evening or Saturday morning." She took a breath. "What do you think? Will that give you enough time to do the cake?"

"I think so," I said.

"Good. Then let's just relax this evening."

After dinner, Francine made a pot of tea. "I don't feel like going upstairs yet," she said. "Would you like to have some tea with me?" She motioned toward the wooden table in the corner of the kitchen. "If you don't mind sitting here for a while longer, that is. There really isn't a decent place where we can sit and chat since I converted the front parlor for my bakery."

"The kitchen is very comfortable," I said, "I like sitting here, and tea would be nice."

It was beginning to get dark. Francine poured tea for us and then switched on a floor lamp that was tucked into the corner. Only the center bulb lit, and it cast a muted light through the opaque glass globe.

"You haven't told me much about yourself," Francine said.

I shrugged. "There's not much to tell," I said. "I came here from Southern Ohio looking for a job."

"You seem a little young to be out looking for work," she said.

"I didn't have much choice. I'm seventeen, and I would have finished high school this year, except my school closed. There wasn't anything for me to do in my town," I said. *Except work at the Paradise Diner with the creep who attacked me,* I added silently. I felt my chest tighten, and I took a deep breath.

"It's terrible that schools are closing," Francine said. "I don't know how people will manage without an education."

"I know," I said. I watched as Francine took a sip of tea. This time she had the cup with the violets. I looked down at mine and saw that it had been painted with roses and forget-me-nots.

"What about your parents?" Francine asked.

"What do you mean? What about them?"

"It must have been hard for them to let you go."

"I guess so," I said. "My mother agreed that I didn't have much choice, though." That was pretty close to an outright lie; the truth was that I *hoped* she understood that I didn't have any choice. I didn't like lying to Francine, so I tried to steer our conversation to safer ground. "You know what I miss the most about school?"

"What?"

"Drawing. My teacher was a really good artist, and he let me stay after school so he could teach me things about drawing. Painting, too. I improved a lot because of him."

"You did a fine job on the carousel," Francine said. "Lucky for me!"

"Lucky for me, too," I said.

Francine smiled. "I would like to see some more of your work. Something drawn in pencil, perhaps, rather than in frosting."

I hesitated. "If you really want to see some sketches, I can show you a few tonight. I drew a little while I was...traveling."

"Yes! Please get them. I'd *love* to see some now."

I got my sketchbook and set it between us on the table next to our teacups. I opened it, realizing that I was about to expose the truth about my travels.

The first page was the little diagram I had drawn to remember how to get to Doris's house. *Steamburg*, I had scrawled across the top. "That page is just a map," I said as Francine looked up from the page, puzzled. "It's kind of a note to myself. The next page is where my drawings begin."

Francine turned the pages very slowly. She looked at the drawings of the hobos in the boxcars, the towns I drew looking out of boxcar doors,

Rita—before I knew she was Rita—and my feet wearing muddy shoes framed by the open boxcar door.

"This is how you came to Auburn?" Francine asked. Her blue-gray eyes were wide with surprise.

I nodded.

"But isn't it dangerous?"

"It's not so bad if you know how to get on and off the trains safely," I said. "I was lucky. Someone showed me."

"But there are many dangers, yes?" Francine said. "Not just getting on and off the trains!"

"Yes," I said, thinking about Blackjack. "And that's why I was wearing men's clothes when I first came to your bakery. But I wasn't alone out there. There's so many people riding the rails—even families with young children are hopping freights to go out West and pick fruit. You can't imagine it if you haven't seen it."

"I know people are desperate," she said.

Francine flipped back several pages and stopped to look at my nearly finished drawing of Rita.

"When I said I wasn't alone out there, I meant as a girl, too," I said. "The hobo in that drawing is also a girl, although I didn't know it right away. Her name is Rita."

"Really—this is a girl? But why didn't you finish the drawing?"

"Well, I meant to. But Rita wasn't exactly a willing model." I chuckled. "We almost came to blows over that drawing. But it turned out all right. We got to be friends."

"Where is she now? Do you know?"

"I hope she's in Pulaski. That's where she was headed. She has a cousin there."

"So she was traveling to Pulaski by train?"

"Yes, ma'am," I said, grinning. "But she was riding the rails, not the cushions."

Francine sat back in her chair and sipped her tea. My sketchbook lay open between us, showing Rita sitting against the boxcar wall. "You draw very well," she said. By now it had gotten quite dark, and the floor lamp only had enough energy to light part of Francine. I could see half of her face and half of her body. Her teacup and the hand that held it were visible, and the hand that supported the saucer nearly disappeared into the gloom. Like a half moon on a dark night, I thought. If you really looked, you could see the dark half of the moon, too.

"If you like," I said, feeling a little shy, "I could draw you."

Francine flashed a smile, which caught for a moment in the weak light. "Yes," she said. "I would like that! Where do you want me to sit?"

I took back my sketchbook and turned to a fresh page. "Stay sitting where you are. In this light, you look very mysterious. From here, I only see half of you, but I can't decide if you're appearing or disappearing."

"Well, if you decide I'm disappearing, by all means, warn me!" Francine said.

I completed several sketches, each a different pose. After drawing her with the teacup, I drew a three-quarter view of Francine with her chin resting on her hand. By then a shaft of moonlight found its way through the kitchen window. I had Francine turn her face toward it so that the light washed over her, and I drew her in profile, concentrating on catching the way the bluish-white light of the moon lit her brow, nose, and chin, and cast a shadow in the hollow of her cheekbone. The moonlight defined her features and gave her an air of elegance.

All the while, Francine sat quietly. Sometimes I was aware of her watching me work, but neither of us spoke.

"You're an excellent model, Francine," I said as I finished the profile. "You don't fidget much, and I wasn't worried at all about you taking a swing at me, like Rita almost did."

"We'll see about that last part," she laughed. "These had better be good!" She stretched, rolled her head back and forth a little to relax her neck, and then leaned forward to look at my work. She studied the drawings carefully, flipping back and forth, comparing all three. "Your drawing skill is remarkable, Maddy. These are very nice."

"I'm glad you like them. You can keep one if you want."

Francine grinned. "No one has ever drawn me before. I would love to have one of these! Which one can I keep?"

"You choose," I said.

"Then I choose the one with the teacup," she said. "You said you couldn't be sure if I was appearing or disappearing, so I must be like the Cheshire cat. This drawing is my proof!"

Friday morning, as the pies we placed in the hot oven started to release their sweet fruity fragrance, Francine drew a little map on a scrap of paper and sent me out to draw Mrs. Hunter's church. "It's here on Williams Street," she pointed, leaving a little buttery smudge on the W. "You'll walk up South Street, past Logan. Williams Street angles off to the left. The Presbyterian church is just down the street from there. It's a large stone building with a circular Tiffany window and two steeples."

She sketched a little extension to the map. "If you want to take a look at the town when you're done, you could keep going up Williams Street. You'd eventually come out onto Genesee Street near the post office, which you'd be sure to notice because it's a grand building with gables and a round tower in the front."

I gathered my sketchbook and several pencils and set off, walking quickly in the crisp autumn air. As I exhaled, my breath turned into little puffs of fog that quickly faded away and disappeared. Go North on South Street, Francine's map showed, and left onto Williams.

The church building was easy enough to find and easy enough to draw, and I finished with it quickly, getting enough detail for the cake but not bothering to capture every little thing. Already, I knew you can do only so much with frosting.

It was Francine's description of the post office that had gotten my attention. I walked up Williams to Genesee to get a view of the entire building. It didn't look anything like a post office. To my eyes, its stone façade with arched entryways, gables, and turrets made it look like an exotic castle.

I found a spot where I could prop myself against a tree and sketch. A little while later, after I had made several sketches I was fairly satisfied with,

I found a newsstand and bought three penny postcards that showed the merry-go-round and dance hall at Enna Jetticks Park. Then I crossed the street, walked up the stone steps of the post office, and went through the heavy arched doorway into that grand building.

"Three postcard stamps, please," I said, sliding a dime under the window.

"Six cents, Miss," he said. He pushed the stamps toward me along with my change. His fingernails were dirty and the skin around his nails was embedded with a dark brown stain. I wondered if he had been working on his car the night before or if he had been coaxing some other piece of machinery into running just a little while longer. I thought of how my mother would have reacted to those hands. *He should have scrubbed a little longer,* she would have said. *After all, when you're dealing with the public...*

My shoes tapped softly on the marble floor as I walked through the lobby, but the walls bounced the sound of my footsteps back at me. They echoed loudly in the empty room and I self-consciously hurried toward a writing table. The walls broadcast my quicker pace and I tried to keep my weight on my toes and walk quietly. I picked up one of the pens lying on the table, avoiding one with a severely chewed top:

> *Dear Henry,*
>
> *I hope you are fine and happy in Pittsburgh. Did you get the job you were looking for? I made it to Auburn, NY and I hope to stay here for a while. I kind of have a job in a home bakery. It's temporary, but for now I have a place to sleep and meals, and the owner is very nice.*
>
> *Thanks for showing me the ropes. I had a little trouble along the way, but I made it here safely because of you.*
> *Please write if you can.*
>
> *—Maddy*

Dear Mom,

I just wanted to let you know I'm in Auburn and I have a job, at least for a little while. I'm working in a family bakery and I'm decorating some cakes and selling pies.

Please write if you're not too mad at me. I miss you and Eddie and Aunt Ruby, too.

Love,
Maddy

Dear Rita,

How are things in Pulaski? I'm still in Auburn and I found some work in a bakery. Part of my job is to decorate cakes by drawing on them with frosting.

Last night, I even drew the owner (on paper, not on a cake), and she didn't try to punch me. Ha, ha.

Write if you can.

—Maddy

I licked the stamps, pressed them neatly onto the postcards, and dropped the cards into the mail slot marked Out of Town.

When I got back to Francine's late in the afternoon, the cake for Mrs. Hunter's volunteers sat on the counter with a note propped next to tubes of colored frosting:

Maddy,

I'm delivering some pies to neighbors. In case you want to get started on the cake, I made up some colored frosting. You'll see I've already put the base of white frosting on the cake. When you're done drawing the church, I'll add the writing and put the piping on.

—Francine

P.S. There's hot coffee in the percolator. Help yourself.

I checked the time. It was about an hour before dinner—long enough to get the church on the cake. I poured a cup of coffee, opened my sketch-book, and grabbed a tube of reddish-brown frosting. I kept one eye on my sketch and the other on the cake, selecting different colors of frosting as I drew the front of the church, the doorway, the steps, the shrubbery; I reached for another tube and added the steeples, which jutted up severely from the roof. As I finished, I looked up from the cake and screamed. A man was standing in the back doorway of the kitchen, watching me.

"I'm so sorry to have startled you," he said. "It appears I have caused you to have a little problem with the decorating." I followed his glance to the cake. One steeple was now sporting a large blob of frosting at its tip. It looked like an oversized pompon on a party hat.

I felt my face flush, but it had nothing to do with the frosting. "What do you think you're doing just walking into someone's house!" I demanded. "If you've come for a pie, you should use the front door!" My heart pounded in my ears, and I eyed the knife that Francine had used to separate the cake from its baking pan. It was within arm's length, and I planned to grab it if I needed to.

"I beg your pardon," he said, "but the house I have walked into is my own!" He grinned, and my eyes were drawn to a dimple forming in his right cheek. "I'm Phillipe, and I think you must be Maddy. My sister has told me about you over the telephone."

"You're Phillipe?" Embarrassment traveled from my toes straight up to the top of my head. I had just been extremely rude to a member of Francine's family, even if it hadn't been on purpose. "I'm pleased to meet you, really. I'm sorry for hollering at you, but I didn't hear you come in—and you scared me." As I looked at him, I could see that he was a younger, masculine version of Francine. His hair was the same light-brown color and his eyes were blue-gray, too, although more intense in color than Francine's. Where Francine was fine-featured and beautiful, Phillipe was angular and handsome. I guessed that he was probably in his early twenties.

"I'm pleased to meet you, too. I didn't mean to frighten you," he said, still standing in the doorway. "I'm sorry about the cake. Can you fix it?"

"I think so," I said. I studied the blob of frosting, picked up a narrow metal spatula, and prepared to slide it under the blob to lift it off the cake.

"Oh, dear," he said as he walked over to the counter. "I'm afraid that you'll have to remove more than that splotch of frosting."

"What do you mean?"

"The cake is for Mrs. Hunter, isn't it?"

"Yes, but I..."

"I'm afraid," he paused, looking sadly at the cake, "that you have drawn the wrong church. Mrs. Hunter's church is the First Presbyterian church, and you have drawn the Second Presbyterian church."

"But Francine said..."

"My dear sister gave you the wrong directions," he sighed. "It's unfortunate, but she often gets right and left mixed up, and north and south are impossible for her to keep straight. I suppose she told you to go north on South Street and turn left onto Williams?"

"Well, yes. And she even drew me a map. I have it right here," I said as I dug into my pocket to retrieve the scrap of paper.

"You should have turned *right* onto Williams." He shook his head as he studied Francine's map. "It's regrettable that she can't even get it right when she puts it on paper. You'll have to forgive her, though. It's kind of a family shortcoming. She comes by it honestly."

"What's really regrettable..." said a voice from the hallway "...is that my dear brother must seize every opportunity to string someone along— even someone he has just met." I looked up to see Francine leaning against the door frame. She was smiling broadly. "I hope you'll forgive him, Maddy. It seems to be a family trait that none of us can resist."

Phillipe threw his head back and laughed, a melodious laugh like Francine's, but accompanied by a rich bass. He and Francine hugged hello. "Couldn't you have stayed away for a few more minutes? I think I would have had Maddy convinced of the 'error.'"

"You would have watched her scrape off the frosting and start over, wouldn't you?" Francine said.

"It's a good thing you came back when you did," I said to Francine, smiling at her, partly because I was relieved that I wouldn't have to redo the cake and partly to show that I got the joke. "He nearly ruined the cake as it is. It's his fault that I blobbed frosting on the steeple."

"Hey, it's not my fault that you're jumpy!" Phillipe protested.

"I'm not jumpy. You..." I said with mock sternness, "were *sneaking*."

Just before suppertime, Phillipe brought up a slightly dusty bottle of wine from the cellar. "This bordeaux was bottled two years before Prohibition," he said. "It is aging nicely. Should we have some with tonight's dinner?"

"Yes. Good choice," Francine agreed.

The three of us sat at the wooden table and shared quiche, crusty bread, and wine. I sipped slowly, enjoying the tart flavor of the grapes. I had never known my father to drink wine, and I wondered why. I knew it was gin he liked, although I had heard Aunt Ruby tell my mother that my father was just as likely to drink rubbing alcohol if his supply of hooch ever dried up. I couldn't tell what my mother thought of that, because she didn't answer my aunt. She had just stared at the diner wall.

There must be something bad about gin, I decided, as I sat there in Francine's kitchen. Then I'll never drink gin, ever, I resolved. I'll only drink wine. There didn't seem to be anything bad about wine. I swirled the red liquid gently around in my glass and looked up to find that Phillipe was watching me.

"Do you like the wine?" he asked.

"Yes, it's very good," I said. "It tastes like there's berries mixed in with the wine, too, but I guess that's just part of the grapes, right? Like the merlot?"

Phillipe looked over at Francine, his eyebrows raised. Francine laughed. "She's like that, Phillipe. She picked out the cherry undertone in the merlot, too."

"Very impressive," he said, lifting his glass to me. "Perhaps when this Prohibition nonsense is over you will become a *viticulteur*."

I didn't know exactly what he was talking about, but it sounded complimentary. I smiled at Phillipe and he smiled back. I watched how the corners of his mouth crinkled slightly when he smiled. Uncle George had lines like that, only more pronounced. *Laugh lines*, Aunt Ruby called them. "Not everybody gets them," she had said. "You have to earn them."

CHAPTER 26

First thing Saturday morning, Mrs. Hunter burst into the front parlor of Francine's bakery in a swirl of self-importance. Francine brought out the cake for Mrs. Hunter's inspection. "It looks quite nice," Mrs. Hunter said. "It's such an improvement over *ordinary* roses and ivy, don't you think?"

"I'm glad you are happy with it," Francine said, ignoring the bait Mrs. Hunter dangled. Instead, Francine called for me.

"Maddy, would you box this cake for Mrs. Hunter while I get her change?" Francine asked.

I had hoped to stay out of sight, but I brought out the cake box and proceeded to package the cake carefully, making sure not to damage the frosting. Mrs. Hunter watched me closely. "Do you live around here, dear?" she asked. "I'm wondering if I might know your family."

"I'm sure you wouldn't know my family," I answered sweetly. "You see, I'm what you would call a *transient*."

The look on her face was pure confusion. I closed the box and taped the side flaps shut. "There you go," I said, and I turned and walked back into the kitchen, feeling just a bit smug. For once, Mrs. Hunter was speechless.

Francine came back with the change, and apparently Mrs. Hunter recovered her voice. "That girl said she was a transient," she said, making it sound like I was a criminal. "Don't you think you should be hiring people from Auburn?"

"I think I should hire the right person for the job," Francine said. "Tell me who you know in Auburn that can draw better with frosting."

"Well, there must be somebody!" Mrs. Hunter said. I heard her scoop up the box and clomp out the door.

"So I guess it was the right church?" I said to Francine, who had returned to the kitchen and was tilting the spout of the percolator over a half-full cup of coffee to warm it.

Her melodious laugh filled the kitchen. "Yes, I am *sure* it was the right church," Francine said, "and I am equally sure that both of us would have heard about it immediately and loudly if it wasn't!" She took her coffee over to the wooden table and sat down. "Did something happen out there while I was getting her change?"

I busied myself with wiping down the already clean countertop. "It wasn't so much what happened out there, it was what happened a few days ago when I first came to Auburn," I admitted.

"Tell me more," Francine said.

"There's not much to tell. She overheard me asking a waitress in the Imperial Coffee Shop about finding a job. Mrs. Hunter butted in and told me that transients weren't welcome. That I should just keep moving."

"Unbelievable," Francine said. "And today she recognized you from the restaurant?"

"I'm not sure," I hedged. I doubted that she recognized me. Who expects a boy to show up later as a girl? My guess is that Mrs. Hunter was trying to remember who else was in the restaurant that day. "Today, she asked if she knew my family."

"That woman gets into everyone's business," Francine sighed. "One of these days, she and I are bound to lock horns, as they say. But for now, her cakes are done. I don't expect to see her again for a while."

I fussed with the canisters of flour and sugar, lining them up in a precise row, trying to delay what was inevitable. My job here was done, as Francine had just said, and she was sure to tell me that it was time that I should pack up my things and be on my way.

"Maddy," she said. "I think the kitchen is in fine shape. Why don't you pour some coffee for yourself and come and sit down?"

My stomach lurched. *Well, you knew this was coming*, I told myself. I did as Francine said, but slowly, so I could stave off the bad news as long as possible.

"Now that Mrs. Hunter's cake is done, I'm wondering if I could interest you in a long day of baking?"

"Sure," I said, feeling hopeful. "Why?"

"I got a telephone call this morning from one of the families on South Street. You've sold quiche to them—the Davises. Mrs. Davis was very upset. She has been planning a party in honor of her parents' fortieth anniversary, but the caterer she hired called her yesterday to say he's going out of business."

But why doesn't he make the food for the party?" I asked. "If he did, he'd make some money."

"Yes, but it's not that simple," Francine said. "Apparently, he owes his suppliers and they won't extend any more credit to him until his bills are paid. The money he would make from the party wouldn't begin to cover his debts. And the reason he owes his suppliers is because he has extended credit to his customers and they haven't paid him. It's a common story," she added. "People lose their businesses and their jobs and can't pay their bills, so more businesses fail and more people lose their jobs. It's a terrible spiral. I don't know where it will end."

I thought of Aunt Ruby and her stack of IOUs. I hoped the Paradise Diner was still open for business. "Will these people be able to pay you?" I asked. I flushed with embarrassment as soon as the words left my lips. "I'm sorry," I said. "I didn't mean to ask about your business. It's just...well, I wouldn't want you to get stiffed either."

Francine leaned over the table and patted my forearm. "Don't worry," she said. "As you know, there are some people in Auburn who barely know that there's a depression, and Mrs. Davis is one of them. Besides, I got half in advance. It's a big job."

"Good. So what do we need to make?"

"Oh, about twenty-five quiches," Francine said. "By tonight."

"Wow, that's a lot, but I suppose if we get started right now, we could do it."

"And twenty-five lemon-raisin pies for dessert," Francine said. A hint of a smile formed at the corner of her lips.

"Fifty pies! Is that even possible?"

"Let's hope so," Francine said. "Or I'm in deep trouble." She stood up from the table. "Let's get started on piecrust. Phillipe is out buying ingredients. We'll do the quiche first and then tackle the raisin pies."

We were up to our elbows in dough and were streaked and splotched with flour when Phillipe returned, lugging in bottles of cream and grocery sacks heavy with cheese and eggs and bacon. Francine assigned rolling out pie crusts to me and charged Phillipe with frying and crumbling the bacon. She grated mounds of cheese and then cracked eggs into a mixing bowl with a quick precision that filled the bowl with bobbing yellow rounds that were soon beaten into froth. We lined up pie pans and assembled the quiches, squeezing as many as possible into the oven without damaging the fluted crusts. While we waited for the first batch to bake, we started on more piecrusts for the lemon-raisin pies.

Francine worked on the lattices, cutting strip after strip of dough and weaving them onto the pies, then carefully fluting the edges. "*Merde!* she said when she had fifteen tops finished. "Ten more to go. I don't know what I was thinking when I put lattice tops on these pies!"

"You were probably thinking that they looked nice," Phillipe laughed.

"Well, they would look just as nice with solid tops—or none at all!"

"Too late for that," Phillipe teased. "You've taught your customers to expect plaid."

By late afternoon, we were dusted with flour and sticky from eggs and raisin filling. The all-day heat coming from the oven raised the temperature in the kitchen to just short of unbearable, and I thought I never again wanted to smell the sweet odor of baking raisins. Finally, I carried the last two pies into the parlor and set them at one end of the long table to cool. I looked down the rows of pies, amazed that we had made so many in one day. The pies closest to me were the quiches; their pale yellow tops were speckled with bits of herbs and pieces of bacon, and each one was circled by a toasty tanned crust. My eyes followed the rings, traveled down the table, and then stopped at the cross-hatching formed by the lattice tops of the raisin pies. The lattices were going every which way, giving this group a wild look, like a wheat field hit by gusty winds that bent rivers of wheat in several directions at once and then froze them in position. I was tempted to arrange the pies so they'd line up neatly, to see what other kind of pattern would be created with the lattices. But before I could move, I heard Francine's voice near my ear.

"They're beautiful, aren't they," she said. "All that's left to do is pack them up and deliver them. This batch of pies will help keep the wolf from the door, for a little while, at least. Oh! We still need the recipe cards."

"You're going to put the recipe with these, too? But Mrs. Davis has it already," I said.

"Yes, but her guests don't," Francine said. She ducked into her office and returned with a thick stack of recipe cards, laying them on the table next to the pies. "I want to be sure that *every* guest gets the recipe for Francine's Lemon-Raisin Pie."

"I've never known a baker who does what you do," I said. "Giving out recipes like that. I know you want to sell raisins, but it still seems like there's a way you could do that without cutting into pie sales."

Francine shrugged. "My grandfather planted grapes that everyone said wouldn't grow here, and I give out my specialty recipe and everyone says I shouldn't." She laughed. "Being contrary is a family tradition, it seems. But, it has worked for the Durrands—so far, at least."

Phillipe called from the side door, "The truck's ready to go. Are the pies?"

"Almost," Francine called back. "Come and help us."

We wrapped, stacked, and packed the pies into cardboard boxes and carried them out to Phillipe's 1927 Model T Ford. A handmade cap of varnished wood covered the bed, offering some protection for the cargo. *Durrand Vineyards* had once been painted in black letters on the wooden sides of the cover, but the paint had faded and was hard to read. I guessed that after the Depression started, no one had bothered with fresh paint.

We fitted the boxes of pies, very carefully, into the bed of the truck. Then the three of us squashed into the front seat, and Francine and I each held two pies that wouldn't fit anywhere else.

"You had better drive *very, very* cautiously, little brother!" Francine said as Phillipe backed out of the drive. I moved my legs to give Phillipe enough room to operate the shifter. "If you have to stop suddenly, there will be a mess such as you've never seen."

"And you and Maddy would have pies in the face," Phillipe agreed.

I giggled, imagining the consequences of Phillipe slamming on the brakes, and then Francine and Phillipe started laughing, too. We were slaphappy—enjoying the silliness that can come from working hard all day with people you like.

"Eggs and raisins everywhere!" Francine declared. "Can you imagine the back of the truck?"

"Mrs. Davis would have to serve the main course and dessert all at the same time," I said.

"True," Phillipe laughed. "Her guests would have to sort it out—from the bed of my truck!"

"They could line up, plates in hand, and scoop out whatever appealed to them," I added.

"No waiting for dessert," Phillipe said. "Everyone could go home early!"

"Poor Mrs. Davis would never recover! But it would be a memorable anniversary party, wouldn't it?" Francine gasped, between peals of laughter. "Oh, please. We must stop! I can't keep a grip on these pies under these conditions." She took a deep breath and tried to put on a serious face. I tried to be serious, too, especially because I was afraid if we kept it up I might drop a pie.

On South Street, we turned into a white gravel driveway that led up to a large, red brick house with green shutters. I remembered the house, but I couldn't recall what the owner looked like. Within seconds, though, a plump, dark-haired woman about Francine's age burst through the front door. I remembered her then; she had been one of my first customers. Today she was dressed for her party. She wore a red skirt and a red-and-white patterned sweater and new red pumps. A string of pearls around her neck and matching pearl earrings accented the white in her sweater.

"I can't tell you how grateful I am," Mrs. Davis said to Francine. She motioned to several women standing just inside the front door. "Ladies," she said. "The pies have arrived." Mrs. Davis's tone left no doubt that the ladies were expected to unload the truck. Three women, dressed in black skirts and white blouses, hurried out. They took the pies Francine and I held, and then they started to carry the rest of the pies into the house. I recognized two of the women as Francine's next-door neighbors. I wondered if Francine had helped Mrs. Davis hire the women to serve the food at her party. I couldn't imagine how else Mrs. Davis would have known them.

Phillipe and I helped unload, too, while Francine and Mrs. Davis talked. Phillipe lifted one box that we must have overloaded with pies, because it looked heavier than the others. I hoped the pies hadn't gotten damaged.

"Thank you so much!" Mrs. Davis said to Francine as the last box was carried into the house. "My guests may think it's odd that for dinner we're having two kinds of pie, but they won't know how close they came to having no dinner at all!"

"I am sure your parents will be pleased that you remembered their anniversary," Francine said. "And perhaps some of your guests would like the recipe for my Lemon-Raisin Pie." She held out the stack of recipe cards.

"Oh, yes. We did discuss that, didn't we?" Mrs. Davis said. "I'll be sure that these are put in a basket near the door so that everyone who wants one can take one. Kind of a party favor, don't you think?" she said. Mrs. Davis handed a fat envelope to Francine. "Thank you again. You saved my party!"

Phillipe, Francine, and I jammed ourselves back into the Ford, which was still full of the savory smell of pies. "Well, that was quite a day's work!" Francine said. "Phillipe, are you staying here through the weekend, or do you have to get back to the vineyard?"

"There's still a lot to be done in the vineyard before winter hits," Phillipe said. "I should go back tomorrow."

Francine nodded. "I thought as much. Too bad you can't stay a little longer, though."

I only half listened to the conversation. I knew that none of it would make any difference to me. I expected to be on my way tomorrow or, if I was lucky, Monday. I thought about Henry and remembered what he had said about hobos. If there was no more work for me here, I had to keep moving. As much as I had come to like these people, I wouldn't take a handout—I wouldn't be a bum.

Francine and I walked back into the house and Phillipe went into the garage to find a broom to sweep out pie crumbs from the truck. Inside, Francine made a beeline for the stairs. "I'm going to go upstairs to take a little nap before dinner," she announced. "Feel free to do the same," she said to me. "This was a long day!"

I was tired, too, but felt too restless to nap. Instead, I surveyed the kitchen. We had cleaned up while the last pies were baking, but some crumbs remained on the counter. I grabbed a sponge and wiped up and then went into the parlor to wipe off the tables that had held the pies. One of Francine's recipe cards had fallen under a table and I bent to retrieve it. It was smudged with someone's footprint and I brushed off the dirt and inspected it to see if it could still be used. For the first time, I read through the entire recipe.

Francine's Lemon-Raisin Pie

2 cups raisins

1 cup sugar

2 Tbsp. lemon juice

2 tsp. grated lemon rind

2 Tbsp. cornstarch

1½ c. water

1 Tbsp. butter

Directions:
Cook raisins and water together until raisins are tender. Dissolve cornstarch in a little cold water and add to the raisins along with the sugar, lemon juice, and the grated lemon rind. Cook until thick and bubbly. Stir in butter. Remove from heat. Fill a 9″ pastry-lined pie pan with the raisin mixture. Top with lattice crust. Bake at 375 degrees for 30-40 minutes, covering the pie crust edges with strips of tinfoil to prevent burning.

Caution: Bricks of raisins may be purchased from Durrand Vineyard for use in your favorite recipes. The raisins can be placed in water for purposes of softening and plumping. However, do not add sugar and put the liquid into a stoppered jug, as fermentation will occur, resulting in wine after approximately 60 days.

Phillipe's voice startled me. "What is it you find so interesting?" he asked. I looked up to see him leaning against the door frame.

"It's Francine's recipe card," I stammered. "I never read the entire recipe before." *A party favor*, Mrs. Davis had called the big stack of recipes Francine brought for her guests. Francine was using her pies to advertise for Durrand's real customers—home winemakers.

Phillipe studied me carefully. "Did you learn something about my sister's pies that you didn't know before?"

I considered Phillipe's question. What I knew about the Durrands was kind of like dabs of paint on a palette. The colors are there, but if you blend a couple of them, you get a new color that you didn't have before. And maybe one that you weren't expecting.

"Not really," I said. "I just figured out that Francine wasn't kidding when she said she hates making lattice crusts."

Supper that evening was simple, quick, and quiet. Phillipe stood at the stove, making omelets with eggs and cheese left over from the day's baking. "It's my specialty," he said. "Francine has her pies and quiches. I have my omelet."

"I don't think it counts as a specialty if it's the *only* thing you know how to make," Francine said. She was smiling, but she sat at the table with her head propped up by her right arm. Even in the dim light, the dark circles under her eyes were noticeable.

"But it's *not* the only thing I know how to make," Phillipe said, pretending to be offended. "You underestimate me, Francine."

"Is that so! And what else have you mastered in the kitchen?" Francine asked.

"Toast," Phillipe said. "I make perfect buttered toast. Sometimes I even serve it with jelly!"

Both Francine and I burst out laughing. "Really!" Francine said with mock seriousness. "Oh, I do hope you're not too tired tonight to make perfect buttered toast for us. It would be the just the thing to accompany your specialty omelet."

Phillipe did indeed make toast for us, although it came out a little too dark on one side. He held the toast over the sink and scraped the black parts off with a table knife. "It's not really burned," he explained. "It's just browned. And it's not my fault, either. It's a toaster problem." He put a plate of scraped toast on the table and firmly set the butter dish and a jar of grape jelly down next to it. "Just slather on a spoonful of jelly and you'll never know the difference."

Phillipe brought the omelets to the table and the conversation stopped as we dug into steaming, folded crescents of eggs oozing with melted cheese. After a few minutes, Francine spoke. "Very tasty, Phillipe," she said. I took a large forkful of my omelet and nodded in agreement. I was also happy that we weren't eating quiche that evening.

"You might even consider branching out," she added. "*French* toast would be a nice addition."

"A related dish, but not too far afield." Phillipe said. "I'll consider it."

"Still a form of toast," Francine said, "but you would eliminate the toaster problem."

Phillipe made a face and Francine chuckled. I was beginning to see that she liked to have the last word, not only with Mrs. Hunter, but when she was joking with her brother, too.

We finished eating in silence, too tired to carry on any more conversation.

"I'll do the dishes," I said, gathering up our plates.

Francine pushed her chair back and stood up slowly. "I won't argue," she said. "I'm really tired. I think I'll take a nice hot bath and go to bed early. Thank you, both. I never could have done this today without you." She headed for the stairs. "Good night, sleep tight," she called as she was halfway up.

Phillipe carried a stack of dishes over to the sink. "Wash or dry?" he said.

"Pardon me?"

"Do you prefer to wash or dry? I don't care which, so you choose."

For a moment I was speechless as it dawned on me that Phillipe was planning to help with the dishes. The only men I knew who ever did dishes were the dishwashers at Paradise Diner, and they were paid to do it. Neither my father nor my Uncle George ever did dishes at home.

"Wash," I said. "But there isn't much to do, so you could go ahead upstairs, if you want. After all, you made dinner."

"You spent all day in this kitchen, too," Phillipe said. "Let's just make short work of it and we can both turn in early."

"Well, okay," I said.

It was an odd feeling to be standing at the kitchen sink, handing hot, wet dishes to Phillipe. Maybe it was because it was different to have a man stick around after dinner and help clean up. But it also felt comfortable, like we had known each other for a long time.

"Francine told me you came to Auburn by train," Phillipe said as he took a dinner plate to wipe. I nodded, and before I could even wonder how much Francine had said, Phillipe asked, "It's true that you were hopping freights?"

"Yes."

"It seems pretty dangerous for a young girl," Phillipe said.

I shrugged. "I had plenty of company. There's a lot of homeless people riding the rails, looking for work. Families with children are hopping freights, too. You mostly have to avoid the railroad bulls. The bad ones don't care what happens to anybody." I decided not to mention Blackjack.

"It seems risky..."

"Not as risky as staying home." I said, cutting him off. I hadn't meant to sound sharp, but even I heard the tone in my voice. Phillipe looked at me quickly, dark eyebrows raised, but he said nothing. I turned my full attention to the plate I was washing, scrubbing it carefully and making sure every speck of egg yolk was removed. After a moment or two I spoke again, quietly this time. "Did you ever try it?"

"Hopping a freight?" he asked.

I nodded.

"No," he said. "It's never occurred to me. I've never had a reason to."

"It's the most amazing thing," I said, "to sit in the doorway of a boxcar on a moving train. There's a rhythm. You hear it and feel it and see it. You have this view of the world—it's kind of like a picture show, except you're not just watching it—you're in it, too. If you see someplace that looks interesting, you can get off the train and spend time there."

Phillipe smiled. "You make it sound very appealing. It's too bad I have to return to the vineyard tomorrow. I might be tempted to hop a freight with you."

I smiled back, trying to mask my feelings. Phillipe had just confirmed what I already knew. Tomorrow, he would return to his family's vineyard, Francine would make more lemon-raisin pies with lattice tops, and I'd be riding the rails again.

We said goodnight as soon as the dishes were done. As I undressed for bed, I heard Phillipe's footsteps travel up the stairs. I slid between the covers and listened to Phillipe move across the floor directly over my room. Then the house became quiet.

My mind, however, refused to be quiet. I lay in bed, restless, with my tired body pleading for sleep as my thoughts collided and churned. Where should I go next? Could I find a job here? It was November and getting very cold in Auburn. Should I try again to go out West to pick fruit, even though the trains were so crowded? At least it would be warmer there and easier to survive. I thought about the Durrands, too. I had grown to like them a lot in a short time. Were they breaking the law by selling raisins for making wine? Could they go to jail for what they're doing?

I tried to distract myself by concentrating on how it felt to lie in a real bed, memorizing its softness and warmth, knowing that I would be sleeping on the cold ground tomorrow night. Finally, the needs of my body won out and I fell into a deep sleep, but it seemed like only moments later I heard the sounds of Francine rattling around in the kitchen.

I laid in bed for just a little while longer, savoring its comfort. Reluctantly, I swung my legs over the edge of the mattress and got up, dressing quickly in my set of men's clothes and packing up my few belongings, making the bindle I would carry.

When I entered the kitchen, Francine was sitting at the wooden table, eating a bowl of steaming oatmeal and reading the *Auburn Advocate*. The smell of fresh coffee, punctuated by the pop-gurgle-pop of the percolator, wafted through the room. A quick pang of sadness stabbed me. *I will miss this*, I thought.

"Good morning, Maddy," Francine said without looking up. "There's oatmeal on the stove and the coffee is almost done. Help yourself." She shook her head, obviously disgusted at what she was reading. "Prohibition laws cause such a waste of taxpayers' money. It's outrageous to spend government resources like this when so many people are out of work! Just listen to this: seventy-five federal agents raided the docks in Brooklyn and sixty men were arrested for smuggling liquor that..." She stopped talking abruptly when she finally looked up at me. "Oh! You're wearing men's clothes today."

I nodded. "I've packed up everything else."

She set down the newspaper as I sat down across from her with my bowl of oatmeal. "You're leaving today?"

"Yes, I guess so. Right after breakfast."

Francine was silent, then she slowly pushed an envelope across the table toward me. "I think you'll need this, then. It's some money for all the work you did yesterday."

"Thank you. I'm sure it will be a big help." I looked at the envelope. Francine had prepared it before I even woke up, which confirmed that there was no more work for me here, that she also expected me to be on my way. I let my thoughts settle around the idea of moving on.

"So—where are you going?" Francine asked.

I shrugged. "I'm still trying to decide. Wherever I can find a job, I suppose."

Francine stared at me for a long minute. "Maddy, I must admit that I'm a little surprised. I know I haven't been able to pay you very much, but I thought you were fairly content with our arrangement."

"I was...I am...I'm very grateful that you let me stay here," I said. "I liked helping in your bakery."

"Then why are you leaving?"

I was speechless for a minute. "Because I thought you and Phillipe wanted me to!" I blurted out. "I thought you didn't have any more work for me."

"Why would you think that?" she asked. "What did Phillipe say? For that matter, what did I say that gave you the impression that I wanted you to leave?"

"Well, it was...I don't know..." I stopped. Phillipe had said, *It's too bad I have to return to the vineyard tomorrow. I might be tempted to hop a freight with you.* I took that to mean that he expected I'd be leaving tomorrow. "You mean you *don't* want me to go?"

"*Au contraire*," Francine said. "I was hoping that you would stay. You have helped my business grow. Pie sales have increased, and so have sales of our raisins." She grinned, pausing for emphasis. "By the way, Phillipe tells me that you now fully understand the importance of raisins." She tapped the envelope that still lay on the table. "I'm afraid I can't offer you any more money than what I have been paying, but if room and board and a small sales commission still suits you, I would like it if you would stay."

"It suits me *perfectly*," I said. In fact, I thought I might burst from happiness. "Thank you!"

I unpacked my few possessions and settled back into what was now truly "my room," at least as long as I contributed to Francine's bakery business. I pondered the two things I had learned that morning: Don't assume anything, and—a stroke of good luck can make you positively giddy.

CHAPTER 27

Frosting became my paint, and cake became my canvas. Francine taught me how to shape roses and violets and add piping to cakes. I learned quickly, and in return, I tried to teach Francine a little about drawing. The cake Mrs. Hunter had ordered for the church volunteers got a lot of attention, and Francine started getting orders for cakes decorated with scenes from Enna Jetticks Park, Owasco Lake, or a child's favorite doll. Francine tried sometimes, but her efforts usually added to my job security.

Most afternoons, I packed a selection of her pies into the Liberty Coaster and took them up South Street and neighboring blocks to sell them. Sometimes, when I just felt like moving, I walked into town, even when the November winds became sharp and brutal. On one of those days, I stopped into the Auburn post office.

"I'm checking to see if you have any letters for me," I said to the clerk. "My name is Maddy Skobel."

"Just a minute, please," he said, and he disappeared into the back. After a couple of minutes he returned, holding two letters. "Here you go, Miss. One letter has been waiting here for a week or so, and the other just arrived yesterday."

I could hardly contain my excitement. I turned the letters over to read the return addresses. One was from Rita, and the other was from—my mother! My heart leapt into my throat. I hurried past the wall of brass letterboxes and out the door of the building. A cold gust of wind nearly tore the letters from my hand as I stepped out onto Genesee Street. I wanted to sit right there on the stone steps of the post office and read the letters, but I was a little worried about what my mother had to say. Her letter was a little thicker than the one from Rita. I stuffed both letters into my pocket and rushed back to the privacy of my room at Francine's. I sat on my bed for a minute and stared at the handwriting on the letters. *Miss Maddy Skobel, General Delivery, Auburn, New York.* Rita's handwriting was large and loopy, in contrast to my mother's, which was small, precise, and neat. I wondered how it happened that whenever we put marks on paper, whether it's handwriting or drawing, part of us shows on paper, too, even if we don't mean it to.

I put off knowing for a few more minutes what my mother had written, and I opened Rita's letter first. Rita's large scrawl filled the lines of a single sheet of notebook paper:

November 5, 1931

Dear Maddy,

I was glad to get your postcard. I'm happy you found a place to live! The Lighthouse Hotel is okay. It's a job, but I don't make much money. I guess people don't have much to spare, so the tips are pretty measly. After I pay my room and board, there isn't much left over. My cousin Irene and I might go to Watertown next week. They're going to have a dance marathon there and the winner gets $500. Can you imagine that much money?!! My aunt says dance contests aren't for respectable girls, but the one in Watertown is sponsored by the American Legion. How bad could that be?

Write again soon!

Rita

I was glad that Rita had made it to Pulaski, but I was sorry she wasn't making much money to send home. I guess Rita, like me, was just lucky to have found some kind of job and a place to stay. I smiled at the thought of Rita being in a dance marathon. It was exactly the kind of thing she would do. She wasn't afraid to try anything.

I set Rita's letter on my bed and picked up my mother's letter. Was she mad at me? I couldn't guess. Finally, I tore it open and began to read:

November 11, 1931

Dear Maddy,

I am so glad you are safe. I've been very worried. I wish you hadn't left the way you did. You should have talked to me first. Raymond says he doesn't know anything about what happened

*the night you left. He says he finished up first and you were still
working when he went home. He says you never liked him and
you're trying to make everyone suspicious of him. He says you
always blame him for everything. I wish I knew for sure what
happened, but I think Raymond is lying about not knowing anything. Ruby said that since we don't know the facts, she doesn't
want to take sides, but she admits that Raymond has been more
trouble than she expected. I'm counting on Ruby and George
deciding to send him back to Chicago.*

*It's probably best that you don't come home for a little while,
if you have someplace to stay. Your father is still in jail, and will
be for a while, and he has to pay a fine, too. I don't think we'll
be able to stay in the house, so Eddie and I will probably move in
with Ruby. You know she doesn't have a lot of room, and Raymond
is still there for now, so—*

I'll write again when things are better.

*Love,
Mom*

My head swam as I read her letter. But there was another page behind
it, and when I turned to it, I recognized Eddie's scratchy, clumsy writing.
Tears welled up unexpectedly in my eyes, and I blinked them back so
I could read:

*Dear Maddy,
    Mom said I could put my letter with hers but I have to be
quick about it.*

*Why did you leave? Mom said you had to go away for a
little while but you'll come back. When are you coming home? I
wish you would hurry up. Things aren't very good around here.
The school is still closed, maybe forever- who knows - and there's
nothing to do but hang around the diner and work. Mom and
Aunt Ruby have kind of been fighting ever since you left, but I*

don't know about what. Mom said I have to help out by washing
dishes because Raymond is probably going back to Chicago as soon
as he gets better. He got a bad infection in his leg and also got into
trouble at the rail yard. He got into a fight with someone but he got
the worst of it. Raymond said it wasn't a fair fight.

    I miss you. Come home soon.

Love,
Eddie

    I folded the letters and put them back into their envelopes. I still
wasn't sure whether my mother was mad at me. At least she had said she
was worried and was glad I was safe. But then, she also said she didn't
think I should come home. It was confusing. Anger welled up inside me as
I thought about Raymond. I should have known he would deny everything
and blame me, to boot. But I had left my torn clothes in the bathroom. My
mother could see that something had happened! Now I was angry that she
didn't stand up for me with Raymond.

    One sentence Eddie wrote about Raymond got me wondering: *He got a*
*bad infection in his leg...*I hoped that infection came from the fork I stabbed
Raymond with. It served him right if it did. I hoped it hurt him plenty.
I hoped it would leave a scar—forever.

    I borrowed some envelopes and paper from the desk in the pantry
and tried to write back to my mother. I held my pen ready, but I didn't
know what to say. I pushed the paper aside and picked up an envelope
and addressed it. *Mrs. Iris Skobel, c/o Paradise Diner, New Harmony, Ohio.*
Maybe if my brain knew for sure that I was writing to my mother, it
would send out some words. I picked up the paper again and waited.
Dear Mom, I'm sorry you were worried, I wrote. Well, that's not exactly
true, I thought. I was glad she was worried. I waited to see what else my
brain would come up with. *I'm happy that you're getting rid of Raymond,*
my brain offered. *Not a good way to start a letter,* I said back. Besides,
there was no guarantee that Aunt Ruby and Uncle George would agree
to send Raymond back to Chicago. *I'm sorry that my father is still in jail,*

my brain said. *No I'm not, everybody's better off when he's not home.* I sighed. This wasn't going well.

I ripped up the letter and picked up my sketchpad. Drawing usually had a side effect of letting me clear my mind, and my mind definitely needed clearing right now. Sitting on my bed, I drew the chair in the corner of my room and the window to the right of it. Outside the window was an oak tree that still had a few brown leaves stubbornly clinging to it. I drew that, too, and behind it, the sturdy old garage that belonged to the house across the street. The angles of the hip roof gave the garage the look of a little cottage. I studied the drawing for a minute, added some shading to the wooden chair, and then I tore the page out of my sketchpad, folded it neatly, and slid it into the envelope addressed to my mother. I took it back out and in the bottom right-hand corner, I wrote *My room. Love, Maddy.* Then I stuffed it back into the envelope, licked the flap, and glued it shut. I added Eddie's name to the front, right under my mother's. Tomorrow I'd walk to the post office and mail the letter.

CHAPTER 28

"I'm going to a meeting tonight of the Allied Citizens," Francine announced as we put lattice-topped pies in the oven. "Would you let Phillipe know? He should be here early this evening."

"Sure," I said, perking up at the information about Phillipe. His work at the vineyard had kept him away from Auburn for the past couple of weeks. Francine was plenty lively all by herself, but it was even more fun when Phillipe was here. "What's the Allied Citizens?"

"It's a group of drys who want to see to it that Prohibition is fully enforced—even strengthened."

I stared at Francine in disbelief. "Why in the world would you want to go to *their* meeting?" I wondered if she had suddenly "got religion." Aunt Ruby had said that about my father once when he quit drinking for a couple of days after getting hold of some bad gin. "I thought you said Prohibition was a stupid law."

"It *is* a stupid law," Francine said. "And it has had some terrible, unintended consequences. I intend to fight for Prohibition's repeal, but the first order of business is to Know Thine Enemy." Francine said these last three words with such emphasis that I knew they were a rule, something like Do Unto Others.

"Oh, so you're going to spy on them?" I asked, grinning.

"Something like that," Francine chuckled. "Although I can hardly be a spy when it's well known in Auburn that my family owns a vineyard. But the more we know about the Allied Citizens' strategy, the easier it will be to form a plan to defeat them." She leaned toward me and added in a near whisper, "At the very least, seeing me sitting in their meeting might make them nervous!" Her musical laugh filled the kitchen.

I delivered pies that afternoon to houses at the north end of South Street and then headed over to Genesee Street to the post office to mail my letter. I didn't really expect that I would have more mail, but I checked anyway; to my surprise, the clerk came out of the back with a letter from Rita. The postmark showed she had mailed it just a few days ago. I tucked the letter into my jacket pocket. After supper I'd find out what Rita was up to.

Francine left early in the evening. "I'm off to 'spy on the drys,' as you put it," she said, grinning. "Please tell Phillipe that I hope to be back by eight."

"Will do. Have fun!" I figured the drys were in for a little trouble tonight.

I brought my sketchpad and Rita's letter into the kitchen, made myself a cup of tea, and settled onto a chair at the kitchen table. I switched on the floor lamp that stood in the corner by the table, and then I tore open the letter and read it in the dim light.

November 13, 1931

Dear Maddy,

It's Friday the 13th and I've had some good luck! You'll never believe this – I got into the dance contest and I'm writing to you while I'm dancing! They have this writing desk contraption that you hang on your neck, so you can write and dance at the same time. They said the audience likes to see things like that. A photographer came and took a picture of me, so I might get my picture in the paper. I was writing to you when the flashbulb popped, so if they print my picture, you'll kind of be in the paper too!

I hate to admit it, but after the first couple of hours, the excitement pretty much wore off. It started to get a little boring, so when they offered the writing desk, it sounded like a good idea. So I guess I'll tell you all about the marathon and that will help pass the time until I win that $500. I hope you can read my writing, though. I have to keep moving. Me and my partner (his name is David – he's a friend of my cousin's boyfriend) have to keep picking up our feet or the floor judge could blow the whistle and disqualify us. One of the other experienced couples, Couple No. 15—their names are Carol and Gregory, said we should conserve our energy during the day, though. They said judges don't care so much what *you do during the day, but at night, when the audience is bigger, they expect you to really dance. They charge people twenty-five cents just to watch, and you better give them a show. Sometimes people in the audience even pick their favorite couple and bet on them.*

We have to dance for 45 minutes, and then we get a 15-minute rest period. You can sleep, but if you want to wash up or go to the bathroom, you have to do it during your rest time. They bring food out onto the dance floor every so often, and you can eat so long as you dance while you stand by the tables. At least they feed us. By the looks of the some of the other couples, they haven't had much to eat lately, and they're glad to see the food being brought out. That was one good thing about working at the hotel. I had plenty to eat, even if tips weren't so great.

Tomorrow night they said they were going to start the Sprints. I'm not sure what that is, but Carol and Gregory said it's like a race and we should pace ourselves during the day. We're coming up to a rest period and my legs are tired, so I'm going to stop writing for now. Root for Couple No. 11—that's me and David, if you couldn't tell, ha ha — (and Couple No. 10, too. That's Irene and her boyfriend.)

—Rita

I folded the letter and pushed it back into the envelope. The crackling of the paper echoed loudly in the empty kitchen, as if the sound was bouncing off the darkness in the corners of the room. Rita was dancing right now, even as I sat drinking tea, and she had already been dancing for several days. If anyone had the guts to win that marathon, it would be Rita. I was positive about that.

I turned the envelope over. It was postmarked in Watertown. She didn't say if I could write back. I got an envelope and paper from the pantry office. *Miss Rita Boyle, c/o American Legion Dance Marathon, Watertown, New York,* I wrote. Surely the post office could find her if they wanted to.

November 17, 1931

Dear Rita,

   I hope the mailman finds you to give you this letter, and you're still dancing like crazy. $500 is a lot of money—I sure hope you win! How is your cousin doing?

   I'm still in Auburn and it seems like I'll have a job here for a while. I hope through the winter. I'm working in the bakery and selling pies in the neighborhood. I have my own room and plenty to eat.

   Write soon if you can!

   I'm rooting for couple number 11—and couple number 10, too.

—Maddy

I sealed the letter and set it off to the side; I pulled my sketchpad in front of me and looked around for something to draw. The kitchen was too neat. Everything had been put away. I got a wooden bowl filled with apples that was sitting on the counter, pulled out several spices from Francine's spice rack, grabbed a fat wooden rolling pin we used for pie crusts, and reached into a drawer for a clean dishtowel. The dishtowel was to challenge me—fabric is hard to draw. I arranged the items, taking one apple and setting it in front of the bowl of apples. I added the sugar bowl and an empty creamer to the still life. I studied the arrangement for a minute and then lifted the lid off the sugar bowl and set it on the table. Still too static. Finally, I tipped the creamer onto its side. It rocked softly for a moment and then rested on its lip.

"That'll do for now," I said, sitting down to draw. I quickly sketched in the wooden bowl and the roundness of the apples, then the sugar bowl—its lid interrupting the dark grain of the wooden table. I took more time to draw the dishtowel, trying to hint at the weave of the material and getting the folds of the fabric just right. Then I sketched in the creamer laying on its side, and on a whim, I drew a pool of spilled cream spreading across the table, seeping around the sugar bowl and heading for the dishtowel.

"Ah...the artist at work," said a familiar voice.

I jumped what felt like three feet off my chair. "Do you *always* have to sneak in?" I said to Phillipe. "Couldn't you clomp your way into the kitchen to let somebody know you were coming?"

Phillipe grinned. "My apologies. I really didn't mean to startle you, although I seem to be pretty good at it." He strode across the kitchen and sat down across the table from me. He peered over the bowl of apples to see what I had drawn and he burst into laughter. "That's an interesting still life you have there."

I knew right away he wasn't laughing *at* my drawing. His laughter was warm, even gratifying. "Some problems find their own solutions, don't they?" he said. "Too bad all spills don't happen with a towel nearby." He leaned back in the chair. "Where's Francine?"

"She said to tell you she'd be back by eight. She went to spy on the drys."

Phillipe raised his eyebrows. "Really! I heard there was going to be a meeting."

I nodded. "Tonight. 'Know Thine Enemy,' Francine said."

Phillipe nodded. "That sounds like my sister." He took an apple from the bowl and bit into it.

"Hey, you're wrecking my still life!" I protested.

"I'm just changing it a bit—that's all," Phillipe said.

"Well, if you're going to continue to sit there, you're going to become part of it, too," I said.

Phillipe shrugged. "Be my guest."

I hesitated for a moment, and then I turned my sketchpad to a fresh page. I sketched in the table, the bowl, and a quick approximation of the apples. Then I started on Phillipe. I drew the shape of his face and the angle of his shoulders, then started on his eyes. His dark brown lashes gave his blue-gray eyes an intensity that at first made me feel very self-conscious. I was drawing eyes that were watching me draw. As I moved away from Phillipe's direct gaze, I became more comfortable. I added his full eyebrows, his straight nose, and his mouth. His lips curved into a hint of a smile, which brought out the dimple in his right cheek that I had noticed the first time I met him. The kitchen lamp cast a dim light that made striking shadows on Phillipe's face. I used the side of the pencil point to apply broad strokes, shading under his cheekbone. I had just started shaping his angular jaw line when the back door clicked open and closed, and Francine came huffing into the kitchen.

"Those people give me a headache!" she said. "I suppose they are well meaning, but they are so self-righteous they simply refuse to consider any other point of view. And they surely refuse to see the facts that are staring them in the face!"

"Well, no one can see *anything* staring them in the face if they keep their eyes tightly shut," Phillipe said. "Isn't that about what you expected? Conserve your energy, Francine. This will not be an easy fight."

"I know that, but it's maddening!" She blew out a sharp puff of air, as if she could expel all her frustration through one breath.

"What happened?" I asked. I was disappointed that Francine was upset. That meant that the drys had given Francine trouble, not the reverse.

Francine paused to look at me, Phillipe, the odd arrangement on the kitchen table, and my sketchpad. "You know," she said, "I really don't want to relive the meeting again tonight. I see that you were drawing. Why don't you get back to what you were doing, and I will fill you in tomorrow with all the infuriating details. I do *truly* have a headache and I think I'd like to go to bed."

Francine's footsteps became fainter as she went upstairs. Phillipe turned toward me. "Please finish," he said, nodded toward my sketchpad.

"You're sure?"

"Yes, of course. I want to see what I look like through your eyes."

His comment flustered me for a moment. I tried to cover it up by picking up my pencil and drawing again. I cleared my throat and attempted a diversion. "Do you think Prohibition will ever be overturned?" I asked.

"I hope so," he said. "But I'm afraid it will be a long, long battle. Alcohol is a problem for some people, that is very true, but the drys are trying to fix one mess by creating another. They're turning decent people into criminals, and for what?"

As he talked, I added shading to Phillipe's cheekbones, neck, and shoulders, drawing his open shirt collar and the U-shape indentation that formed where his collar bones met. I returned to his head and sketched in his hair. Finally, I erased some of the pencil shading in his hair, which had the effect of adding highlights.

"People will not stop drinking because the Volstead Act requires it, and the law will not stop some people from drinking to excess. Drunks will always find a way to get drunk," Phillipe said.

"I know," I said. "My father is one of them."

Phillipe looked steadily at me for a minute. "I'm sorry, Maddy, about your father."

"I am, too," I said. I studied my drawing. I couldn't believe I had so easily told him about my father. I looked over at Phillipe and back at my drawing. Phillipe's face gazed at me from both directions. "Done," I said, feeling satisfied that the Phillipe captured on paper reflected the Phillipe who sat across the table.

"Oh, good. Let me see," he said. He came around the table and as he bent over to get a better look, he rested his hand on my shoulder. My mind leaped wildly from one thought to another: New Harmony, Raymond, Paradise Diner, the jungle, Henry. This was the first time I had let any man touch me since the night I had gone looking for Henry in the jungle. I had resolved then that I wouldn't let what Raymond had done keep me from being close to people I cared about. I focused my thoughts on Phillipe and on my drawing, shutting off the commotion in my mind.

"It's a striking portrait—and a flattering one, I think," Phillipe said.

"I didn't draw it to be flattering," I objected, standing up to start dismantling the still life. "It's exactly how I see you."

"I wish I could draw," he said. "Then you would know exactly how I see *you*." He pulled me to him and gently kissed me, his lips soft against mine, lingering, his fingers lightly touching my face, then stroking my hair. Phillipe's touch sent a surge of warmth through my body and I kissed him back, as gently as he had kissed me. I tasted the faint, sweet flavor of apples.

I wanted to memorize how Phillipe felt, the pleasure of his closeness. But I also found that his kiss made me feel unsettled and a bit intimidated, and so I pulled away.

"I have to be up early tomorrow," I said as I scooped up the still life and quickly put everything back. "Good night, Phillipe." I could feel him watching me, but he didn't answer right away.

"Good night," he said, finally. "See you in the morning, Maddy."

CHAPTER 29

"All the infuriating details" of the meeting, as Francine had put it, were printed across several columns in the next morning's *Auburn Advocate*. "Dry Campaigners Hold Spirited Meeting," the headline announced. It was a headline I found funny after I was fully awake and could appreciate its double meaning. "Tightening of Prohibition Against Alcohol Is Stressed," said the subheading.

I was the last one up. Francine and Phillipe were both sitting at the table, sipping coffee and eating oatmeal topped with brown sugar and apple slices. Francine was reading out loud: "...more than 400 persons bowed their heads...good morning Maddy...and repeated after Rev. Wheeler, 'God help us win this fight. We vow to defeat those who would defeat the 18th Amendment. God is on our side.'"

"Good morning," I answered. I spooned oatmeal into a bowl and sat down next to Francine. Phillipe smiled at me from across the table; I smiled back, feeling shy as I thought of last night's kiss. Francine continued to read. "Mrs. Edward Hunter introduced the guest speaker, Doctor Robert Barrow, who is traveling to 85 cities over the winter months to organize the dry campaign."

"*Mrs. Hunter?*" Phillipe groaned. "Doesn't that figure!"

"I wasn't surprised to see that Mrs. Hunter was involved," Francine said. "But I *was* surprised at the size of the crowd. The church was packed! I had hoped, naively I now realize, that I could speak to the group, which I thought would be small, and present the facts about the unintended consequences of Prohibition." She sighed, "But the group clearly had its mind made up. I'm sorry to say that I didn't dare speak out."

"I think you would have been shouted down or even mobbed if you had tried." Phillipe said. "There will be a time for speaking out. First, we have to organize the opposition to Prohibition. If we speak as a group, our voices are more likely to be heard."

"You're right," Francine said, "but it is a monumental battle, I'm afraid." She continued to read the article, this time to herself, shaking her head in disbelief. "Now a local chapter of the Allied Citizens is forming, and guess who is heading up the Women's Division!"

"My wild guess," Phillipe said, "is Mrs. Hunter."

"Of course!" Francine said. "Well, I have just this minute decided that I will help to organize the Auburn chapter of the Women's Organization for National Prohibition Reform."

Phillipe whistled softly. "I predict that it's going to be a warm winter! If you and Mrs. Hunter go head to head, sparks are sure to fly!"

"We'll see," Francine said.

Turned out that Phillipe's predictions were right—both about the warm winter and sparks flying between Francine and Mrs. Hunter. The sparks quickly turned into fireworks. In the days that had passed since the "drys" had met, Francine, true to her word, had been busy making phone calls and writing letters—working to organize Auburn's Prohibition dissenters.

Late one afternoon, Mrs. Hunter hurried up the front walk. Both Francine and I saw her coming. "I don't think she has come for another birthday cake," Francine said, muttering under her breath. I beat a hasty retreat into the kitchen and Francine waited in the parlor.

"Hel-lo, Fran-cine," Mrs. Hunter greeted her. "I do hope you have some of your quiches left today. With all of my organizing for the Allied Citizens," she gushed, "I just didn't have time to prepare dinner tonight!"

"I understand completely," Francine said. "With all the Prohibition activity going on in Auburn, I barely have time to bake my usual number of pies."

"Francine, I can't tell you how delighted—and surprised—I was to see you at the meeting the other night. It's wonderful that despite your family's past...um...history, you are on the side of sobriety. Perhaps you see joining the Allied Citizens as an opportunity to, well, frankly...to make amends."

"I'm afraid you assume too much, Mrs. Hunter," Francine said in a sweet, clipped tone. From the kitchen, I marveled at how both ice and fire could be present at the same time in one voice. "First, there is *nothing* in my family's history that requires making amends. My family prospered in this state through hard work—cultivating vines that thrived in this climate and making quality wines for people's *enjoyment*. I see no shame in that! Second, I came to the Allied Citizens' meeting to hear what people had to say and to present another viewpoint. But I quickly realized there was no room for dissent. Therefore, I have been spending a great deal of time these past few days organizing a chapter of the Women's Organization for National Prohibition Reform. Perhaps you would like to come to a meeting to hear another view of Prohibition?"

"I have no interest in your meeting and I'm sorry to hear that you're involved in such a thing!" Mrs. Hunter snapped. "And frankly, Francine, you can consider this pie as the last one I'll be buying from you—until you come to your senses."

"Mrs. Hunter," Francine said. "Again, you are quite mistaken. You can consider the pies you bought several days ago as the last ones you'll be buying from me. These pies are not for sale!"

I waited, barely breathing, to hear what would happen next. There was a moment of utter silence followed by footsteps—foot*stomps*, actually, traveling across the parlor—followed by the slamming of the front door. A minute later, Francine stormed into the kitchen. *"Merde, merde, MERDE!"* she said, and she plopped onto a wooden chair. "Maddy, we're going to have to find some new customers...to replace the ones I'm sure to lose when Mrs. Hunter finishes telling her friends about this incident."

"Well, at least you won't lose many customers from the rich people on South Street," I said. "They buy a lot of raisins."

She chuckled. "They do, don't they? Well, we'll just have to see." She shrugged, as if a quick little shoulder movement could shake off any trouble Mrs. Hunter was sure to cause. "So...do you have a taste for quiche for supper tonight? I just happen to have extra."

Phillipe listened intently as Francine and I took turns telling him about the afternoon's showdown. "Very impressive, Francine," Phillipe said. "You'll pay a price for that confrontation, though."

"I know. Mrs. Hunter can be spiteful when someone crosses her, but she stepped over the line when she insulted our family and suggested that

we had something to be ashamed of! Anyway, I'm not easily intimidated,"
Francine said. "I'm already working on a plan. There are many people
in Auburn who don't support Prohibition and won't be sympathetic to
Mrs. Hunter."

"We can find more customers," I said. "I'm sure of it. I'll just have to
walk farther." I was a little worried—I didn't want the lack of sales to cause
me to lose "my" room. But I remembered something Francine said when
I first came here. "You said the bakery doesn't provide your only income,
right? So it's okay if finding new customers takes a little time?"

Francine and Phillipe exchanged glances. "The bakery helps out,"
Phillipe said. "But mostly we depend on selling grapes and juice from the
vineyard. And raisins, of course."

He started to say more, but Francine stood up suddenly, pushing her
chair back noisily over the wooden floor. "I nearly forgot about the quiche,"
she said. "I put it into the oven to warm. I don't want it to dry out! I hope
you two are ready for supper."

Phillipe looked a little amused. I waited, expecting him to tease
Francine about her quiche or Mrs. Hunter, but instead, he disappeared into
the cellar and returned with a bottle of wine. "Tonight, let's celebrate my
sister's mettle." He poured three glasses and then lifted his for a toast. "To
Francine," he said, as the three of us touched glasses.

Unlike the other two wines I had tasted at the Durrand's, this wine
was nearly clear, but tinged with pale gold. I took a little sip and paused to
enjoy its warming effect. "This smells so...grapey! It tastes fruity, too, and
it's a little sweeter than the other wines," I said.

"Right again!" Francine said. "It's our Riesling, which is a fruity
white wine, and it does have a touch of sweetness." She took another sip.
"Mmmm. This one has mellowed so nicely!" She turned the bottle to look
closely at the label. "1917," she said, sighing. "Fourteen years ago! I hope
we can defeat Prohibition soon so we can legally make these wines again."

That night, as I drifted off to sleep, a low murmur wedged its way into
that narrow place between slumber and consciousness. At first the sound
was a soft hum, then it became louder, more energetic. A few words drifted

by—*trust, juice, family*—words that seemed unrelated, yet they pulled me slowly back to consciousness. With a start, I realized I was hearing an argument between Phillipe and Francine. More awake now, I tried to listen, but they had lowered their voices and I couldn't make out what was being said. I worried, feeling the unease I had always felt when I heard my parents argue—knowing that things weren't as they should be and I had no say. My heart sank, and I wondered if I would soon be riding the rails again.

The voices stopped, then footsteps traveled across the floor above my head, and then there was silence—the kind of enormous stillness that fills every corner of a room and presses loudly against your ears. I lay awake in the dark, restless, unable to return to sleep. I gave up trying. I pushed off the covers, switched on the light, and pulled out my tools and the nickel I had started before I arrived in Auburn. For the next several hours, I was absorbed in the sound of metal scraping against metal. As I put the finishing touches on the nickel, sleepiness returned, and I crawled back into bed feeling that I had done one small thing to control my future. I made up my mind to work on other nickels during whatever time I had at Francine's, and then I turned my attention to the bed, memorizing how it felt so that I could remember it the next time I had to spread my blanket on the ground.

CHAPTER 30

Morning came quickly. When I joined Francine and Phillipe for breakfast, they both looked up, wished me a good morning, and returned to reading sections of the *Auburn Advocate*. I couldn't tell whether they were avoiding talking to each other, or to me, or if their silence was due to being interested in the news.

My uneasiness faded somewhat as the day unfolded. Phillipe left to return to the vineyards, which was disappointing because I really liked it when he was around, but it was also reassuring because that meant it was an ordinary day. Francine and I got to work rolling out dough for her lemon-raisin pies, and I knew I wouldn't have to pack up and go—at least not right away.

"I came down to get a drink of water late last night and your light was on," Francine said, as she cut strips of dough for the lattices. "Were you not feeling well?" She looked at me closely, and I wondered if she was really trying to determine if I heard the argument.

"I couldn't sleep, so I got up to work on...a drawing," I said. It was a half-truth, but I didn't want to explain the nickel, or its purpose. If she was already thinking about sending me on my way if she lost customers, I wasn't going to make it easier by letting her know I was preparing for it.

"Oh," Francine said, and then she got quiet again.

A cold wind pushed icy snow pellets into my face, but I kept my promise to walk farther in search of new customers. That afternoon I established a route that stretched over the western part of Auburn, walking the blocks from South Street to Division Street and then north to Genesee Street right into town.

Mrs. Hunter had wasted no time talking to her friends. At several houses, women shut the door in my face. "I'm a dry. I'll *never* buy a thing from a wet," one woman snarled as she slammed the door. "I'm not wet," I yelled back through the closed door, "I'm cold!"

Still, I managed to sell all but three pies, and I was determined to do even better tomorrow. When I came to the post office on Genesee Street

I hurried inside, more to warm up for a few minutes than expecting to find mail waiting for me, but the postmaster handed me two letters, both addressed in Rita's loopy handwriting.

I leaned against the brass letter boxes and with numb fingers, I tore the first envelope open.

November 16, 1931

Dear Maddy,

Here I am with that writing desk around my neck again. It feels heavier today than it did yesterday. Guess I'm getting a little tired. Last night I found out what the Sprints are. The orchestra, which they only have at night—in the daytime they just play records on a phonograph—plays a fast piece, like a jitterbug, and you have to dance that kind of dance exactly. If you don't dance full out, you can get disqualified. That happened to two couples last night. The man in Couple No. 19 dislocated his knee, and they had to carry him out on a stretcher. And the girl in Couple No. 6 had such a swollen ankle that she couldn't jitterbug, so the judge threw her out. Carol and Gregory said that happens all the time. Now we're down to 20 couples. Did I tell you that David and I are Couple No. 11? And my cousin Irene and her boyfriend are Couple No. 10.

If you was here, you could root for us.

Rita

The second letter had been postmarked only two days later than the first. This one had a newspaper clipping in it. I unfolded it and saw a photo of Rita on the dance floor. She was wearing a dress, which looked funny to me because I had only ever seen her in trousers and a shirt, and hanging from her neck by a thick strap was a slant-top writing desk. She was holding up a pen and smiling into the camera. I read the caption under her picture.

Miss Rita Boyle, from Detroit, Michigan, writes to family and friends from the Watertown Dance Marathon. An article followed, but Rita had clipped away everything but the headline. *Hopeful Couples Vie for $500 Prize.*

November 19, 1931

Dear Maddy,

The postman brought your letter to the dance hall today, and the promoter brought it out to the floor along with the writing desk. They liked you writing back and even made a little announcement about it. I'm glad, too, but I swear this desk gets heavier every time they hang it on my neck. Maybe they're adding lead weights to it during our rest periods, ha, ha. Remember I told you that a photographer took my picture? Well, it was printed in the newspaper! Imagine that! They brought me some copies of the paper, so I'm putting a clipping in this letter so you can see. If you look close, you can see the paper I was writing on. That was my letter to you!

Tonight is Friday night and they're expecting a big crowd, so they're going to run a Derby. I don't know what the rules are yet, they said they'll explain them during our next rest period, which I don't think is fair. I want to sleep, even it is for only 15 minutes, not listen to their stupid rules. I'm getting a blister on my foot and the nurse looked at it and put some salve and a bandage on it. It hurts when I dance, but I'm trying to keep my mind on the $500 instead of on my foot. Root for Couple No. 11.

Rita

I folded the letters and pushed them into my jacket pocket. Already Rita had been dancing for more than a week. As I walked back to Francine's, I pulled the wagon with one hand and crossed the fingers on my other hand, hoping to send her some luck.

I wrote back to Rita that evening.

November 22, 1931

Dear Rita,

I was glad to get your letter. I hope you're doing okay and still dancing. I'm still in Auburn, but I'm a little worried about staying here. Francine, the woman who owns the bakery, got into it with a customer—well, she's a former customer now—about Prohibition, and now I have to find some new customers for the bakery. I'm pretty sure I can if I walk farther and knock on more doors, because I'm selling her pies door-to-door, but if I can't, I'll probably have to leave. Francine's family owns a vineyard, so they want to make wines again. But they can't unless Prohibition is repealed. So that's what the argument was about.

I hesitated, wanting to tell Rita about Phillipe, but felt unsure about what to say. Finally, I wrote:

Francine also has a younger brother who comes to Auburn every weekend. Weekdays, he works at the vineyard. Phillipe is very nice, and good-looking, too. I think we're becoming friends.

Well, that sounds stupid, I thought. Still, I didn't want to write about Phillipe's kiss. No telling who might get ahold of my letter at the dance marathon, and I wasn't about to share that kiss with the whole world.

Hope your cousin is doing okay, too. Write if you can.
—Maddy

Francine sold plenty of pies that week because of Thanksgiving, a holiday I would have forgotten about if it wasn't for the pies. The wealthy people on South Street had ordered in advance, and Wednesday morning Francine and I got up extra early to get started. We rolled out piecrust after piecrust as the sun came up.

"Let's get the lemon-raisin pies out of the way first," she said, sighing. "I could just kick myself for making those lattice tops to begin with, but they looked so nice and made the pies look special. It seemed like a good way to sell our raisins."

"Maybe now that people know about your raisins, you could make the pies with regular crusts," I said.

"I tried that once, but customers complained," she said. "Some people don't like change."

I knew Francine was right about that. I remembered one time when Aunt Ruby changed her chili recipe and she ended up with a bunch of surly railroad workers sitting at the counter griping at her. *Why'd you go and change it?* they asked. *If something was wrong with your chili, we would've told you*, they said.

"Don't mess with people's food, Ruby," my mother said after watching all the fuss, and she laughed out loud, which she didn't do very often. Ruby just made a face at my mother, but I don't believe she ever changed a successful recipe again.

By mid afternoon we had lined up about two dozen pies on the tables in the parlor. After the lemon-raisin pies, we made half a dozen pumpkin pies, too, which Francine made only because they were special requests. But they were easy; they had a bottom crust but no top crust.

"I'm going to have to make several trips to deliver all these pies," I said. "There's no way we can stack all these in the wagon without damaging them."

"Didn't I tell you?" Francine said. "Phillipe will be coming home shortly, and we'll use the truck to deliver the pies."

"Oh, good!" I said, looking forward to spending a little time with Phillipe again.

Francine looked at me oddly. "I thought you didn't mind going out with the wagon."

"I don't mind—not at all!" I said, worried that Francine would think I didn't want to earn my keep. "But it's fun to make deliveries in the truck, too, like when we took all those pies to Mrs. Davis."

"Yes, that was quite a project!" Francine said. "You'll take some more pies to Mrs. Davis today, too. She called several days ago and placed an order."

We wrapped and labeled all the pies and then boxed them in groups, carefully stacking the larger orders inside cardboard cartons that Francine had saved from the grocer's. As Francine marked down the addresses for delivery, Phillipe pulled into the drive.

"Good timing," Francine said to Phillipe when he walked into the kitchen. "We can load up the truck and off you go." She handed me the list. "You won't need to travel far. All but three pies go to homes on South Street."

"Aren't you coming?" I asked.

"There's no need for three of us to squeeze into the truck to deliver this batch. I'll stay here and finish cleaning up. Then I'm going to treat myself to a nice hot bath."

We loaded Phillipe's truck and climbed in. Phillipe put the truck into reverse and as he backed out of the drive, the smell of baked pumpkins and raisins filled my nose. It seemed like we had backed right into the scents.

The first stop was Mrs. Davis's house. I consulted my list. "Hers is the box marked DAV. She wanted both lemon raisin and pumpkin pies," I said, looking at my list.

Phillipe jumped out and picked up two cartons. One was marked DAV, but I couldn't see the marking on the other one. "You can get our next delivery ready," he said. "I'll be right back."

"But you've got too many boxes!" I called after him. "Someone's going to get shorted."

"I've got it—it's fine!" he said, and he hurried up the front walk to the house.

I double-checked the orders for the next group as Phillipe bounded back down the walk and jumped into the truck. "I hope you got Mrs. Davis's delivery right," I said. "I don't think that was what Francine wrote down."

"It's right," Phillipe said, touching my knee. "Don't worry. Francine told me about a last-minute adjustment just before we left." He backed out of the drive as I puzzled over the adjustment, distracted by the warmth of Phillipe's hand.

We made six more deliveries on South Street and then drove over to Garrow Street to finish. I checked off each delivery from Francine's list, sure that something wouldn't work out right because of the delivery to Mrs. Davis's house. But everything worked out as planned, just like Phillipe had said.

Phillipe turned down Swift Street and as we got about a block away from home, we saw that two Auburn police cars, lights flashing, were parked in the driveway to the house, and Francine was standing on the porch, gesturing to the cops. There was no mistaking her expression. Francine was livid.

"*Merde!*" Phillipe exclaimed. He gunned the engine and the truck flew forward, covering the short distance to the house in a few seconds.

"What's going on?" I asked, but Phillipe had pulled onto the grass, cut the engine, and was already out the door. I threw open my door, scrambled out, and followed him, catching some of the discussion as I ran.

"What's the problem?" Phillipe asked.

"The *problem*," Francine yelled, "is that these men think we're selling bootleg liquor and they want to search the house." She turned to the cop closest to her, a short, balding man. "I suppose Mrs. Hunter put you up to this! I know she has a nephew on the police force..."

"Miss Durrand," he interrupted, "we can't reveal the source of our information. But your family owns a vineyard and it's a well-known fact that you started the Auburn chapter of that women's group that's pushing for Prohibition reform."

"So that makes me a bootlegger!"

The second cop, a taller man with dark hair and bushy eyebrows, crossed his arms on his chest and leaned back on his heels. "It might," he said.

Francine stepped toward the cop, "Did the Eighteenth Amendment also amend my freedom of speech? This is political harassment, plain and simple!"

Phillipe stepped between Francine and the cops. "This request you've made to search our house—is it accompanied by a search warrant?"

The taller cop rocked back on his heels and smiled smugly. "As a matter of fact, it is."

"I'd like to see it, then," Phillipe said. He showed no expression, in contrast to Francine, who looked "mad enough to spit nails," as my mother liked to say.

The balding cop reached into his jacket and sighed, handing Phillipe a folded document, acting like it was a big pain and he was doing Phillipe a favor. Phillipe unfolded it and read it, which was when I noticed how my heart was pounding. In New Harmony, and in Auburn too, it seemed, contact with the police only meant trouble.

Phillipe refolded the warrant and handed it back. "Francine," he said, without looking at her, "we'll have to let them in."

Francine exploded in anger and started yelling at the cops again, this time in French. *"C'est scandaleux! Vous n'etes rien que deux fantoches arrogants et egoistes, et la loi Volstead est idiote!"*

"What'd she just say?" growled the balding cop.

"My sister says she understands that you are just doing your job, and she assures you that she is a law-abiding citizen who respects the Volstead Act," Phillipe said, casting a quick look at Francine, who glared at him. "Certainly you can understand that she is a little upset at having our home invaded."

Francine turned on her heel and stamped into the house. The cops went inside right behind her. Phillipe motioned for me to come inside and put his hand lightly on my shoulder as I stepped through the doorway.

"Who's the girl?" the taller cop asked, meaning me.

"None of your damn business," Phillipe answered. He squeezed my shoulder lightly.

Both cops made a beeline for the cellar steps, and Francine, Phillipe, and I followed close behind. I'd never been anywhere but the main floor of the house, and I didn't know what the Durrands kept in their cellar. Except I knew that both Francine and Phillipe had gone into the cellar to bring up wine for dinner. My palms were sweaty and I clung to the handrail as I walked down the wooden steps, which creaked under my feet. Cool air rose up to fill my nose, and the air seemed full of rich, earthy odors of old wood and wines. I wondered if I would be arrested along with Francine and Phillipe.

As we stepped onto the cellar floor, Francine flipped a wall switch and bathed the room with yellow light from three bare bulbs hanging from the floor supports. Stretching the full length of one cellar wall was a built-in wine rack crafted of oak. It was beautifully finished in a warm, honey-colored stain that showed off the wood grain, and it was artfully designed to cradle hundreds of bottles of wine. It held exactly five bottles.

"Here's the bootleg liquor you were looking for," Francine said. The scorn in her voice was as unmistakable as the disappointment showing in the face of both cops. "Are you going to arrest me for possessing five bottles of wine bottled fourteen years ago?"

The balding cop hurried over to the nearly empty wine rack and pulled out one of the bottles. "Durrand Wines, Pinot Noir, 1917," he read, pronouncing it like *peanut nor*. Even I knew that wasn't right. He pulled out another. "Riesling, 1917." The taller cop bit his lip. "Well, let's check the rest of the cellar and the house," he said. He drew himself up to look as tall as possible. "You know, if we wanted to, we could arrest you just because of these bottles of wine. The Volstead Act clearly states," he continued in a sing-song voice, "the possession of liquors by any person not legally permitted under this title to possess liquor shall be prima facie evidence that such liquor is kept for the purpose of being sold, bartered, exchanged, given away, furnished, or otherwise disposed of in violation of the provisions of this title..."

Phillipe interrupted the cop's chant with a peal of laughter. "You and I both know that if you arrest us for possessing five bottles of wine, any judge would throw you right out of court. Clearly, what little wine we have is for personal use, which is not a violation of the law!"

"We'll see about whether you're violating the law," the balding cop said. "We haven't finished searching the house yet."

Phillipe spread his arms in a gesture that said the cops should hurry up and be done. The cops then walked around the cellar, an action that seemed downright silly. The cellar was empty except for the furnace and two things that were visible right from the base of the stairs—a wringer washer and a laundry basket half full of clothes waiting to be washed. It was obvious that there was nothing else stashed anywhere.

"You go on up and check the second floor," the taller cop said to the balding one. I'll search the main floor."

We all traipsed back up the stairs. Creaking steps rhythmically marked each person's passing. Francine followed the balding cop upstairs, and

Phillipe and I watched as the taller cop made a quick tour through the parlor, my room, and the kitchen. Then he went through the items in Francine's pantry. I wondered if he really believed that cases of wine might be hidden among the sacks of flour and blocks of raisins. Someone like my father might hide a bottle or two back there, but anybody could see that you couldn't supply a bootleg business from narrow shelves crammed with baking supplies.

"Just make sure you put things back where they were," Phillipe said. "My sister is very fussy about her pantry!"

Finally, everyone returned to the kitchen. "I hope you're satisfied!" Francine said. The cops said nothing. They looked at each other, and then they turned to leave. "Have a good day," the balding cop said as they walked out the front door.

"You give Mrs. Hunter my best!" Francine called after them, her voice dripping with sarcasm.

Both cops ignored her, but the taller one muttered to his partner, "I still don't believe it."

The three of us watched as the cops drove away. Francine was still seething. "That does it!" she said, "If I needed any more motivation to work hard to defeat Prohibition, this was it! I'm holding a meeting here on Friday for the Women's Organization for National Prohibition Reform and I'm determined to have a good turnout! I could strangle Mrs. Hunter!"

"You watch your back, Francine," Phillipe said. "You won't be the only person with something to prove. Those cops weren't pleased at coming up empty handed, and Mrs. Hunter isn't going to be happy, either."

"You're right, Phillipe. But I'm not letting Mrs. Hunter intimidate me. Francine said. She turned to me. "Maddy, you haven't said a word! Are you okay?"

I nodded. "I didn't know what to do," I admitted. "I've never had an experience like that before. Even with the railroad bulls. I was worried that you might be arrested. And maybe I'd be arrested, too."

Francine shook her head. "Idiots! For five bottles of wine!"

"I say we make it four!" Phillipe said.

"Amen!" Francine said, and Phillipe stepped lightly down the cellar stairs again, returning with the pinot noir. He poured the rich, red liquid into three stemmed glasses. "It's the finest *peanut nor* that the *Doo Rands* ever made," he said, making Francine laugh with his mispronunciations. "And now, a toast!" The three of us touched our glasses together. "*A la Sante,*" we said in unison. It was the first French phrase I had ever learned.

"A la Sante—now that is the true 'French toast,'" Phillipe said with a grin. "Not the breakfast dish that is made of fried bread, which isn't French at all."

"Is that true?" I asked. Phillipe just shrugged. "So they say," he said, opening his eyes wide.

Francine laughed. I couldn't tell if Phillipe was "stringing me along," so I let it drop. Eventually, I looked it up in an encyclopedia in Auburn's library. Turned out that Phillipe might have been right. One version claims that French toast was invented by a tavern keeper in Albany in 1724. His name was Joseph French, but he didn't understand possessives. So he called his dish French toast, instead of French's toast.

CHAPTER 31

Thursday was Thanksgiving. That afternoon, as I watched Phillipe carve a whole turkey, I thought about families. In New Harmony, my family's Thanksgiving Day never looked like the illustrations in *Harper's Weekly* or the *Saturday Evening Post*. Our dinner table was the white tile counter at Ruby's Paradise Diner, and the specials were always sliced turkey breast or pork chops—your choice. Stuffing came with both, and mashed potatoes and string beans. I had never been part of a dinner where just one big, plump, stuffed and roasted golden brown turkey with drumsticks was brought to the table whole and served at one time.

I thought about how there were two kinds of families: the ones made up of people related by blood, which you're automatically part of, like it or not, and about the families you choose for yourself. Ruby chose to include the railroad workers, and today Francine and Phillipe chose to include me. I knew I was lucky, because there was a very large hobo family out there that didn't have enough to eat.

"I'm sorry you won't get to meet Armand and Louise and the boys today," Francine said as she passed me the bowl of green beans. "They went to visit Louise's family in Philadelphia for the weekend."

"I'd like to meet them sometime," I said.

"I'm sure you will," Phillipe said. "But in the meantime, I'd like you to see our family vineyard. How about if you and I drive over there tomorrow morning? Francine is going to be busy with the Reform group—right Francine? You're not planning to do any baking tomorrow, so Maddy and I can enjoy the day together."

"Well that's true," Francine said. "But do you think it's a good idea to go to the vineyard, Phillipe?"

"I think it's a fine idea," he said. "How about it, Maddy?"

"Sure. I'd love to see it," I said. Francine frowned, but didn't say anything more. I wondered if she thought Phillipe ought to have a day off from the vineyard.

"Great. We'll leave at eight." He picked up the bottle of Riesling Francine had opened for dinner. "Anyone care for some more 'bootleg liquor'?" He poured more wine into each of our glasses and then lifted his to Francine. "To my sister. Really, Francine—*deux fantoches*!"

Francine brightened. "Well, they are!"

"You said that to the cops, didn't you," I asked. "What does it mean?"

Francine started to giggle. "It means 'two political puppets.'"

Phillipe chuckled. "My sister told those men that they were arrogant, pompous puppets and that the Volstead Act is an idiotic law."

Both Durrands erupted into laughter at the shocked look on my face. "I only spoke the truth," Francine said.

"We're all lucky that neither of them understands French," Phillipe said. Then he and Francine burst into laughter again. This time, I joined them.

We bumped along in Phillipe's truck Friday morning, following the road along Seneca Lake and enjoying a spectacular view of the water reflecting the intense blue sky. Stark gray-brown skeletons of maples and oaks covered gently sloping hills that framed the lake. Here and there, patches of green pines interrupted the grayness. As we turned down a dirt road, acres of grapevines stretched out on both sides. Row after row, the vines lined up, looking like stitching on a quilt—parallel brown threads that seemed to anchor the earth. I guessed that the green leaves had melted away with the first hard frosts, but the vines looked sturdy and orderly—and patient. I thought about how the plants would endure the coming winter as they had many previous winters and emerge again in the spring, full of new energy, pushing out leaves from woody stems and forming buds that would produce delicious, fragrant fruit by fall.

Pride nearly oozed from Phillipe as he surveyed the vineyard. He looked over at me and grinned. "It's beautiful, isn't it? Many of these vines were planted by my grandfather. I've also propagated more of this stock and planted it—adding to his legacy."

"What about your father? Did he plant some of these vines, too?" I asked, instantly regretting my question. What if Phillipe and Francine's father was a drunk, like mine?

"My father helped build the business because it was expected of him—but making wines wasn't his passion. He was a master craftsman with wood. You'll see when we go into the house. His handiwork is everywhere."

Phillipe didn't say more. I decided that since I'd already opened the door, I'd go ahead and barge right through it. "Does your father still make things?" I waited to see if Phillipe would slam the door shut.

"My father died in 1915," Phillipe said. "I was pretty young—only seven years old. Truth be told, I don't remember much about him. Francine has a better recollection. She was fifteen."

"I'm sorry," I said, as Phillipe turned the truck into a driveway leading to a white two-story farmhouse. The front porch immediately grabbed my attention. It extended along the front of the house and then turned a corner and wrapped all the way around the right side. It was supported by elegant white columns and a fancy white railing. The roof of the porch was trimmed in a shorter version of the railing, and on its peak was a cursive letter D.

"Did you father build that porch?" I asked. "It's beautiful!"

Phillipe nodded. He parked the truck and we got out for a closer look. "That's one thing I do remember—my father building the porch. He turned every bit of the railing himself, on a lathe. He'd let me hand him a piece of lumber and then make me stand back, away from the lathe, while he worked. When a piece was done, he'd let me pick up the curls of wood he'd shaved off the rail."

Phillipe's eyes got a faraway look. "It took him all summer. He worked on it in the evenings because most days he and my grandfather worked out in the vineyard. I remember my father always seemed happy when it rained. Later, I figured out it was because he could spend the whole day working with wood. He loved the winter, too, for the same reason." Phillipe looked at the porch and then over at me. If there is such a thing as time travel, I saw it right then—I watched Phillipe snap back from the past into the present. "He only got to enjoy his porch for one season, though. By the following summer, he was dead of a heart attack."

"But look at the porch," I said, thinking about how I felt when I was drawing. "The real joy would be in building it."

Phillipe looked at me with a strange expression in his eyes. Quickly, I thought about what I had just said, and I flushed with embarrassment.

"I didn't mean that the way it sounded. It's sad that he didn't have more time," I said, tripping over my words. "It's just that when I'm drawing, it's such a pleasure to push my pencil over the paper, and I think you probably feel like that when you're growing new grapevines, and if your father loved working with wood, then he probably felt like that too as he built this porch...anyway, I really am sorry he wasn't around when you were growing up. I didn't mean to sound unsympathetic."

"I know," Phillipe said. He drew me toward him and kissed the top of my head and then gently kissed my mouth. He held me close for a moment and then pulled away to look at me. "You have such a different view of the world. That's why I like you so much."

I felt my face color again. "Thank you." The odd thing was that Phillipe made me feel, well, *visible*. Not like how I had felt most days at the diner, or even when I knocked on doors selling Francine's pies. That person was transparent—that person could be anybody. But with Phillipe I felt visible, like *I* mattered. I wanted to find a way to say this to Phillipe, but instead I slipped my arm around his waist. "I like you, too. Very much," I said. It was safer. Phillipe put his arm around me, squeezed my shoulder, and then took my hand and led the way onto the porch and into the house.

As Phillipe had said, it was clear that a master craftsman in wood had lived here—his work was everywhere, from the ornate oak stairway with its turned and detailed banister to the wide crown moldings and woodwork framing every doorway.

"Your father did all this? It's beautiful!"

Phillipe smiled. "Most of it, but not everything. Armand inherited my father's talent, and he's made his mark on this house as well. Come on, and I'll give you the grand tour."

We walked across hardwood floors through the parlor and into the dining room, which had rich wood wainscoting, built-in china cabinets in two corners, and a window seat that invited you to sit and look out over the vineyard. In the large kitchen, floor-to-ceiling cabinets lined one wall. Along the opposite wall, base cabinets supported a long butcher-block countertop.

"This woodworking is amazing," I said. "By the looks of this, there must have been a lot of rainy days—or long winters!"

Phillipe laughed and led me through the pantry and down a wide set of steps into the cellar. "When he built this house, my grandfather planned this cellar to be his first winery. That's why the steps are wide and the cellar walls are quite tall. It's not your typical cellar."

It certainly wasn't like any cellar I had ever seen. It was spacious and warmly lit, cool but not damp. Along one long wall, large wooden barrels were neatly lined up, resting on planks of wood. Two more layers of barrels had been stacked on top of the bottom barrels, each layer separated with planks.

"All of this is sitting idle," Phillipe sighed, shaking his head. "My grandfather had these barrels built and shipped over from France. Each one holds about 60 gallons, but they were hand built, so no two are exactly the same size." He pointed to red numbers painted on the face of each barrel. "This number tells how many gallons each barrel holds." I looked down the row and read some of the numbers: 56, 59, 61, 63.

"Right now the barrels are full of water," Phillip said. "They can't be stored empty because the wood will shrink and crack and the barrels will be ruined. I hope someday we can use them again to age our wine."

Along one of the short walls in the cellar were dozens and dozens of large stoneware jugs. "We use these to transport our grape juice in the fall," Phillipe said. "This is just overflow from the warehouse. They've all been washed and sanitized. They're being stored until the next harvest." He shook his head. "It still pains me to sell our juice for jams and jellies, and not for wine."

We turned to the other short wall, which held a wine rack that was a twin to the one in Francine's cellar. This one was totally full of bottles, but all were empty. "The wine rack is Armand's handiwork," Phillipe said.

"Your brother made the rack at the other house, too?" I asked.

"Yes, and there's still another in the warehouse, but not so fancy. We have thousands of empty bottles to store."

I walked along the wall, looking at row after row of dark green bottles lying on their sides, cradled in the diamond-shaped compartments of the rack. Down at the end, something on the floor caught my eye. My heart jumped.

"Phillipe! What's this?"

"What?" He rushed over to where I stood and looked where I was pointing. Something dark was seeping out from under the rack. I couldn't make sense of what I was seeing; it looked like a puddle of blood.

Phillipe's face drained of color. "Oh, my god. Maddy, this is not at all what I wanted to show you." He hurriedly pulled a vertical strip of trim off one section of the rack and pushed. It moved—easily. That section of the rack separated from the rest and swung silently on a hinge. It was actually a door into another smaller room, which was packed with wooden barrels like the other ones in the cellar. The red puddle was coming from a larger pool that had collected under one of the barrels.

Phillipe entered the room and I followed, feeling stunned and a little shaken at this discovery. It was easy to see what had happened. One of the planks supporting a barrel on the upper tier had cracked. The barrel had shifted slightly and wine had dripped out from around the large stopper on the top of the barrel.

He took hold of the cracked plank and wiggled it carefully. "It's wedged in there good," he said. "I'm glad of that. If that barrel had rolled off, it would have destroyed some of the other barrels and smashed through Armand's wine rack in the process." He studied the tilted barrel. "It looks like it stopped dripping. The wine must be level with the opening now. That's good at least."

Phillipe turned to look at me. His expression was somber—more serious than I had even seen before. "Maddy, I have to clean this up and put everything back in place. Then you and I will have to talk."

I found my voice. "I'll help you. Where's a mop and a bucket?"

"Under the stairs," he said. "All the cleaning supplies are there."

We worked together and mopped up all the spilled wine and then washed the area with soap and water, but the wine had discolored the concrete. When Phillipe closed the "door" to the hidden room, the shadow of the puddle was still visible. He stood frowning at it. "We'll let it dry, and then I'm going to have to figure out how to get that stain out." Phillipe turned to me. "Now we need to talk."

"Not just yet," I said. I wanted some time to sort out my feelings about this discovery. "You brought me here to show me the winery. I'd like to see the rest of it, okay?"

"You've already seen much more than I intended," Phillipe said. "All right. Let's go look at the warehouse."

We went upstairs and walked outside toward a long building situated a short distance from the house. The sun was nearly overhead, but the air was cold. I watched my breath turn to vapor. "Phillipe, the wine rack that's in the cellar at the house in Auburn. Is it...?"

"Yes."

I nodded. "I never would've guessed."

"That's the idea," he said.

We reached the warehouse and went inside. More wooden wine casks were stacked inside, along with hundreds and hundreds of crockery jugs.

"Are these barrels filled with water, too?" I asked.

Phillipe nodded.

"Only water?" I said, testing Phillipe's mood. He shot me a quick look and then relaxed a little as he realized I was teasing. Still, his body was tense and his face looked grim.

Phillipe showed me the equipment room with grape presses, filters, and the corkers. "My father used to brag that he could fill and cork fifty bottles an hour," he said. I smiled but bit my lip, leaving my question unasked. As if he read my mind, Phillipe said. "Forty-six. When I'm in good form, I can do forty-six."

We stepped back outside and turned toward the house. "What is this...?" Phillipe said.

I followed his gaze and we both watched as two cars turned into the driveway from the vineyard road.

Phillipe swore under his breath. "Not today!"

The cops who got out of the cars were the same ones who had come to the house in Auburn. My heart plummeted right into my shoes. I thought about the mess we had just cleaned up in the house, and the stain in the concrete. I knew we would both be arrested.

"See if you can stall them," I whispered as the cops swaggered over to us. I wanted a chance to see what the cellar floor looked like.

"So what brings you out here today?" Phillipe asked the men. "Let me guess. Mrs. Hunter sent you." He crossed his arms and exhaled. "You don't give up, do you?"

"Just doing our job," the bald one said.

The tall one pulled a paper from his jacket pocket and handed it to Phillipe. "Here you go. You can read it if you want, but it's just like the other search warrant."

Phillipe took it and slowly opened it. I stamped my feet in the cold. "Phillipe, I'm freezing. I'm going to wait in the house, okay?"

"Okay. I'll be there soon."

I turned to go and the tall cop looked like he might follow me, but Phillipe said, "Look, this is bullshit. Let's get this done and then you two can get off my property." He strode toward the warehouse with both cops right behind him, and I walked quickly to the house.

I ran down the steps to the cellar and over to the wine rack. I looked at the floor and fear rose up in my throat. The concrete had partly dried, but the wine stain was unmistakable, and obviously fresh. There might as well be a sign announcing *This is a false wall.* I sat on the cellar steps for a minute and tried to think about what to do, but all I could think about was going to jail.

Well, don't just sit here quietly on the chopping block, I told myself. *If those cops are going to haul us off to jail, make them work for it!* I got up and started lugging stoneware jugs from the other side of the cellar, sliding them on the floor in front of the wine rack, covering the wine stain. I worked quickly, not knowing how much time I had. I set down a row of seven jugs, three deep, and then pulled several unused planks off the top of the wine barrels. I laid these on top of the jugs and then placed another layer of jugs on top. I stepped back and looked at the stack, hoping that it looked like normal storage; there wasn't anything more I could do.

Upstairs, I settled onto the window seat in the dining room to wait. As I looked out at the view over the vineyards, I felt like I had crossed over a bridge that morning, and then the bridge had collapsed behind me. There was no going back.

The clues about Francine and Phillipe had been there all along, I just hadn't put it all together. The raisins, the Durrand's attitude about Prohibition, the family winery, which Francine hadn't been happy about Phillipe showing to me. Even Wednesday, when Phillipe and I had delivered boxes of pies—there was the unexplained box that he took in to Mrs. Davis, and somehow we didn't end up short. And then I remembered the first time we delivered pies for Mrs. Davis's anniversary party. Phillipe carried in a heavy box then, too. It made sense now. Once you discover the truth, it's hard to figure out how you missed it to begin with.

Soon I heard voices, and Phillipe and the two cops entered through the back door. "It's no different here than in the warehouse," Phillipe was saying. "We use the cellar to store the overflow from the warehouse." Phillipe's voice sounded very tight. The three men went down the stairs and I held my breath. One of the cops asked a question, but I couldn't make out what he said. Phillipe answered, "Yes, as I explained before—all our wooden casks have to be kept full of water or they'll be ruined."

Then I heard the scraping sound of stone jugs on concrete. Phillipe's voice carried up the stairs. "Just like in the warehouse, every one of those jugs is *empty* and has been cleaned for storage." After what seemed like hours, footsteps sounded on the stairs and the three men came through the kitchen into the dining room where I sat. I looked up, waiting to see what would happen next.

The two cops came through first. "We still have to check the rest of the house," the tall one snarled. Phillipe made eye contact with me as he followed them, and he smiled just a little. I breathed out some of my tension. Unless the Durrands had another surprise I didn't know about, we weren't going to be arrested.

The men went through the house, upstairs, and even into the attic. Finally, they came downstairs and Phillipe let the cops out through the front door. As they left, he said, "You've now searched both of my properties. If this isn't the end of it, I'm going to file a complaint!"

Phillipe sat down next to me on the window seat, put his arms around me, and hugged me hard. "Thank you. That was a brilliant idea to move those jugs."

"You're welcome. I'm just glad it worked," I said. "I was worried when I heard them moving some around."

"Me, too. But they just picked up a few to see if they were empty. It didn't occur to them, thank goodness, that the jugs were hiding something."

We sat in silence for a few minutes, then Phillipe spoke again. "Maddy, I don't have to tell you how serious this is. I need to know what you think about what happened—and about what you saw," he said.

"It's very strange," I said slowly, "because you and Francine never told me what you were doing, even when I was helping with deliveries, and it feels like I shouldn't trust you because you hid the truth from me. But you and Francine trusted me and gave me a place to stay in exchange for helping out. So how can I *not* trust you?"

"Does it upset you—what you saw?"

"Are you asking me if I care that you're illegally selling wine?"

"You know I am," he said.

I thought for a minute. "No and yes," I said. "'No, because I think Prohibition is pretty useless. I already told you that my father is a drunk. Prohibition was supposed to dry him out, but it never will. I don't remember a time when he didn't smell like booze. And it seems like anyone who wants beer or wine can either make it themselves...or find the right people to buy it from."

Phillipe smiled a little.

"And yes I care that you're doing something illegal, because I don't want you or Francine–or *me*–to go to jail!"

Phillipe nodded. "Then we must continue to be very careful."

We sat quietly, each thinking our own thoughts. "You sure looked like you had seen a ghost when you saw that puddle of wine," I said, giggling a little.

"Well, you looked pretty horrified yourself," Phillipe said, chuckling. "Did you think I was an ax murderer?"

"How did you know? For a minute, I did wonder if it was blood!" I said. I felt all the tension of the day slip away, and laughter bubbled up from inside me. "You and Francine!" I said, laughing harder. "Bootleggers!"

Phillipe laughed harder now, too. "Please, don't make us into such common criminals—we're *French* bootleggers! French bootleggers have some class, you know!"

"Oh, sure. 'Dear Mother,' " I said, writing an imaginary letter in the air. "'Please don't worry about me. I'm staying with a nice family of bootleggers in New York. *French* bootleggers! They make the best wine!'"

"Well, of course, we *do* make the best wine," Phillipe said, kissing me.

Francine was in high spirits when we came back late in the afternoon. She greeted us with a big smile and a rush of words. "Oh, I'm so glad you're back! I can't wait to tell you about the meeting—it went so well! Sit down. I'll make some fresh coffee." She bounced around the kitchen, setting up the percolator and grinding coffee beans.

As Phillipe and I moved toward the table, he drew close to me and said under his breath, "Don't say anything yet. I'll fill her in when the time is right."

"I just got home myself. Attendance was so good," Francine was saying, "that we had to move our meeting! Mrs. Davis came and brought several of her friends. And a lot of other women from Auburn came, too. Mrs. Davis offered her house when it got too crowded in here. So we spent the afternoon organizing and we're going to concentrate on two things: we've formed a speaker's bureau to make our case to the public, and we're supporting candidates who are working for repeal of Prohibition."

Francine finally took a breath, but only enough to recharge. I started thinking that she must have had plenty of coffee at Mrs. Davis's house. Maybe making a fresh pot wasn't the best idea.

"The Women's Organization for National Prohibition Reform is growing fast! We signed up a lot of new members today, and do you know that the last WONPR newsletter said that nationally there were over 500,000 members? I really think we have some momentum to repeal Prohibition!"

"It sounds like a very successful meeting," Phillipe said. "I hope the momentum continues. Wouldn't it be wonderful to harvest our grapes and legally make wine again?" Phillipe cast a quick look at me. I wondered if he was working up to breaking the news to Francine.

"It truly would," Francine said. She turned to me. "I'm so sorry, Maddy. I've been going on and on about my day, and I haven't even asked you about yours! So you saw our family vineyards—what did you think?"

"They're very impressive; I think the vineyards are beautiful even this time of year," I said. Out of the corner of my eye, I saw Phillipe smile a little and raise an eyebrow. Francine kept looking at me, clearly expecting to hear more. "Phillipe showed me the house and the warehouse and..." I searched for something else to say. I glanced at Phillipe, wanting him to take over the conversation. "I learned a lot about your family's business," I said, finally.

At that, Phillipe laughed out loud, startling Francine, who turned toward him. "What...?"

"Francine," he said, growing serious, "Maddy got the grand tour today, and I do mean that she saw *everything*."

"You don't mean..."

"Everything," he said, pronouncing each syllable.

Francine looked stricken. "But...oh, Phillipe, *why?*"

"It wasn't my plan," he said. "But there was a leaking cask and some wine seeped under the wall and into the main cellar. It had to be taken care of. I had to go into the room, and we had to clean it up."

Francine was so upset she could barely listen to Phillipe. I felt bad for her. She had been so happy about her meeting, and now she had to hear about the day's events at the vineyard.

"Oh, Phillipe! That's *one* of the reasons why I didn't think it was a good idea for Maddy to..."

"That's not all, Francine," Phillipe interrupted. "In the middle of it, the cops came again with a search warrant. Apparently, Mrs. Hunter has pretty long arms."

Francine turned white and sat back on the kitchen chair. "No," she said. "No, they couldn't have...How did you...wait, but you weren't arrested. So what was...tell me what happened!" She stood up, sat down, and then stood up again.

"Francine, please. Sit down," Phillipe said. "Things turned out fine, but it would not have been so good if Maddy hadn't been there. While I was out in the warehouse with the cops, trying to stall them, Maddy was in the house covering up the evidence. The leak left a stain in the concrete that was quite obvious. Maddy put together a storage area for the jugs right on top of the stain. The cops picked up some of the jugs to see if they were empty, but they didn't move enough of them to uncover the stain."

When he finished, Francine sat back in her chair and looked at me. "I don't know what to say," she said. "But thank you for what you did." She stood up. "Let's have some coffee." She poured three steaming cups and set them on the table. Then she sat down across from me and studied me keenly with her blue-gray eyes.

"Maddy, certainly you understand why we never told you about our... activities. I know that you knew people bought our raisins for purposes other than to make pies, but that part of our business is entirely legal. We could never be arrested for selling raisins, no matter what our customers do with them. But of course, selling wine is different. We have much to lose if the wrong people find evidence of our dealings."

I nodded. "I know."

"So here we sit, and today you have information that could ruin us. I'm a little angry with Phillipe for taking you to the vineyard—I was afraid that you might somehow find out what we are doing. It wasn't that I felt you were untrustworthy. It's just that it's better if no one who isn't directly involved knows about the cellar." She took a deep breath. "Yet, if you hadn't been there and hadn't made the effort to conceal the spill, the cops would have gotten the evidence they needed. So I must ask you, is this something you can continue to keep to yourself?"

I recognized the same kind of predicament I had faced earlier today. On one side of the scale, Francine hadn't wanted to trust me, and on the other side, now she *had* to trust me.

"Phillipe asked me about this, too," I said. "I'm not on the side of the drys. Nobody can make someone else stay sober. They're just plain wrong in thinking that they can keep a person from being a drunk, if that's what he wants to be. But most people aren't drunks, so it doesn't make sense to have a law that doesn't do a thing to prevent what it's supposed to prevent." I took a sip of coffee. Francine was silent, waiting for me to finish.

"But I kind of wish you and Phillipe weren't...bootleggers...," I said, hesitating to use that word with Francine, wondering if she would take offense, "because I don't want you to get arrested. I'm very grateful that you gave me a place to stay, and a job, and I'd never tell anyone about your activities."

Francine nodded. "I'm glad to hear you say that." She relaxed against the back of her chair. "When you first came here and I offered you a room in exchange for help with my bakery, it was mostly a business decision. You needed a place to stay and I needed your drawing talent for those darned cakes. Then you helped my bakery business grow, which also helped our wine sales, which I'm sure you've figured out by now. But I'm also glad you've stayed here because as it turns out, I like you a lot, as does Phillipe," she said, glancing at him, "although he might not think I've noticed—and besides, I'm happy to have some female company in this house."

Phillipe grinned, unruffled by Francine's remark.

"If you're still willing to help with our family business, knowing what you now know, I'd like you to stay," Francine said.

"I'd like to stay, too, at least for awhile," I said. "When I hopped off the freight train in Auburn, I never expected to find friendship and a job all in the same place. I know I'm very lucky." I also knew, although I didn't say it, that eventually I'd have to figure out what was next for me and make my own way.

Turns out that the WONPR meeting was also good for Francine's business. More people came to Francine's house to buy pies and quiches, and sales of raisins really picked up. Still, each afternoon I loaded the Liberty Coaster and pulled the wagon up and down the neighborhood streets until I sold most of Francine's excess pies or until it got late enough that I knew people were already getting their supper on the table. Then I'd stop at the post office because Rita was writing almost every day.

November 25, 1931

Dear Maddy,

After last night's Derbies, we're down to 17 couples. They make you race—like horses, only in couples—around the dance floor. And the last couple to cross the finish line is eliminated. They did that three times last night! The third time, David and I almost got eliminated. We were second to last. My blister was really hurting and it was hard to run.

Then the girl in Couple No. 2 stepped on my foot, accidentally, she said, and I almost fell, but David held me up and we crossed the finish line in front of them. So Couple No. 2 got sent home. Serves them right.

I hope things work out okay for you at the bakery. If you find more customers, will they let you stay? Tell me more about Phillipe! It'll give me something else to think about. Right now, all I can think about is the next rest period. I want to curl up on a cot and sleep until next week.

Root for Couple No. 11.

Rita

November 27, 1931

Dear Maddy,

Four couples gave up this morning and went home. I heard one of the men got squirrelly and was talking but not making any sense. So now we're down to 13 couples. Hope that's not an unlucky number, ha, ha. Couple No. 3 just announced that they're getting married after this contest is over and people in the audience threw some coins at them. The promoter said that's called a silver shower, and the couple got nine dollars and 50 cents, which they get to keep. Maybe David and I should say something like that, so we get some money to inspire us while we're waiting to win that $500.

We heard there's going to be plenty of Sprints and some Derbies
tonight. Root for Couple No. 11.

Rita

I had some trouble reading the last letter from Rita because her
handwriting had turned into a scrawl. By now, she had to be so exhausted
that it would take a great effort to write. I thought about the picture of
her wearing that writing desk and wondered if they made her write letters,
even if she didn't want to.

I sat down to answer her. I picked up the second of the two letters
and looked at the date. November 27. Friday after Thanksgiving—the
same day I was as close as I ever wanted to get to ending up in jail. So
much had happened to me in the past week, but I couldn't tell her all of
it, especially the part about the bootleggers I happened to be living with
at the moment.

November 30, 1931

Dear Rita,

It sounds like the dance marathon is getting really hard! I
hope you win soon so you can get some sleep!

I'm still in Auburn, and we've gotten more customers to re-
place the ones we lost when Francine argued with that busybody.
I helped them get more customers, and Francine and Phillipe are
happy about that, so they told me I could stay. I think I'll be here
through the winter and then I'll figure out what to do in the spring.

I'm still rooting for Couple Number 11.

Maddy

I reread my letter. It didn't sound anything like what my life here was
really like. *Tell me more about Phillipe! It'll give me something else to think about,*
she had said. But my feelings about Phillipe didn't seem like something

I could put in a letter—how he was fun to be with, and easy to talk to, and how I felt safe even when I was alone with him, and how I felt when he kissed me. Maybe someday I could tell Rita—face to face—about all this, but not now. But I knew a way to give Rita something else to think about. I went to my sketchbook and tore out a blank page, then turned to the drawing of Phillipe behind the bowl of apples. I made a new sketch, using the earlier one as an example. When I was satisfied, I wrote "Phillipe" across the bottom and folded the sketch in with my letter. Then I opened to a fresh page in my sketchbook and worked on some drawings of the vineyards, trying to make the pictures in my mind spill onto the paper.

Toward the end of the week, the mail clerk handed me a letter from Rita and a postcard—from Henry! I read both pieces of mail right there in the post office, leaning on the wide ornate column at the base of the dark marble steps that led to the second floor.

> *Dear Maddy,*
>   *I'm glad you're okay and found a place to stay in Auburn. The job in Pittsburgh turned out to be a rumor, but I'll keep trying. I been on the circuit again from Pittsburgh to New Harmony.*
>   *Saw Reedy and Professor last week. Professor got beat up by some thug on a train who wanted Professor's new boots. He's all right, but hopping mad about losing those boots.*
>   *You keep off the trains if you can. It's dangerous out there. Keep in touch.*
> *Henry*

I felt bad for Professor, but I was sure glad he was okay. He didn't seem like much of a fighter, so I suppose that's why someone decided to pick on him. I wondered where Henry was staying. I wanted to write back, but he didn't say where he'd be.

Rita's letter was short, and her handwriting was uneven and strayed all over the page.

November 28, 1931

Dear Maddy,

Bad news. Couple No. 10—Irene and her boyfriend—got eliminated in a Derby last night. So did five more couples. There's only seven couples left and the crowds are getting bigger. They smell blood I guess, which includes my foot. My blister keeps getting worse and worse and I can't put my shoe on, so I dance with one shoe on and one shoe off. I've never been this tired in my entire life. Carol and Gregory worked out a way so that one of them hangs from the neck of the other one and sleeps for a couple of hours. It's against the rules but the judges don't say anything now as long as one person keeps moving. David and I tried it, but my arms fell asleep when it was my turn to sleep, and I got pins and needles in them and David is too heavy for me to hold and his knee almost touched the floor and if the judge sees that happen we're cooked.

I never want to hear jitterbug music again.

Rita

I worried about Rita. The dance marathon sounded like it had turned into torture, and Rita seemed so exhausted I was afraid she'd "get squirrelly" herself. I decided not to write back for a few days. Maybe my letters only made it worse for her, especially if they were bringing out that desk and making her write.

A few days later, there was another letter from Rita, but this one looked different from the others. Her handwriting looked loopy and readable again, and when I checked the postmark, it said Pulaski. I tore it open, hoping it was good news. Wouldn't that be something if she won the $500!

November 30, 1931

Dear Maddy,

It was down to four couples Saturday night and they called a Sprint followed by a Derby. I swear they were trying to kill everybody. I swear the judge turned his back, too. Carol and Gregory pushed past us in the Derby and Gregory bumped David on purpose, which made David lose his balance and he stepped on my bare foot while he was trying not to fall. It hurt so much I couldn't put any weight on it for a few seconds, and we lost the Derby. Eliminated, just like that! And the judge didn't see a thing except that we came in last. So after all that time, we didn't get any share of the prize money. I could've cried if I wasn't so awful tired. It was in the paper that Carol and Gregory won, too. I hope they choke on that $500. They didn't win it fair and square.

So now I'm back in Pulaski and I slept for two days without getting up for much else than breakfast and dinner. I guess I'll be back working at the Lighthouse Hotel tomorrow.

Write to me.

Rita

I walked home, dragging the wagon behind me, hunching against the cold wind that blew through Genesee Street and made the news of Rita's defeat feel even worse. All that pain and exhaustion for nothing. Carol and Gregory had won by cheating, and they got away with it, too.

Francine was sitting at the kitchen table writing letters when I got back to the house. I knew that the small stack of envelopes, addressed and stamped, meant she'd been working on her Prohibition-repeal activities. "There's some hot water in the kettle if you want tea," she said. "You must be frozen. The wind is miserable!"

"It *is* miserable," I said, meaning both the weather and Rita's ordeal. "How were sales?"

"Good. I came back empty today." I poured some hot water for tea and brought my cup over to the table. Before I sat down, I fished around in my jacket pocket for the pie money and laid it on the table.

Francine looked at it and then looked up at me. "Wonderful," she said. "I'll settle up with you later, all right?"

"Sure."

She studied me for a moment. "Is something wrong? You don't seem quite like yourself."

"I'm kind of upset right now," I admitted. Francine raised an eyebrow. "It's about my friend Rita. Do you remember me telling you about her? I met her in a boxcar—you saw the drawing I did of her."

Francine nodded. "I remember."

"Well, we've been writing to each other, and I got a letter from her today. She spent fifteen terrible days in a dance marathon, trying to win a $500 prize. Can you even imagine going without sleep for that long, and having to dance, too? They even made them race! But Rita hung in there, and when they were down to four couples, one of the other couples tripped up Rita and her partner and made them lose. The judge said he didn't see a thing, so Rita and her partner were out. Then she heard that the couple who tripped them won the $500. It makes me mad, and I feel sad for Rita, too. I really think she would have won if that other couple hadn't cheated. That girl has guts!"

"I'm sorry it turned out that way," Francine said. "I've heard some bad things about dance marathons. It seems like a cruel way to make money, doesn't it? But if there wasn't a big audience, the promoters wouldn't hold them. They're the ones who rake in the money."

"Why do you think people go to those? I can understand someone entering a marathon, like Rita did, hoping to win the big prize. Her family really could've used the money. But why would people pay to watch?"

"I don't know," Francine said. "Maybe it makes people feel better to watch people worse off than themselves." She made a face. "I suppose it's human nature."

"Maybe," I said. "But if that's true, it doesn't make me feel very good about human nature."

A week or so later, another letter from Rita made me feel even worse about human nature:

December 2, 1931

Dear Maddy,

Today I got your letter that you sent to the dance hall. At least they sent it on to me. So that drawing is Phillipe! Is he really that handsome, or did you just draw him that way? (Just kidding!)

There's a big hoo-ha about that dance contest I was in. Seems that the company that ran the contest skipped town without paying their bills. They owed for food, for the orchestra, and for the Legion Hall. Can you believe it? They stiffed the American Legion! Then it came out that the American Legion in Syracuse had the same trouble with them, and Carol and Gregory were in cahoots. Carol and Gregory always "win" these marathons, because they're supposed to. They get paid by the company that runs the contests, but they don't get $500. The marathons are fixed! Just like a horse race, Irene said. I guess I was stupid for believing they were real. I just wanted to win that $500 real bad. I could've helped my folks a lot with that money.

More bad news. I got a letter just yesterday from my mother, and she said my brother lost his job at Ford last week. They shut down the plant Daniel was working in, and now Daniel's got nothing, plain and simple. Sales were bad, Ford said, and they've been shutting down plants and are retooling to make a new model. The V-8, my mother said. Nobody knows when they'll be hiring again.

It makes me mad that people don't know what goes on there. Henry Ford is a big fat liar. He said he was paying $7 for an 8-hour day but nobody really earned that. And he got rid of higher paid workers and farmed out some of the work to shops that paid 14 cents an hour! Then he cut everybody's pay from $6 a day to $4, and for 10 hours a day of Ford's speedups! Everybody's *so desperate, they'll work for $4, even though you can't support a family on those wages. It's not right to take advantage of people like that. Nobody in Henry Ford's family is hungry or needs a roof over their head, that's for sure.*

I'm worried about my family now, but I guess there's nothing I can do except keep working at the hotel and hope for some super-duper tips! Sorry I didn't have any good news to tell you. Hope things are still good for you in Auburn.

Write soon,

Rita

I folded up Rita's letter and stuffed it back into the envelope, wishing I could stuff my feelings of gloom in there with it. I squeezed the envelope in my hands and wondered how such a small rectangle of paper could hold so much grief.

CHAPTER 32

For a while, I got a taste of normal life, at least as normal as anyone could expect at the Durrand's during the Depression. I sold pies and sometimes, because now I knew the Durrands' secret, I delivered wine. I wrote letters to Rita and I worked on my drawings—and I went out on real dates with Phillipe. When he came home for the weekends, we'd often go to the picture show. We'd watch the newsreels and then Phillipe would take my hand or put his arm around my shoulders and we'd laugh at the Marx Brothers or watch some wild western like *Cimarron*.

Afterwards, when we returned to the house, we'd make a pot of coffee or Phillipe would pour some wine, and then we'd sit at the kitchen table and talk. Once, over a glass of merlot, I asked him if Francine had ever been married.

He shook his head. "She never took the plunge."

"Why not?"

"She's a strong woman," Phillipe said. "Most men don't like that. She was very interested in a man from Skaneateles several years ago, but when it came right down to it, he always expected to have things his way. Francine finally broke it off."

I nodded. All the men I knew—my father, my uncle, the railroad men—expected their wives to go along with whatever they decided. The men always wanted the last word.

"What about you," I asked. "Do you like strong women?"

"Apparently I do," he said, grinning, as he raised his glass to me. "I certainly like *you*."

I was speechless for a moment. I hadn't thought of myself as strong. But I had left home determined to make my own way, and if that made me appear strong, I was glad of it.

"Thank you," I said, touching his glass with mine. "Then I guess it's fair to say I like men who like strong women." As we sipped our wine, I felt the same as I had at the Durrand vineyards—like I had crossed a bridge of some kind and could not, or would not, go back. I think that's what happens when you grow up. You cross bridges and never go back.

That night, at the end of our date, Phillipe walked me to the door of my room as he usually did—walking me home, he called it—and he bent to kiss me goodnight. But this time he pulled me close and kissed me with an intensity that was new to me. His body was warm against mine and I felt the power in his arms as he held me. For a second his strength scared me, but I knew I was safe, and I let myself enjoy the pleasure of his mouth kissing mine and his caress. Finally, reluctantly, I pulled away, needing to let my swirling feelings settle down enough so I could take a good look at them.

"I should go, Phillipe," I said. "Goodnight."

"All right," he answered, touching my cheek. "Goodnight, *cher*."

After he went upstairs, I laid in bed, unable to sleep, and listened to Phillipe moving around in the room above me. I thought about my feelings for him and wondered if I was falling in love. But I didn't know anything about love. I wished I had someone to talk to. I supposed that most girls could talk to their mother, but even if I could talk to mine, I wouldn't have trusted what she had to say about love. Maybe my parents loved each other once, but if they still did, I couldn't see it. They fought a lot, and I didn't want my life to be like theirs. And Aunt Ruby and Uncle George got along well enough, but there wasn't much of a connection between them. They worked together at the diner, out of necessity, for sure, but also kind of out of habit, it seemed to me; I never saw a spark between them. I didn't want my life to be like that, either.

But being with Phillipe made me happy, and I definitely felt a connection to him—and a spark every time we were together. I knew I cared, very deeply, about Phillipe. Was that love?

I turned in bed to curl up and try to get some sleep, and then I noticed that Phillipe hadn't gone to sleep yet, either. The faint glow of his light illuminated the branches of the tree outside my window.

Phillipe returned to the vineyard for the week, which made me feel a bit glum. It seemed like a long time until the next weekend. But a stop in the post office brightened my day when the clerk handed me an envelope with Eddie's handwriting. I waited until after dinner to read it, letting the pleasure of hearing from him simmer, like a tasty stew.

> *Dear Maddy,*
>
> *Yesterday I went into town with Aunt Ruby and we stopped at Woolworth's. There was an attendant at this new photo booth they just put in, and she let me take my picture so she could test how they came out. So I got a strip of pictures for free! I put one in this letter. How do you like it? Do they have a photo booth in Auburn? Maybe you could send me a picture of you.*
>
> *Mom said to tell you thanks for sending the drawing. She said she has a lot on her mind right now, so she'll write another time. Dad is still in jail and Mom and I are going to move in with Aunt Ruby and Uncle George. I help out a lot. There's not much else to do around here. Raymond is still sick. The infection in his leg won't go away. Uncle George said he might have to send Raymond back to Chicago even though he's sick, so the doctors there can take a look at him.*
>
> *I hope you'll come home soon. I miss you.*
>
> *Love,*
> *Eddie*

I picked up the picture Eddie had included in the letter and turned it over. Eddie's face grinned up at me and I felt an ache grow in the pit of my stomach. I really missed my little brother. I wondered how long it would be before I saw him again, but I had no intention of going back to New Harmony, even if they sent Raymond away to Chicago. I wasn't sorry his leg was still infected, either. I hope it hurt him—a lot. He deserved it.

That night, I wrote back to Eddie:

> *Dear Eddie,*
>
> *I got your letter and I'm really glad to have your picture. That was lucky that you were in Woolworth's when they were testing the*

photo booth. I miss you a lot, but I can't come home right now. It might be a long time before I come home.

I'm glad you're helping out. Maybe school will start again soon, if times get better.

I like working in the bakery and I've made some friends here, too. If Mom is worried about me, tell her I'm fine.

Love,
Maddy

P.S. I don't know if they have any photo booths in Auburn, but I'm sending you a picture anyways!

I took my sketchbook and, looking into the small mirror in my room, drew a self-portrait, which I included with my letter.

A couple of weeks later, I got an answer back from Eddie. His letter came during a week of unseasonably warm weather that even made headlines in the Auburn newspaper. I bounced into the kitchen after an afternoon of selling Francine's pies.

"Everybody's in a good mood, today," I said to Francine, who was putting groceries away in her pantry. "I sold all the pies again!"

"I don't know how anyone could be grumpy on a day like this!" Francine said. "What a treat, to have such warm weather in the middle of winter!"

"Yes! It was so nice to be outside. And to top it off, I got a letter from my brother today, too."

"That's good," Francine said, her voice muffled by the bags of groceries.

I sat at the kitchen table and opened Eddie's letter.

Dear Maddy,

I hung your picture on the bulletin board by my desk in my room. You draw really good. Thanks for making that picture. It makes me feel better when I look at it, but I still miss you a lot. I go down to the rail yard sometimes, but it's not as much fun without you.

Remember I told you about Raymond and his infection? Well, Uncle George sent him back to Chicago so the city doctors could take a look at him, but they didn't help him, either. Aunt Lydia sent us a letter and said that Raymond had a bad flare-up. He got a high fever and the infection went into his blood and then into his heart – and he had convulsions and died! I can't believe it. We used to go fishing together and now he's dead. Aunt Lydia is mad at everybody here, and everybody here seems mad at everybody else, because no one is being very nice to anyone.

I wish you'd come home so I'd have someone to talk to.

Love,
Eddie

I gasped. Raymond had died! I couldn't think. It served him right. I hated him for what he did to me. I wanted him to be punished. But I don't think I wanted him dead. But maybe I did. And maybe I killed him. I stabbed him with the fork, which he deserved, didn't he? But if it caused his infection, then I killed him, didn't I? There was so much noise in my head that I couldn't hear myself think anymore.

"Maddy? Maddy!" Slowly, I became aware of another voice. It finally registered that Francine was talking to me. "Maddy, are you all right? What happened? Did you get bad news?"

"I can't believe it," I said. "Raymond is dead."

She looked stricken. "Who is Raymond? Is he your brother? Oh, I'm so sorry!"

"No, *Eddie's* my brother; Raymond is—was—a cousin, kind of," I said. "He was my uncle's sister's son. He came to live with my aunt and uncle and help out at the diner." And then the whole story spilled from me and I felt like it had just happened yesterday. I felt the pain in my jaw, the feeling of suffocation when he had pushed me face down into the booth, and the stinging heat of the hot bath all over again. Huge sobs surged up from somewhere deep in my body, and I couldn't breathe.

I heard Francine pull a chair next to me, and she sat down and gently put her hands on my shoulders. I felt the warmth from her fingers, and her touch helped calm me. Finally, I wiped my eyes and said, "I might have actually killed him because of stabbing him with that fork. I don't know what to think... And I don't know what I should do."

"You go on with your life, just like you have been," Francine said. She was dabbing at her eyes, too. "One thing you must believe is that what you did to Raymond was exactly the right thing to do. It got him off of you and got you out of the diner. You don't know what he was thinking. It could have been even worse for you if you hadn't gotten away."

"But he's *dead*!"

"You were defending yourself. *You* could have been dead! Don't ever forget that. If, and it's still an *if*, Raymond's infection was from being stabbed, he paid a big price for what he did, but *he's* the one who attacked *you*."

"I know, but..."

"It's not your fault, Maddy," Francine said.

We sat in silence for a few minutes, and I thought about what Francine had said. Part of me knew that she was right—it wasn't my fault. But another part of me was horrified that I might have caused Raymond's death.

Finally, Francine spoke. "Now that Raymond is gone, are you going to go back home?"

I shook my head. "If I went back home, they'd expect me to work in the diner, and I couldn't. I won't go back into that diner again. Ever."

Francine nodded. "I understand—I don't blame you."

"And besides, Eddie and my mother are moving in with my aunt and uncle. They wouldn't have room for me, even if I wanted to go back, which I absolutely don't." At that moment, reality struck me with full force. I truly had become a hobo. I didn't have a home anymore, and I was working to earn my keep.

Later that week, I wrote back to Eddie.

Dear Eddie,

I'm sorry so much has happened—you moving in with Aunt Ruby and Uncle George—and even Raymond. Raymond was a terrible person, but I didn't want him to die.

I miss you, too, but like I said in my last letter, I can't come home right now. But I'm sending you something I made that you can put in your pocket and when you pull it out and look at it, you can think of me. I learned how to make these from some friends I met before I got to Auburn. I hope you like it. And if you ever need a meal or a place to sleep for the night, it'll buy you that, too, if you ask the right person.

Love,
Maddy

I picked out one of my carved nickels—a man with a derby and a beard. I wrapped it in a square of paper, taped it to the letter, and folded it into an envelope.

CHAPTER 33

The newspapers barely had enough room on the front page to cover the two big stories that unfolded in early March of 1932. One was the kidnapping of the Lindberg baby, and the other was the riot at Ford's River Rouge plant in Dearborn, Michigan. Neither one turned out well.

Phillipe had gone back to the vineyard for the week, and Francine and I sat at the kitchen table and read the news while the first batch of pies baked.

"That's where Daniel, Rita's brother, worked," I said, looking at the headline. *Four Killed in Riot at Ford Plant.* Below it, in smaller letters, *Police Fire on Marchers. Fifty Injured.* "Wow! It says there were 3,000 marchers. I wonder if Daniel was there? I hope he didn't get hurt if he was!"

Francine shook her head. "It's terrible. So many people out of work! All those people were unarmed and the police shot at them. I don't know where all of this is going to end."

When we were done baking, I jotted a quick note to Rita and mailed it that afternoon on my way home from selling pies.

> *Dear Rita,*
>   *I read in the paper about the riots. Was your family there? Is everyone all right? Please write back soon.*
>
> *Maddy*

By the end of the following week I got an answer. Phillipe and Francine were both in the kitchen when I hurried in, waving the letter. "It's from Rita," I said, not bothering to sit down before I tore the letter open.

"What does she say?" Francine asked.

I read the letter out loud.

> *Dear Maddy,*
>   *I finally heard from my mother about the riot. I've been on pins and needles all this time. I knew Daniel and my pop*

would've been part of the demonstration, and I was right. Pop and Daniel inhaled some tear gas, but they are both okay. They went to show their support for the committee that went to Ford, and all the committee wanted to do was present a petition, but Ford saw to it that people were tear-gassed and had firehoses turned on them in freezing cold weather. Then they shot at people and blamed the whole thing on Communists. It's Ford that caused the riot!

Do you know what was in the petition? The committee wanted some pay and some coal for all the laid-off workers, relief from foreclosures, and for the men who were still working, a shorter work day, two 15-minute breaks, and slowing down the assembly line that Ford keeps speeding up. Boy that sure sounds like Communist stuff, doesn't it — ha, ha.

I heard the ACLU is trying to press charges against Henry Ford and the Dearborn police. Fat chance. You wait and see.

Anyway, my mom said their only hope to keep the house is if my pop gets his bonus from the service. Right now, I'm the only one with a job, and it sure don't pay much.

Write soon.

Rita

"I'm glad Rita's family wasn't hurt," Francine said. "But what are they going to do without a job?"

"I'm afraid there's not much chance of Rita's father getting that bonus, either," Phillipe said. "Hoover already vetoed it once."

"What kind of bonus is Rita talking about?" I asked.

"Congress drew up a bonus for veterans of the World War to help make up for the income they lost while they were in the service. They got a certificate for their bonus money, but they won't be paid until 1945. Veterans have been trying to get the money now, instead of later, because they're so desperate."

"Why won't the government give it to them?" I asked.

"Hoover thinks it would break the bank," Phillipe said. "Of course, Hoover has a roof over his head, doesn't he?"

"I don't understand how he can just sit back and watch people suffer," Francine said.

"Maybe he'll lose his job," I said. "Then he'll find out what it's like."

"Let's hope," Phillipe said.

"Yes, we can hope," Francine said. "But even so, Hoover will never know what it's like to be without money and without prospects."

The second Monday in April, I rolled out of bed and carried a secret with me into the kitchen. It was April 11, my birthday, and today I was eighteen. There'd be no fuss—I hadn't told anyone in Auburn that it was my birthday—but I added a little extra brown sugar and apple slices to my oatmeal that morning to celebrate, and I looked forward to the afternoon, when I was done selling pies and could stop at the post office. I felt fairly sure there'd be a card or letter from my mother.

The day dragged by slowly, and it took longer than usual to sell all the pies. I worried that the post office would close before I could get there, but I ran up the steps with just a few minutes to spare.

"Mail for Maddy Skobel, please," I said, still breathless.

The clerk glanced at the clock, sighed, and then disappeared into the back. He returned a minute or two later, empty handed. "Sorry, miss," he said.

Are you sure? I wanted to ask. *Maybe you missed it because you're in too much of a hurry to go home.* But he pulled the shade down over the window and I heard him walking away. I swallowed my disappointment, but it sat like a stone in my stomach.

"Not too hungry tonight?" Francine asked, eyeing my dinner, which I had barely touched.

"I guess not," I said. "I'm pretty tired. I think I'll just turn in early."

"You go ahead, then," Francine said. "I'll clean up supper dishes."

In my room, I sat on my bed, cross-legged, and stared out the window into the dusk. I wondered if my family had thought about me today, if anyone had remembered it was my birthday. I wasn't ever going to go back to New Harmony, but I didn't want to be forgotten about either. Is that what had happened? How could I pass my eighteenth birthday so invisibly?

Well, maybe it doesn't have to be invisible, I thought. I picked up my sketchbook and a pencil and sat in front of the mirror. When I finished my self-portrait, I wrote neatly across the bottom: Maddy, at eighteen. April 11, 1932.

Tuesday, I checked again at the post office, just in case, but again there was no mail for me. *Accept it*, I said to myself. *She forgot.* I tried to put it out of my mind, and I purposely avoided the post office for the rest of the week, but on Friday, I stopped once more, and the clerk handed me a piece of mail bearing a New Harmony postmark. My spirits lifted, but I waited until I pulled the wagon home and poured a cup of coffee before I opened the card. On the cover was a bouquet of flowers with Happy Birthday printed across the top in gold. The inside was blank, except for my mother's writing:

> *Dear Maddy,*
> *Sorry this card is a little late, but I hope you had a happy birthday.*
> *Love,*
>
> *Mom*

I looked at the postmark on the letter. April 12. I was surprised that it mattered so much, but I wanted to know why it had been mailed a day after my birthday. Had my mother had lost track of time, or had she lost track of me?

I took a second look inside the envelope. Nothing from Eddie, either, which was another disappointment. I sighed, pushing the card away from me as I sat at the table.

Francine walked in a few minutes later. "You look a bit glum, Maddy. Is there something wrong?"

"Not really," I said, fingering the card again. "It's just kind of weird," I hesitated, "that I got this card from my mother, and she mailed it the day *after* my birthday. I'm trying to figure out if she forgot."

"Your birthday?" Francine asked. "I didn't know. When was your birthday?"

"Monday," I said. "She didn't even mail the card until Tuesday."

"I'm sorry," Francine said. She looked like she might say more, but she was quiet for a few minutes. "It's good that your mother remembered, though, no?" she offered.

"I suppose so," I said, frowning. "But she didn't say much. And Eddie didn't write, either."

"Maybe they're distracted because the times are so hard," Francine said. But she didn't sound convinced.

"Yeah, that's probably it," I said. I didn't believe it, either.

Saturday afternoon, when I returned from selling pies, Phillipe and Francine were chatting animatedly in the kitchen, but they stopped and turned to look at me as I walked in.

"How were sales?" Phillipe asked.

"Good," I answered. I dug into my pocket to retrieve my notes. "And Mrs. Davis ordered several quiches for her club meeting next week–and another, uh, special order."

"Wonderful," Francine said. "We'll make sure she has what she needs."

"We were just discussing dinner," Phillipe said. "Francine has a chicken casserole in the oven. I'm hungry—are you?"

"Sure," I said. "Just let me wash up."

When I came back into the kitchen, Francine was setting the casserole on the table and Phillipe was opening a bottle of wine.

"We're ready, Maddy," Francine said. "Have a seat." I walked to my usual place at the table and stopped in my tracks. In the middle of the table sat a gaily decorated two-layer cake trimmed with green piping. A row of pink miniature roses trailed over the sides of the cake, and the top was loaded with candles.

"Happy birthday, Maddy!" the Durrands said in unison.

"I never expected...you didn't...this is..." The words tried to tumble out, jostling each other in the rush. "I'm so surprised. Thank you so much!" I felt like I could burst from happiness. I leaned over to take a closer look at

the cake and then I did burst—into laughter. Francine had drawn a deliberately clumsy version of the carousel that she had struggled with the first
day I met her. The carousel looked like an old umbrella, and the horses were
stick figures with squiggly manes.

She and Phillipe were both grinning. "We have many reasons to
celebrate your birthday," Francine said. "I thought I'd remind you of one
them."

Phillipe poured wine into our glasses and lifted his, signaling a toast.
"A la Sante, Maddy," he said, his blue-gray eyes keeping contact with me
long enough to create warmth deep inside me.

"Thank you," I stammered, "thank you both. A la Sante."

After dinner, Francine cleared the dishes and brought small dessert plates to the table. Phillipe took a kitchen match, flicked it with his
thumbnail, and the match tip sprouted an orange-yellow flame. He lit the
candles and then he and Francine sang Happy Birthday to me in French.
When they finished, I took a deep breath, ready to blow out the candles,
and then I hesitated for a moment. What should I wish for?

I thought about Eddie and I wished that school would open again so
he wouldn't be stuck in the diner; I wished my father would stop drinking;
I wished my mother would be happy; I wished that the Durrands' boot-
legging would remain secret; I wished that somehow I would become an
artist. It was too many wishes for one birthday cake. Finally, I blew out the
candles, wishing only that today wouldn't have to end.

Francine cut the cake, giving me a generous first piece. Phillipe disappeared into the pantry and returned carrying two rectangular packages
wrapped in blue tissue paper, topped with white bows. He set the packages
next to me and leaned over and kissed me lightly. "Happy birthday, again.
Francine and I thought you should have these."

I was stunned by the gifts. "I don't know what to say. I never expected
this."

"Well, good," Phillipe said. "It wouldn't have been much of a surprise
if you had been expecting them."

"Please. Open your gifts!" Francine urged.

I opened the smaller package first, stripping away the blue tissue to reveal a box holding an array of pastels. "Oh, this is wonderful," I said. "I got to use pastels sometimes in school, when Mr. Otis was teaching me how to use color in my drawings, but I never had any of my own." I touched the sticks of color, feeling their smoothness against my fingertip. "I love these! I can't wait to use them."

"Open the other package," Phillipe said, grinning.

I reached for the other gift and unwrapped a slim pad of beautiful textured paper, exactly right for the pastels. "Oh—these gifts are perfect! How did you know?" I asked.

"Mrs. Franklin was a great help," Francine said. "She's a talented artist who joined our anti-Prohibition group not long ago. I talked to her early this morning, and Phillipe was able to find the supplies in town."

"I don't know what to say. 'Thank you' isn't enough."

"You're welcome, Maddy," Francine said. "I'm looking forward to seeing your artwork."

"I might even let you draw me again," Phillipe said, "to see what I look like to you in color."

I thought of the night I included Phillipe in my still life and felt a spot of color bloom in my cheeks as I remembered his kiss. I wouldn't mind one bit including him in one of my still lifes again.

That night, I was still too keyed up to sleep. Francine and Phillipe had gone to bed and the house was very quiet. I wanted to try out the pastels, but I also wanted to talk to someone. I got out a sheet of writing paper and started a letter:

April 16, 1932

Dear Rita,

I've had the best day today, and I wish I could tell you about it in person. But since I can't, I'll write to you instead.

It all started on Monday, really, which was my birthday, but nobody knew because I didn't tell anyone. But Francine found out yesterday, when I got a card from my mother. And tonight

Francine and Phillipe surprised me with a birthday cake and presents! They even sang to me in French.

The presents were drawing paper and pastels. (They look like chalk, but the color is richer. It's kind of like drawing with sticks of dry paint.) So now I can make drawings in color! But what I keep thinking about is that these gifts were from <u>friends</u>. I've never gotten a birthday gift from anybody but family, and those gifts were always things I needed, like a new hat or a scarf, or even underwear. Don't get me wrong, I appreciate those things, but they're things that <u>everybody</u> needs. But tonight's presents were special things that were picked just for me, because <u>I</u> needed them, because I love to draw!

So I'm feeling happy and even flabbergasted that Francine and Phillipe made a celebration for me the very next day after they found out about my birthday. I hope you take this right—I'm not bragging—I'm just very happy and wanted to tell you my good news. I wish you could have been here, too. I would have given you a big piece of cake!

I hope things are going okay for you in Pulaski. Write soon.

Maddy

I folded the letter and tucked it into an envelope, and then I reached for the pastels to test them out on an old drawing in my sketchbook. I wanted to get confident using them before I tried drawing on the good paper.

I spent every spare minute the next week or two drawing and working with the pastels. Finally, I felt ready, and I took a piece of the special textured paper and made a light sketch in pencil. Then I started using the pastels, thrilled with how the paper grabbed the bits of pigment and held on to them. I learned how to rub and smudge with my fingers to blend lines and colors, and I took special care with the dark browns and greens, knowing that if I made a mistake, it would be difficult to correct.

Finally, when I was satisfied, I carefully laid the finished drawing on some newspaper and slid it under my bed.

When Friday came, I waited until after dinner, when Phillipe and Francine were enjoying coffee, and then I went to my room to retrieve my drawing. I carried it out carefully and placed it on the table. "This is my gift to you," I said. I looked with a critical eye at the image of Durrand Vineyards on paper. The house with the ornate front porch sat among acres of neatly planted grapevines. Off to the right was the warehouse. I thought the angle of the roofline could be improved a little, but I was pleased with how I had used the pastels to catch the pale yellow light of morning. The vibrancy of the pastels gave a glow to the picture. Not too bad, I thought.

"Wow. You've really caught the vineyard," Phillipe said, studying my drawing. "This is wonderful."

"I agree. It's marvelous. Thank you, Maddy," Francine said.

"I'm so glad you like it," I said. I didn't know what else to say. No one had ever been so enthusiastic about my work before.

By mid week, the clerk at the post office handed me a letter from Rita.

April 27, 1932

Dear Maddy,

I'm glad you had such a good birthday. Are you doing lots of drawing? I wish I had money to buy a gift for you, too, but it's pretty slow here at the hotel, and I'm sending home whatever I can. Daniel hasn't found another job yet, but sometimes he or my pop finds an odd job, so my family is just scraping by. I hope things get better soon.

Not much else to say. Write soon—I like to hear what's going on in Auburn.

Rita

May 2, 1932

Dear Rita,

　　I wish things were better for your family so you wouldn't have to worry. Too bad I couldn't send them some pies somehow. I know Francine wouldn't mind. There's nothing much different to report from here. I'm still making and selling pies and trying to improve my drawings when I have time. Oh—One thing new is that I gave Francine and Phillipe a pastel drawing of their vineyard, and their brother Armand made a handsome frame for it. They put it on the wall in their parlor where everybody can see it. I never had anything I drew displayed like that before, but Francine's customers make a fuss about it and I admit that it makes me feel very pleased.

　　I'll keep practicing, and maybe next time I see you I can draw you in color.

　　Write soon.

Maddy

Within two weeks, another letter from Rita arrived:

May 15, 1932

Dear Maddy,

　　Things are going from bad to worse for my family. My pop says if he could just get that bonus, they would be okay for awhile—at least maybe they could hold out until times get better. He said there's a group of veterans that are going to Washington to try to persuade Congress to pass a bill to give them their bonus early, and my pop and Daniel are going to go. Pop said they've got nothing to lose.

　　A lot of the veterans are bringing their families, seeing as how they've got no place else to stay anyway. Pop said the more people that show up, the more likely it is that they'll get their bonus. My mom can't go because she's been sick, but I've been thinking that I'm going to go and meet up with Pop and Daniel. My cousin doesn't mind if I leave for a couple of weeks, and the owner of the Lighthouse Hotel has a brother who was in the World War, and he said if I want to go and help his brother get his bonus, I'll still have this job when I come back.

And if you was to decide to go to Washington with me, that would be swell. We could meet somewhere – maybe Syracuse – and then find a nice dry boxcar and travel together. The truth is, I'd really like it if you'd go with me.. You could even bring your sketchbook and draw the demonstration.

Send me a postcard and tell me if you can come. I'll wait to hear from you but I hope to leave soon.

Rita

I thought about Rita's letter as I walked back home. It didn't seem right that people in the government were holding on to money that veterans could use right now. The vets had certificates that promised them money, but wasn't that like giving a starving man pictures of food and telling him he could trade them for the real thing in about ten years? It was cruel, wasn't it, when so many people were desperate? And the vets had earned the money, hadn't they? Henry must have earned that bonus, too. Maybe if they paid it, he'd have enough money to stop riding the rails and he could marry Anna after all.

I walked into the kitchen and found Francine sitting at the table, writing away. "Are you working on anti-Prohibition letters?"

"Yes, these are going to members of Congress," she said without looking up. "The WONPR is conducting a letter-writing campaign. We're going to make sure that Congress hears our voices, too, not just the noise from the drys."

"That's good," I said, weighing what Rita had written about the bonus march and thinking about Francine's cause. "You spend a lot of time trying to defeat Prohibition. It's important, isn't it?"

"Yes. If you don't make your beliefs known, nothing will change," she said as she licked the flap of an envelope and sealed a letter.

"Remember when we talked about the veterans' bonus a couple months ago?" I said, sliding into a chair at the kitchen table. "Rita said her father was trying to get his."

"Yes, I remember," Francine said. "There's been something about the bonus in the paper again, too. There's a group, out in Oregon I think, that's trying to make people pay attention."

"Yes. Some of the veterans are planning to march into Washington to show Hoover how bad they need their money," I said. "Rita sent me a letter telling me about it. Her father is going, and so is her brother. I guess whole families are going to show their support for the vets."

"That's good," Francine said. "Maybe that will get the attention of Congress. They'll have to pass another bill, though, and then they'll probably have to override Hoover's veto."

"Rita said she's going, too." I hesitated. "The thing is, she asked me to go with her."

Francine raised her eyebrows. "Really?"

"Francine," I said, swallowing hard. I felt like I was about to jump off a cliff. "I think I'm going to go. She's my friend. Maybe it's one way I can help. Like you said, if you don't make your beliefs known, nothing will change. The more people that go on this march, the more Hoover has to pay attention—don't you think?"

"Maybe," Francine said. She looked at me intently but didn't say more.

I took a deep breath. "So what I'm wondering is, if I go – will you still want me to come back? Would I still have a job?"

Francine set her letters aside and sighed. "Well, I guess this is as good a time as any to tell you about my plans."

"What do you mean? What plans?"

"You know how crowded it can get in the kitchen. I've been wanting more countertop and cabinet space, so I've been thinking about expanding the kitchen into the pantry area. That means I'd need to convert your room into a pantry."

"Oh," I said. "I suppose you *could* use more room for your bakery." The tightness in my throat made my voice sound strained and small. I bit back my disappointment and looked down at the table. With my fingertip, I traced the lines of the wood grain.

"Yes. Well, I haven't quite decided. It's either that, or I'm going to rent your room out to Mrs. Hunter so she can keep a better eye on what we're doing here."

I looked up quickly and Francine burst into laughter. Relief flooded through my body. I should have known she wouldn't miss a perfect opportunity to string me along. "I thought you were serious!"

"Yes, I could see that," Francine said, still chuckling. She leaned across the table and touched my arm. "Maddy, you're more than just 'bakery help' to me. You must know that I also consider you my friend. You do what you have to do and come back when you can. I'll manage, and you'll still have a place to stay and a job, such as it is."

"Thank you. I'm glad I have a friend like you."

"How long do you think you'll be gone?"

"I don't know. Probably a couple of weeks."

Francine nodded. "How are you getting to Washington?"

"We'll ride the rails," I said.

Her expression turned serious. "It's dangerous, isn't it? I could lend you the price of a ticket. Then I wouldn't have to worry about you."

I shook my head. "I really appreciate your offer, but I can't accept it. It would take me a long time to pay you back, and Rita couldn't ride with me. It's safer if we travel together. We'll be careful. Don't worry."

The next day was Friday, a day I always looked forward to because Phillipe would be coming home. Sales went exceptionally well that afternoon—I finished my rounds early, quickly selling all the pies in my wagon.

I stopped at the post office, wrote two sentences on a postcard to Rita, and dropped it in the slot marked Out of Town.

> *Dear Rita,*
> *Forward march!*
> *Where and when should I met you?*
>
> *Maddy*

I skipped down the steps of the post office, feeling full of energy. The warm and sunny afternoon added to my cheerfulness, and the soft air carried the sweet scents of trees in bloom. It was too beautiful to be inside. I hurried home, grabbed my sketchbook, and jotted a quick note to Francine, who was out somewhere, too – *Had a great day selling pies. I'll be down by the lake if you need me. Maddy.*

Enna Jettick park hadn't opened yet for the season. The merry-go-round building was still shuttered, but workers were getting ready, cleaning up the grounds. I sat between two white columns on the steps of the porch surrounding the ballroom and looked out at the lake. A line of tall, graceful lampposts curved along both sides of a long walkway that led down to the water, which shimmered deep blue, mirroring the cloudless sky. I was tempted to wade out in the water's blueness, but I knew if I did, I'd also be turning blue. That water would be icy cold in May.

I sat and sketched, spending a blissful couple of hours drawing scenes from the park, listening to birdsongs, feeling warm spring air traveling over my skin, and inhaling the crisp, clean smell of fresh lake water. I moved to a park bench to get a better view of the roller coaster and concentrated on sketching in the curves of the coaster's framework against the bright sky. Someone sat down on the bench next to me, startling me, and I looked up to see Phillipe grinning at me.

"Great day, isn't it? I saw your note to Francine and I knew I'd find you here with pencil and paper in hand," he said. He kissed me, twice—unhurried kisses that created a shiver of pleasure in my body.

"Well, you were right," I said. "It's a perfect day to sit and draw."

"Care to show me what you've drawn?"

"Why not?" I shrugged, turning back the pages to show him my afternoon's work.

"Nice!" he said, lingering over one view. "You've made the park look like it's just waking up."

"I think it is," I said. "Workers have been very busy today. Do you know when the park will open?"

"Next week. The park always opens for Memorial Day." He leaned back in the bench and stretched his legs out in front of him.

"Hmm. Maybe I'll get to see it in action."

"Sure, let's come down here together for the holiday."

"I might not be here." I said.

"What?" Phillipe sat up straight on the bench and turned to me. "Where are you going?"

"Remember my friend Rita? I'm going to go with her to Washington, D.C. to march with the Bonus Marchers. I'll probably be gone for a couple of weeks."

"Well, this is a bit of a surprise." The edge in Phillipe's voice made it clear that he wasn't pleased. "When were you planning to tell me?"

"I thought I just did."

"Does Francine know about your plans?"

"Of course," I said. "I talked to her yesterday." Phillipe's displeasure knocked me off balance, and I scrambled to pull my thoughts together.

"And she was fine with it?"

"Yes, she said I should do what I needed to do and she'd manage while I was gone. She said it's important to stand up for what you believe in, to make your beliefs known," I said, hoping my tone of voice suggested that he ought to adopt the same attitude as Francine.

He crossed his arms and scowled. "I see. Then please bring me up-to-date. When exactly are you leaving, and how are you getting to Washington?"

I drew a deep breath, feeling surprised and annoyed by Phillipe's attitude. "I don't know *exactly* yet when I'm leaving, but as for *how* we're getting to Washington...well, we considered a luxury Pullman car," I said, "since we have so much money, but we decided instead to ride the rails for the sheer thrill of it."

"I don't appreciate your sarcasm, Maddy." Phillipe's voice got louder and louder. "Hopping freights is very dangerous! And why do you need to go to Washington anyway? You're not a veteran!"

"And I don't appreciate your shouting at me!" I answered, half aware that I was shouting back at him. "I know riding the rails is dangerous! That's how I got here, remember? I also know *a lot* more about it than you do, including *how* to do it!" I felt the heat of anger in my face. "As for *why* I'm going—I already told you. It's to show support for the veterans, which happens to include Rita's father—and Henry, who is the hobo who showed me how to ride the rails to begin with!"

Phillipe stood up. "I don't understand why you didn't discuss it with me before you said you'd go!"

I stood up, furious, looking him in the eye. "I don't understand why you think I need your permission!"

We stood, glaring at each other. "I'm going back to the house," he growled. "Come on. I'll give you a ride back. We can finish our discussion at the house."

"Our discussion is already finished!" I said. "And I'd rather walk!"

"Fine!" Phillipe said as he turned and stalked off toward the parking lot.

"I thought you said you *liked* strong women!" I shouted at his back. "The truth is, you only like strong women if they're doing something you agree with!" Phillipe acted like he didn't hear me, but I knew he had. I plopped back down on the bench, still seething. I looked down at my sketchbook at the half-finished drawing of the roller coaster. The outside edge of the paper had wrinkled from the pressure of my hand. I took my pencil and with the flat side of the point, I threw down quick, broad strokes, forming ugly storm clouds over the roller coaster. Then I slammed the book shut and strode out of the park.

All the way up Lake Avenue, I replayed our "conversation" in my mind. I felt stung by Phillipe's anger and confused by his attitude. By the time I turned down Swift Street, I had walked off much of my anger, but I still felt unsettled, the way I had often felt in New Harmony when my father would lash out at Eddie and me for no good reason. It was unfair, and coming from Phillipe, it especially hurt.

When I walked into the house, Francine was checking on a casserole she had put in the oven. Phillipe was sitting at the kitchen table, flipping through the day's mail.

"Hello, Maddy," Francine said. "Did you have a good session down at the lake? It was a gorgeous day, wasn't it!"

"It *was* gorgeous," I said. "And my *drawing* went well." Phillipe didn't look up, but there was a hard edge to the set of his mouth.

"Good!" she said. "Dinner should be ready in twenty minutes or so."

"Thank you, but I'm not very hungry. I think I'll just spend some time in my room *getting ready for my trip*," I said.

"Oh...well...that's fine." Francine looked at me questioningly and then at Phillipe, who still didn't look up from the mail, but now a scowl creased his forehead. "Maybe you'll be hungry later," she said.

"Maybe." The truth was that I was hungry right then, but I couldn't sit across the table from Phillipe and eat dinner, knowing that the afternoon's tension would be sitting right there on the table between us—an ugly centerpiece.

I went to my room and firmly closed the door. Then I pulled out my nickels and the manicure set, which held my jig and files, and I set to work. I tried to shut out everything else and concentrate on my work, but I was aware of an undertone of conversation between Francine and Phillipe. I didn't want to hear any of it. I started humming *Wildwood Flower*, incorporating the rhythm of the music into the strokes of my file. Outside my window, darkness replaced the orange light of sunset, and I switched on my lamp and kept working late into the evening—well past the time I heard Phillipe's footsteps in the room above me—until I was so tired that I knew I could finally sleep.

Very early Saturday morning, hunger woke me and would not be ignored. I went out to the kitchen and started a pot of coffee and then made two pieces of toast, which I heaped with grape jelly. I wolfed them down to quiet the hunger pangs, and then I dug around in the cabinet for a pan to make oatmeal. I heard footsteps coming down the stairs and was relieved to hear Francine's cheery voice. *Good*, I thought, Phillipe wasn't up yet.

"Good morning!" Francine said. "I'm glad to see that you've got your appetite back today. If you're making oatmeal, will you make enough for the three of us? I'm sure Phillipe will be down soon."

"Okay, oatmeal for three," I said, hoping Phillipe would sleep late.

A few minutes later, Phillipe appeared in the doorway, muttered a good morning, and sat down, immediately opening the newspaper. And there it was. Tension occupying a place at the table like a surly fourth person. We all did our best to pretend it wasn't there. Over breakfast, Francine and I planned the day's orders, and Phillipe put down the paper long enough to discuss his weekend deliveries with Francine. But Phillipe and I didn't speak to each other.

After breakfast, Francine and I started making pies while Phillipe made numerous trips to the cellar, loading up his truck with cartons that I knew held bottles of wine. Then he came back into the kitchen and made a couple of sandwiches. "I have a lot of deliveries. I won't be back for lunch," he said to Francine.

"Dinner?" she asked.

"Yes, probably," he said. And then he was out the door and we still hadn't spoken and I felt miserable and angry, all rolled into one.

Dinnertime brought a repeat of the mood set at breakfast. Francine and I talked, Phillipe and Francine talked, and Phillipe and I pointedly ignored each other. Partway through dinner Francine said, "I think this quiche would be much better with some Riesling, don't you?" And she disappeared into the cellar to get a bottle. Phillipe and I sat awkwardly in silence, avoiding eye contact.

When Francine returned, she set out three large-bowled, stemmed wineglasses and poured a taste of wine for each of us. "Oh, that's better," she said as she sipped the light amber liquid and finished her piece of quiche. "I think the French have the right idea, don't you? It's much more *civilized* to have wine with dinner. Don't you think?" she insisted, looking at both of us. I nodded, unsure why Francine was being so persistent. Phillipe looked a little puzzled, but muttered, "Yes. Of course."

"Good!" Francine said. "I'm glad you both agree." She picked up the bottle, poured a little more for herself and then leaned over and filled our glasses almost to the brim, emptying the bottle. "Because I'm going to finish my wine upstairs and I suggest that the two of you drink your wine and work out your disagreement in a *civilized* manner!" She stood up and swept out of the kitchen. "I'm leaving the clean-up to you."

Phillipe and I sat motionless; both of us were stunned. I focused my gaze on my overfull glass and tried not to show how unnerved I felt. Then I picked up the glass carefully and took several big gulps of wine, feeling it warm me as I swallowed. As I set the glass back on the table, Phillipe reached over and touched my hand. "Francine is right, you know. We need to work out our...disagreement. Yesterday, you said there was nothing to discuss. Will you please talk to me tonight? At least hear me out."

I looked directly into his blue-gray eyes. "I'm going to go to Washington, Phillipe."

"Yes, I suppose you are, and I suppose there's no way I can talk you out of it."

I sat up stiffly in my chair.

"And," he added quickly as he watched me start to stand up, "I suppose I was wrong to get angry at you. But please, let me explain." I hesitated and then sat back down.

Phillipe took a long sip of his wine. "You and I have gotten very close over these past months, and...I admit that I was a little hurt that Francine knew you were going before I did. And so I got angry, partly because of that, but mostly because I don't want you to leave...and because I'm afraid for you. Riding the rails, as you call it, is so dangerous. I don't want anything to happen to you."

Phillipe looked very unhappy, and I felt some of my anger melt away. "I'll be fine," I said. "I know the trains are dangerous, but I know what to do. I had a good teacher. And I'll be traveling with Rita—that's good, too." I took a deep sip of wine. "I got upset with you because it seemed like your anger at me came out of nowhere. I couldn't see how I deserved that...and it felt like how it was at home. My father would get mad for no reason and I'd be the target. I don't want any part of that anymore."

Phillipe stood up and came around the table. He took my hands and lifted me to my feet. "I'm sorry I hurt you," he said. "I didn't mean to. I care about you very much." He gently kissed me, and then he pulled me close and held me. My anger was gone and I relaxed against him, enjoying the warmth of his body against mine and his breath against my hair.

I pulled away a little so I could look at him. "I care about you, too. Very much. And I didn't mean to hurt you, either."

He held me close again and then released me. "Let's have a toast. It just so happens that we still have a little wine in our glasses."

I laughed, and we picked up our wine and touched the glasses together. "To a safe and *short* trip," Phillipe said.

"To a safe trip, and to standing up for what you believe in," I said, making eye contact with Phillipe to emphasize my point, although the wine I had drunk made holding eye contact a little tricky. I giggled.

Phillipe chuckled and kissed the top of my head. "Tomorrow you can stand up for what you believe in! Tonight, you're not too steady on your feet!"

I set my glass down and gestured at the table, which was still littered with dishes from supper. "I guess we'd better do something about this. After all, Francine said she was leaving the clean-up to us."

"I don't think it was supper dishes she was referring to," Phillipe said, grinning. "But yes, let's take care of the kitchen."

When the last dish had been put away, Phillipe put an arm around my waist and pulled me toward him. With the other hand, he smoothed my hair and touched my face. "When are you leaving?" he asked.

"As soon as I hear from Rita. Probably in a couple of weeks."

He sighed. "Maybe Rita will change her mind?"

I glared at Phillipe.

"I know, I know. Just hurry back, all right?"

"I'll come back as soon as I can."

We said goodnight by sharing a deep, lingering kiss. Phillipe spoke softly into my ear, "Promise me that you'll come back to Auburn?"

"I promise," I said.

CHAPTER 34

The first Monday in June, I picked up a letter from Rita:

June 2, 1932

Dear Maddy,

I am so happy you're going to join the march! My pop and Daniel left with a large group of vets from Detroit, so he said to look for them on the steps of the Capitol building when we get to Washington.

Can you meet me in Syracuse on Wednesday (June 8)? My cousin said that in the center of town, on Washington Street, is the Yates Hotel. Let's try to meet there-sometime between 11 a.m. and 1 p.m.? I'll wait awhile if I don't see you, but if you're not there by 3 o'clock, I'll figure that something happened and you're not coming, and I'll go on to Washington by myself.

My cousin said the trains run right through the center of town, if you can imagine that, so maybe it will be easy to catch out!

See you soon.

Rita

Only two days away! I hurried back to the house. "I have to leave on Wednesday," I said to Francine, waving the letter in the air. "I'm going to meet Rita in Syracuse and from there we'll go to Washington."

"So soon?" Francine said. "All right. Tomorrow we'll need to let our customers know you won't be delivering pies for a little while, but they can come here to pick them up. Now, what do you need for the trip?"

"Some food would help us out," I said. The memory of being so hungry I could barely stand up would never leave me. I never wanted to feel that pain again. "I have a little money saved from bakery sales that I can use to buy food, but sometimes when you get off a train, you're nowhere near a town."

Francine nodded. "I'll make sure you have food. What else do you need?"

"I'll be okay. I've got my bindle—my bedroll," I said, "and I'll wear the men's clothes I wore when I came here."

"I remember." Francine said. "I can probably find a pair of trousers and a shirt if you need a change of clothes."

I hesitated. "I don't have a change of men's clothes," I admitted, "but I don't want to ask for anything more..."

"You didn't ask. I offered," Francine said. "I'll see what I can find." She sighed. "I do wish there was another way for you to get to Washington. I'm going to worry about you on the trains."

I hoped Francine wasn't going to try to talk me out of riding the rails. "Now you sound like Phillipe," I said, smiling a little.

"Yes, but I won't fight with you about it," she said, returning my smile. Then she became serious. "You must know that because my brother cares for you very much, he's finding your trip to Washington...difficult."

"I know...Phillipe doesn't want me to go, but I think he understands why I have to. And I promised him I'd come back."

Tuesday, I stopped at every customer's house to explain that Francine's delivery service would be canceled for a couple of weeks. Then I gave everybody a little card with her address and phone number and hoped that they would call in and pick up their orders. I didn't want Francine to lose business became of me.

"Phillipe called earlier this afternoon to confirm a special order," Francine said, using the wine sale code words. "I told him you would be leaving Wednesday morning and he said to tell you 'Be safe and hurry back.'"

"Thanks," I said. I swallowed my disappointment at not being at the house when he called. I might have been able to talk to him for a few minutes, even though it was a long-distance call. "When you see him, tell him I'll be back as soon as I can, okay?"

Francine nodded. "You'll find a shirt and pair of trousers in your room. The trousers belonged to Armand's older boy; I kept them to wear sometimes for gardening, but they're still serviceable. The shirt is Phillipe's. He insisted that you take it."

"Oh...thank you," I said, surprised at the way my feelings churned, knowing that Phillipe wanted me to have his shirt.

"Now, tell me what kind of food you need," Francine said.

"I can't carry a lot," I said. "But if I could have some bread, some peanut butter, a can of beans, and maybe some coffee?"

"Yes, of course," she said. "What time are you leaving tomorrow?"

"Probably about nine. I need to allow plenty of time to catch an east-bound freight and find my way to Syracuse. But I can help get the piecrusts started before I go." I felt like I needed to do that in exchange for everything Francine was doing for me.

She shook her head. "That's not necessary. You do whatever you need to do tomorrow morning to get ready to go."

"There isn't much to do," I said. "I'll just roll up my change of clothes, my hairbrush, and my sketchpad inside my blanket. Then I'll get dressed and I'll be ready to go."

I awoke at dawn Wednesday morning; it felt like my body was tuning in again to the rhythms I had learned nearly a year ago as I traveled east from Cleveland. The friendships and life that I had found in Auburn were important to me, but I was drawn that morning to the excitement of what lay ahead. I looked forward to going to Washington and to being part of a march that might make life better for people who were suffering. I knew I was lucky. I had a place to come back to, but many veterans and their families had nowhere to live.

There was no sense in staying in bed any longer. I threw off the covers and walked quietly into the kitchen to have breakfast, savoring every spoonful of oatmeal and every sip of coffee. I knew I'd be eating bread and peanut butter for a while, and coffee made over a campfire left a slurry of grounds you had to be careful to avoid.

It was still very early when I finished breakfast—too early to get ready to go—so I pulled out the flour and lard and started making piecrusts. If I didn't find a channel for my energy, it would just be sitting there idling, like a motor with no job to do.

There was something satisfying about taking a lump of cold dough, setting the heavy wooden rolling pin on top of it, and then pushing two strokes forward, two strokes backward to flatten the dough into an oval. Then two strokes right and two strokes left to change the oval into a circle. If I used the right amount of pressure on the rolling pin, I'd have a good piecrust in eight beats. Then into the pie pan and on to the next crust. By now, it was a familiar, pleasing rhythm.

I was rolling out the ninth piecrust when I heard Francine's footsteps on the stairs. "Maddy, for heaven's sake! I said you didn't need to worry about the pies today," Francine said.

"I couldn't sleep any longer," I said, "and besides, I wasn't worried about the pies, exactly. I needed something to do."

Francine shook her head and poured herself a cup of coffee. I lifted the flat circle of dough and set it in a pie pan. "How many lemon-raisin pies do you need today?"

"A dozen, I think."

I rolled out two more bottom crusts and added them to the lineup while Francine retrieved a piece of yesterday's ham quiche from the Frigidaire for her breakfast. "Tell me—how will you know which train goes to Syracuse?" she asked, spearing a chunk of ham.

"If it's going east out of Auburn, it ought to get me there," I said. I rolled out more piecrust to make the lattice tops.

"That's all there is to it?"

"It's not usually that simple," I laughed, "but Syracuse isn't that far. It'll be a little more complicated to get to Washington, but going south from Syracuse is the most important part."

Finally, it was time to get ready. I changed into my men's clothes, dampened my hair and pinned it up so that it would stay hidden under my cap, and then rolled my few belongings into my blanket, making my bindle. I slipped some dollar bills into my shoes and put several of my carved nickels into my trouser pockets, along with several lengths of twine for tying my pant legs. Then I hung my "girl's clothes" on the hooks in my room and took one last look in the mirror. I tugged my cap a little lower over my face and felt satisfied that I would pass as a young man.

When I walked into the kitchen, Francine called to me from the pantry. "I'm getting some food together for you. Come and see if I have what you need." She looked me as I came to the doorway. "Quite convincing," she said, eyeing my clothes. "Here's some peanut butter, a couple of cans of beans, some coffee—and there's bread in the kitchen, too." She looked at the small pile. "It hardly seems like enough. I'd like to give you more."

"Francine, I can't carry a lot. It makes it hard to get on and off the trains. This is plenty. I won't go hungry."

"You're sure?"

"Positive." I hugged her. "Thanks for everything. I'll be back as soon as I can."

Francine hugged me back. "You be very careful!"

"I will."

I stepped out the back door and was shocked to see Phillipe standing in the driveway, leaning against his truck. He looked as shocked as I felt.

"Maddy?" he said.

"Phillipe, what are you doing here?" I asked. "It's Wednesday. You're never here on Wednesday!" I felt anxiety rise up inside me. Was he going to try one more time to talk me out of leaving?

"You look like a boy," he said.

"I'm *supposed* to look like a boy."

"I know, but I've never seen you dressed like a boy. It's very unsettling."

"Why are you here?"

"I know you said you can handle yourself on the trains," he said, "but please, let me take you to Syracuse. At least I won't have to worry about you on that leg of your journey."

I didn't know whether to be happy or mad. My thoughts swirled into tangled confusion. He should have trusted that I can get to Syracuse safely...He left the vineyards very early this morning to get here in time... He doesn't want me to go...He came to see me off safely...I sighed and mentally stepped away from the knotted mess.

"All right," I said. I crossed my arms. "But you *will* take me to Syracuse, right?"

"Yes, I promise," he grinned. "Although I would much rather take you to the vineyard."

I tossed my bindle into the bed of the truck. "Okay, then. To Syracuse." I tipped my cap in a gesture of thanks.

Phillipe half smiled and shook his head. "It's very strange to see this male version of you," he said.

"Did Francine know you were coming?" I asked as Phillipe drove up Lake Avenue to Genesee Street and headed east.

"No, and unless she looked out the window this morning, she still doesn't know. She'll be surprised to see me later today." Phillipe put his hand on my knee. "After I got off the phone with Francine yesterday, I decided to persuade you to let me drive you to Syracuse."

I studied his hand as it rested on my leg. It was muscular from his work at the vineyard, but not coarse. A line of light brown hair extended from his forearm, over his wrist, and tapered off along the outside of his hand. I placed my hand on top of his, and Phillipe looked at me for a moment in a way that made me feel deeply connected to him. We sat quietly for a little while, not needing to speak.

Eventually, Phillipe broke the silence. "Tell me what it's like to ride a freight train," he said.

I thought for a moment. "When I left home and caught my first freight, I sat in the doorway of an open boxcar, rocking with the rhythm of the train and looking out at this huge countryside. All the ties you have to a place seem to drop away and you have this wide view of the world. Things seem...possible," I said, trying to find the right words. "I guess that's why so many desperate people are riding the rails. Because if you're moving, there's hope."

"What about you? Were you also desperate?"

I took a deep breath and let it out slowly. "Yes, I'd have to say that I was desperate. A lot of bad things had happened, and there was no hope for things to be better if I stayed where I was, that's for sure."

Phillipe looked over at me. "What happened, Maddy?"

I shook my head. "Not now. When I come back, maybe we can talk."

"All right."

I wasn't sure how much I wanted to tell Phillipe, either, about why I left home. It was still very painful to think about, so I turned my thoughts to something else.

"Maybe, when I get back," I said, "you'd like to take a ride on a freight train—ride in a boxcar and see what it feels like. We could catch out in Auburn and see where we end up."

Phillipe laughed. "*Catch out.* I just might take you up on that," he said.

"I hope you will," I said.

At first glance, Syracuse looked like any normal city with blocks of storefronts, churches, banks, and movie theaters lining both sides of the streets and people walking along the sidewalks. But the buildings were gritty looking, and where the rain had tried to wash away the grime, dark streaks stained the brick walls. Within a few minutes, a locomotive pulling a short line of freight cars came through, spewing choking clouds of black soot, on tracks that ran right through the center of town, just like Rita had said.

"I've never seen a city like this!" I said as we waited for the train to pass. "Trains usually run along the edge of town, not through the middle of it!"

"The city grew up right along the tracks, I think," Phillipe said.

Further down Washington Street stood a massive, six-story building that took up an entire city block. I pointed to the sign on its roof. "There's the Yates hotel. It's a good thing we're a little early. It's going to take some time to find Rita. The hotel is huge!"

"I'll park the truck and we can look for her together," Phillipe said.

"She probably isn't even here yet. If she's still on her way, it might even be a couple more hours before she gets here. You can just drop me off. I'll find Rita eventually."

"I don't mind waiting," Phillipe said.

"It's not necessary," I said. "I appreciate that you brought me to Syracuse, but you should get back to your work."

He pulled the truck over to the curb, not far from one of the entrances to the hotel. "All right," he sighed. "I suppose I have to let you go...for now."

We both got out and he came around the truck as I lifted my bindle out of the bed. "I wish I could drive you all the way to Washington," he said, putting his hands on my shoulders.

"I know. Don't worry about me, okay?"

"Of course I'm going to worry," he said. "Be safe, all right?" He leaned over and quickly kissed me, then strode around the truck and climbed in. I picked up my bindle and walked past a row of plate glass windows toward the hotel entrance. Might as well start by checking the lobby, I thought. The windows reflected a slightly wavy view of the street—and the young man passing by, who was me. Past the reflection, on the other side of the windows, another young man grinned and waved. It took a moment to register—it was Rita! We both moved toward the door, but Rita burst through it first, greeting me on the sidewalk with a hug.

"I'm so glad I got here early enough to see the little scene you created!" she said, laughing.

"What are you talking about?"

She rolled her eyes toward the lobby. Inside, several people with very sour expressions looked toward us.

"What's the problem?" I asked.

"A minute ago, they watched two men kiss," Rita chuckled, "and it's obvious they don't approve. My guess is that they don't think much of two men hugging, either."

I burst into laughter as I realized Rita was talking about Phillipe and me, and then our hug. "So who needs their approval?" I asked, turning toward the people in the lobby who were still watching us. I mimicked their sour expression and then Rita and I hurried away, in case one of them decided to pick a fight.

Trains ran frequently through the center of Syracuse, but there were too many people around for us to catch out unobserved. We walked away from town, following tracks that led south, until we heard the measured chugs of a locomotive coming behind us. We watched as cars clanked slowly past us. I spotted an open boxcar and pointed.

"Okay?" I yelled to Rita.

She nodded. We trotted alongside the car, tossed our bindles in, then I grabbed the handhold and swung myself up and in. Rita followed right behind me. We propped ourselves against our bindles and sat back. The car swayed gently, and my body rocked in comfortable rhythm. I felt as much at home here as I did in my room in Auburn.

We traveled south through New York, into Pennsylvania, and at every town and whistle stop, we saw veterans get on the train. At first it was one or two, and then sometimes groups of five or six. Tired-looking veterans, some carrying army knapsacks and wearing tattered shirts or pants from their old uniforms, helped their buddies or their wives and children find a place to ride.

Rita turned to me. "People keep getting on the trains, but the railroad isn't making a fuss about it," she said. "I can't believe it."

"I know," I said. "It's almost making me nervous. The crew has to know what's going on."

"Some of them railroad men are veterans, too," said a man sitting next to Rita. He drew his knees up to his chest and shifted his weight. He wore his old army boots, but his toes peeked through the sides where the leather had split. "They think the government ought to do the right thing and pay the bonus, so they ain't makin' a stink about people riding."

Rita brightened. "Well, that's good news!"

"Don't you go thinking it's gonna be a cakewalk, buddy," the man said. "Didn't you hear what happened in Cleveland?"

"No, what?"

"There was over a thousand veterans that piled into the freight yard in Cleveland, and the police came and rousted them. The veterans fought back, though, and some of them took over the roundhouse. The papers said they stopped all freight traffic for something like fourteen, sixteen hours."

"What happened?" I asked.

The man shrugged. "Eventually some big old transport trucks came and they loaded up the veterans and took 'em to the city limits." He grinned. "Wasn't too far out of Cleveland that they hopped the train again, though. I imagine they're in Washington by now."

"Well, maybe we'll be lucky," Rita said.

"Maybe," the man said. "But I wouldn't count on it. I ain't countin' on nothin'."

The next afternoon, somewhere past Wilkes-Barre, our train pulled into a rail yard to take on water and coal while a switching engine removed and added some cars. These stops had a rhythm of their own and we knew we'd be parked for a while. Everybody would take that time to go find a patch of woods or just stretch their legs. There would be a ripple of people moving away from the cars, and later the current would shift and flow back to the cars.

Rita and I walked past some veterans at the edge of the woods who were watering the brush, but we went deeper into the woods to be sure we'd have privacy. When we got back, a crowd of angry veterans had gathered near the train.

"What's going on?" I asked a man who was standing close by.

"The railroad ain't letting anybody back on the train," he said. "They brought in a bunch of bulls and some railroad hotshot said they ain't leaving this yard with anybody riding the train."

"Then the train ain't leaving this yard, either," another man said, and he took off up the tracks and disappeared between two boxcars.

The bulls were striding, in pairs, up and down the tracks. It looked like each pair had been assigned a section of the train to keep clear of riders. The veterans were clustered in groups, buzzing angrily, but no one wanted to pick a fight with the bulls, especially with women and babies in the crowd. We heard the locomotive build up a head of steam, and then the familiar clanking of couplings grabbing traveled toward us. Up ahead, the train started moving, but the cars in front of us stood stock still. A cheer went up from a group of veterans. "That's a pretty short train!" someone yelled from where the boxcar had been uncoupled, leaving most of the train behind.

The brakeman signaled frantically and the locomotive stopped. They backed up the locomotive and got the boxcar recoupled, then tried again. This time, the train came apart at another place. Again, it was reconnected, and again, a car in a different place was uncoupled, breaking the train every time it started to move forward. For a good hour, this act of defiance went on, and finally, the train stopped and a red-faced engineer came huffing toward several of the bulls.

"What the hell are you doing back here?" the engineer yelled.

"There ain't enough of us to keep them from uncoupling the cars and keep 'em off the train, too," said a bull.

"We tried getting the police to come in and help us, but they said it was railroad business, not police business," another bull explained.

"Jesus H. Christ," the engineer bellowed. "Then let these people get on the goddam train so I can get out of this yard!"

"But the office said..." the first bull stammered.

"I represent the railroad, too, and this is my goddam train! I want it out of here in fifteen minutes. And I mean all of it! You got that?" he barked. Then he turned on his heel and huffed back toward the locomotive. The bulls signaled the rest of the bulls to come to the front of the train, and behind them, a jubilant crowd piled onto the train.

Rita and I settled into a boxcar with a group of men and their families, and within fifteen minutes we were jerked toward the back of the car as the couplings grabbed like a proper line of dominoes. At the back of my boxcar, a veteran with stripes on his sleeve spoke up. "If I had any money to bet," he said with a big grin, "I'd lay money on the engineer being a vet, too."

"How are we going to find your pop and your brother?" I asked as we picked our way Friday morning across the tracks near Union Station.

"Pop said to wait for him on the steps of the Capitol. Eventually, we'll find each other," Rita said. "He knew I was leaving on Wednesday, so he'll be looking for me every day now."

"At least it won't be hard to find the Capitol," I said, pointing. Ahead of us, only a few blocks away, the Capitol dome rose grandly against the skyline, looking important even from the train station.

We shouldered our bindles and set a solid pace toward the dome. Everywhere I looked, block after city block was filled with stone buildings rising from concrete. In one way, it was thrilling to experience such a grand city. Through my eyes the pictures of Washington, D.C. that I had seen in books had transformed into a living, breathing city. But the magnitude of the city left me feeling very small and insignificant. I wondered if Rita and I had been silly to think that we could change anything by coming here. But then, as we got closer to the Capitol and the entire building came into view, we could make out a sea of movement.

"Look at all those people!" Rita said. "There must be thousands of marchers!"

I was speechless for a minute. "I've never seen anything like this," I said. My feelings of doubt disappeared. Excitement welled up inside me and pushed me forward, eager to get a better look at the marchers and become part of them. Rita quickened her steps to match mine.

"This is exciting," Rita said. "With so many people here, Congress has to listen, don't you think?"

"I don't see how they could vote against the bonus when they see how many people need it," I agreed.

Rita was beaming. "Oh, that bonus money will help out my family so much!"

"Well, don't go spending any of it yet," I said, grinning. "So far, Congress hasn't voted for it."

"But look at all these people. Congress has got to vote for it!"

"They just might!" I said.

We made our way to the Capitol steps, through throngs of men in tattered clothes, rundown shoes, and tired hats. The men looked thin and worn-out, but they also had a look of strong determination about them that you could see and feel. My fingers itched to sketch them.

We found a place to sit on one of the lower steps and propped ourselves against our bedrolls to watch for Rita's father and brother. I studied the crowd. There were women and children, but the majority of faces belonged to men in their thirties and forties. Veterans who shared a past and a purpose, I thought. I pulled out my sketchbook and got to work.

Rita impatiently walked up and down the steps, looking for her father. She'd sit for a few minutes and watch me draw, commenting on some of the men or pointing out something she thought I should draw next. Then she'd stand up and walk farther up the steps to try to get a better look at the crowd. "You know, I think I'm going to walk around a little and try to spot my pop," she said.

"Okay, I'll be here," I said, concentrating on a sketch. A short time later, I sensed a presence behind my left shoulder. I turned to see who was there and looked directly into the curious blue eyes of a young boy. His sandy brown hair had recently been bowl-cut, and his skinny arms poked out awkwardly from the sleeves of a worn, too-big tan shirt. He might have been eight years old.

"Hi," I said.

"Hi," he said. "You draw good."

"Thanks. What's your name?"

"Leo. What's yours?

"Matt," I said, remembering to use my "traveling" name.

Another boy suddenly appeared right next to Leo, with the same sandy-brown hair, the same scrawny body, the same blue eyes—and even the same face.

I chuckled. "I bet you two are brothers," I said to the twins.

"Yeah. I'm Lester," the second boy said, elbowing his brother a little. "I'm older than Leo."

"Only an hour older!" Leo protested.

Lester looked at my sketchpad. "Hey!" he said, his blue eyes widening. "That's a swell drawing!"

"Thanks. Want me to draw you?"

"Yeah!" they said in one voice.

I had them sit a few steps higher than me so that the Capitol would be in the background. I quickly sketched in the plane of the steps and then started on the boys. Lester sat hugging his shins and Leo propped his elbows on his knees, resting his chin in his hands. Both boys watched me intently, pleased to be subjects of attention.

"Where are you boys from?" I asked. I sketched Leo's too-big shirt, the frayed hem of his trousers, and worked my way to his shoes. The left one was starting to split, and his toes were poking out.

"Daddy says we're from Washington now," said Lester. "He says there's no place else to go."

"Yeah, but we used to live in Kentucky," Leo said. "Till they kicked us out of our house."

I started drawing Lester, working on the way his skinny arms wrapped around his legs. A shrill whistle pierced the air and both boys jumped up. "That's our daddy. Gotta go!" They disappeared into the crowd.

I finished Lester—drawing him wasn't much different from drawing Leo, and as I sketched in the pillars of the Capitol building, I heard Rita's voice.

"Maddy, I found them! Come meet my family," she said.

I stood up to greet what was definitely the Boyle family. All three had dark hair, dark eyes, and round faces. Rita introduced me to her father and brother. Mr. Boyle spoke first. "I'm glad to meet you, Maddy" he said, "and I'm glad you came with Rita. I didn't like the idea of her traveling alone."

Daniel stuck out his hand. "You and Rita don't look half bad as guys. Good to meet you," he said.

I shook his hand. "Good to meet you, too," I said.

"What's happening with the march?" Rita asked. "I've never seen so many people in one place before!"

"I have," Daniel said, scowling. "And we got tear gassed and four people died."

"Well, this isn't Detroit," Mr. Boyle said. "Let's hope Congress votes the right way so we can all go home soon."

"Is anything happening yet?" Rita asked.

"Today, we'll see," Mr. Boyle said. "The bonus bill got tabled in May, and the rules say that the first time it could come up for a vote is June 13."

"But today is the 10th," Rita said. "So why did you say we'll see today?"

"Because the House is scheduled to adjourn today," Mr. Boyle said. "If they adjourn, they kill the bonus bill."

"Then they better not adjourn!" Rita said. "We didn't travel all this way for nothing."

"We'll find out what's more important to them," Daniel said. "They're supposed to adjourn so they can go to the Republican National Convention and nominate Hoover for four more years of misery."

"Wait and see, Daniel," Mr. Boyle said. Daniel only shrugged.

Late in the afternoon, a buzz of excitement filtered down the Capitol steps.

"Something's happened!" Rita said. "What's going on?"

Daniel hurried toward a group of veterans and came back smiling. "Pass the word," he yelled. "The House is staying in session." Shouts of "the House is in session" and "no adjournment" carried throughout the Capitol grounds.

Mr. Boyle was beaming. "That's good—there's hope! It's possible that they'll vote on the bonus bill next week." He turned to look at Rita and me. "We might as well go back to camp," he said. "Can't do anything now until Monday."

"Where's camp?" I asked.

"Across the Anacostia River," he said. "Some of the vets are staying in abandoned government buildings on Third Street, but so many people came in, they started another camp across the river. That's where Daniel and I are, and there's room for you, too." He paused, looking at Rita and me. "There's women and children over there, but you're probably better off staying dressed like you are. You'll blend in better."

"Glad you think so, Pop," Rita said. "Because we didn't bring any girl's clothes."

We crossed the Eleventh Street drawbridge over the Anacostia River, and the sight of that camp stopped me in my tracks. Stretched out across the Anacostia Flats was the biggest Hooverville I had ever seen. It was also the oddest and most orderly. Camp Marks, it was called. Camps were set up in long rows, like city blocks, and they were a mix of army tents, wooden shacks, and makeshift cardboard structures. Everywhere, over block after block of these shelters, American flags flew, creating a motion of red, white, and blue that made me catch my breath. All the people in that giant Hooverville were desperate—and destitute—but somehow they still had faith in America. I hoped the men in Congress would live up to that faith.

Inside the camp, we walked through the huge field, down grassy rows that divided veterans into sections. Arizona, Ohio, Indiana, West Virginia, Kentucky—each state claimed its own area. It was a well-organized camp of shabby ex-military men and their families.

Mr. Boyle and Daniel led us to the Michigan section. "We've got two tents," Mr. Boyle said. "Daniel and I will share one and you two can share the other."

Rita and I ducked inside briefly to toss our bedrolls into the tent designated for us. A wave of steamy air smelling of overheated canvas and grass wilting in the hot afternoon sun pushed against my face.

"Wow! Let's hope it gets cooler tonight," Rita said.

"Yeah, let's hope," Daniel said from outside the tent. "It's been damn hot!"

Rita and I spent the weekend getting our bearings within the camp. The first thing Mr. Boyle showed us was the mess tent, where we could get something to eat. "Where does this food come from?" I asked as the four of us stood in a long line, waiting our turn.

"From a lot of places," Mr. Boyle said. "The government set aside some money to feed us, some of the states have sent food, and there was even a big boxing event last week that was a benefit for the marchers."

The weather stayed beastly hot, but every day more veterans came, undeterred by the heat, full of determination to get what the government had promised them. We were lucky to have the tents. People scrounged whatever they could for shelter. One couple had a large crate that had been used to ship a piano. Another veteran and his buddy lived in their battered car, which they had painted with slogans. *We Done a Good Job in France, Now You Do a Good Job in America* was printed on the side of the car. On the back, they wrote simply *We Need the Bonus*.

The camp emptied out early Monday morning as nearly everyone made their way across the drawbridge to wait on the steps of the Capitol. People got restless in the hot sun, but there was no action on the bonus. By the end of the day, a discouraged horde walked back to Camp Marks.

"What were they doing?" Rita asked her father. "Why didn't they consider the bonus today?"

Mr. Boyle shrugged. "There's no telling."

"They see no reason to hurry," Daniel scowled. "They'll go home to their nice houses and have a good dinner. We'll go back to camp and have some stew."

"Let's just be patient," Mr. Boyle said.

"Pop, you've been patient for eight years, ever since Congress first promised the bonus."

"Then I guess I can wait a couple more days," Mr. Boyle said.

Tuesday's crowd was even bigger because day and night, more people were streaming in from all parts of the country. Mid-morning, as I sat drawing a group of vets who were playing cards to pass the time, word traveled through the crowd that the bonus bill was going up for debate in the House. The energy level of the crowd grew as people's hopes rose. I felt the change all around me, but I couldn't find a way to grab it and put it in my drawings.

Some members of the B.E.F., short for Bonus Expeditionary Force, which is what the veterans were calling themselves, watched the debates from the gallery. After each representative spoke, someone came out to report on what was said. Rita worked her way up the Capitol steps to listen to the reports and then she'd come back to tell me about it. The first congressman spoke for the bonus, the second spoke against it, the next one supported it—and the debate went on.

It had been a while since Rita's last report, and I wondered if some representative was being particularly long winded. If that was the case, I hoped it was a speech in favor of the bonus. Finally, Rita came back, but she wore a serious expression on her face.

"What's wrong?" I asked. "Did they vote it down?"

"Something terrible happened. They said a congressman from Tennessee started giving a speech and then he collapsed. There were three doctors that tried to revive him, but word is that the congressman died. And to make things worse, his wife was there to listen to his speech, so she saw it all happen."

"Oh no—that's awful!" I said.

"The House adjourned. I guess everyone out here is heading back to camp for now. No one is sure what to do."

That night, there was a lot of discussion, and the vets decided what to do. Wednesday morning, all the flags in the camp flew at half staff. Wednesday afternoon, the dead congressman was being taken from a funeral home to the train station so he could be buried in Tennessee. Rita, Daniel, Mr. Boyle, and I stood with thousands and thousands of veterans who lined the route and paid their respects, heads bowed, as the procession made its way to Union Station.

That same day the House took a vote, and they passed the bonus bill. "The vote was 211 to 176," Daniel said, "It's up to the Senate now, and they're going to vote on Friday." Daniel's mood was a little brighter and I saw a little glimpse of what Daniel might be like in better times.

"At least there's hope now," Rita said.

I looked at Daniel, Mr. Boyle, Rita, and then at the veterans sitting near us. Everybody wore faded, threadbare clothes, worn out shoes, and faces that were tired and creased with worry. That vote was probably the first piece of good news that anybody in the camp had heard in a long time.

Thursday was a day of restlessness. Groups of vets from Camp Marks took turns going to the Capitol to keep a presence, but we had a lot of time on our hands. "Hurry up and wait," Mr. Boyle said. "Just like the army."

The summer heat was so stifling that you couldn't stand to be inside a tent, but there wasn't any shade to be found, either.

"Let's go down to the river," Rita suggested. "We can wash up a little and maybe cool off."

"Great idea!" I said. "I really need to wash these clothes, too." I took the spare pants and shirt Francine had given me, and Rita grabbed her one change of clothes. But as we got close to the river, we could see that hundreds of veterans had the same idea. The banks of the river were thickly occupied by nearly naked men who were bathing and washing their clothes in the muddied water. Rita and I glanced at each other and, hiding our grins, quickly walked further down the river, past all the men in their skivvies, until we reached a spot where we could have a little privacy. We hurriedly stripped down to our underwear and swam out into the murky river until we were neck deep in water. We washed ourselves and our clothes quickly in the deep water and returned to shore to dress, not trusting that we could bathe for long without being seen.

"I feel a lot better!" Rita said. "But I wish we dared to swim around longer."

"I know. At least we cooled down a little," I said. As I buttoned the shirt Phillipe had given me, I felt a stab of emotion, remembering that Francine said Phillipe had insisted that I take it. I missed him, and Francine too. I hoped her bakery business would stay steady enough until I got back. Maybe I'd leave Washington on Friday, after the vote.

Rita's voice interrupted my thoughts. "It's a good thing I've got some twine." She threaded a length of it through the loops on her trousers, which hung loosely on her hips. She hitched up her pants and knotted the twine. "I guess that'll do," she said. "What about you? Need some twine?"

The trousers Francine had given me were a little loose, but I tucked in Phillipe's shirt and it took up the slack between me and the waistband. "No. I'm okay," I said.

"You've got quite a bit of room in that shirt," Rita said. "I guess everybody is getting thinner, though."

"Well, that's probably true," I said. Some days the food donated to the camp had to be stretched pretty far. "But this shirt would be big on me anyway. It's Phillipe's."

"Wow," Rita said, raising her eyebrows. "The man gave you the shirt right off his back. He must really have a case for you!"

"It wasn't right off his back," I said, feeling color rising in my face. "He just said he wanted me to take it." I hesitated and then grinned a little. "But you might be right about that case."

We took our time walking back to the Michigan encampment, walking up and down the long rows of the giant Hooverville, reading the signs pleading for the bonus and marking the states—Oregon, Texas, Georgia, New Mexico.

"How can they refuse to help all these people?" I wondered out loud.

"Let's hope they don't refuse tomorrow," Rita said. She mopped her forehead with her sleeve. "God it's hot! I wish we could find some shade."

"People just have to make their own," I said, looking ahead at the Pennsylvania block. Someone had suspended a tattered blanket from four poles, making an awning in front of their tent. As we drew closer, Rita pointed to a dog sleeping in the small rectangle of shade the awning provided. His ears flicked to fend off flies, but he was dreaming, his little brown and white legs jerking rhythmically.

Rita laughed softly. "Wonder where's he running to?"

"Someplace cool, I bet. Or maybe he's swimming in a nice cold...wait... is that...oh my gosh...I think it's..."

Rita jerked her head around to look at me. "What are you talking about?"

"Jigger!" I called. The brown and white dog raised his head and looked around warily, trying to get his bearings.

"Are you nuts?" Rita said. "Why are you yelling?"

"Jigger!" I called again. This time, he jumped up and came trotting over to me, tail wagging furiously. I knelt down and gave him a good scritching behind his ears. "It's good to see you, boy," I said as he bobbed around excitedly, licking my arms.

"You know this dog? How?" Rita asked.

Before I could answer her, a man strode over to us. From ground level, all I saw were his faded khaki trousers and worn out shoes.

"Looks that way," the man said. "My dog ain't that friendly with strangers. Can't say that I recognize you though."

I stood up. His face was shaded by his hat, but he was scowling a little, just the way I remembered from the very first time I met him down at the river.

"Well, that's probably because you haven't seen me in about a year, Henry," I said, grinning.

"Holy cow!" he said, and the scowl made way for a big grin as his face registered who I was. He shook my hand, covering it with both of his hands and pumping my arm up and down energetically. "How are you

Maddy? I wonder about you every time I go back to New Harmony, but I never expected I'd see you here." He took in my men's clothes and then looked closely at Rita. "Birds of a feather, looks like. Glad to see you're not traveling by yourself," he said to me.

"Henry, meet Rita Boyle," I said. "Rita, this is my friend Henry O'Connor. He's the one who taught me how to ride the rails."

"Pleased to meet you," she said, shaking Henry's hand.

Henry pointed to the makeshift awning. "If you want to get out of the sun, sit for a while."

We settled onto the prickly grass under the awning, which cast a shadow just barely big enough to shade the four of us. Jigger settled back down for another nap, and his panting became a rhythmic undertone to our conversation.

"I never would've expected to see you here," Henry said to me. "You got family that served?"

"No, not me," I said. "I came with Rita to show support."

"My pop served," Rita said. "He was overseas for two years. He earned that bonus, just like everybody else who was in the war. And like everybody else, he needs it now." And she told him about her father and Daniel and Ford Motor.

Henry nodded. "Ford bought steel from the mill I worked in Pittsburgh, but we heard he wasn't no friend of the working man. Word gets around." Henry uncrossed his legs and recrossed them, changing which leg was in front. The hem of his right pant leg was fraying, and he pulled off a loose thread. "So, how did you two meet? Did you both work at that bakery you wrote me about?"

"No, I met Rita in a boxcar on the way to Auburn," I said. "We almost got into a fistfight."

Rita laughed. "Well, if you'd been minding your own business, I wouldn't have gotten testy."

"If I'd been minding my own business, we never would have become friends," I said.

"You've got a point there," Rita admitted. "And I'd be traveling by myself and hating it." She turned back to look at Henry, "I was on my way to Pulaski, New York, which is where I spent most of the winter—except when I was nearly killing myself in a crooked dance marathon—and when my pop wrote me about the bonus march, I wrote to Maddy and she I met up again and rode the freight trains to Washington." She took a breath and I took the opportunity to jump in.

"What about you, Henry? Did you find any work?"

"Some odd jobs. None of 'em lasted very long. Helped me get through the winter, though."

"That's good. You said you'd been back to New Harmony..." I stopped, not knowing what to ask, but wanting to hear some news.

"Yup. Found a couple of odd jobs there, too." He looked at me intently. "One time I washed dishes for a couple of days at that diner near the rail yard. Those were good days—I sure ate well. But the job didn't last too long. Just long enough to let the regular dishwasher start seeing straight again. He'd been in a fight and had two shiners. Couldn't hardly see."

I remembered Eddie's letter. He told me Raymond had gotten into a fight with someone—that he got the worst of it.

"I might have heard something about that," I said. "I believe he, the dishwasher, claimed it wasn't a fair fight."

"Funny how the first ones to complain about things not being fair are the ones who ain't fair to other people," Henry said. "I heard he had it coming."

I looked closely at Henry. It seemed like he knew a lot about that fight, but he didn't offer anything more.

"But that must have been a while ago," I said.

Henry nodded. "It was. Why?"

"Because I also heard," I said, "that the dishwasher died."

Henry raised his eyebrows. "That so? What from?"

"From an infection. It got into his blood and killed him."

"Could be true," Henry said. "I stopped there a week or two before I came here to Washington. They didn't need any help, but a young boy was washing dishes."

Eddie, I thought.

"What happened to your job at the bakery?" Henry asked.

"Nothing, I hope," I said. "Francine—the woman who owns the bakery—said she'd be okay for a couple of weeks while I came to the march. As long as her business stays steady enough, I'll still have a job when I go back." I was a little worried about the bakery sales, but I didn't say so.

"Well, you didn't tell him the best part," Rita chimed in. "Francine's got a swell-looking brother, and he's got a case for Maddy."

I felt my face warm up.

"That so?" Henry smiled. "Well, good. I'm glad for you."

"Do you suppose we should head over to the mess tent?" I asked, desperate to change the subject. "I'm getting hungry."

We found Daniel and Mr. Boyle and introduced them to Henry. Then we all took our place in the mess tent line, which was already getting long. But it turned out that a fresh donation of beef had arrived at camp in the afternoon, allowing for a savory stew full of nice chunks of meat that satisfied my hunger for a long while. A full stomach lets you turn your attention to other things, and Rita and I sat with the three men long into the evening, talking about the bonus, the Depression, unions, Ford Motor, and listening to Mr. Boyle and Henry trade war stories.

By the time Rita and I crawled into our tent, it was close to midnight. But it was too hot to sleep, and my mind kept churning around thoughts of the Paradise Diner, Raymond, the attack, stabbing him with the fork, Eddie, my mother, my father in jail, Raymond dead. I barely slept, except for little bits of time when exhaustion won out, and at the first light of morning Rita and I were up, visiting the latrines before making our way to the mess tent. It seemed like most of the camp was stirring, and Mr. Boyle, Daniel, Rita, and I stood in a line that had already formed at the latrines. Even early in the morning, the air was warm and thick with humidity, and it reeked of human waste that had collected over several weeks and heated up every afternoon in the summer sun. I breathed as shallowly as I could, but still the stench filled my nose and turned my stomach. When it was finally my turn, I held my breath as I took care of business, although I thought my lungs might burst before I finished up and got far enough away to start breathing again.

"Whew!" Daniel said as the four of us approached the mess tent. "I heard that they're working on a temporary hookup to the city's sewer system. I hope that happens soon!"

"Well, if the Senate approves the bonus today, there won't be such a need to hook up the latrines. People will be going home," Mr. Boyle said. "At least those who have homes. They'll get some money to keep the devil from the doorstep a while longer." He shook his head, "But for some of the others, it's already too late." His eyes looked sad and his forehead creased with worry. I wasn't sure which group his family was in.

The plan was for a large group of veterans to go to Capitol Hill that Friday morning to hold a vigil for the vote. Even though the vote probably wouldn't take place until the end of the day, they wanted to make sure the senators saw thousands of veterans as they arrived at the Capitol for the day's session. Later in the afternoon, when the vote was getting near, the rest of the veterans in Camp Marks would cross the Eleventh Street bridge and join the others.

Mr. Boyle and Daniel went over with the early group, and Rita and I stayed back, waiting impatiently with thousands and thousands of veterans and their families. I tried to find Henry and Jigger, but Henry wasn't in the Pennsylvania encampment.

Finally, it was time to go, and a huge contingent of men, women, and children gathered to march together out of Camp Marks to the Capitol. We moved steadily, accompanied by a quiet hum of conversation that seemed to unify us and underscore our purpose. But after a short while, the forward movement stopped, and then a wave of agitation traveled through the crowd. The quiet hum turned into an angry buzz.

"What's going on?" people behind us yelled. "Why aren't we moving?"

Nobody seemed to know, and then from up ahead, a voice cried out, "They've raised the drawbridge! No one is allowed to cross."

Outrage ricocheted through the crowd as the news was passed.

"Those sons a bitches," another man shouted. "They got no right to keep us from crossing. But there's other bridges we can cross and they ain't drawbridges."

A large group broke away to find another way, but word came back that the police had closed the other bridges, too. Blue-uniformed cops were standing shoulder to shoulder behind a line of police cars they had parked crosswise to block the other bridges.

Rita and I worked our way closer to the Eleventh Street drawbridge to see for ourselves. The steel bridge stood upright, like a sword drawn, a deliberate act of aggression. A long line of policemen, maybe 50 or more, stood stiffly near the base of the bridge.

"I don't believe what I'm seeing," Rita said. "Why would they do this?"

"Maybe the Senate took a vote and it went bad," a man nearby said.

"Maybe they tear-gassed the men at the Capitol and hauled them off to jail," another said.

"I hope Pop and Daniel are all right," Rita said.

"I know. And Henry, too," I said.

The crowd grew angrier and angrier. "Lower the bridge! Lower the bridge!" men chanted.

One of the cops grabbed a bullhorn. "Return to your camp. The bridge is closed," he said.

The men shouted him down. A group of veterans scrambled down to the bank of the river, intending to cross by boat, but the cops turned them back.

The people in Camp Marks were united, and their outrage took a new shape, like it came from one mind, not many. I took a deep breath and swallowed hard—I was sure that trouble would erupt any minute.

Then suddenly we heard the sound of metal against metal, and slowly the gears engaged and clanked, and the drawbridge was lowered. The cops stepped away and we surged across the bridge, a throng of seething people pushed along by a wave of indignation.

A large group of furious veterans waited on the other side of the bridge. As the two groups of veterans merged, we heard pieces of information that explained what happened. It seemed that the crowd of veterans at the Capitol kept growing larger and larger, and it made the police nervous. To stop the flow of veterans into the capitol grounds, a police inspector by the name of Edwards ordered the drawbridge raised and the other bridges

sealed. What he hadn't counted on was raising the ire of the commuters in
Washington, whose way home was across those bridges.

"Idiots!" Rita said as we hurried toward the capitol. "If there'd been a
riot, the police would have been the cause of it."

"And they would have blamed the veterans," I said.

We got closer to the Capitol and saw that it was packed with veterans
and family members.

"Wow! What a crowd! I wonder if we'll be able to find Pop and Daniel,"
Rita said.

We threaded our way through hordes of people and stopped to watch as
the U. S. Army Band started to set up on the lawn.

"Look, the Army Band!" I said to Rita. "Are they supporting the
B.E.F?"

A gray-haired man wearing a ragged khaki uniform overheard me. "I
hope they are," the ex-soldier said, "'cause they might find themselves in
our boots someday, but that's not why they're here. They play on the lawn
of the Capitol every Friday night. This Friday night's the same to them as
any other, I s'pose."

The band started warming up, drowning out any possibility of conversation. We moved on and then Rita pointed to a crowd gathering to her
left. "There they are," she shouted.

Daniel and Mr. Boyle were standing near a food wagon that had been
brought in. Veterans were getting stew and coffee.

Mr. Boyle spotted us, too, and raised his arm to get our attention. "It's
a good thing we found each other now," he said. It's getting dark."

Daniel's mouth was full of stew, so he just nodded at us. "Man am
I hungry!" Daniel said between bites. "What took you so long? Did you
have a hard time finding us?"

"Didn't you hear about the bridges?" Rita asked.

Daniel noisily sipped his coffee. "No, what happened?"

We found a place to sit near the steps, which were packed with veterans, and as Rita described the scene at Camp Marks, I opened my sketchbook and drew some quick sketches of the sea of men. Then I turned my
attention to the Boyles and drew a family portrait, adding detail to each of

the Boyles until it got so dark I couldn't see what I was doing. Then there was nothing to do but wait.

Finally, late into the evening, a bugler sounded a call from the Capitol steps. "There's news!" Daniel said. And the voices of the veterans echoed the call for attention in a low murmur that vibrated through the crowd. The Army band stopped playing. Everyone immediately stood up and turned to the Capitol, and the humid night air became thick with tension.

We strained to see who would speak. "Who's that standing on the steps?" Rita asked her father.

"Walter Waters," Mr. Boyle said. "He got this march started, all the way from Oregon. He was a sergeant in the war, I heard."

Mr. Waters picked up a bullhorn and the crowd became silent. "The bill," he announced, "is beaten. We have received a temporary setback."

A great wave of boos erupted from the crowd.

"But we will stick it out. We are going to get more men as fast as we can and stay here until we change the minds of these men," he motioned toward the Capitol.

Cheers rose from the veterans.

"The result doesn't alter our plan to stay here until we get results, and to get more and more men to join us," Waters continued.

"I can't believe it," Mr. Boyle said, his face crumpling in defeat. "How could they look out on all these men who served and let us suffer?"

A veteran next to me said, "It's not a handout we're asking for. It's owed to us, for chrissake!"

Daniel shook his head. "I don't believe it!"

"This won't be the end of it!" someone else said.

Above the noise of the crowd, Mr. Waters finished his speech. "We are ten times better Americans than those who voted against us," he said.

The marchers roared their agreement. The rumble of angry voices created a thunder that surged through the night air and threatened to explode into a storm at any minute. The hair on the back of my neck stood up, and my heart pounded as I waited for the violence that was sure to come. Then, from somewhere near the Capitol steps, another wave of sound rolled through the crowd. I strained to hear what was happening and then stood confused for a minute as my brain tried to make sense of it. The words came in snatches—"...in brotherhood...shining sea..." The veterans were singing "America!" Soon, the entire crowd was singing. The Army band joined in, and when the last verse was sung, the mood had changed. Everyone started to walk back to their camps, grim and disappointed and determined not to give up. But the danger had passed, at least for now.

CHAPTER 35

June 20, 1932

Dear Francine and Phillipe,

I hope you both are fine and business is good—or at least good enough. I'm fine, but so much has happened here I hardly know where to begin. I wonder if the paper in Auburn has been printing reports about the bonus march. Maybe you've heard some news.

There's thousands and thousands of people here. Some veterans are staying in abandoned government buildings in Washington, but so many people came that they had to make a huge camp near the Anacostia River. That's where I'm staying. Camp Marks, it's called. It's divided into sections by state, and there's veterans and families all living here. Some people have noplace else to be.

Yesterday, some things happened that I'm never going to forget. First, the police closed the bridges connecting the camp to the Capitol so that nobody from the camp could join the group already at the Capitol. We had every right to peaceably march, but they stopped us, and for no good reason except we were making them nervous. They finally had to let everybody through because the commuters were mad when they couldn't get home, but they ended up causing a traffic jam that took two hours to sort out, the D.C. papers said, and they got the veterans riled up, too. In this morning's paper, the police chief even apologized to the marchers.

Once we got across the bridges and gathered at the Capitol, there ended up being thousands of veterans and their families waiting for the vote. Even so, the Senate voted down the bonus! When word went out, people were so upset I thought there might be a riot. I was pretty scared. But things calmed down and finally everyone went back to their camps for the night.

This weekend, there were many meetings, and the veterans have decided on their next course of action. They put out a call for more and more veterans and their families to come to Washington from all over the country. They said they won't leave Washington until they get their bonus. "No Pay – All Stay" is their new slogan.

The reason I'm writing you about all this is because when I left Auburn I said I would be back in a couple of weeks and I don't want to go back on my word. But the Boyles have asked me to stay if I can. Mr. Boyle said every single person counts, that it's important to get as many people here as possible. I know he's right about needing many people here, although it doesn't seem like one person—me, for instance, would make any difference. But then if everybody felt that way, no one would be here, would they?

And so I've been thinking a lot, especially about your work to defeat Prohibition and how you stood up to Mrs. Hunter, even if it cost you sales. I see so many people here who are desperate and suffering, and I know this march is very, very important. If they don't get the bonus, I don't know how they're going to make it. It makes me angry that the government could help all these veterans right now and the Senate won't give it. So I have to stay for a while longer. I'm going to stand up for what I believe. I hope you understand, and I hope you won't be mad. I know you're missing out on bakery sales if I'm not there to pull the wagon around town, and if you have to hire someone else to sell the pies, I understand, but I hope you won't have to, and I hope I'll still have my job when I come back.

Please don't think I'm ungrateful. I know I'm lucky to have a job that pays room and board, and I'm also lucky that we became friends, too. I miss you both very much and I hope to come back soon.

—*Maddy*

I reread my letter and then flipped through my sketchbook. I chose a drawing that showed the Capitol building with the steps packed full of veterans. Some were sitting on the steps and some were carrying signs identifying their states and their divisions, reminding Congress that they had served. Carefully, I tore the drawing out of my sketchbook and folded it in with the letter. Then I carried the letter over to the tent that the Salvation Army—Sallies, they were nicknamed—had set up, complete with a lending library and a real post office.

"Thank you, young man," a woman dressed all in black, and wearing a black bonnet, said to me as she took my letter, stamped it, and put it into a cardboard box that held hundreds of other letters. "This will go out first thing in the morning," she said.

For the next few weeks, more veterans streamed into Washington while Congress fretted. The papers said now that the vote was done, the veterans should go home. Congress could only wish they would.

Conditions at the camp got worse, partly because of the rain, which turned the campground into a muddy, slippery mess, and partly because food supplies were getting low. There were rumors, started by the FBI we heard, that the B. E. F. marchers were Communist.

Mr. Boyle sneered at that. "That's what they say to try to turn people against you."

"They tried that in Detroit, too," Daniel said. "Henry Ford claimed it was Communists that got the workers all stirred up. Couldn't have been Ford's rotten treatment of his workers, could it."

"Look at all the men in this camp," Henry said, who had by now become good friends with the Boyles. "They all served in the World War. Since when do Communists defend democracy? A lot of men didn't come back, and some who did ended up shell shocked. Either way, it's a big price to pay." He spat into the mud. "Communists. Like hell."

"Well, there's going to be a Fourth of July parade," Mr. Boyle said. He had gotten a deck of cards from the Sallies, and he was dealing five cards to each of us for a round of poker. "I suppose they'll claim that Communists are marching in the Independence Day parade, too."

But the rain delayed the parade, and it turned into a protest rally on July 5 because Congress announced it was planning to adjourn on July 16.

A few days later, a contingent of veterans came in from California, led by a man named Robertson. They set up camp on the Capitol lawn and

delivered letters to the Vice President and Congress telling them that they
were going to occupy the Capitol grounds until they got their bonus or
Congress adjourned.

The police must have been wary about taking immediate action
because of the flak they had caused several weeks ago at the drawbridge.
They ignored the Robertson army the first night as they slept on the lawn,
but the second night, the police turned on the sprinklers, which got all
the veterans hopping mad. Then the chief of police told Robertson that his
group had to keep moving. I suppose the chief thought that would be the
end of it, but it turned out to be another miscalculation, because Robertson
kept his men moving all right—moving single file in a slow shuffle around
and around the Capitol building, past the offices of the Senate and of the
Vice President. People started calling it "the death march," and word got
around fast. It drew a huge audience, not only from Camp Marks, but of
Washingtonians. The crowd got so large they had to close the Capitol.

We went back to Camp Marks for the night, but the next morning
everybody went back to see what was happening, and Robertson's men
were still shuffling around the Capitol.

"They look exhausted," Rita said. "And I know exactly how they feel.
It's just like being in a dance marathon. They haven't been able to sleep and
they have to keep moving!"

"You're right. They're exhausted," Henry said. "I believe they need
some reinforcements." He gathered a small group of his army buddies and
they walked up the steps and stepped into place in the line snaking around
the capitol. More veterans from Camp Marks joined in, too, and soon, the
Californians who had been marching all day and all night were able to
quietly leave the march and sleep. The shift change went unnoticed by the
public and the press, and the death march went on and on.

At the crack of dawn on July 16, Camp Marks was stirring and the first
wave of bonus marchers trudged across the drawbridge to see what action
Congress would choose—voting again on the bonus or adjourning.

I joined the next wave of marchers, mid morning, with the Boyles, but
we couldn't get very close to the Capitol.

"What's going on?" Mr. Boyle asked a veteran who was walking toward us.

"There's a standoff with the police," the veteran said. "A line of them are blocking the way to the Capitol steps. They won't let us get close to the building."

"What about the death march?" Mr. Boyle asked.

"Stopped," said the veteran.

"Who stopped it?" Mr. Boyle asked, but his question was drowned out by a roar of voices. The crowd moved forward, and then it halted.

"I'm going to go find out what's going on," Daniel said, and he disappeared into the sea of people. I watched his plaid cap zigzagging through men, women, and children, and then I lost sight of him.

Not long after, the sound of singing drifted back to where we stood. This time it was "Hail, Hail the Gang's All Here." Then they started changing the words to the songs, and Rita and I joined in to sing "My Bonnie," except that the words were "My Bonus Lies Over the Ocean."

Daniel came back a short while later with an update. "It's crazy," he said. Waters had been arrested, released, arrested again, and released again."

"Why?" all three of us asked at once.

"They said he got belligerent when the police wouldn't let people get close to the Capitol. Waters got them to agree to let us on the steps if the sidewalks are kept clear."

"So is Waters arrested?" Mr. Boyle asked.

"No, I don't think so." Daniel said. "They said he was going to get to meet with the Speaker of the House."

By late afternoon, Congress was still in session and nothing had happened with the bonus. We went back to Camp Marks to get a bite of supper, although that evening's stew was pretty thin, and then we walked back to the Capitol to wait. The death march had resumed, and I sat where I could see to draw the men circling the Capitol. Henry was there, and soon after, Daniel joined the group to take a turn.

It was after 11 p.m. that the announcement was made. Congress had adjourned for the year. This time, there was no singing of "America." The death march disbanded, and groups of disheartened men walked back to their camps for the night. Nothing had been done for the veterans, except that they were allowed to borrow against their bonus to buy a rail ticket home. Some did in the next couple of days, but the word was that still more veterans were on their way to Washington to pressure Congress to go back into session.

July 20, 1932

Dear Francine and Phillipe,

Congress adjourned without giving any help to the veterans. It looks like there isn't anything else to be done, so I will be returning to Auburn very soon.

Mr. Boyle said there's a plan to picket the White House to try to get some action from President Hoover, but that will have to wait a few days because Mr. Hoover left town. Daniel said Hoover was running scared, and he might be right, because a smaller group picketed the White House and Hoover locked himself inside. Daniel said every gate was chained and the secret service was everywhere.

I wonder if you are reading anything about this in the papers?

I hope both of you are fine. I'll leave Washington as soon as the Boyles are ready to go.

Maddy

I opened my sketchbook again and removed one of the drawings I had done of the death march. *P.S.* I wrote at the bottom of the letter, *This is what the death march looked like. Daniel is the fourth man from the left, and Henry is right in front of him. (Henry is the one who taught me how to ride the rails.) Jigger is the name of Henry's dog; he walked right next to Henry for hours some days. Sometimes he'd find some shade and take a nap. Smart dog, huh?*

I took the letter to the Sallies' tent. They were packing up to leave, but one of the women in black took my letter and promised to mail it.

Early the next morning, Mr. Waters met with groups of veterans from all the camps. "The police say we're going to be evicted," he announced.

"They've decided that since Congress has adjourned, there is no longer any need for veterans to camp anywhere. They want to start demolishing the government buildings where men are camping, and they want everyone—men, women, and children—to leave the other camps."

"We got nowhere to go!" one man shouted.

"Tell 'em when they give us the bonus we'll go," shouted another.

"Orders are one thing, but making people follow them is another," Mr. Waters answered. "If they push women and children out of the camps, the newspapers will print the pictures and there'll be hell to pay."

"All stay! All stay!" One veteran started the chant and the others took it up.

Mr. Waters let it go on for a few minutes and then raised his hand. The men got quiet.

"I'm going to try to get a meeting with President Hoover as soon as he returns to Washington. Then we'll decide what's next."

That afternoon, we heard a plane flying low overhead. As Rita and I watched, the plane circled over Camp Marks and belched a plume of smoke. But the smoke broke into bits and pieces and fluttered to the ground. Everywhere, people bent down to investigate the clutter of paper that skidded over the muddy, well-trodden field.

"It's a flyer or something," Rita said. She picked up a sheet and read out loud. "Eviction Notice."

"What the hell," said one man, scooping up one for himself.

I picked up a leaflet and read it. "Can you believe this? They say they're going to take back all the equipment from the mess tent by August 4," I said.

"Those sons a bitches," someone said. "Well, we still ain't leaving."

A bearded veteran scooped up several leaflets and stuffed them into his pockets. "These'll come in handy at the latrines," he said. "I'm going to wipe my ass with them," he growled.

There was mood of nervous restlessness in the camp that week as groups of veterans decided what they were going to do. Henry went to meet with some of his buddies who were camped in the abandoned buildings on Pennsylvania Avenue.

"They got cranes with wrecking balls parked next to the buildings, ready to go," Henry said. "Some of the men are moving out to the other camps, but most of them aren't budging." He shook his head. "It's getting tense. Even Waters is telling the men that they should get off federal property now and move to the other camps, but the men ain't going."

Mr. Boyle looked concerned. "You think the police are going to get rough?"

"Worse," Henry said. "I think they might call in troops to roust everybody."

Daniel scowled. "It figures. Anytime they don't like what you got to say, they kick your butt."

"It'll be a sad day if they call out the military to roust veterans. Brothers against brothers," Mr. Boyle said.

"I've got some good buddies in those billets," Henry said. "I'm gonna go back there and see if I can get them to come here."

"Probably a good idea," Mr. Boyle said.

"Be careful," I said.

"Don't you worry, kid," Henry said. A soft smile warmed his face for a quick moment.

I thought about how Henry had helped me back in the hobo jungle in New Harmony, and how he had made sure I knew how to take care of myself on the trains. And now he was looking out for his buddies from the war. I wondered how it was that some people got ugly and mean in tough times, and other people, like Henry, were always willing to give something to people who needed it, even if it was just a kind word or a smile.

Daniel went off to see what news he could find and came hurrying back within an hour. "They're trying to haul men out of the billets, but the men ain't going. Police are trying to get into the buildings and lines of veterans are keeping them out. So far, it's a standoff," he said. "I rode out on a pickup truck with some other men from here and I saw it. Then the police shut down traffic around Pennsylvania Avenue so none of us could get close enough to help the B.E.F. They ain't gonna stop us, though. We need all the men from the camp to go into the District. They can't stop thousands of men on foot." Daniel ran off to spread the word in the camp. Already, men were streaming toward the Eleventh Street bridge.

"I'm going," Mr. Boyle said. He turned to Rita and me. "You two should stay back until we see what's what."

Rita looked like she wanted to argue, but Mr. Boyle's mouth was firmly set and Rita sighed. "Okay, Pop. But if we hear that more people are needed, we're coming in."

Mr. Boyle frowned but didn't say anything. He started walking off in the direction of the bridge but then turned back toward us. "I want you to stay out of harm's way," he said. "Bad enough that I have to worry about Daniel."

By mid afternoon, we heard reports from veterans returning from Pennsylvania Avenue that there were tanks waiting to be unloaded from transport trucks.

"I'm going into the District," I said to Rita.

"But my pop wanted us to stay back," Rita said.

"That's between you and your pop," I said. "But he's not my pop, and when I first decided to come to Washington with you, it was so I could stand up for what I believe. I can't do that if I stay here while veterans are getting rousted." Maybe even Henry, Daniel, and your Pop, I thought. "So you decide whether to come with me or stay back," I said. "Either way, I'm going."

Rita looked distressed. "I want to go, but if my pop comes back to camp and doesn't find us...me..." She fidgeted for a moment. "I guess I'll stay here for a little while longer. If they don't come back soon, I'll go looking for them—and you."

"All right. Suit yourself." I pinned my hair securely under my cap and pulled the visor low on my face. Then I joined up with a small group of veterans striding toward the Eleventh Street bridge. We got to Pennsylvania Avenue, but the police had cordoned off the street. Veterans were on one side, standing near the billets, and spectators were on the other side, restrained by nervous-looking police. We worked our way up closer to the billets. "What's the news?" one of the men from my group asked.

"A scuffle broke out a little while ago," someone said. "Men were shouting, and bricks and stones went flying, then there was a gunshot and then another. We heard one man was dead and another was pretty badly hurt. They brought in an ambulance, and they took them away, and that's all we know."

The demonstration was calm now, but it felt like we were teetering on the brink of trouble. The veterans were edgy—their voices tight and their faces grim. Then, coming from the west on Pennsylvania Avenue, we heard a clatter. At first, it was hard to make out what the sound was. We strained to see the source of it and then a veteran on my right shouted, "For chrissakes, it's troops and cavalry!"

"It's a military parade," another veteran said. He started clapping. "Let's show 'em our support." A few men joined in the applause.

"That ain't no military parade," someone said. "They've come to give us trouble."

We watched as they came closer. There were hundreds of infantrymen, all carrying guns with fixed bayonets. Behind them were cavalry—hundreds more men on horses—and the glint of their swords flashed ominously in the late afternoon sun.

"Jee-zuz Christ," a man yelled. "They're all putting on gas masks!"

My heart pounded in my ears, mixing with the sound of horses' metal shoes on the pavement; there was a rush of motion and confusion—and then bedlam. The veterans surged along the street and I was shoved backward. I turned to try to get my balance and caught someone's hard elbow or shoulder, cutting my upper lip. I tasted blood. I ran along the street a little ways and suddenly I couldn't see. My eyes burned intensely and my lungs felt like they were on fire. Tear gas, it registered. I couldn't breathe and I started coughing so hard it nearly made me vomit. I tried to get off the street, to get away from the tear gas, but I wasn't sure which way to go. I stumbled and heard horses' hooves right next to me, and then I was struck with such force that I went flying, tumbling over the pavement and into some dirt. Pain streaked through my right arm. As I laid there gasping and choking, I heard the sound of children shrieking, and I knew that it wasn't only the veterans who'd been tear-gassed. I scrambled to my feet as I heard a loud drone and more metal clanking. I turned to try to see, and squinting toward the sound, through the tears that were flooding my face, I could make out tanks rolling behind the horses. My mind swirled with confusion as I struggled to grasp the idea of tanks grinding through the streets of Washington. Troops were actually attacking the veterans.

I caught a whiff of gasoline and where the billets were turned into a sea of glowing orange. Everything was burning.

Someone yelled, "They're not stopping! They're going to attack all the camps!"

I still could barely breathe, and I sank to my knees again in the grass. I remembered I had a handkerchief in my trouser pocket and I fished around for it to wipe my face, mopping up tears mixed with blood from my lip. My right arm and shoulder throbbed, and just the effort of lifting my hand to my face caused sharp pain to shoot up my arm.

I've got to warn Rita about the troops. My mind bounced around from thought to thought. *She's got to get out of Camp Marks...We've got to find Mr. Boyle and Daniel...Where's Henry and Jigger?*

I stumbled along in what I hoped was the direction of the camp, and as I gulped fresher air I started to breathe a little better. It seemed like people were running everywhere, but the troops and tanks were now ahead of me. I tried running to catch up, to get to the camp to find Rita, but violent coughing made me stop. Finally my eyes and head cleared enough that I made to the Eleventh Street bridge, but there was a line of soldiers blocking the bridge. One pointed his bayonet at me as I got close.

"Nobody goes in," he said, stopping me from crossing.

"But my friend is in there," I said, my voice still raspy from the tear gas.

"Too bad. You better hope he comes out soon," the soldier said.

Other veterans were trying to cross, too, and all were being held back by bayonets. People were straggling out of the camp, a few carrying their belongings. I searched for Rita, Daniel, Henry—anybody I knew—but found no familiar face. And as I stood near the drawbridge and night fell, the sky lit up with yellow and orange flames coming from Camp Marks. It felt like all of Washington was burning.

CHAPTER 36

I stood, numbly, watching refugees exit the camp. A lucky few carried what little belongings they had; most were empty handed. One woman pleaded with the soldiers to be permitted to go collect her children's clothes, but they wouldn't let her go back in. Slowly it dawned on me that my few clothes, bedroll, and even my sketchbook were burning.

Exhaustion crept into my bones, and finally I gave up hope of finding any of the Boyles or Henry that night. I turned back and wandered toward the Capitol, past small groups of people sitting on steps, in doorways, and on patches of grass. Some pressed wet handkerchiefs to their eyes. Everywhere was the sound of coughing.

I found a place to rest where I could see the Capitol building, hoping that maybe the Boyles or Henry would return to the steps. Beyond the Capitol, the billets on Pennsylvania Avenue still glowed, still burning. I sank to the ground under a tree, curled up on the grass, and fell into a disturbed half-sleep, jumping at any sound. Sometime later, in the middle of the night, a soft rain starting falling, soaking me to the skin as it dripped off the leaves above me. My wet clothes stuck to me, chilling me to the bone.

When morning came, I was hungry, miserably cold, and for the first time since I left home—bewildered. I didn't know it was possible to feel so young and so old all at once. I wanted someone to take care of me—to warm me and give me food and tell me what to do next. I had been tear-gassed and physically hurt as troops attacked veterans. *Brothers against brothers*, as Mr. Boyle had predicted. I never would have believed it was possible, and the knowledge that it had indeed happened made me feel old. I remembered my mother once telling me that wisdom comes with age, but if this was what wisdom felt like, I didn't want any more of it.

I pulled myself to my feet and slowly started walking. My arms and legs were stiff from the cold and I shivered in my wet clothes. A couple of blocks away from the Capitol, I came upon a bakery. I stood on the sidewalk and dug around in my trouser pockets to see how much money I had. I knew I only had some change, but there were the two nickels I had carved. I fingered one of them and started for the door, but I stopped in shock at what I saw in the bakery's plate glass window. There stood a scruffy young man with wrinkled, dirty clothes and a droopy, shapeless cap pulled over his forehead. One side of his face was puffy, and a smear of blood marked his right cheek. I stared at the young man and then raised my right arm to touch my cheek. So did he. A shot of pain traveled up my arm into my shoulder as I realized he was me.

I pushed open the door, hoping for a bit of sympathy from whoever was working in the bakery, but the woman behind the counter greeted me with a look of horror.

"Good Lord!" she said, "You been in a fight?"

"I suppose you could say that," I said. "A fight with the government."

"You one of them bonus marchers?"

"Yes, ma'am."

"You're too young to have fought in the World War," she said, looking at me suspiciously.

"My friend's father served. I came to help him get his bonus."

"Hmmph," she said, crossing her arms. "Seems to me you all should have gone home when Congress adjourned. Wasn't nothing left to do after that. That's what the papers said."

Did the papers say that most people had nowhere to go? I thought, but I didn't say it. I didn't want to start an argument. All I wanted was something to eat. The smell of fresh, yeasty breads made my stomach growl all the more.

"Still," she continued, "it was shameful for the army to drive the veterans out and burn their billets."

"Yes, ma'am," I said. I paused. "Could I possibly use your washroom? I'd be grateful if I could wash up just a bit before I buy something to eat."

She looked critically at me. "You're a mess, all right. Yes, I suppose you can use the washroom. It's through there," she said, pointing to a short, dark hallway at the back of the bakery. "Just past the broom closet."

"Thank you," I said, hurrying past her.

"Just shameful," I heard her mutter just as I closed the washroom door. I wasn't sure if she was commenting on my appearance or the army's behavior.

It was pure bliss to stick my hands under warm, running water. I soaped up my arms and held them under the faucet for a few minutes, just letting the warm water run over them. Then I gently soaped up my face and splashed water on it to rinse. I peered into the mirror to look at the damage. My upper lip was cut, but no longer bleeding, and my cheekbone was tender and purplish. *You're a mess, all right*, I said to my reflection.

I did the best I could to re-pin my hair without having a comb, and I tried to reshape my soggy cap as I secured it over my hair. I couldn't do anything about my wet clothes, but if the sun came out, they'd dry pretty quickly in the 80 or 90 degree heat that I'd come to expect in Washington.

I heard the bakery's bell jingle a couple of times, but when I stepped out of the washroom, the customers had come and gone. I was glad. It made my request easier. I dug into my pocket and pulled out a carved nickel.

"Thank you very much for letting me use the washroom," I said. "Now I'd like to buy a cup of coffee and something to eat." I put the nickel on the counter. I thought of Owen again and used his words. "I don't have much money, but I wonder if you'd like to trade some food for this special coin?"

"What do you mean, a special coin?" she asked, frowning. She picked up the nickel and examined it. "Haven't seen one like this before," she said. "It looks like a nickel, but there's a man with a derby on the front of it." She flipped it over. "Well, there's the buffalo on the back. Is it something new?"

"In a way it's new. I carved it."

"You carved it?"

"Yes, I change the Indian into another person...and I make each one a little different."

"You make a lot of them?"

"No, ma'am. They take a lot of time."

She studied it for another minute without saying anything. My stomach growled loudly.

"What do you want in trade?" she asked.

"I'd take whatever food you think is fair," I said. "And a cup of coffee." I really needed to feel that hot liquid warming me.

"All right, then. But you got to take your food outside. I don't want you in here scaring off customers. You're still a mess."

She picked a large cherry turnover from a tray. "Will that do?"

"Yes, ma'am. Thank you."

She bagged her selection and handed it to me. "You got something to put coffee in?"

My heart sank. Everything I had brought with me had burned in Anacostia. "No ma'am. I'm afraid not."

"Hmmph. Well, let me see what I can find." She disappeared into the back room and came out with a thick white ceramic mug shaped kind of like an hourglass. Exactly the kind of mug Ruby served coffee in at the Paradise Diner.

"Here," she said, filling it with steaming hot coffee. "You can take it with you."

"Thank you," I said, transferring the bag to my right hand and wrapping my left around the mug. The pain in my right shoulder made my hand too unsteady to depend on it to handle hot coffee.

I sat in the doorway of an empty storefront just a few doors down from the bakery. I set my coffee on a ledge and carefully pulled out the cherry turnover. With every bite, bits of sweet flaky pastry clung to my lips, and I made sure to clean off every morsel with my tongue. I chewed slowly, rolling pieces of cherry around in my mouth. Between bites, I took tiny sips of coffee and tried to make this food last.

When my coffee was finished, I sat quietly, turning the heavy white cup around and around in my hand, thinking about what to do next. Finally, I decided. I'd go back to sit on the Capitol steps for a while, at least until my clothes dried more in the sun. I hoped to find Henry or the Boyles, but if there was no sign of them by mid afternoon, I'd start my journey "home"—to Auburn.

CHAPTER 37

It was a short walk from the Capitol building to Union Station, but along the way I passed group after group of bonus marchers. People were dazed and anxious; they scanned the faces of anyone walking by, in search of a husband, a wife, an army buddy, or a brother. Sometimes I'd hear someone cough, still suffering from the aftereffects of tear gas. The rain had cleared the atmosphere of tear gas, but the stink of last night's fires hung low in the air, the smoldering remains of a terrible confrontation.

Police seemed to be everywhere. I slipped behind Union Station and ran alongside a line of railroad cars, staying low and close to the trains, hoping to be unnoticed. Finally, I reached a protected area and ducked into it, only to discover that I was not alone. A large group of men had gathered there. Some of them looked up at me as I entered the area, but most sat quietly on the ground or leaned against tree trunks. Some were sleeping. I moved to the edge of the group, trying not to call attention to myself while I figured out what to do.

A grizzled veteran in a tattered khaki shirt came up to me. "We've all agreed to wait until dusk to catch a freight out of here," he said. "Less chance of being seen—or reported."

"Suits me," I said in a low voice.

"Good." He moved away and I sat down, trying to be inconspicuous. I pulled my cap a little lower over my face, but peered out from under it, trying to see if I recognized anyone. Nobody. I sighed and wrapped my arms around my knees. Dull pain traveled through my shoulder, and I released my right arm. I shifted my weight a little, trying to get comfortable. It would be quite a few hours before dusk.

A pair of work boots appeared at my left side and then someone sat down next to me. I stiffened, not wanting to risk being discovered as a girl, but then a voice asked, "You okay?"

I turned to look. "Daniel!"

He smiled slightly. "I've been watching all the new arrivals here, and I saw you come in."

"Is your pop here, or Rita...?"

He shook his head. "I can't find either of them. But I thought you and Rita were together. I was with Pop when the trouble first started, but then he went back to Camp Marks. He wanted to get you and Rita out of there and warn people in the camp that troops were coming. Don't you know where Rita is?"

"No. I left the camp first and Rita stayed back. She said she might catch up with me." I didn't tell Daniel about his pop telling us to stay in the camp, but now I wished I had insisted that Rita come with me.

"Shit," Daniel said. "I hope they're both all right." He looked at me. "What about you? Your face don't look so great."

"I got hit by a cop or horse or something," I said. "I can't say what because I couldn't see. Tear gas."

Daniel grimaced. "Too bad."

"What about you? Are you okay?"

He held out his left arm, which was wrapped in what was once a white tee shirt. Only now it was dirty and bloody.

"Jeez, Daniel! What happened?"

"I got stabbed with a bayonet," he said. "Some soldier had to prove his manhood." He lowered his arm and carefully tucked it against his stomach.

"Looks like it still hurts a lot," I said.

Daniel nodded. "Soon as we get out of this godforsaken town, I've got to find a doc to look at it. Good thing I got a good right arm to pull myself onto a train."

"Yeah. That's good. Well, today I have to be a lefty," I said.

Daniel frowned. "Why?"

"I took a pretty bad spill when I got hit," I said. "And I wrenched my right shoulder when I fell."

"Are you gonna be all right getting on a train?"

"I can do it," I said. *What choice do I have?* I thought.

More bonus marchers found their way into our patch of woods, and each time someone slipped in, Daniel and I hoped to see his pop, Rita, or Henry. But there was no familiar face.

We sat and waited as freight trains rumbled by. People grew restless as the afternoon passed, and finally, as evening came, word spread that we'd catch the next freight out. Then we heard the sounds of a train being made up and everybody stood up and pressed toward the edge of the trees. We heard the whistle, and down the track, the slow chugs of the engine started, then got louder and quicker. My heart was thumping. I knew we didn't have any choice but to hop a moving train, but I was scared. By the time it got to us, this train would be moving faster than any other one I had ever gotten on.

The engine roared past us, laboring to pick up more speed, and then, as if there was a silent signal, everyone rushed for the tracks, running along-side the cars and pulling themselves onto the train.

Everything Henry had taught me raced through my mind. I ran, trying to match my speed to the speed of the train. But there were no open boxcars that I could see. In a few more seconds, the train would be going too fast for me to get on.

"Go, go, go!" Daniel yelled from behind me.

I got up even with the ladder on a boxcar and reached out with my left hand, pulling with all my might, lifting myself up and bringing my left foot onto the bottom rung. My foot slid along the metal and pushed my leg to the back of the rung. I brought my right foot onto the same rung and then climbed up. My right shoulder throbbed, but I scrambled to the top of the car and sprawled onto it. Then I turned to look to see where Daniel was.

He was on top of the same boxcar as me, but at the back. He crawled on his belly toward me. "Christ, Maddy! I was afraid you weren't going to get on." I barely heard him as the wind carried his voice away from me.

"I wanted to get into a boxcar, not on one!" I shouted at him.

"No choice," he shouted back.

I shrugged. He was right, but we had taken a big chance. And Daniel had taken an even bigger one. Henry had warned me never to get on at the back of a moving car. If you miss, he had said, you'll probably fall onto the couplings between the cars and end up greasing the rails.

I wanted to tell Daniel what Henry had said, but the train had picked up more speed, and the rush of wind made it difficult to talk. I'd have to wait until later to pass on what Henry had taught me.

The boxcar swayed on the tracks and I heard Henry's voice in my mind as I unbuckled my belt with shaking hands and threaded it through a metal support so that I wouldn't fall off. I motioned to Daniel to do the same, and I was relieved to see that he did. Then there was nothing to do but ride and think. Laying on top of a boxcar was such a contrast to my first ride. There was no sense of freedom, no watching the countryside, and no thoughts of discovering possibilities. There was only the sound of the wind, the clatter of the train, the rocking of the boxcar, and icy fear. It was starting to get dark, and even though Daniel was riding next to me, I felt very alone.

The train passed through towns but didn't stop; it slowed, and then picked up speed as soon as it got through the city limits. Every so often, I could see a veteran or two jump off the train when it slowed, usually taking a tumble into the dirt and cinders and disappearing into the twilight.

Daniel tapped me on the shoulder and yelled to me. "I'm getting off at the next town!"

I shook my head vigorously. "It's too dangerous. We've got to stop to take on water soon. Wait until then."

"Can't! Gotta do something about this," he said, motioning toward his arm. The tee shirt wrapped around his arm was soaked with dark red blood.

"Jeez!" I said. "What happened?"

"I banged it getting up here. It won't stop bleeding!"

I didn't know what to say. His arm looked really bad. Still, if we stopped soon, he could get off and find help.

Not long after, the train started slowing down again. Daniel fumbled, using his good arm to unbuckle his belt from the metal support. He scooted up to the edge of the car and swung one leg over to the ladder at the front of our car.

"Be careful!" I yelled.

He nodded, then swung the other leg over and took a step down. The train slowed a little more and then jerked sharply. Daniel went flying over the edge. I reached out to grab him and caught hold of his wrist. Searing pain shot through my shoulder and my hand clutched Daniel's wrist. His weight pulled me forward and my belt strained hard against the metal support, and then, as seconds ticked by slower than I ever thought possible, his hand slipped through mine and Daniel disappeared between the boxcars.

"Daniel! I screamed. There was no answer. The train gave another lurch and then sped up again.

CHAPTER 38

We stopped for water maybe fifteen minutes later. *If only Daniel had waited*, my mind kept chanting, like a broken record. I slowly climbed down from the top of the boxcar, but I was shaking so badly that I had to plant every foot carefully on a rung and hold on to an upper rung with both hands, even though it made my shoulder pound. *I told him to wait. Why didn't he wait?* Finally, I dropped to the ground and stumbled away from the train, trying to get control of my limbs. Even my teeth were chattering, as if my body knew what my mind was denying.

He was getting down from the front of the car, I reasoned. He could have bounced off the car and got thrown off to the side. I started walking in the direction the train had just come from. There was no telling how many miles it was back to where Daniel fell. I'd just have to keep walking until I got to the town we passed last and could find some help.

How am I even going to find him in the dark? I wondered. The clouds were so thick that there'd be no moonlight tonight. *He's okay, he's okay, I just have to find him.* I walked for a very long time. The darkness was punctured every so often by the light of another train passing, but it quickly disappeared. Then the racket of metal on metal faded, and the night returned to the sounds of cricket and cicadas.

Finally, in the distance, I saw the lights of a town. It had to be the same town the train had been slowing down for when Daniel climbed over the side of the boxcar. I tried to quicken my pace, but my legs refused to move any faster. I kept my eyes on the town, but it seemed like a mirage. I moved forward, but the lights didn't seem to get any closer.

Then I became aware of the smell of wood smoke. I kept walking and the smell became stronger. I caught a momentary flicker of orange in the woods but it disappeared. I stood on the grading and stared hard into the darkness. There it was again. It *was* a fire!

Cautiously, I worked my way toward it. As I got closer, I saw that there were three campfires, spaced apart so that everyone in the large group of people could hover around one. It wasn't hobos milling around the fires, either. I saw children, several women, and men dressed in khaki. It had to be a group of bonus marchers.

I approached the closest fire. Twigs snapped under my feet and several people turned quickly to look at me.

"I need help," I said. My throat was parched and my voice croaked.

"What the hell?" a man asked, staring at me.

"I need help," I tried again. "My friend fell off the train."

"Where'd you come from?" another man asked. "Ain't been a train passing by here in a little while."

"I've been walking a long time," I said. "From up the tracks somewhere."

Several people spoke at once. "Jesus, you look terrible."

"You better sit down."

"Where'd your buddy fall?"

"You a bonus marcher?"

Someone handed me a battered enameled cup filled with steaming coffee. My hands shook, but I accepted the coffee gratefully. "We left Washington with a lot of veterans. We had to ride on top of a boxcar. My friend was hurt. From the march." I took a breath and tried to collect my thoughts so my explanation would make sense. "He got bayoneted when the troops attacked and his arm was bleeding. He tried to get off when the train slowed for that town." I pointed in the direction of the lights I had seen from the tracks. "But the train jerked and Daniel…" I fought back tears. "He fell."

"From the top of a moving train?" a man asked.

I nodded. I looked around at the group and several people looked away. "That's too bad," someone said.

"Would you help me find him?" I asked.

"Do you know where he fell? Was it near a signal or switch or anything?"

"I don't know. I don't think so. It happened just as we were coming into the town."

"We're going to have a helluva time finding him in the dark."

"But we've got to try. He could be hurt and he might be just laying there…in pain." I squeaked out the last two words.

Nobody spoke and nobody would make eye contact with me. I knew what they were thinking but I refused to believe it. I stared at the fires deeper into the woods and watched as someone added some sticks, causing flames to flare brightly.

"All right. Let's spread the word and round up some volunteers," one of the men said. Two or three men headed for the other campfires.

"My name's Ben," said the veteran who had sent men off for volunteers. He stuck out his hand.

"Mine's Matt." I shook his hand and then grabbed my shoulder, grimacing. "Bad shoulder," I explained. "I got hurt in the march, too."

Ben shook his head. "Never thought I'd live to see such a thing, those soldiers attacking."

Within a few minutes, a sizeable group of recruits had gathered. "Here's what I think," Ben said. "We should start right out and walk both sides of the tracks. Chances are we're not going to find him until we get to the far side of town, but we should start looking now," he paused, "in case he got dragged."

I looked down at the ground. I didn't want to think about what might have happened.

"It'll be slow going because we can't see much. So when we get closer to town, a few men should split off and report the accident to the sheriff. They can bring lights and help us search."

"I'll walk the west side of the tracks," someone said.

"I'll cover the east side," another man said. People started dividing into groups.

"When we get close to town," a familiar voice said, "I'll go with Ben to get the sheriff." I picked up my head and searched for the man who had just spoken.

"Henry?" I said.

A figure stepped out of the shadows and into the firelight. "Who called my name?" He took a closer look at me. "Madd...uh...Matt?"

I nodded.

"It's *your* buddy we're about to search for?"

I nodded again.

"Holy Christ." Henry's face was grim.

"You two know each other?" Ben asked.

"Yep, we sure do," Henry said. "You go ahead and start searching—give me a couple minutes alone with my friend. I'll catch up with you."

"Okay," Ben said. Everyone moved toward the tracks, and Henry guided me away from the fire toward a couple of fallen logs.

"Let's sit," he said. "You look like hell. Are you all right?"

"No...yeah...kind of," I said.

"What happened? Who fell off the train? I know it ain't Rita."

"It was Daniel," I said, my voice nearly a whisper.

Henry's face crumpled. "Jesus," he said. "Jesus H. Christ. Tell me what happened."

I couldn't hold back any longer; sobs erupted from deep inside me as I told Henry the story. Henry's face was gray and serious when I finished. "He could still be alive," I insisted. "He's out there somewhere and he needs help!"

"You got to prepare yourself, Maddy," Henry said. "More than likely, he's dead. And it ain't going to be pretty if we find him. Maybe you should stay back while we look."

"No. I have to help." I took a breath. "I made him use his belt to lash himself to the boxcar, Henry, just like you showed me. I tried to tell him it was too dangerous to jump off, but he was bleeding really bad..." I started to cry again.

"Don't go blaming yourself," he said, putting his hand on my shoulder and standing up. "It ain't your fault. It's just a damn shame, that's all."

"And the Boyles," I said. "I don't even know where they are. What if Rita or Mr. Boyle got hurt at the march, too?"

"I don't know where John Boyle is, but I do know about Rita. I was just about to tell you."

"What? Is she okay?"

"Yep, she's okay. She's here. We were lucky enough to find each other in Washington. We got a ride out of town in the back of an army vet's pickup truck. He could only get us to the Maryland border, though, so we hitched a freight from there."

"Where is she?"

"Last I saw, she was back by the fire. With Jigger." He pointed to the farthest of the three fires. "Telling her about her brother ain't gonna be easy." He looked at me again. "You really do look like hell. When's the last time you ate?"

I had to think for a minute. "This morning, I guess."

"I'm going to get you some stew," he said.

"Henry, I don't think I could eat."

"I think you better eat while you have the chance," he said. He went off to the middle campfire and came back with a tin of thin stew. "You eat while I talk to Rita."

"All right." I took a spoonful and forced myself to swallow, but my stomach threatened to send the food right back up. I set the tin down and waited. A few minutes later, Henry came back with Rita on one side and Jigger at his heels. Rita was capless, and her hair was unpinned and falling into her face. She was still crying as she hugged me. "Oh, Maddy—what happened?"

"I tried to get back into the camp to warn you about the troops, but they wouldn't let me," I said. "I even waited on the Capitol steps, hoping to find you. I gave up and got to the edge of the rail yard at Union Station, and that's where Daniel spotted me. There was a lot of veterans there and we all hopped a train at once." My throat got tighter and tighter as I talked. "There wasn't any open boxcars, so we had to climb on top of one. I didn't want to, but...." I sucked in a big gulp of air. "And Daniel's arm was cut pretty deep from a bayonet and it was bleeding...bad. So he tried to get off near town and he...." I couldn't go on.

"That's when he fell?" Rita's voice came out in a squeak.

I nodded, choking on tears.

"We got to find him," Rita said.

"There's a group of people already gone looking for him," Henry said, his voice gentle and sad. "Why don't you two stay here by the fire and I'll let you know as soon as I know anything."

"No!" both Rita and I said at once.

"I'm going to look for him," I added.

"So am I." Rita said.

"There's plenty of people out there already looking for him. You might not want to be there if they find him," Henry warned.

"You'd do the same if it was your brother," Rita said. "You wouldn't just sit back, would you?"

Henry looked at Rita for a long minute. "No. I guess you got a point. I wouldn't sit back, either." He exhaled heavily. "All right. Let's go. We'll take Jigger, too. He might be helpful."

The four of us moved steadily toward town in the dimly lit night. Jigger crisscrossed the tracks, sniffing, trotting out ahead of us, and circling back, as if he knew why we were out there.

As we got closer to town, we caught up with the other searchers. "No sign of him yet," one man said.

"I don't think we'd find him here, though," I said. "It was on the other side of town where he fell."

"Maybe," another searcher said. "But people get dragged a good distance sometimes."

"Just shut up, Jack," a man muttered. "The kid don't need you to be painting any pictures."

After that, we walked in silence, except for the crunching of our footsteps in the gravel, which sounded unnaturally loud in the dark night. When we got to town, Ben took a group of men to notify the sheriff, and Henry stayed with us. Maybe ten minutes later, Jigger's nose went up into the air and he started sniffing keenly. Then he started zigzagging tightly along the track bed, concentrating, his ears pricked forward and his nose working loudly. Jigger broke into a fast trot and made a beeline for something.

"He's onto something," Rita cried, and she took off running after him.

"Wait!" Henry said, but Rita ran ahead, not answering.

A moment later, Rita's voice pierced the night. "Oh, no!" she screamed. The sound of that cry drilled deep into my heart and froze a piece of it forever. We ran toward her and found her sitting at the side of the tracks with Daniel's head cradled in her lap. Tears streamed down her face. "No, no, no, no," she moaned as she rocked.

Jigger was still circling around near Rita and then he stopped a little farther up the tracks and waited. Henry ran after Jigger and then he stopped, too. "His body is over here," he said.

CHAPTER 39

The sheriff's search party drew arcs of yellow light in the darkness as unidentified men lifted and lowered flashlights and lanterns around Daniel's body. They wrapped him in a dark blanket and carried him to an ambulance that had been driven alongside the track bed as far as possible, until a tangle of weeds and blackberry canes blocked it.

"Someone here can identify the body?" the sheriff asked, looking around.

Rita stepped forward. "His name is Daniel Lewis Boyle," she said.

"And who are you?" the sheriff asked, holding up a lantern to see Rita's face.

"Rita Boyle. I'm his sister." She squinted, turning away from the lantern rudely thrust at her.

"Are you going to claim the body?"

"Yes...well...I don't know what you mean...I already told you...He's my brother."

Henry moved into the space between Rita and the sheriff. "Give the kid a break, willya?" He turned to Rita. "They're going to take him to the morgue tonight," he explained. "Tomorrow you have to decide what to do." Henry turned back to the sheriff. "That right, officer?"

"That's right," the sheriff said, sounding like he just wanted to get back home and go back to bed.

"We'll come to your office tomorrow morning then," Henry said.

"Fine," the sheriff said. Doors were slammed shut and we watched the ambulance drive off toward town, leaving all of us standing in the dark. Nobody spoke, and then Henry's voice sliced into the night.

"All right," he said. "Let's go back to camp and try to get some rest."

We all turned and walked back toward the camp, silent except for the slow rhythm of our feet beating out the sound of a funeral march in the gravel. The fires were still burning as we returned; they had been tended by the people who had stayed back, waiting for news.

I dropped down onto a log near the closest fire and wrapped my arms around my knees. Exhaustion had wrung out every muscle, and I was having trouble organizing my thoughts. All around me, people's voices swirled.

"What happened?"

"Did you find him?"

"Was he dead...?"

"... someone get the sheriff?"

"so sorry..."

"...identify the body"

"burial tomorrow..."

"get some sleep..."

I felt someone's hand on my shoulder. "Get some sleep," I heard again. I looked up and focused on Henry. "You need to get some sleep and Rita needs a friend close by," he said.

I nodded, looking around. "Where's Rita? We can sleep here by the fire."

"She went back to where we set up camp. She's got your bindle back there, too. Come on."

"She's got my stuff? I thought it all burned up when the soldiers attacked!" I followed Henry and Jigger deeper into the camp. Rita was unrolling her blanket. A few feet away sat my bedroll.

"You saved this from the fires," I said. "Thank you."

"I couldn't carry everything, so I left the tent behind," she said. Tears were welling up in her eyes. "I figured Pop and Daniel were together and they'd be all right. But I thought you'd need your things, if I could find you." She sat down heavily on her blanket. "Oh, God. How am I going to tell Pop about Daniel? I don't even know where my Pop is! What if he got hurt...And my mother..." Rita sobbed and wiped her eyes with her sleeve. "What are we going to do without Daniel?"

I had no answer, and no words that could help. My heart broke to see Rita in such distress, and I reached out to hug her. She hugged me back and we stayed like that for a few minutes, not talking at all. Then she pulled away, saying, "I suppose we ought to try to get some sleep. I don't know what I'll have to do tomorrow."

I spread my blanket on the ground near Rita's and laid down, looking at the murky sky. "I'm sorry, Rita," I whispered. "I tried to hold on to Daniel. I just couldn't."

"I know," she whispered back. "I know you tried."

I closed my eyes and felt sleep pulling me into the darkness, and then I saw Daniel's face just before he slipped between the cars. Daniel's face turned into Eddie's and my body jerked awake in panic. I turned to stare at the campfire, to think about something else, hoping sleep would come, but my mind saw the fires of Anacostia. I shut my eyes tightly and made myself listen to the cicadas and count the chirps of the crickets, and finally the night sounds faded and I slept fitfully, waking up off and on through the night to the sounds of Rita's sobs. "I'm sorry," I murmured again and again.

Daniel was buried the next day, at the back of the city cemetery in an area for paupers. Henry, Rita, and I, and some of the bonus marchers stood watching as they lowered the rough pine box into the grave.

"I hate to leave him here," Rita said, her eyes still red and puffy. "Maybe someday we can pay for a headstone..." Her voice broke. "They said there'd at least be a small marker so we can find it later."

Henry cleared his throat. "There was kind of a meeting early this morning, while you was still sleeping. The vets dug into their pockets, if they had anything in them, and collected enough money to buy you a ticket home to Detroit. People didn't think you oughta be catching a freight, considering."

Rita's eyes widened and then filled. "Thank you," she said, her voice just louder than a whisper. She looked around at everyone. "I'll never forget this."

The marchers slowly made their way back toward the camp, and Henry and I walked with Rita to the train station. Henry paid for her ticket and we waited with her until it was time for her to depart. "My bedroll and clothes," she said as she hugged us both, "would you give them to somebody who needs them? That's all I've got to give to say thanks."

"We'll be sure somebody gets them," Henry said.

Rita stepped into the doorway of the Pullman and turned to us. "I wish you both could come with me. I hate to think about you riding the rails. You be careful, okay? Extra careful!"

"Don't you worry," Henry said.

"Write, okay?" I said through a tight throat.

Rita waved and disappeared into the car.

CHAPTER 40

"I'm never riding on top of a boxcar again," I said to Henry. "I don't care if I have to wait for days to find an open boxcar. I'll just wait." I was tying up my bedroll and Henry was putting out the last embers of the morning's fire. We had stayed one more night after seeing Rita off and I felt a little more rested, although I still had to count crickets to get to sleep.

"That's a good rule," he said. "Hope you never have to break it." He kicked dirt onto a hot coal, suffocating it. "Where are you heading now? You going back up to Auburn?"

"Uh huh. I hope they're not too mad at me. I've been gone longer than I said. What about you?"

"I'm going north to Ohio and Pennsylvania. Work my usual route along the branch lines, try to find odd jobs." He sighed loudly. "Sure would have made a difference if we could've got the bonus."

"I know." I hoisted my bedroll onto my right shoulder and immediately dropped it. "Shoot!" I rubbed my shoulder. "Sometimes I forget to favor this side."

Henry frowned. "That ain't good to be riding freights if you don't have two good arms."

"It can't be helped," I said. "I can't very well wait until my arm heals. I'd starve."

We gathered our bindles—this time I lifted mine with my left arm—and walked out to the tracks. "Well, what's it going to be?" Henry asked. "We either head toward town and hope to catch out on a slow train, or we head toward the water tower and hope to catch out when a train stops for water."

"Definitely the water tower," I said. I had no plans to get on a moving train today, either.

"They don't all have to stop to take on water, you know," Henry said. "Just depends. We might have to wait a while."

"I'll wait." I said.

"All right. I'll wait with you."

We sat behind the water tower, just inside the tree line. A soft breeze carried the scent of pine on cool air from deeper in the woods and I inhaled deeply, taking in some of the freshness as it swirled past us and moved out over the tracks.

"Henry, you're such a good friend," I said. "You helped me through the two worst things that ever happened to me—first when I was attacked and now this, with Daniel and all. I wish I could repay you somehow."

"You don't repay friendship, Maddy. It ain't no bank loan."

"I know. I didn't mean it to sound like that. It's just, well...I'm really grateful. I wish I could do something for you, too."

"Well, you did. You came to the march. That was something good, even though it didn't turn out right." He shook his head. "Never thought I'd see the day that soldiers would turn against their own. Least not in my country."

"I still can't believe it," I said. "I think about all those men and all those families I saw. Everybody was so poor. Anybody could see how bad they needed that bonus, and the march was peaceful! Nobody deserved to get tear gassed—or bayonetted." I fought back tears. "In my mind it's Hoover's fault that Daniel died. And Congress's fault, too. They're supposed to be protecting the people, not killing them!"

"I know," Henry said. "I know."

We heard the rumbling of an approaching train, but it roared by the water tower, not even slowing down. Henry looked over at me and shrugged. About twenty minutes later, a second train came through. That one stopped to take on water. Henry and I kept out of sight until we found an open boxcar. Henry boosted Jigger in first. Then we tossed our bindles in and hoisted ourselves inside. It was awkward for me because I had to grab with my left hand and pull myself in backwards. Henry watched me, frowning, but didn't say anything.

Not long after, the slow drum roll of couplings grabbing came traveling toward us. It passed through our car, jerking us backward a little, and continued on down the line. Then slowly, we started moving forward. I settled back against my bedroll, ready for the comforting side-to-side rocking of the boxcar. Outside the door, I watched as we picked up speed and moved farther from the town, passing fields of wheat and corn.

When I woke up, Henry had a game of solitaire spread out on the wooden floor. Jigger was curled up into a tight little ball, barely succeeding at keeping one eye open.

"I guess I fell asleep," I said. Cautiously, I stood up. My legs had cramped and I moved slowly, feeling my circulation returning as I stretched. "Where are we now, do you know?"

"'Bout halfway through Pennsylvania," Henry said, placing a seven of diamonds below an eight of spades in a line of cards. "You been asleep for a while."

"Oh. Then I guess we must be getting close to where you'll be getting off." I was sorry I had fallen asleep. Henry would be on his way soon, and there was no telling how long it would be before I saw him again.

"We'll have to change trains pretty soon," he said, "but I been thinking that I might go north into New York. Maybe I'd have some success with the branch lines up there. If not, I can make my way back to Pennsylvania." He turned up a six of clubs and slapped it down on the red seven. "That way, I can see that you make it to Auburn all right. I don't like it, you traveling with a bad arm. Ain't safe."

Henry's words touched me deeply. I didn't want to admit that I'd been worried, but I was relieved to know I wouldn't be alone. "I'd be grateful to have your company, Henry. And when we get to Auburn, I want you to come with me to meet my friends. They'll see to it that you get a good meal and a place to sleep."

It was tougher than I expected, getting through Pennsylvania and New York. The railroad bulls seemed to be everywhere, on the lookout for the crowd of defeated bonus marchers that had been flooding the freights, trying to get out of Washington. I was very glad Henry had stayed with me. Near the New York state line, he spotted a bull who had seen us getting on and was heading for us with a club in his hand. Henry pushed me to the door, grabbed both our bindles, tossed Jigger down and pointed to the woods. "Run like hell," he said, jumping down. And when we finally found another train to get on, he had to boost me into a boxcar because the grab handle was missing and I couldn't get myself on using my one good arm.

We changed trains a couple more times and camped another night in southern New York before our feet hit the cinders along the tracks that ran through Auburn.

"It's not much farther now," I said. We walked east on Clark Street and turned onto South Street, passing houses I had visited many times while delivering pies or bootleg wine. We reached Swift Street and I slowed for a minute to take a fresh look at how the porches lined up from one house to the next.

"This is the house," I said, leading Henry up the steps of the porch. I pushed on the front door, making the bell jangle. I turned to Henry and grinned. "I've missed hearing that sound."

CHAPTER 41—1946

The bell bumped and jingled against the door like it had done thousands of times before. But this time it was different. It would be Eddie's hand opening and closing that door. I stood up from the wooden kitchen table, my heart suddenly racing, and walked toward the doorway of the parlor.

"Hello? The sign said to walk in," a deep male voice called out.

"Yes, come in!" I answered. How could such a deep voice belong to my little brother? Four more steps took me into the parlor to where a tall young man stood. I saw my father's nose, my mother's eyes, and an uncertain grin that was all Eddie's.

"Hello, Maddy," he said.

"I'm so glad you came," I said, hugging Eddie. "It's been so long!"

"Yeah, like fifteen years," Eddie said.

"I know, I know," I said, leading him into the kitchen. "Please, sit and rest. It was a long drive, wasn't it? Let me get you something to drink. Tea, coffee, wine? Something stronger?"

"Coffee sounds good," he said, settling his lanky frame onto a chair. "Maybe something else later."

I poured him a cup of coffee and set cream and sugar on the table. "You look really good, Eddie. Being in the Army must have suited you."

"Well, it ended up being better than what I had in New Harmony. When they started the draft in 1940, I had just turned 21. I knew it was only a matter of time before they'd call me up, so I enlisted instead." He stirred a teaspoon of sugar into his coffee. "In the Army, I made some friends, learned something about keeping a tank running, and I survived the war, which was the biggest surprise of all. At least to me."

"Well, I'm glad," I said. "You were one of the lucky ones." I studied the grown-up Eddie. He had dark brown hair and blue eyes, like me, but a longer face and a square jaw that gave him a determined look. I wondered if he had a girlfriend. Women would find him attractive, I was sure.

"So what are you doing now that you're out of the Army?" I asked.

"Well, that's one of the reasons why I came to visit," he said. "I wasn't planning to jump into it so soon. But, since you asked..." He took a big breath and suppressed a grin. "The thing is, I saved some money when I was in the Army. At first, I sent money home, but then I found out that Mom didn't get hardly any of it. Dad took it and drank it. So I sent Aunt Ruby a small amount every month and asked her to give it directly to Mom. I saved the rest, and when I got my discharge from the Army, I had enough saved up that...well, the thing is, Aunt Ruby and Uncle George are ready to get out of the diner business—not work so hard, you know? So they've agreed to sell the diner to me! I have enough for a down payment, and I can pay off the rest of it in installments."

His excitement brought out the young boy I remembered. Behind that adult face I saw Eddie, the 12-year-old brother I had left behind in New Harmony. "That's great, Eddie. I'm happy for you."

"I know I can make a real go of the diner," he said, "and I have some ideas to, well, update it a little."

I chuckled. "You better go slow with that. The railroad men are still going to want Paradise chili for lunch. Remember what happened when Ruby tried to change her recipe? She nearly caused a riot!'"

"Yeah, I know," he laughed. "But here's what I'm thinking," he said. "You and me, we could work the diner together. We could expand the bakery part, and you could oversee that. And I would do the daily specials, and the chili, of course, and..."

I felt like I was looking at Eddie through the wrong end of a telescope. Even his voice was distant and faint.

"Whoa, Maddy. What's wrong? I thought you'd like the idea! I mean, I know you'd have to move and all, but I thought it would be fun to work together again and run the diner our way. Paradise, right?"

I took a deep breath, trying to clear my head and settle all the thoughts that were swirling and colliding, smashing into each other in a rush to be the first one out. "It's not possible," I said, hearing in my own ears how curt I sounded. I tried again. "Eddie, when I left New Harmony, I vowed never to go back. Especially to the diner."

"Why not?" Eddie's face registered hurt feelings.

"Don't you know what happened the night I left? Why I left?"

Eddie shook his head. "Not really. I remember I had been night fishing off the bridge, and when I got back to the house, nobody was there. When

I went up to the bathroom, there were wet towels on the tub, so I could tell you'd been home, but then I couldn't find you. I was kind of scared, because it was pretty late and I didn't know where anybody was. I thought something bad had happened."

"Something bad did happen, Eddie."

"Well, yeah. I know. Mom came home a little later and told me about Dad being in jail. That was the first time, anyway."

"That's not what I mean."

"What? What do you mean?"

"Raymond is what I mean. He attacked me, that night, in the diner. After Mom and Ruby went to the police station."

"What do you mean, he attacked you? I know you two didn't get along, but..."

"He hit me...and raped me, Eddie."

"Oh my god," he said. He looked at me and then down at the table. "I didn't know. I'm sorry."

Neither of us spoke for a few minutes. Finally, Eddie broke the silence. "I was really young when you left, Maddy. I remember turning twelve a month later, but it wasn't the same...you not being there on my twelfth birthday to celebrate. I missed you and was mad at you, all rolled into one. I didn't understand why you left." He looked at me and his mouth curved into a sad smile. "You know, I remember seeing your clothes in the trash can in the bathroom. I didn't know why you had put them there, but Mom was so upset at Dad and I was worried that she'd be mad at you, too, for throwing away good clothes. So I took out the trash."

"So Mom never knew?"

Eddie shook his head.

"Do you know when she found my letter?"

"I don't remember. Maybe a couple of days later. I heard her tell Aunt Ruby you left a note. But all Mom told me was that you left because you were upset that the school closed. I thought that was what you wrote. Did you tell her what happened?"

"Not exactly. I told her she should ask Raymond why I left. It was too hard for me to write down what Raymond did. I thought Mom would figure it out, but she didn't, I guess. And I told her to keep Raymond away from you."

"Well, she got that part," Eddie said. "I wasn't allowed to go anywhere with him. It was probably just as well, because he got beat up pretty badly at the rail yard soon after. I might have gotten caught up in it if I had been with him."

I poured fresh coffee for both of us and put a plate of lemon tea biscuits on the table. "I remember you wrote me about that. You said he claimed it wasn't a fair fight. Do you know what happened?"

"I don't know much. He said he got jumped by a gang of bums camped near the tracks. I guess one of them had a dog and Raymond got bit, too."

I nearly choked on my coffee. It had to be Henry and his friends that Raymond ran up against, and I felt sure it wasn't happenstance. "What about that infection? What do you remember?"

"God, Maddy. I don't know. All I remember is it started in his leg. Maybe the dog bite got infected. Why?"

Or maybe it was from being stabbed in the leg with a fork, I thought. "I just wondered if you knew, that's all." *Because I want to know if I killed him—or if Jigger did.*

I picked up my coffee cup and took a long sip. "So when do you take over the diner?"

"Soon. There's some papers to be drawn up, and then it'll be mine." Eddie hesitated. "I'm sorry about what happened to you in the diner. But are you sure you won't change your mind? After all, it was a long time ago that you were...that Raymond...."

"Sure it was a long time ago!" I said. Anger flashed through my body. "And sometimes it seems like it was yesterday. Things that happened years ago can still reach out and grab you by the throat when you're not expecting it. And not just me, either! I know lots of people whose lives changed forever because of things that happened during the Depression, including some veterans who suffered terribly because they didn't get what had been promised to them. There are some things you can't forget, no matter how long ago they happened." I thought about Rita, sitting at the side of the tracks, holding her brother's head.

"All right, all right. I'm sorry!" Eddie sat back in his chair, stunned by my anger. I felt a stab of guilt and spoke again, quietly.

"Eddie, even if Raymond hadn't attacked me, I wouldn't move back to New Harmony. I have a life here. This has been my bakery for thirteen years, ever since Prohibition ended and the Durrands went back to making wine." *Legally*, I added silently. "I have friends here, the man I love is here, and with running the bakery, teaching drawing classes part-time at the high school, and helping the kids paint the scenery for their school plays, I make a living here."

Eddie relaxed a little and reached for a biscuit. "I guess I can understand that, but I have to admit I'm disappointed. Other than Ruby and George, I don't have anybody in New Harmony. Dad is still there, at least he's officially on the census, but he's so drunk most of the time he doesn't know where he is. And you knew Mom finally gave up on him and went to live with her second cousin in Indiana, right?"

I nodded. "We're not in touch very much, but she sends me a birthday card from there every year," I said. "What about you, Eddie? Do you have a girlfriend?"

"I've been seeing someone," he said, and his blue eyes lit up for a moment. "But it's too soon to tell if it's going to lead to anything permanent."

"Well, I hope you'll find someone who makes you happy."

"Thanks. Time will tell, I guess. But what about you? You said the man you love is here. Does that mean you might get married?

"He's asked me to marry him," I smiled, "every Christmas since 1932. I always turn him down."

"Why? You said you love him."

"Because the way things are, a woman loses her identity and even her ability to support herself when she gets married. When times are bad, women take the brunt of it. Don't you remember how they fired the married female schoolteachers during the Depression? And now that the war is over, they want the married women to give up the factory jobs they held for all those years and go back home. Be dependent on their husbands."

"But you have your own business. It wouldn't be like that for you, would it?"

"You sound like Phillipe," I said. "Marrying changes the balance for women. I'm never giving up my independence. I can love Phillipe without marrying him." I stood up, signaling I was done talking about it. "Would you like some wine? I happen to have a pretty good selection of Durrand wines. They're the best around."

"Sounds good," Eddie said.

I opened a bottle of 1933 merlot and poured the ruby liquid into two long-stemmed wine glasses. "This is one of the first wines the Durrands made when Prohibition ended. It's aging wonderfully," I said. I touched my glass to his. "A la Sante. And to the success of your diner."

"To Paradise," Eddie said. We clinked glasses and sipped slowly, savoring the deep, rich flavor.

"This is an excellent wine," Eddie said.

I nodded, holding my glass up to the light, swirling the wine, watching it cling slightly to the sides of the glass before gravity pulled it back into the bowl.

"Hobos," I said.

"What?"

"It was hobos that were camped by the tracks. Raymond got into a fight with hobos, not bums."

"Hobos, bums. What difference does it make what you call them?" Eddie said.

"It matters to hobos," I said. "Hobos work for a living, bums don't."

"How do you know?"

"Because for a time, I was one. A hobo."

Eddie set his glass down. "I think there's a lot more I need to know about you before I head back to New Harmony."

"Are you serious?" I grinned.

"You bet I am."

"Then stay for a couple of days. Tomorrow we'll go to the winery so you can meet Phillipe, Francine, and Henry. But tonight, I have something to show you." I put a quiche in the oven for our dinner and then walked into the pantry. I pushed aside cans of tuna and soup, moved several bags of egg noodles out of the way, and pulled out the box marked Durrand Vineyards that I had wrapped tightly with string so many years ago. I was surprised at how light it was, considering all the history it holds.

I set the box on the table and pulled a pair of scissors out of the gadget drawer. Then I cut the string, releasing all that pent-up history. Eddie watched as I reached in and, one by one, pulled out the odd collection of artifacts: the manicure set, several buffalo nickels, the jig I had used to carve the nickels, a finished hobo nickel with a bearded man wearing a top hat. He had a darned good ear, I noticed.

Eddie picked it up and studied it. "You sent me one of these. I still have it."

"You kept it?" I said.

"I carried it with me during the war," he said. "For luck."

My throat tightened and I tried to clear it softly. "I'm glad it brought you good luck, Eddie."

I picked up my worn-out shoes, and for a moment, they were back on my feet and I could feel the gravel of the track beds through the thin soles.

"Not much left of those shoes," Eddie observed, pulling me back into the present.

"No, there isn't," I said. "But they got me through a lot of hard times." I reached inside the left shoe and repositioned the twenty dollar bill folded up and wrapped in cellophane.

"Would you really wear them again?" Eddie asked.

I shrugged. "You never know. I learned a long time ago that you don't always have a say in what happens to you. You only have a say about how you react to those things. Anyway, if a time came when I had to leave again, I'd be ready."

Eddie was silent for a minute. "Is there more?" he asked, motioning toward the box.

"Yes, there's more." I reached in and pulled out several sketchbooks. "These tell my story." I hesitated. "But maybe it's more than you want to know."

Eddie reached for the smallest sketchbook, the one that had traveled nearly as many miles as my shoes, and flipped it open. I waited silently as he turned the pages, and I looked at upside-down portraits of Henry, Professor, Red, Owen, Rita as a hobo, Phillipe, Francine, the Boyles—all people whose lives had intersected and entwined with mine, sometimes pulling and shaping my life, and sometimes profoundly altering it.

There were scenes from Durrand Vineyards, Enna Jetticks Park, and the Auburn post office. There were sketches for cakes I had decorated, and the self-portrait I had drawn on my eighteen birthday. I remembered how alone I had felt the night I drew that sketch, and I was surprised to see a very determined-looking young woman looking out from the sketchbook.

When Eddie got to the pages of Bonus March drawings, he studied the scenes on the Capitol steps, the sprawling encampment of Camp Marks, the Death March, and the drawing of government buildings burning.

Finally, he looked up. "Let's talk," he said.